RECLAIM

FINDING PROVIDENCE

BOOK THREE

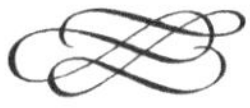

JILL BURRELL

Cover Design © 2022 Kelli Ann Morgan at Inspire Creative Service.
Editing by Daniel Rodrigues-Martin.

First edition: July 2021
Library of Congress Control Number: 2021910270

ISBN: 978-1-955507-06-6 (eBook)
ISBN: 978-1-955507-07-3 (pbk)

To my children,
You fill my life with joy.

Content Warning: Victims of domestic violence may find some scenes in this book disturbing.

CHAPTER 1

Jessie cradled her right arm against her abdomen as she stepped down from the bus. Despite being careful, pain jolted through her head, side, and wrist.

The doors of the bus closed, and the rumbling beast eased away, leaving her in a shroud of exhaust. A heavy mist--typical of Seattle's weather, despite it being mid-July--hung low in the air.

She looked across the parking lot at the entrance of the University of Washington Medical Center. The illuminated letters spelling Emergency were barely visible through the thick fog. The shadows surrounding her sent an ominous shiver racing through her.

"I'll kill you if you ever leave me." Patrick's threat rang in her ears, as though he stood right behind her.

Her feet remained rooted to the sidewalk. *It's only a hundred yards to the doors.*

One hundred yards to freedom.

"You can't escape me." Right on cue, Patrick's words mocked her, triggering another shiver.

"You deserve better than this, honey." Her mother's words echoed in her head.

After so many years of being beaten down and letting Patrick control her, Jessie struggled to believe she didn't deserve everything she'd suffered at his hands.

She stepped off the sidewalk and started the lengthy walk across the parking lot. *Never again.*

How many times had she promised herself that?

"I mean it this time." Her voice sounded small, even to her own ears. The dense fog swallowed up her words. She brushed away the tears that wet her cheeks and cleared her throat. "Never again," she said. Louder this time.

The words didn't instill the confidence she needed.

Taking the final five steps to get through the door proved harder than she'd anticipated. This wasn't the first time she'd gone to the hospital after one of Patrick's beatings.

This will be the last, she promised herself. If she could find the courage to tell the truth, that is. It had been easy to lie last time because she really had fallen down the stairs--with Patrick's help.

Jessie forced herself to walk through the door and approach the reception desk.

The receptionist's eyes raked over Jessie. She frowned as her gaze settled on Jessie's battered face. "How can I help you?"

Jessie took a deep breath, sending a sharp prick of pain through her side. "I think I have a broken wrist."

There was a possibility she had a couple of broken ribs as well. But she was pretty sure they were only bruised. Even though her side killed, it wasn't nearly as painful as the last time she had two broken ribs.

The receptionist studied the way Jessie cradled her arm against her abdomen. She fired off a series of questions as her fingers flew across the keyboard.

Jessie gave her name, birth date, address, and insurance information.

"How did you injure yourself?"

An icy chill swept over Jessie. She wrapped trembling hands around herself, favoring her right wrist.

"I'll kill you if you ever try to leave me, Jessica."

Fighting the urge to race out the door, she wiped the damp palm of her good hand on her designer jeans. Dizziness threatened to overwhelm her, so she focused on the clock on the wall behind the receptionist. She watched the big hand jump from one little black line to the next.

For the first time in four years, Jessie told the truth about her injuries. "My husband...did this...to me."

Concern filled the young receptionist's eyes as she searched the room behind Jessie. "Did he drive you here?"

"No. I rode the bus."

It was the only way she could get to the hospital without Patrick knowing. She'd made it a point to leave her cell phone and car at home since Patrick used them to track her location. And she couldn't take a taxi or a ride share because he'd be alerted if she used the credit or debit card. The little cash she had on hand left the bus as the only option.

"Have a seat and someone will be with you soon."

Jessie turned to the near-empty waiting room and braced herself for the barrage of questions she'd soon face. Fortunately, the wait was brief, and she soon found herself behind a curtain with a petite nurse clad in navy blue scrubs.

"Can you tell me what happened?"

"My hus-band..." a tremor filled Jessie's voice. She watched the curtain, expecting Patrick to push it aside and drag her out of here. She swallowed and tried again. "My husband got angry when I asked him if he was having an affair with his coworker."

What was I thinking? She'd practically asked for this beating by confronting Patrick about his relationship with Tina. But Jessie refused to bend to Patrick's will while he had an affair.

No more criticism. No more manipulation.

Tears filled her eyes. No matter how hard she tried to be the wife Patrick expected, he'd still turned to another woman. She should have been happy he spent less time at home and fewer nights in her bed, but it was just another reminder of her failures.

Sympathy filled the nurse's face as she asked follow-up questions, taking copious notes. Then she left, saying the doctor would be right in.

Dr. Adams, a tall man with graying hair, came around the curtain a short time later, followed by a social worker who introduced herself as Janet Denton. She stood in the corner while the doctor examined Jessie and asked many of the same questions as the nurse. Then he asked additional questions concerning her injuries as he examined her.

"Has your husband ever hurt you before?"

"Yes." The word came out little more than a whisper as another shiver racked her body.

Ms. Denton stepped to the side of the bed. "You realize, Mrs. Pendleton, that by law we have to report this to the police."

Jessie met the social worker's kind eyes for a moment before lowering hers and giving a solemn nod.

"They'll ask if you want to press charges. I hope you tell them yes. Every time I've seen this level of violence, it has never gotten better."

Jessie hugged herself again, hating the way her shoulders hunched in defeat. Every time she got a glimpse of the Patrick she'd fallen for, she thought things might change--hoped they would get better. But they never did, and each fit of rage was worse than the last.

"I want to..." Jessie choked on the words. She cleared her throat and tried again. "I want to press charges."

Dr. Adams ordered x-rays, and someone soon whisked away Jessie. She returned to find two female police officers waiting outside her cubicle, talking to the social worker.

For the next twenty minutes, Jessie stared at the smiley-to-frowny face pain scale on the wall and recounted what happened after Patrick announced his plans to spend the weekend at a work retreat. She couldn't look at the officers' faces--she'd fall apart if she allowed herself to see the sympathy or doubt there.

When they lived in New York, Patrick always took her with him to his quarterly retreats. Things changed after his transfer to Seattle a year ago. He said they didn't invite spouses to the retreats that occurred monthly here. At first, Jessie hadn't minded. With Patrick gone, she didn't have to worry about what little thing might set him off. But ever since she accidentally saw the text from Tina last month saying, *I can't wait for our next weekend together,* Jessie had decided she was done. In fact, she suspected the work retreats didn't happen nearly as often as Patrick claimed.

Is that why I provoked him today?

Now that the pain meds were kicking in, she could admit she was glad she did. It justified her leaving, but at the time...

"I thought...he was going to kill me," she told the officers, her voice weak and strained.

The officers asked more questions as they filled out the paperwork to press charges and file a restraining order.

When they left, Ms. Denton stepped close to Jessie's bedside. "Do you have a safe place to go after you're released from the hospital?"

"I need to borrow a phone to call my mom."

The social worker pulled a cell phone from her bag and handed it to Jessie. Her fingers trembled as she took the phone and attempted to punch in her mom's number.

"Here, let me." Ms. Denton took the phone and waited for Jessie to give her the number. She handed it back to Jessie. "I'll wait outside."

Jessie gave her a grateful nod.

"Hello?" Her mom's voice, soft and lilting, came through the phone.

"Mom--" Jessie's voice broke, and then came the tears.

CHAPTER 2

Sheriff Robert Winters lifted his gaze from the budget report on his desk when Janice, the receptionist and dispatcher, stuck her head through his door. He welcomed the reprieve from the spreadsheet he'd been poring over for the past hour.

The Adams County Sheriff's Department had more money than ever thanks to a generous, anonymous donation last year, but he was responsible to make sure they spent the funds wisley. He was up for re-election this year, and he didn't want to do anything to mess that up. Rumors circulated that someone planned to run against him for Sheriff.

"You have a *visitor*," Janice said, rolling her eyes.

The emphasis she placed on the last word meant not only did the visitor not have an appointment, but it was also someone he'd rather not see. In this close-knit community, there was only one person who met both requirements.

"Debbie Wheeler?" He leaned back in his chair and stretched.

Janice gave a curt nod. "Bingo."

Debbie always dropped in unannounced. Robert wanted to refuse to see the needy young widow, but he didn't want to get on her bad side, especially during an election year. Despite her flaws, she did a lot of good in Providence with her money.

Her visits to his office were rarely police related. They were personal, and that's why Widow Wheeler--as some people thought of her--was one of his least favorite people. Especially now that his cousin Ben and his brother Jake were both married.

Robert had always been straightforward in telling Debbie he wasn't interested, but like a trained attacked dog, she wouldn't let go until someone called her off. Unfortunately, there was no one to call Debbie off.

Stifling a groan, he rocked forward in his seat. "Send her in."

"If she's still here in ten minutes, shall I make sure you receive that important call you've been waiting for all day?" Janice winked.

"Please." He wasn't expecting a call, but he wouldn't let Debbie know that.

Good breeding brought him to his feet when Debbie entered his cramped office. He didn't care for the woman, but his mother would box his ears if he didn't show her respect.

"Debbie, what a surprise," he said with only a tinge of sarcasm. He gestured to a chair opposite his desk. If he didn't keep the desk between them, Debbie would invade his personal space. "What can I do for you?"

Debbie sat and fluffed her red hair with a hand that sported three--or was it four?--flashy rings. "I've been thinking about the anonymous donations made in Providence last year." She batted her eyelashes and lick her lips. "I'd like to make some similar donations. I'd love your opinion on how my resources could benefit our town."

Although the generous donations were given anonymously, it hadn't taken the citizens of Providence long to figure out where the money had come from. Robert's new sister-in-law, Emily, moved to town around the time of the donations. Her move and the donations came on the heels of the sale of her father's billion-dollar computer programming and software development company. A business deal that made national headlines.

"You donate generously to the town already, Debbie. Everyone knows you funded the new community center, swimming pool, and city park."

"That's just it." Debbie pouted and leaned forward in her chair, exposing her cleavage. "Everyone knows where and how I spend my money."

Robert stared at the wall behind Debbie. "I thought you liked it that way."

The comment sounded rude, but when Debbie returned to Providence four years ago, she'd been very vocal about where her money came from and the fact that her aged, wealthy husband left the bulk of his estate to her on the condition that she donate a certain amount every year to charity.

Debbie shrugged and studied her nails. "I used to, but now I think that maybe it's better to give for the sake of giving."

Robert shook his head. "I don't understand. What's changed?"

Debbie gave a mirthless laugh, and her gaze met his for a moment before dropping to her hands again. She really was quite pretty, with shiny red hair the color of ripe cranberries and striking blue eyes. But she tried too hard. She wore too much make-up, too much flashy jewelry, too tight of clothing that hugged her slender, yet busty figure--a figure many speculated was surgically enhanced. And she came on too strong.

"It's taken me a long time to realize money can't buy happiness. Not lasting happiness, anyway."

Debbie had never used this tactic before, and it left Robert speechless. He'd seen her pouty, clingy, weepy, and even angry--the woman was quite the actress--but he'd never seen her like this. What was this, anyway?

He leaned back in his chair and scratched his jaw. He'd regret it, but he had to ask. "What is it you think you need for lasting happiness?"

Keeping her chin tucked, she looked at him through long, thick eyelashes--they were probably fake too. "All you have to do is look at Ben and Amy or Jake and Emily to see how happy they are. We all want to be loved and need someone to love."

Robert grimaced as a crawling sensation swept over his skin.

Ben and Jake were nauseatingly happy with their new brides. As happy as he was for them, he was acutely aware of his role as the fifth wheel. Unfortunately, there was little chance of that changing anytime soon.

Yes, he wanted what they had, but it wouldn't be with Debbie Wheeler. The woman was at least five years older than him and had been married twice. She had thrown herself at Ben, then Jake, and now at him. She reeked of desperation.

He clenched his jaw. He refused to give her the satisfaction of acknowledging her not-so-subtle hint.

"What does that have to do with making anonymous donations?"

She shrugged. "I guess I don't want to be so transparent anymore. I want people to wonder about me."

"Aren't you afraid Em--uh, I mean the other anonymous donor will receive credit for your donations?"

"Silly, if I make the donations anonymously, it means I don't want credit for them."

Robert shook his head. He couldn't understand what game Debbie was playing. How would making anonymous donations make someone fall in love with her? She saved him the trouble of asking.

"I want people to like and respect me for me, not for my money or what it can do for them or this town." She shrugged. "I don't want people to feel intimidated by my wealth."

She should have thought about that before she built that mansion on the outskirts of town. It wasn't her wealth that intimidated upstanding men. She simply came on too strong and made no secret of the fact that she was looking for husband number three.

Again, Robert was at a loss for words.

"Will you help me?"

"Uh..."

"I'm trying to turn over a new leaf here."

"The best way to do that is to attend the city council meetings," Robert said. "We'll be having one next Wednesday."

"That's a great idea, but I'd like to come up with a list of ways or places to donate before then. Maybe we could go out to dinner and brainstorm ways I could help?"

There it is. Robert's jaw clenched, and his hands curled into fists. Every one of his run-ins with Debbie ended in an invitation to talk over lunch or dinner where she ended up invaded his personal space.

He held up a hand. "Sorry, Debbie, I've made it clear I have no desire to socialize with you on a personal level."

Debbie's lips turned down in a pout. "But this would be on a professional level--for the benefit of the community."

Low blow. Everyone knew how much he loved this town, and many were aware of what he'd given up by staying in Providence.

"I'd be happy to make a list of donations you could make as they come to mind, but I will not go to dinner with you. Tonight, or ever."

Debbie's eyes narrowed to slits as she raised her chin.

Just as he'd thought. It had all been an act. She'd almost had him convinced.

His cell phone vibrated on the desk, and relief shot through Robert. Saved by the bell. Jake's face popped up on the screen, and he snatched it up before Debbie could see it wasn't an official call. "Sorry, I need to take this."

She huffed as she stood and walked out of his office with her heels clacking on the floor.

He closed the door behind her. *Good riddance.*

"SHERIFF WINTERS," Robert answered with his official title, in case Debbie was still close enough to hear. He kicked back in his chair and put his feet on the corner of his desk when his brother's cheerful greeting came through the line. "Hey, Jake. What's up?"

"I have some news to share with you." Jake said, his voice a little higher than normal.

"Sounds like good news from the sound of your voice."

"Emily's pregnant. You're going to be an uncle." The pride in Jake's voice brought a smile to Robert's face.

"Congratulations. But that's not news to me."

He'd noticed Emily's struggle not to give in to the nausea the other night, just like Amy had been doing the past couple of months. When Emily placed her hand on her lower abdomen--like Amy always did--it was a dead giveaway.

"Who told you? I haven't even told Mom yet."

"Good thing, unless you want the entire town to know."

Robert loved his mother, but she was about as big of a gossip as they came, *and* she was eager to be a grandma.

"No one told me, bro. Emily looked as green around the gills as Amy did the other night at dinner."

"When is Emily due?"

"About a month after Amy," Jake said.

That meant late January. Ben and Amy were expecting in December, and Robert couldn't be happier for them.

"Congratulations, Jake. I'm happy for you both."

"Thanks. Uh...hey, don't tell Mom yet, will you? I don't think we're ready for the entire town to know yet."

"You got it."

The call ended a short time later, and Robert planted his elbows on his desk. *An Uncle.*

He already felt like an uncle to Ben and Amy's daughters. Kallie and Cassey were the cutest three-year-olds.

Now, Jake and Emily, who had only been married five months, were expecting a baby this winter as well.

A heaviness filled his chest. This wasn't how things were supposed to turn out. As the oldest, he should become a father before he became an uncle.

If anyone had asked him five years ago where he saw himself at thirty-one, without hesitation, he would have responded, "Married with a couple kids." Back then, he knew exactly who the mother would be.

But things hadn't turned out like he'd planned. This one-horse town was too small for the only woman he'd ever loved. Jessie needed more. More than he could give her.

His head shot up at a knock on his office door. He gripped the cell phone he still held. If Debbie had come back, he might do or say something that could hurt his chances for re-election.

The door opened, and Robert sucked in a sharp breath.

"Have you got a minute?" Sylvia Sorenson, the woman he'd thought would be his mother-in-law, stood in the doorway. Her resemblance to Jessie--tall, slender, with dark hair--brought a pain to his chest.

Had his thoughts of Jessie conjured her mother? Too bad they couldn't summon Jessie. That would be an amazing feat since she lived in New York. Not only was she about as far away from Providence as she could get without leaving the country, she was married to another man.

"Mrs. Sorenson, come in." Robert stood and extended his hand. "Have a seat."

"Robert, we left formalities behind a long time ago. Call me Sylvia, please."

Robert dropped back into his seat. "How have you been, Sylvia?"

"I'm doing good, but..." her words died on her lips.

He took in the silver threads in her dark hair and the lines around her eyes. She was still a beautiful woman, but she'd aged over the past five years since he'd hung out at her house.

"Is something wrong?"

She sucked in a deep breath. "I need your help. I know this is asking a lot, but I need you to help me bring Jessie home."

Robert's heart pounded against his ribcage. "I'm sorry, I don't understand." He rubbed damp palms against his thighs.

"Jessie has been living in an abusive relationship for the past four years. I've finally convinced her to leave Patrick. But she's scared--" Sylvia's voice caught.

How had Jessie ended up in an abusive relationship? How could anyone hurt such an amazing, creative, beautiful woman?

Robert cleared his throat. "Why don't you explain what's going on."

"Years ago, I suspected Patrick was abusing Jessie, but she wouldn't admit it. Last year, they moved to Seattle. I've visited her occasionally, and my suspicions were correct. I've been trying to get her to leave him, but she's too afraid. Patrick threatened to kill her if she ever left him."

Robert's hands balled into fists under his desk.

"She called me from the hospital an hour ago. Patrick beat her pretty badly before he left for a work retreat."

"The hospital? Is she okay?" This kept getting worse.

"She has a mild concussion, a broken wrist, and some bruised ribs. They're keeping her overnight for observation."

Robert bolted to his feet and walked the few steps to the window. A band tightened around his chest. He took slow, steady breaths as he looked out at the back parking lot. Domestic violence one of the most difficult things he dealt with in his job.

"And she says she's ready to leave him?" He spoke through clenched teeth. He couldn't bear to help her if she wasn't ready to leave the jerk.

"She is, but she's afraid he'll come after her. I know this is a lot to ask, considering your history with Jessie, but I need you to help me bring her home and...keep her safe. If I take her to my house, Patrick will find her in no time and force her to go back."

Robert stared at his fleet vehicle, a Chevy Tahoe. Bring Jessie home and keep her safe. Could he do that without providing round-the-clock detail? Despite hiring two more officers after receiving the anonymous donation last fall, he didn't have those kinds of resources.

He had enough personal leave built up that he could take a full month off. But he couldn't protect her himself. As sheriff, he had responsibilities he couldn't shirk, nor could he spend that kind of time with her. He feared he'd fall for her again, and he couldn't afford to let that happen.

An image of his family's cabin on the lake came to mind. He could take her there. It was remote enough Patrick wouldn't find her. She'd be safe, and he wouldn't have to provide constant protection.

"Will you help me?" The pleading in Sylvia's voice pulled at him, and he looked at her.

Staring at her, he saw not only her concern for her daughter, he saw glimpses of the woman he'd fallen in love with. He sucked in a sharp breath. It had taken him years to rid his mind of Jessie. And just like that, she was back in his head.

"I'll help keep her safe, but..." Robert rubbed his jaw. "It might be better if you took one of my deputies to bring her home. I'm not sure Jess--"

Sylvia scooted to the edge of her chair. "She was so scared on the phone. I promised I would bring you along in case Patrick showed up. It was the only way I could convince her to leave him."

"You're sure she wants *me* to come?"

Sylvia nodded.

"When do we need to leave?"

"She'll be released from the hospital in the morning."

This might be the toughest protection detail of my life.

CHAPTER 3

Robert opened his closet door. His gaze shifted from his jeans to his uniform and back to the jeans again.

The uniform would be more intimidating if Patrick showed up, and it would instill more confidence in Jessie. And in him. He reached for the hanger, unsure why he needed the confidence of the uniform to face his former girlfriend.

When he opened the top dresser drawer to get his badge and gun belt, the little velvet box he'd kept there for five years slid forward. He picked it up. It sprang open with the slightest pressure to reveal an engagement ring, a solitaire surrounded by smaller diamonds. Memories of that night five years ago swept over him.

Warmth filled him as he recalled the hours spent with Jessie at his family's cabin, canoeing and hiking. The surprise on her face when they'd returned from watching the sunset, to find a candlelit dinner laid out on his mother's china was exactly the reaction he'd hoped for. Jake and Riley had followed his instructions down to the tiniest detail.

Everything was perfect, including a blazing fire, the roses everywhere, and the soft, lilting strains of romantic music. He could still smell the scent of the pine firewood mingled with the fragrant roses.

Stop it!

Snapping the box closed, he shoved it to the back of the drawer, then slammed the drawer closed. This wasn't the first time the box had worked its way forward. Not the first time he regretted the way things had turned out.

I should have pawned it years ago.

He finished dressing and went to the kitchen for a bowl of cereal. Too restless to sit down to eat, he leaned against the counter, holding a bowl of Frosted Mini Wheats. His gaze roamed the great room, consisting of the kitchen, dining room, and family room.

Five years ago, when he built this house, he knew Jessie would love the openness of this layout. But she never got to see it.

His gaze rested on the portrait above the mantle. A gift from Jessie for his twenty-fifth birthday. He sat astride his horse, Goliath, who, although large, wasn't really a giant in the horse world. But the Belgian had looked like a giant to Robert when he got him on his eighth birthday. It had nearly broken his heart to put the horse down two years ago after he went blind and kept injuring himself.

Robert had been overcome with emotion when she gave the painting to him, because she'd done such an amazing job. It didn't take a skilled artist to appreciate the detail she'd captured in not only Robert's expression, but in Goliath's as well.

He'd been torn about putting the portrait up after the house was finished because Jessie was gone. But any other piece of art wouldn't have felt right.

Would he get to see more of Jessie's amazing work?

ROBERT DROVE his personal truck rather than his fleet vehicle. He didn't want Jessie or Sylvia--whoever ended up in the back seat--to feel like a criminal. He flipped down the visor as he pulled up in front of Sylvia's house. The brightness of the sun on this mid-July morning did not fit his mood.

A mood that only grew darker as he listened to Sylvia talk about what Jessie had been through during the drive to Seattle.

"I suspected for a while Patrick was abusing her." She wrung her hands as Robert rounded a long bend of I-90. "She always hurried to end our calls whenever he came home. It got so she wouldn't answer if he was home. I wanted to go to New York to visit her, but she kept putting me off with silly excuses." Sylvia angled the AC vents toward her face and adjusted the neck of her blouse for the third time since they'd started the drive.

Robert's grip on the steering wheel tightened as he remembered Jessie telling him how abusive her father had been before he walked out on his family.

"Even after they moved to Seattle, he refused to let her come visit me." Sylvia spoke again. "I dropped in a few times when I was sure he'd be at work and often saw bruises on her. She tried to deny he was hurting her. But I recognized too many signs." Her voice grew husky. "I feel like this is all my fault. If I'd left Ted sooner, when the girls were younger, maybe Jessie wouldn't have thought Patrick's behavior was normal."

"Sylvia, don't do this to yourself. This is not your fault. You had no idea Jessie's husband would end up being abusive."

"No, but I should have known he was controlling when he refused to come to Washington to meet me before the wedding."

Robert doubted he could say anything that would alleviate Sylvia's guilt, so he kept quiet.

"Did you know he refused to let her get a job when they moved to Seattle?"

Robert shook his head. He couldn't possibly answer right now and sound civil. Unfortunately, he'd seen this kind of thing too often. Men who distanced their wives and girlfriends from their family and friends to gain control over them. Those women became so dependent on their husbands they felt like they could never leave.

Sylvia continued to make comparisons between her ex-husband and Jessie's husband as they entered the heavily forested Okanogan-Wenatchee National Forest. Much to Robert's dismay, the sun still shone as they reached the coast.

It'd be easier to bear the heaviness that had settled in the SUV if he could blame it on the weather, rather than the things he'd learned about Jessie.

His stomach bottomed out as he pulled to a stop in the hospital parking lot. It had been five years since Jessie walked out of his life. Did she really want him to be the one to bring her home?

His footsteps slowed as they neared Jessie's door. He rubbed damp palms down his thighs when Sylvia walked into Jessie's hospital room. He froze in the doorway, unable to make his feet carry him any farther.

He couldn't see Jessie, but her choked, "Mom," closed a vise around his heart.

Jessie and her mother had always been close. The past four years must have difficult for Jessie.

Sylvia hugged her daughter and stepped aside, revealing him standing in the doorway. His eyes met Jessie's wide ones. At least, he thought it was Jessie. The woman in the hospital bed not only had a black eye and a swollen lip, she had long, blond hair.

He'd never seen Jessie with such long hair. She'd never let it grow past her shoulders because she loved experimenting with hairstyles and colors--often including a strip of blue, pink, or purple. It was the artist in her. She'd never gone full blond, though. There was something else different about her too, but he couldn't figure out what before she tore her eyes away.

"Mom, you brought Robert?" Jessie's voice sounded like she'd been betrayed.

"Yes, honey, I told you I'd bring Sheriff Winters." Sylvia patted her arm.

"I thought you meant his uncle, not...*him*."

Of course, she didn't want Robert. If Sylvia told him she'd bring Sheriff Winters, Jessie would assume her mother meant his uncle Dawson, who was Sheriff when she left Providence.

Had Sylvia intentionally led Jessie astray, knowing she'd never agree to come home if Robert was the one bringing her.

Sylvia waved a hand in dismissal. "I'm sure I told you Robert was elected Sheriff a few years ago."

Jessie gave a slight shake of her head and looked everywhere but at him.

Robert stepped into the room and cleared his throat. "Listen Jessie, I know this is...awkward, but I promised your mom I'd bring you home and keep you safe and I--"

"I know. You always keep your promises," Jessie said. "I'm sorry, Robert. Forgive me. I just wasn't expecting..." Her voice was full of remorse.

His name on her lips sent a jolt through him.

"I know. Maybe I should just wait out here." Before either of the women could say anything, Robert retreated to the hallway. He took several steps before collapsing into a chair.

What have I agreed to?

As soon as Robert left, Jessie dropped her head back against the bed and groaned. "I can't believe you brought Robert." She couldn't believe the man whose shoulders looked broader and stronger than ever was even better looking than she remembered.

"Honey, I know you and Robert have a history, but that was all a long time ago. Neither of you are the people you were years ago." Her mom fluttered around Jessie's bed as though searching for something to focus her attention on.

Which meant she'd intentionally led Jessie to believe she was bringing Sheriff Dawson, not Sheriff Robert. Jessie had only gotten a quick glimpse of Robert standing in the doorway, but something had changed about him. He was still tall, dark, and handsome, but something about his eyes had changed. His usually smiling eyes were guarded and brooding. And it was her fault.

"Don't worry, honey, Robert holds nothing against you."

Doesn't he? He had every right to. Her mother's choice of words reminded her that the way things had ended between her and Robert was all her fault.

"You know he's a man of his word. He'll keep you safe."

"I know, but this is so..." Where did this feeling of dread to face her former boyfriend come from? Was it humiliation? Shame?

"I hurt him when I left, Mom. And whether he holds it against me or not, I do."

She thought of the years she and Robert had spent apart during college, rekindling their relationship every summer. They'd endured additional separations when he went to the police academy and then again when she went on a lengthy study abroad program. Each time they reunited, their love for each other grew stronger.

But Jessie had felt so claustrophobic when she returned home from Europe--trapped in that one small corner of the world. There was no occasion for her to use her art degree in Providence. So, when the opportunity to escape that one-horse town came, she took it. Her choice put an abrupt end to her relationship with Robert, but she couldn't settle down in that small town without ever knowing what might have been.

The disappointment in his eyes when she told him she was leaving had nearly made her change her mind. But she knew she could never be truly happy if she felt like she was settling.

"It's all water under the bridge now, honey."

Jessie gave her mother a doubtful look. "Is he married?"

Her mom didn't meet her eyes. "No, but I hear he dates a lot. He's got quite the reputation as a ladies' man."

Jessie remained quiet.

Were there even that many women to date in Providence? She doubted he had difficulty finding dates. He was certainly handsome enough. Had she damaged him so badly when she left that he couldn't commit?

CHAPTER 4

After she signed the discharge paperwork, Robert asked Sylvia for a few minutes alone with Jessie. He couldn't commit to helping her if she wasn't prepared to make a clean break from her husband

As soon as Sylvia stepped out of the room, he turned to Jessie. "Did you press charges against your husband?"

"Yes," Jessie whispered, avoiding eye contact.

"Did you file a restraining order?"

She nodded and looked up at him through long, thick lashes. "And I plan to find a lawyer and start divorce proceedings." She lowered her eyes again.

His gaze narrowed on her face. The lashes were obviously fake, but there was something else about her eyes he couldn't put his finger on. He waited for her to look at him again. He didn't have to wait long.

She lifted her blue eyes to his, and a jolt shot through him.

Blue?

Robert clenched his jaw. He didn't know why the realization startled him so much, but it did.

His Jessie had the most beautiful brown eyes he'd ever seen. Technically, they were more gold than brown except for the dark ring around the irises. Eyes that flashed when she got angry or excited. Eyes that he'd fallen in love with when he was seventeen.

She must wear contacts.

Jessie looked away and shuffled her feet, clearly uncomfortable with his scrutiny.

"Good." He cleared the huskiness from his throat. "Your mother said your husband..." Boy, was that word hard to say. "He's away for the weekend? Should I expect trouble when I take you home to pack your things?"

"He shouldn't be there." Her voice wavered. "Unless he...comes home early."

Robert gave a curt nod and walked from the room, trying to ignore the fear on Jessie's face. He pulled his truck up to the entrance and waited for Sylvia and Jessie to come out. Jessie was clearly as uncomfortable with his presence here as he was. Maintain a professional air would be difficult.

Once Sylvia settled in the seat beside him, with Jessie behind her mother, Robert pulled out into traffic. Sylvia had tried to insist Jessie sit in the front, but she refused. Robert figured she had no desire to sit that close to him, but he wished she had, because every time he looked in the rear-view mirror, he saw her face.

While Sylvia helped Jessie pack her bags, Robert wandered through Jessie's house. The large house in a pricey neighborhood was decorated in a contemporary style with a lot of black leather, glass, and chrome. Robert studied the few pieces of art on the mostly bare walls. He didn't recognize a single piece as Jessie's.

Did she change her style that much over the past few years?

He didn't care for this new style. It felt passionless. He searched the corners of the works for Jessie's signature mark. He found no curvy J.S. or even J.P. in the corners.

In fact, he found nothing that matched Jessie's personality. The entire house felt sterile. Cold. Had her husband been so controlling that he'd gotten rid of everything that meant something to Jessie?

He searched for her studio and again found nothing. No easel, no canvas, not even a single art pad or paintbrush. The tightness that filled his chest yesterday when Sylvia walked into his office contracted.

Sylvia's voice reached him as he stepped out of the room next to the master bedroom. "Do you want to pack any of these dresses or pant suits?"

"No," came Jessie's clipped response. "Patrick bought those. He rarely let me dress casually even if I didn't leave the house."

"Well, all you have packed are a few blouses and these silk pajamas."

"Let's pack my yoga pants, track suits, and jeans."

"Those are the fanciest track suits and jeans I've ever seen."

"Everything had to have a designer label," came Jessie's quiet voice.

Robert sensed a hint of self-recrimination in Jessie's tone.

The poor woman couldn't even buy her own clothes.

Robert's hands balled into fists as he walked away. He paced the family room until Sylvia and Jessie brought out two suitcases. His fingers brushed Jessie's when he took the case from her, and an electric jolt shot through him.

Jessie jerked back, wide-eyed, as if he'd burned her. She stepped toward the hall. "Give me a minute, please."

Robert's eyes followed her. She pulled her wedding ring off before entering the master bedroom. When she returned a few minutes later, tears clung to her lashes, and her ring was absent from the hand that sported fake red nails.

Apparently, she'd broken her habit of biting her nails.

Robert looked away. He was an easy-going person and never took things too seriously, but right now, an anger festered inside him like nothing he'd ever known.

Needing to get out of this house before he said something that might hurt Jessie even more. He grabbed the second suitcase and headed for the door.

Sylvia and Jessie followed.

"Wait, I need to get something." Jessie hurried to the kitchen, returning moments later with a black book that looked like a large journal.

"I'm ready," she said, her voice thick with emotion.

Eager to get Jessie away from here, Robert put her luggage in the back of his truck and climbed in. Again, Jessie sat in the back, and again, he wished she'd sat beside him. It would have been easier to keep his eyes off her.

She stared out the window, wiping away the occasional tear. Was she upset because she was scared or because her marriage was ending?

Surely, she couldn't still love the jerk after all he'd done to her. After the changes he'd no doubt forced upon her. Blond hair, blue eyes, fake fingernails, and designer clothes. None of these things were Jessie.

What kind of man marries a woman then changes every wonderful thing about her?

Robert had seen too much of this in his career, and every time it got to him.

Keeping a white-knuckled grip on the steering wheel, he focused on the road. Sylvia must have sensed his tension because she didn't attempt to make conversation.

He forbade himself to look at Jessie again, because the anger surging through him made him a distracted driver. He clenched his jaw so tightly he was certain to have a headache by the time they reached Providence.

He had a feeling this tension would become an unwelcome companion in the coming weeks.

JESSIE'S STOMACH twisted when she spotted the billboard for Charity's diner two miles before the exit to Providence. How many times had she and Robert climbed up on that billboard? They'd spent hours there talking, counting cars on the freeway, and gazing at the stars. They'd even made out a time or two up there to give the passersby something to talk about.

She pressed a hand to her abdomen as a flood of memories from her years in this small town assaulted her. She'd like to chalk her nausea up to motion sickness, but the thought of facing people she knew and admitting she was a battered wife threatened to make her lunch come up.

They exited the freeway and within minutes the pink and white striped awnings of Charity's Diner came into view. A warmth settled over her. She had so many happy memories of the diner where she'd worked after school and during her summer breaks.

She loved this beautiful little town, but she'd felt so trapped when she returned here after traveling Europe, only to realize there wasn't a future for her here. Nothing except Robert.

He should have been enough. She'd loved him with all her heart, and it nearly killed her to leave him, but she needed to do more with her life.

Making an occasional pot in the school's ceramics lab or painting a picture for a friend or family member's birthday wasn't enough anymore.

The sharp pangs of failure filled her. Jessie had wanted so badly to succeed in her career as an artist and eventually become a museum curator. She'd experienced a tiny glimpse of success with her art and her career, but her success had made Patrick jealous. He'd slowly taken away everything she treasured.

She wrapped her arms around herself as she remembered the first time Patrick got angry with her for spending so much time painting. He'd mocked her skill, saying anyone can paint. Then he'd taken her largest paint brush, swiped it across her pallet, collecting a variety of colors, then smeared it across her canvas in sharp, erratic movements. He'd ruined the picture she'd worked on for two days.

The move to Seattle last year helped further Patrick's career, but it ended hers. He'd refused to let her get a job, insisting that with the stress of his new job, he needed her support and attention.

What little dignity and creativity Jessie had maintained to that point had withered. And when the crate containing the few remaining pieces of her work mysteriously vanished in the move, Jessie died inside.

Nothing mattered anymore.

She'd tried so hard to please him--to be exactly what he wanted her to be. But she'd failed. Miserably. No matter how hard she tried, it was never enough.

She'd failed in her career and her marriage. But worst of all, she'd failed herself.

~

"THE CABIN IS FURNISHED and has all the amenities," Robert said as they entered Providence, even though Jessie knew that. She'd gone there with him many times. "It has some emergency essentials and food, but I can't guarantee what's there."

"Let's stop at the grocery store before we go to the cabin," Sylvia said. "I'll buy some food."

Robert pulled into the parking lot of Knight's Grocery store and parked.

Sylvia climbed out and looked at Jessie. "Aren't you coming in with me?"

"Mom, I can't." It was little more than a whisper.

Sylvia's brow wrinkled.

"You know how small towns are. I'm just not ready to see anyone yet," Jessie said.

Sylvia gave Robert a pleading look, as if asking him for help. He shook his head, telling her to let it go. With a sigh, Sylvia closed the door.

The silence in the truck grew stifling, and Robert's gaze drifted to the rear-view mirror. Despite Jessie being tall, she looked delicate and fragile.

"Thank you," came Jessie's quiet voice from the back seat.

Robert shifted in his seat to turn and look at her. "Don't worry about what people think. It took great courage to leave the situation you were in. I admire you for that."

"A situation created by my own choices." There was the self-recrimination again.

He dropped his gaze. What could he say? Life would be drastically different for them if they...she...had made different choices. He'd lived with plenty of regret for the past five years but dwelling on the what-ifs wouldn't change anything.

"I'm sorry, Robert."

"For what?" His eyes sought hers.

"That my mother pulled you into this." Jessie looked away. "And for leaving five years ago."

A prickling sensation raced across Robert's skin. How many times had he wished Jessie would come back and apologize for leaving him? Now, she'd done exactly that, but it brought no joy, like he thought it would. She'd come back to Providence, but not back to him.

"It's a little late for apologies." He didn't intend for his tone to sound so sharp. Was it because he still fumed over the way her husband had treated her?

No, the turmoil that ate at him was personal. *Am I still angry with her for leaving? Or myself for letting her?*

It killed him to admit that after all these years, the answer was both.

"I know I hurt you." She didn't make eye contact as she said the words.

A part of Robert wanted to lash out at her, telling her how badly she'd crushed him, but Jessie had been hurt enough.

He stared out the window as he made his own admission. "And I imagine I hurt you by letting you go."

She dipped her head. "But I'm the one who left. I really am sor--"

Robert raised a hand, cutting her off. "Don't apologize for something that's not your fault. Apologies won't change anything at this point." He shook his head. "We've both made mistakes and we both have regrets, but we can't play the blame game."

Jessie lowered her gaze again. "We don't need to play the blame game," she said. "It's my fault. The pain I caused you when I left...everything I've suffered since. It's all my fault."

Robert wanted to assure her she was wrong, but he couldn't get the words out. "He really did a number on you, didn't he?"

Jessie's gaze jumped back to meet his.

"The Jessie I knew would never apologize for following her dreams and should know I wouldn't expect her to."

She blinked rapidly as she stared out the window again. The silence stretched on.

"I heard about your father... I'm sorry for your loss, Robert. I wanted to call and express my condolences, but..."

"But what?"

"I figured I was the last person you wanted to hear from."

He would have loved hearing from her, but she was married by the time his dad passed away and it would have been a painful reminder that he'd lost more than his father.

"Besides, Patrick..."

Robert kept his gaze on her face, waiting for her to look at him again. When she finally did, he asked, "Patrick what?"

"Never mind."

The more Robert learned about Jessie's husband, the more he loathed him. The man didn't deserve Jessie.

CHAPTER 5

Robert propped another short log on the chopping block. Picking up the ax, he threw it down into the log. With each chop, he wondered what all Jessie had endured.

He swiped the sweat from his brow and surveyed the pile of split logs. It was more than enough to last Jessie a few days, especially since the cabin had a furnace fueled by propane if she needed it. They rarely used the furnace throughout the summer months, but it still got chilly in the mornings and evenings this close to the lake.

Everywhere he looked, he saw Jessie. On the dock, where he'd taught her to fish. In the lake, where they'd canoed and swam. In the tree house, where they'd hidden away and made out until his little sister and cousin interrupted them.

Robert loaded his arms with split logs and marched into the cabin. After filling the woodbox, he caught himself staring at the couch where he'd held Jessie in his arms as they planned their future together. His insides churned as he remembered how he'd planned to propose to her here on that fateful night five years ago. But Jessie had crushed him before he had the chance.

He strode back out the door, not stopping until he reached the lake. *Why did I think bringing Jessie here was a good idea?*

Yes, it was safer than letting her stay at her mom's, where Patrick was sure to find her. Safer, maybe, but not easier.

Not for him, anyway.

Did Jessie remember the times they spent here together? Did they mean anything to her, like they apparently still did to him?

He picked up a flat rock and threw it with practiced precision. It skipped across the lake, each bounce rippling out in broad circles before dropping beneath the surface.

Jessie removed herself from his life years ago, and he'd moved on. Well, he'd tried anyway. His career had moved forward, but that was about it.

He bent and picked up another rock.

SYLVIA HUGGED JESSIE. "I'll come visit you tomorrow after I get off work."

Robert caught the fear that flitted through Jessie's eyes. Leaving her alone wasn't ideal, but Sylvia needed to maintain a normal routine so she could honestly say Jessie wasn't there when Pendleton showed up at her door.

No way could Robert stay here with her. The spacious cabin felt too cozy. The scent of the fresh-cut pine logs and the golden rays of the setting sun coming through the picture windows gave the great room an ethereal feeling. One that could be construed as romantic.

He waited at the door for Sylvia to step outside. "I need to talk to Jessie. I'll be out in a minute."

He turned to lead Jessie to the couch in the great room, then deciding he couldn't sit on the same sofa they had made out on, he changed directions. He led her to the dining table, trying not to remember their last night here together.

Keep it professional.

"Your mother and I will take turns checking on you. If you need anything, let one of us know and the other will bring it the next day."

Could he stand to visit Jessie that often?

He pulled his mind back to the task at hand. "I want to be on guard for when we might expect trouble from your...from Pendleton. When will he get home?"

"Probably around six tomorrow evening." Jessie wrapped her arms around herself.

"An officer will most likely be waiting to arrest him. By Monday though, I'm sure he'll have made bail and he'll be banging down your mom's door."

Jessie's brow furrowed. "Have I put her in danger by coming home?"

"I'll keep an eye on your mom. Is he volatile enough to hurt her if she's not cooperative?"

"Yes," she whispered.

"Okay. I'll see if I can talk her into staying with my mom and Aunt Charity."

"I'm sorry to cause so much trouble for everyone." Jessie stuck a bright red nail between her teeth, then apparently remembering she didn't bite her nails anymore, pulled it out.

"Don't be. My deputies and I will be vigilant, and we'll keep everyone safe. I'm going to take care of you Jessie."

Robert reached out, intending to put a comforting hand on her shoulder. Then, remembering the shock he'd experienced when he took the suitcase from her, he pulled back. He couldn't touch her right now. He was having a hard enough time as it was.

Robert stood and walked to the door. "It's best if you stay inside and keep this door locked at all times."

Robert closed the door behind himself and waited to make sure Jessie locked it. He hoped he wouldn't end up regretting helping her.

AFTER DROPPING OFF SYLVIA, who insisted on going home, Robert headed back toward the Double Diamond. He longed for the carefree days of his youth. Even though he had no interest in working with animals for the rest of his life, he'd never trade the childhood he'd enjoyed on the forty-thousand-acre ranch.

He pulled up to his childhood home and shut off the engine, asking himself why he was here. He needed to talk to someone, but he wasn't sure he could talk about any of it.

Seeing Jessie looking so different but still so beautiful had rocked him. And recognizing how thoroughly her husband had beaten her down--until she felt the need to apologize for every little thing--ate at him.

He didn't want to feel sorry for Jessie. He didn't want to feel anything for her, but apparently, he still did, because hearing her apologize for leaving and hurting him after all these years pierced something deep inside him.

He'd waited so long to hear those words. But it wasn't supposed to be like this. She should have come back years ago, saying she couldn't live without him. Not five years later, as a married woman who was so different from the woman he'd loved.

Robert rapped on the front door, then walked in to find Jake and Emily snuggled on the couch. Judging by Jake's messy hair and Emily's rosy cheeks, Robert had interrupted something. Coming to the ranch house was awkward nowadays. He liked Emily, and he was happy for Jake, but things were different now. And even though Jake insisted he should just walk in, Robert was always leery to find exactly what he'd found tonight.

"Hey, Robert," Jake said, pulling back from Emily but keeping an arm around her shoulder. "What's up?"

Robert shrugged and plopped down on the other couch with a sigh. "Guess I needed something more than my own thoughts for company."

"What's going on?"

"I'm not sure I want to talk about it?"

"Suit yourself," Jake said. Quiet fell over the room. "So, what do you want to talk about?"

Robert groaned. "Nothing...everything."

Emily and Jake chuckled and waited, eyebrows raised.

Robert scratched the stubble on his jaw and looked at Jake. "Guess who I spent the day with."

"Who?" Jake asked.

"Sylvia Sorenson and her daughter."

"I didn't know Chelsea was in town. Why did you spend the day with them?" Jake's eyebrows furrowed. "Isn't she married?"

Robert worked to keep his voice even as he met his brother's gaze. "Not Chelsea."

"Oh," Jake said, understanding filling his face. He'd been the one to keep Robert from going into a deep depression after Jessie left. "Where did you see Jessie?"

"Sylvia and I picked her up from the hospital in Seattle and brought her back to Providence. I took her to the cabin."

Jake's eyebrows rose again. He withdrew his arm from around Emily and leaned forward. "Jessie is at the cabin, right now?" At Robert's nod. Jake said, "Whoa."

"She's the one, isn't she?" Emily asked, her gaze fixed on Robert.

Robert's eyes jumped to Emily.

"This Jessie is the one who broke your heart years ago, isn't she?"

Robert shifted in his seat. "No offense, Emily, but I'm not in the mood to be psychoanalyzed tonight."

His new sister-in-law put Ben--Robert's best friend and cousin--to shame. Ben always knew when something bothered Robert, but Emily knew exactly what bothered him. The two of them made him feel vulnerable.

He hated it.

Emily crossed her legs and clasped her hands around her knee, giving him a "we'll-see" smile.

Jake spoke again. "She's married, but you picked her up from the hospital and brought her to the cabin? Where's her husband?"

"He beat her up, then went to a work retreat." Robert's chest tightened, as it did every time he thought about what Jessie had been through. "She's been living in an abusive relationship for the past four years. Sylvia convinced her to leave him, but she's scared. He threatened to kill her if she ever left him."

Jake's fists balled. The only person Robert knew who hated the thought of a woman being abused more than he did was Jake. "Do you think he'll come after her?"

"Jessie thinks so. He thought nothing of leaving her so battered she ended up in the hospital." Robert sucked in a deep breath, reining in his anger. "He's crushed her. She is not the same woman I--" He stopped himself from saying she is not the same woman he used to love. "She's changed. And not for the better."

"Changed how?"

"What was the only thing that meant more to Jessie than--" he almost said "me" but stopped himself again. "Anything?"

"Her art," Jake said without hesitation.

Robert nodded. "There wasn't a single piece of her work in their house, no studio, no easel, not even a paint brush. Her husband took everything away from her."

The muscle in Jake's jaw clenched as he shook his head.

Emily's brow furrowed, and her lips pressed into a thin line.

Just thinking about what Jessie must have endured incensed Robert. He came here hoping for distraction, so he could get his mind off Jessie, but it wasn't working. Now that she was back in Providence, he feared she would occupy his thoughts far too often.

"So, you're supposed to be like her bodyguard or something?" Jake asked after a lengthy silence.

"Something like that. I promised her I'd keep her safe."

Jake's voice was quiet when he spoke again. "Can you afford to make that promise?"

Robert raked both hands through his hair, then propped his elbows on his knees and dropped his head into his hands.

Why did I make Jessie a promise I'm not sure I can keep?

He'd do his best to protect her from her husband, but it would be difficult to do when he could barely stand to be around her. He couldn't seem to separate the woman who needed protection from the memories he'd shared with her.

Bolting to his feet, he headed to the door. "I'd better go. I shouldn't have come here, right now."

"Don't leave," Jake said, springing up from the couch.

"Robert," came Emily's soft voice. He looked at her, bracing himself for the harsh truth she was likely to speak--he was acting like an idiot. But her words surprised him. "You are a strong, intelligent man. You're confident and capable. Despite finding this situation difficult, you are not the same person you were five years ago. You are in control of this situation, and you can decide how it plays out."

Robert absorbed her words like a dry sponge. They were exactly what he needed to hear. Ever since Sylvia walked into his office yesterday, he'd felt his life spiraling out of control. He'd struggled to separate the past from the present, because it filled him with the same old emotions and regrets.

Emily's right.

He wasn't the same person he was before. He was confident and mature. He was the sheriff, for goodness' sake. He'd dealt with harder things than this. He needed to determine how to control the situation and decide what he wanted the outcome to be.

One thing was for sure: he wouldn't open his heart again. He couldn't bear to be hurt a second time.

He could be a protector, but that was it.

CHAPTER 6

Jessie stood from lighting the fire and rubbed her hands on her arms. Despite it being July, the luxurious cabin with hardwood floors throughout was chilly this early in the morning. She couldn't justify turning the furnace on for only herself. Besides, Robert chopped enough wood to heat the spacious cabin for a month.

She put the kettle on to heat water for the herbal tea her mother had bought, hoping it would settle her stomach. Her tummy growled, reminding her she'd skipped dinner last night. She'd been so tied in knots she couldn't eat anything. Despite being hungry this morning, the anxiety lingered. She'd be lucky if she could get some toast down with her tea.

She paced around the large kitchen while waiting for the water to heat. Spotting a sweatshirt on the hook by the back door, she grabbed it. Her hand stilled when she realized it was Robert's Washington State University hoodie. Bringing it to her nose, she inhaled. The scent was faint, but it still smelled like him. Tangy and woodsy.

She slipped it on, trying not to remember the many times she'd borrowed his sweatshirts or jackets and the way he'd warmed her by wrapping his arms around her.

A few minutes later, she stood in front of the floor-to-ceiling picture window, cradling a steaming mug in her hands. She stared out at the lake shrouded in the shadows of pre-dawn light.

The sun's golden rays peeked over the mountain as she sipped her tea, turning the lake a splendid emerald color. Jessie sucked in a sharp breath at the beautiful scene, wishing she had some art supplies.

She retrieved the black book she'd grabbed on her way out of the house yesterday and searched the kitchen for a pencil. A thrill shot through her when she found one. It was a far cry from the sketching pencils she was used to, but it would have to do. She pushed a comfortable armchair toward the window and sat with her legs curled beneath her.

She opened the book that held her secrets. Her deepest sorrows, darkest fears, and greatest regrets.

Robert's name appeared more than once early in the book.

At first, she'd used it as a diary, pouring out her heart on its pages. Then when Patrick punished her creativity, this book had become her only outlet. She'd sketched her emotions many times when he wasn't home, keeping it hidden where she knew he'd never find it--under the kitchen sink, behind the cleaning supplies. He never helped with the cleaning. In his opinion, caring for the house was a woman's responsibility.

The book was the only place she'd sketched anything for the past two-and-a-half years. Most of the images were dark with heavy strokes. She used the words and the sketches to document the abuse she'd suffered at Patrick's hands, even adding in photos occasionally.

She searched for a blank page and began sketching. With quick, light strokes, she sketched the outline of the lake and the stately pine trees surrounding it. The motions soothed her, and she willed herself to relax. For the first time in four years, she didn't have to worry about discerning Patrick's mood when he walked through the door.

Peace was slow in coming, however. She felt vulnerable here, alone. It was only a matter of time before Patrick found her.

Robert had promised to keep her safe, but could he do it when he couldn't stand to be around her? At least that was the vibe he'd given off yesterday.

Patrick wouldn't give up without a fight. It was only a matter of time before he figured out where she was. She hoped her decision to leave Patrick didn't get her mother or Robert hurt.

Jessie continued to sketch as a flock of geese settled on the lake. It was all so beautiful. She loved this lake and this cabin. Memories of this place and Robert had assaulted her all night.

Her hand stilled as her gaze drifted to the dining table where Robert's brother and sister had laid out a romantic dinner for them five years ago. There had been a look of excitement and anticipation on Robert's face. That is, until she'd crushed it.

It was at that table, with candles flickering and the smell of roses filling the air, that she'd told him of the internship her professor had recommended her for at the MET.

"The Met?" Surprise registered on Robert's face. "As in the Metropolitan Museum of Art? In New York City? Are you planning on applying?"

"I did a few weeks ago." Excitement bubbled in Jessie. "I didn't mention it to you because I didn't think I'd get it."

Robert's face fell, but he quickly recovered. "You got it? That's amazing, Jess!" He sprang to his feet and pulled her into his arms. "I can't think of anyone more deserving."

"Thank you. I was afraid you'd be upset." Jessie grimaced.

They took their seats again.

"Why did you think I would be upset?"

"Well, we've been making plans for the future..." Jessie's voice faded.

Robert's gaze dropped to the table. "When do you leave?"

"I have to be there in two weeks." Jessie fiddled with her napkin.

"Two weeks?" Robert's eyes widened. "That's soon."

"I know, and there's so much to do."

"How long does the internship last?"

"It's only a year, but if all goes well, I'll get a permanent position at the MET."

"A permanent position?" His voice squeaked a little. "So, you'll stay in New York?"

At her shrug, Robert stood and walked to the picture window. He shoved his hands deep into his pockets and stared out into the darkness.

Jessie studied his rigid posture. He was upset. She didn't blame him. She hadn't bothered to tell him about the internship, thinking that if they rejected her, the disappointment would be easier to bear if no one knew about it.

They'd accepted Jessie, though, and she couldn't wait to follow her dreams. But she was torn. She loved Robert and didn't want to leave him.

Robert's heart was here in this small town where he knew everybody's name, where he could hike or ride all day without seeing another person. He'd never be happy in New York City.

As much as Jessie loved him, she couldn't stay here without ever trying to achieve her dreams when they were within reach.

She stepped up behind Robert, slipped her arms around him, and laid her cheek against his muscular back. "I'm sorry I didn't tell you. I honestly didn't think I'd get the internship."

Robert unwrapped her arms and stepped away. "But you did."

She stepped toward him. "We still have two weeks together."

"And then what?" Anger laced his words as he took another step away.

"I don't know." Jessie's throat ached as she blinked back tears. "I love you and I don't want to leave you."

"I love you too, Jessie, and I've waited a long time for things to work out for us, but I can't... I won't wait anymore." Robert choked before turning his back to her and folding his arms over his chest. "Have you accepted the internship?"

He looked over his shoulder long enough to see her nod.

"Then you've already made your choice."

Pain ripped through her chest at the coldness in his voice. She wanted to cry and scream at him. She wanted him to beg her to stay--

to make her choose him over her dreams. Wanted him to fight for them.

But he would never do that. He knew working at the Met was Jessie's lifelong dream, and he would never ask her to give that up. Just like she could never ask him to leave Providence.

In stony silence, Robert cleaned up their meal. She wrapped her arms around herself, fighting the chill that filled the room despite the fire.

The thirty-minute drive home felt like an eternity. The powerful hands that had held hers so many times kept a firm grip on the steering wheel. He kept his gaze focused on the road, so Jessie stared out her window into the darkness, wondering if she would ever travel this road again.

When he stopped his truck outside her house, she turned int her seat. "I'll turn down the internship and we can get married, like we talked about. I love you that much." A pinch of regret stole her breath.

Why did she have to choose between the two best things that had ever happened to her?

"I know you do, Jess." He reached out a hand but stopped before he could touch her face. "And I love you too much to ask you to give up your dreams. You'll never be happy if you settle and don't find out what might have been. And I'd never forgive myself for letting you." Then he got out of the truck and walked around to open her door.

She swiped at her tears as she slid down from the truck seat.

Robert swept her into his arms for a brief, tight hug, then released her. "Follow your dreams, Jess. Be happy and know that I will always love you." Then he was gone, taking a piece of her heart with him.

She trembled as his taillights disappeared into the night.

Jessie looked down at the indiscernible image she'd drawn in her book, remembering the rush of long-forgotten attraction she experienced at the hospital yesterday when she first saw Robert again.

Coming home felt like Jessie's only option, but now she feared it might be the hardest thing she would ever do.

~

TIRES CRUNCH ON GRAVEL OUTSIDE, and Jessie bolted upright from the couch where she'd been resting. Heart in her throat, she crept to the window.

He didn't find me already, did he?

She let out a sigh of relief when she recognized her mother's blue Toyota Camry.

Jessie watched as her mom pulled a cardboard box from the back seat. She held the door open for her mom, who hugged her with one arm while balancing the box on the other.

"I brought a few of your old clothes and things." Her mom set the box on the sofa, and Jessie stared at it as though it were a snake.

Do I want to know what's inside?

"I brought some groceries for dinner, too. I'll be right back." Her mom patted her arm before walking back out the door.

The box pulled at Jessie. She couldn't recall a single thing she'd left behind when she moved to New York. She'd been so torn when she packed, wanting the life that lay ahead, but not wanting to leave the life that lay behind. The way Robert had dismissed any chance of them working out one more separation between them broke her heart.

She lifted a soft, red sweater from the box. Robert had given it to her for Christmas the year before she left. "I love how it makes your eyes spark like little twin flames," he had said. "It's the same look you get when you're angry."

She'd punched his arm for that comment, but he'd laughed and pulled her into his arms. "It's also the same look you get when you're passionate about something."

Jessie had been passionate about two things: Robert and her art. And she couldn't have both.

She'd made the wrong choice, and she'd live with the regret for the rest of her life.

She set the sweater aside, swallowed the pain of the memories. Smiling, she pulled out her favorite threadbare pair of jeans and two t-shirts. Robert had given her the first one, the second she'd borrowed from him to use as a nightshirt.

At the bottom of the box, she found the bottle of perfume he gave her for her birthday. She pulled the lid off and sniffed. The combination of flowers and fruit sent a warm flush surging through her as she remembered the way Robert often buried his face in the curve of her neck and inhaled.

She heard the low, husky timbre of his whisper. "You smell like summer and sunshine." His breath against her neck sent a tingle through her every time.

She dropped the perfume back into the box. *I left these things behind on purpose.*

She held up the sweater and rolled her eyes as her mom walked back into the cabin. "Really mom?"

Sylvia set the bag she carried on the coffee table and sat beside Jessie.

Looking at her mother, Jessie felt like she was looking in a funhouse mirror that age her twenty years. Fine lines had deepened around her mom's eyes, and streaks of gray now accented her hair.

Sylvia patted Jessie's arm. "It's chilly in the mornings and evening this close to the lake, I thought you'd need it."

Her mother's feigned innocence didn't fool Jessie.

"But this sweater? Of all the ones I left behind?" She couldn't remember if she'd left any others behind. She'd packed most of her sweaters--because New York winters were cold--but she couldn't bear to take this one with her.

Mom sighed and took Jessie's hand. "Honey, is it so bad for you to remember you were happy here?"

But it wasn't enough. Jessie swallowed the sting of tears as she remembered how her pursuit of art had ultimately led to a life devoid of it.

"Coming home doesn't mean things will be the same, Mom. I'm not the same person I used to be."

Sylvia tucked a lock of hair behind Jessie's ear. "No, you're not. I know you feel damaged and broken right now, but you're a fighter and a survivor. It'll take time, but you're going to be okay. Wounds heal, even ones as deep as yours. I'm living proof of that."

Jessie remembered how abusive her father had been before he walked out on them. Sixteen-year-old Jessie had wondered if she'd been a better daughter, would he have been nicer? Would he have stayed? But then she felt guilty because they were definitely better off without him. It had left her confused and lacking confidence.

Her mother had been a strong woman, though, and had insisted the girls go to therapy with her. It had taken a long time and the friendship of a nice boy--Robert--before Jessie found her self-worth.

And she'd let Patrick take it all away.

Why didn't I see him for what he really was?

"You're a stronger woman than I am," Jessie whispered.

"No. If I'd been stronger, I would have left your father when you girls were little." She lowered her gaze. "And maybe you wouldn't have ended up in the situation you did."

Jessie squeezed her mother's hand. She understood how terrified her mother must have been to leave. "It's not your fault, mom. None of it is."

Sylvia's eyes glistened as she held Jessie's gaze. "And what you've been through is not your fault. You are stronger than you think. You had to sacrifice love to chase your dreams."

"And look where it led me."

Mom wrapped an arm around Jessie's shoulder and squeezed. "I am. It led you right back here. Give yourself time to heal, honey." She rested her hand on the sweater. "Then look forward to the possibilities."

"You mean Robert? Mom, that won't happen. He can barely stand to look at me let alone be in the same room with me."

"He's not the same person he used to be either. I imagine this is as hard on him as it is on you."

Maybe, but that didn't mean Jessie deserved a second chance with Robert.

CHAPTER 7

Patrick took in the dark windows of his house as he turned onto Magnolia Way. He was later than he'd planned, but Jessica shouldn't be in bed already.

Had he hurt her worse than he thought?

The enjoyment of his weekend dissipated, and his grip tightened on the steering wheel. Coming home sometimes fell like a burden. Maintaining the control he needed to have in his home often took its toll on him.

Jessica was a beautiful woman, but she had no fashion sense. She cared more about her art than how she looked. As a prosperous investment broker, he had an image to uphold. He couldn't go out in public with a wife who preferred jeans and a paint-splattered t-shirt over evening attire.

No. He'd needed to teach her what it meant to step out on his arm.

It was a pity, really. She was an incredibly talented artist, but she'd let it consume her. Her art meant more to her than he did. He couldn't tolerate that. He needed to be in control, and if she had her art, he didn't have control of her.

So, it had to go. All of it.

He pulled his Lexus LC into the garage, noting Jessica's silvery-blue Infiniti Q50 in its usual spot. *Good, she's home.*

He hated to think about who might have seen her if she'd gone out.

Patrick had left her bruised enough that if she ran into someone she knew, they would ask questions. In fact, he may have come down a little too hard on her, but when she'd confronted him about Tina, he'd snapped.

He'd been under an immense amount of stress since taking this job in Seattle, and he'd relied heavily on Jessica playing the part he needed her to play--the quiet, doting housewife. Like his mom always did. If Patrick could make good at this brokerage firm, maybe he'd finally make his father proud.

He didn't enjoy putting Jessica in her place, but sometimes she needed a reminder that he was in charge. She should have known better than to question him about where he was going and who he'd be with.

He parked his car and walked into the house after grabbing his duffel bag and the dozen roses he'd bought as a peace offering. He'd treat Jessica like a queen for the next few days to make up for his outburst.

"I'm home," he called as he hung his keys on the hook beside Jessica's.

Silence.

"Jessica!" he called through a clenched jaw.

Still no response.

He tossed the roses on the counter. So much for treating her like a queen.

Flipping on lights, he walked through the house, ending in the master bedroom. He dropped his duffel bag on the perfectly made bed.

"Don't play games with me, Jessica! Where are you?" His muscles tensed as heat radiated through his body.

He pulled his cell phone from his pocket and checked Jessica's location. It showed her at home, as she'd been all weekend. He called her cell.

Jessica's ring tone echoed from the kitchen. Following the sound, he spotted it on the counter.

His stomach plummeted as if pulled down by a led weight.

Jessica was gone, and she'd left her car and cell phone behind so he couldn't find her.

Heat coursed through his veins. Cursing, he picked up her phone and flung it across the room.

It struck a cabinet, fell to the granite countertop, then clattered to the tile floor.

Jessica would pay for making him do that.

He darted back to the master bedroom and stepped into the closet.

"Where is she?" he shouted at the rhinestone stilettos he'd given her for her birthday last week.

He turned in a circle, examining her clothes. Very little was missing, but a gaping spot in the corner mocked him. Two suitcases were missing. Cursing, he kicked the remaining carry-on suitcase.

He walked back into the bedroom, where a glint of light from the top of the dresser caught his eye. He stepped closer.

Jessica's wedding rings.

His shoulders bunched from the waves of fury coursing through his body. "So help me, Jess--"

He jumped at the ringing of the doorbell.

That had better be her!

He stormed through the house, vowing to teach her a lesson she'd never forget as soon as he let her in. His blood practically boiled, causing the edges of his vision to blur.

He threw open the door and doubled his fists. But it wasn't Jessica on the doorstep.

Two uniformed police officers stood there. "Mr. Pendleton, we have a warrant for your arrest for assault and battery."

ROBERT PICKED up the paper with the image of Patrick Pendleton off the laser printer. Blue eyes stared back at him from a reasonably good-looking face. It was just a driver's license photo, but nothing in the blue eyes made Pendleton look menacing. He didn't look like a man who would hurt a woman, let alone break her wrist.

But Robert had learned in his job that evil came in all shapes and sizes. He remembered the contempt in the man's face who tried to kill Emily last year. One look into the hit man's eyes was enough to chill him to the bone. But the eyes of the man who kidnapped Ben's daughter had been filled with fear.

Dale, the senior most deputy, stuck his head through Robert's office door. "Hey, boss, Rudy just walked in. Everyone's here, now."

"Thanks, Dale. I'll be right there." Robert took a deep breath, straightened his tie, and picked up the box of cinnamon rolls he'd picked up from Aunt Charity's diner this morning.

He usually sent out important information to his deputies via email. Saturday night was the first time he'd sent out notice of a mandatory meeting in over a year.

Robert had to tell his deputies they needed to be on the lookout for a dangerous man who'd threatened to kill his wife while acting like this was just another assignment.

The moment he stepped into the crowded squad room with the cinnamon rolls, uniformed officers surrounded him. Someone lifted the pastry box from his hand and passed it around.

"Save me one of those," he called over Vickie's head.

He waited for the excitement over baked goods to die down before speaking. Hiring two new deputies over the past year had seriously cramped the room. He needed to get the plans for the addition to the sheriff's office finalized soon.

"I know this mandatory meeting is unusual, but a situation has arisen that I suspect could bring trouble as early as this afternoon."

"What kind of situation?" asked Kyle, the newest and youngest member of their team. He'd only been with the Adams County Sheriff's Department for six months. The rookie stood beside his desk--stiff and formal--leaving his sweet roll on his desk for later.

In sharp contrast, Brady and Dale both had their feet up on their desks and were already licking their fingers clean.

"Many of you know Sylvia Sorenson's daughter, Jessie." Robert watched a few heads bob before continuing. "Jessie left her abusive husband this weekend and has returned to Providence from Seattle." He paused to see if anyone made the connection between him and Jessie. Only Brady's eyes narrowed. "She pressed charges of assault and battery against her husband, Patrick Pendleton, and filed a restraining order against him."

He distributed the pictures of Pendleton and the description and license plate number of Patrick's car.

"He threatened to kill Jessie, and she believes her life is in danger. Even though this is the first time she's pressed charges against her husband, I'm asking you to treat this as though her life is in peril. I want you to be on the lookout for Pendleton day and night. Regular patrols will now include hourly sweeps past Sylvia Sorenson's house. Even though Jessie is not at her mother's house, I fear Pendleton won't hesitate to harm Sylvia to discover Jessie's whereabouts."

"Where is Jessie staying?" Brady asked, his eyes fixed on Robert.

"Somewhere safe." *I hope.*

He trusted his deputies--with his life, even. Vickie and Kyle, the department's newest deputies, hadn't been here very long, but they were good deputies, and he knew they'd have his back in an emergency. But people said things without thinking, things that got passed on. Small towns were notorious for their gossip.

And anyone who knew his and Jessie's history would gossip about the fact that the sheriff's former girlfriend was back in town. Robert didn't want anyone gossiping about Jessie. And he didn't want people linking his name with hers again.

"I'm keeping Jessie's location classified for now, but I want you to contact me immediately if you spot Pendleton or have any concerns as you patrol past Mrs. Sorenson's house."

He studied the face of each deputy, making sure they took this assignment seriously, before saying, "Rudy and Kyle, go home and get some sleep."

Rudy and Kyle didn't need to be told twice. With quick waves, they headed out the door. Their night shift had technically ended over an hour ago. Dale and Vickie discussed who would take which patrol today, which left Brady to follow Robert from the squad room.

Robert sensed his friend behind him, but he kept walking to his office. Although Brady was three years older than him, Robert had grown closer to Brady than anyone else on the squad.

Brady leaned his tall, muscular frame against the doorjamb. "You okay?"

"I'm fine. Why wouldn't I be?" Robert kept his voice steady.

Brady shrugged. "You and Jessie used to be pretty close."

"That was a long time ago. We all have a job to do, and I'll do mine just like everyone else."

"If you say so." Brady straightened up and nodded his blond head. "But I'm here if you need to talk, man."

Brady turned and walked away, and Robert dropped into his chair. If Brady could see through him that easily, what would everybody else be able to see?

What would Jessie see?

CHAPTER 8

Patrick brought his Lexus to a crawl on Cyprus Street and checked his GPS. He came to a stop in front of a brown brick house.

This is it?

Sylvia Sorenson's house, though not a complete eyesore, wasn't much to look at. He studied the small brick home, surrounded by an equally small, well-kept yard with an older model Toyota Camry in the driveway.

No wonder Jessica preferred jeans and a t-shirt over the dressy clothes that showed off her figure. She looked amazing no matter how she dressed, but just the memory of her in the red satin evening gown she wore the night they met still turned him on.

Making her dress up for him was a matter of principle. He deserved a wife who always looked her best.

That's why he insisted on calling her Jessica. "Jessie" was such a plain name, but *Jessica* was alluring and graceful, just like he'd trained his wife to be.

He smirked at himself in the mirror as he smoothed his hair. Jessica had been such an easy target. Her reluctance to accept compliments on her art the night they met showed her lack of self-esteem. She didn't stand a chance once he turned on the charm. Initially, he'd planned on making her a quick conquest, but her strong morals had kept him at bay.

Her refusal of an easy, physical relationship presented a challenge that intrigued him. Determined to win her over, he'd focused all his attention on her until he'd become addicted to her. Some might say he fell in love with her, and maybe he had, but one thing was certain: He would not let her walk away from him.

She belongs to me. I've worked too hard to let her slip back into her country bumpkin ways.

She'd cost him a day's worth of work and the humiliation of having to ask his father to bail him out of jail. For that, she'd pay.

"I did not raise a convict." His father's voice had boomed over the phone line. "You should know better than to lose control."

Like his father ever practiced what he preached.

Patrick shook his head to clear it. Did Jessica honestly think she could run home to mommy and pick up where she left off?

He got out of the car and strolled to the front door of Sylvia's house. *Play it cool. Apologetic.*

He scowled at the wooden door in need of a fresh coat of stain before knocking. At a quiet noise on the other side of the door, he pasted on his most charming smile.

The door didn't open, though. Instead, a curtain in a nearby window fluttered.

His smile faded.

He heard a faint voice speaking in hushed tones on the other side of the door and caught the word, "*hurry.*"

He knocked again. "Sylvia? Are you there? It's Patrick. I need to talk to you. I'm worried about Jessica." The best defense was offense.

"Why are you worried about Jessica? What happened to her?" Her alarmed voice came through the door.

He didn't know Sylvia well, but he doubted the alarm in her voice was genuine. That, coupled with the fact she didn't open the door, told him she knew exactly where Jessica was.

He doubled up his fist and banged on the door. "Open the door, Sylvia, and let me talk to my wife."

A muffled shriek sounded from behind the wood, and he grinned. The woman was as big of a coward as her daughter. He grabbed the doorknob. If she wouldn't open the door, he would.

But the knob didn't turn. He cursed. *I should kick the door down and teach them both a lesson!*

He caught himself. If he forced his way in, then Sylvia would believe every lie Jessica had told her about him. He drew in a deep, calming breath and rolled his shoulders.

"You can draw more flies with honey than with vinegar." One of his dad's pet sayings rang in his head.

Patrick had learned well from his dad how to get what he wanted, but he'd always been more partial to turning on the charm then turning up the heat method. Patience was not his strong suit.

He turned toward the street at the sound of a vehicle approaching. A momentary weakness threatened his legs at the sight of a white Chevy Tahoe with the word Sheriff emblazoned across the side in large black letters.

It had been less than twenty-four hours since two officers arrested Patrick at his home in front of his gawking neighbors. They'd hauled him to the police station and fingerprinted and photographed him like a common criminal.

An officer wearing sunglasses climbed from the SUV and started up the walk.

Patrick wiped clammy hands down his slacks. *Play it cool. If you act guilty, he'll think you're guilty.*

He sized up the officer as he approached. Tall--at least two inches taller than his own five foot ten inches. Solid, rugged build. Something about the broad shoulders and dark hair looked vaguely familiar, but Patrick couldn't figure out why. He was certain he'd never seen the man before.

How could he? He'd never stepped foot in this backwoods town before.

If he had his way, as soon as he had Jessica, he'd never come back to this Podunk town again.

"Can I help you?" The officer stopped an arm's length away.

Patrick licked his dry lips and swallowed hard. The man had at least twenty pounds of pure on Patrick. The snug fit of the sheriff's uniform wasn't caused by a bullet-proof vest.

Sheriff.

According to the gold star on his chest, Sylvia hadn't called a lowly deputy. She'd called in the top dog.

Smiling, Patrick extended his hand. "I sure hope so. I'm Patrick Pendleton, Sylvia's son-in-law. I'm trying to tell her I'm worried about my wife, but she won't open the door."

The sheriff ignored his outstretched hand. "Why are you worried about your wife?"

Patrick dropped his hand. "She's missing."

The door clicked, then eased open. Sylvia poked her head out. "Jessie isn't missing. She left you because you put her in the hospital."

Hospital.

The officers who arrested him last night had mentioned a medical report that stated a concussion and a broken wrist, but they hadn't said Jessica had to stay in the hospital.

Maybe he'd overdone it by breaking her wrist, but how dare she press charges against him for assault? She deserved the punishment she got. She had no right to question him about Tina.

He clenched his teeth and drew in a long breath through his nose, trying to tamp down the fury rising in him. He couldn't lose his cool in front of the sheriff.

He turned imploring eyes on Sylvia. "I admit, I may have been a little harsh with Jessica, but I love her. I need to tell her how sorry I am."

"A little harsh? You broke her wrist!" Sylvia's penetrating gaze pierced him.

An uncomfortable tightness gripped his chest. "Please, Sylvia. Let me talk to her so we can work this out."

"I'll do no such thing. You're supposed to stay away from her."

"I can't... I can't live without--" Patrick stopped himself as a bitter taste filled his mouth. He'd meant the words as a platitude, but the crawling sensation that swept over his skin attested to their truthfulness.

How on earth had he become so obsessed with Jessica? He should be glad she'd left, then he wouldn't have to hide his relationship with Tina. But right now, he didn't want Tina. He wanted his wife back.

He set his jaw and choked out his next words. "Please let me make this right with Jessica." He turned a soulful look on Sylvia.

Sylvia's eyes narrowed as she regarded him.

Women were usually easy to read, but he'd never bothered to get to know his mother-in-law, so he couldn't tell if she was softening or not.

She squared her shoulders and lifted her chin. "The only way to make this right with Jessie is to stay far away from her." She waved her hand at the sheriff. "As you can see, I won't hesitate to call the police. You're not welcome in my house."

"And I won't hesitate to come." The words came from behind him.

Patrick turned to find the sheriff only a foot away.

The tall man took off his sunglasses, and Patrick bit back a growl as recognition dawned on him. He'd seen those brown eyes framed with dark lashes in the photos he'd caught Jessica staring at. The photos he'd burned in a jealous rage.

Watching the smiling face of the brown-eyed Casanova curl up and turn black--while Jessica pretended her heart wasn't breaking--had given him great satisfaction.

She'd not only run home to Mommy, she'd run back to the arms of her high school sweetheart.

If Patrick wasn't so furious, he would have laughed. A roaring filled his ears, accompanied by a surge of adrenaline that shot straight into his fists. It took every ounce of his willpower to keep from lashing out at the cocky sheriff who had kept him from winning Jessica's heart.

The man in front of him was the reason she'd left, and Patrick had been arrested.

"Let me remind you, Mr. Pendleton, Jessie has a restraining order against you. The simple fact I'm not slapping handcuffs on you right now should tell you Jessie isn't here."

She must be here. Jessica doesn't have anywhere else to go. He'd made sure of that. She had no friends or coworkers to turn to.

"You're lying," Patrick spat out. He rocked forward on his toes and looked over Sylvia's shoulder. "Jessica! Come out please, honey! I just want to talk to you!"

A firm hand clamped down on his shoulder, forcing him back onto his heels. "It's time for you to leave. Jessie's not here, so you can stop harassing Sylvia. In fact, consider this your one and only warning to leave Sylvia--and Jessie--alone." A hard edge filled the sheriff's voice.

But Patrick couldn't back down after finally coming face-to-face with the man his wife had never stopped loving. She may as well have been cheating on Patrick for the past four years, because there was a part of herself she'd never given to him.

He stepped closer to the sheriff, getting in his face. "Or what?"

The sheriff's jaw clenched as his eyes narrowed. "I'll throw you in jail."

Perspiration pricked Patrick's brow. "Touch me without cause, and my lawyer will have you wrapped up in a lawsuit so fast your head will spin."

"Your lawyer?" The sheriff laughed, showing off perfect white teeth. "Guess what, I have one of those, too, and an uncle who is the justice of the peace here in Adams county. Oh, and another uncle who's a Supreme Court Judge. How about you? Do you have those kinds of connections?"

Patrick's pulse skyrocketed, and the edges of his vision clouded as he stared at his nemesis. He was at a loss for words. Never had he felt so livid.

"Sylvia has made it clear you're not welcome here. That means you're trespassing." The sheriff smiled again. "Tell me, does your lawyer enjoy dealing with trespassing charges?"

Patrick glared at him, his entire body trembling with the desire to wipe the smile off the other man's face. Engaging in a physical altercation would not end well.

He turned back to Sylvia and spoke through clenched teeth. "Tell Jessica I am truly sorry, and I hope we can work things out."

Sylvia crossed her arms over her chest. "Don't hold your breath."

He gave the sheriff another glance--still fighting the urge to punch him--before stepping off the porch. Climbing into his car, he slammed the door. He drove out of the subdivision, intending to stop somewhere, away from the prying eyes of the sheriff, and regroup.

Patrick had just hit main street when he spotted the sheriff's Tahoe tailing him. He smacked his palm against the steering wheel. He hadn't planned to leave this hick town without Jessica, but the sheriff didn't give him much choice.

He'd just have to come back when Sylvia and the sheriff weren't expecting him.

CHAPTER 9

Robert grabbed the bag Sylvia sent with him for Jessie, took a deep breath, and climbed from his Tahoe.

This was the first time he checked on Jessie and he wished Sylvia had accompanied him. He could use a buffer.

He repeated Emily's counsel in his head as he knocked on the cabin door. *I'm smart and intelligent. Confident and capable. I control--*

The cabin door swung open, and the air rushed from Robert's lungs.

There stood golden-eyed Jessie in his WSU sweatshirt, looking adorable and all too feminine despite the baggy hoodie.

Memories rushed back to him of sharing his jacket and sweatshirts with Jessie, then wrapping her in his arms when they weren't warm enough.

"Hi, Robert." Jessie gave him a hesitant smile.

"Hi." He sucked in a quick breath and stepped into the cabin, catching a whiff of the perfume he gave her for Christmas years ago. Man, he loved the way it smelled on her.

The scent put his senses on high alert, and the temperature inside the cabin skyrocketed. Resisting the urge to fidget, he held out the paper bag from Sylvia. "Your mother sent a few things."

When she reached for the bag, he shifted his fingers so they wouldn't accidentally touch, like they did when he took her suitcase the other day.

Jessie frowned but said nothing.

He stepped away, but watched as she pulled two books from the bag. He glimpsed the titles *Life After Divorce* and *Overcoming Abuse.*

Jessie's face reddened, and her posture stiffened.

"Um, I'm going to go chop some firewood," he said in a rush, before darting out of the cabin.

For the next thirty minutes, he berated himself for still being attracted to Jessie and feeling bad for her discomfort. Except for the hair color and the defeat and uncertainty in her eyes, she looked like the woman he used to love.

After dumping his second load into the woodbox, he shuffled his feet. The energy spent on splitting the wood wasn't enough to chase away the attraction or the memories.

Jessie sat with her legs curled beneath her in a chair near the window, watching him.

"So, how have you been?" He rubbed his palms on his uniform pants.

She gave him a small smile. "Good. Bored."

"You're uh... Pendleton showed up at your mom's house this afternoon."

Gasping, Jessie swung her legs out and leaned forward. Her brow furrowed. "Did he hurt her?"

"No. She refused to let him and called me. I hurried over there and managed to convince him you weren't there and that he needed to leave."

Jessie frowned. "Just like that?"

Should he tell Jessie he'd been sure her husband wanted to throw a punch at him? A part of Robert wished he had. He'd have loved to throw the jerk back in jail.

Robert grinned, trying to lighten the mood. "We had a bit of a stand-off, but he realized I'm bigger and stronger than him, so he did the smart thing and walked away."

She didn't smile like he expected. The furrow between her brows only deepened. "He'll be back. He's never been one to give up easily."

Robert doubted that, but he wouldn't tell Jessie so. He didn't want to offend her or make light of the pain she'd suffered.

He shifted from one foot to the other. It would look rude for him to leave so soon, but he couldn't stay in the cabin filled with so many memories.

"So, um... would you like to get out of the house and go for a walk?"

"Yes!" Jessie sprang from her seat so fast; Robert fell back a step. "Give me a minute to get my tennis shoes on."

Too restless to sit, Robert wandered around the great room after she disappeared down the hall.

A black book--the one Jessie had gone back after--lay open on the couch. Jessie had always kept a diary of sorts. He stepped closer to the couch, curious whether she still sprinkled drawings throughout her journal.

The haunting image of a dejected mother bird, worm in mouth, sitting on the edge of an empty nest, filled the page.

Robert's chest tightened. It had been a long time since he'd seen a drawing so well done that it evoked this kind of emotion in him. Not since Jessie moved away.

Knowing he violated her privacy but unable to stop himself, he flipped the page to another dark image of a hand extending from the flames of a fire. The fist gripped a human heart. Words surrounded the disturbing image.

"Indescribable pain."

"Anguish."

"Broken heart."

He recognized Jessie's neat script in heavy ink.

Robert's breath grew shallow, and a heaviness settle over him. This was Jessie's escape. Where she tucked all the emotions she had to keep hidden from Patrick.

Shoulders bunched, he reached out to flip the book closed. A photograph slid out, the unmistakable bruises in the shape of a man's fingers around the creamy white flesh of a wrist.

He bit back a curse as a chill swept through him. Pendleton had been cocky today, and Robert had read the determination in his eyes, but the man hadn't looked dangerous.

This proved otherwise.

He tucked the picture back into the book and closed it. Judging by its thickness, the book was nearly full. He feared almost every page was full of similar images and writing. And how many photos did the book hold?

Jessie's husband was a dangerous man.

"Okay, I'm ready." Jessie's voice came from down the hall.

Robert hurried toward the door so Jessie wouldn't know he'd intruded on her privacy.

Within minutes, they were on the trail leading around the lake.

Jessie tipped her head up to the sky. "I've been dying to get out of the house. I'm bored out of my mind. You'd think I'd be used to it since I haven't worked for the past year, but Patrick always had a list of things for me to do that helped fill at least part of my day."

"What kind of things?" Robert didn't want to talk about her husband, but he couldn't help himself. He had to know what Jessie had seen in the man.

"Go to the gym, volunteer at the hospital or senior citizen's center, drop off and pick up his dry cleaning, hair and nail appointments, clean the house, fix dinner." Jessie ticked the items off on her fingers.

"I can't imagine your house got very dirty with just the two of you."

"It didn't, but he often had clients over for small dinner parties and everything had to be perfect." Jessie hugged her arms around herself as she said the words.

Robert could guess what happened to Jessie if things weren't perfect.

"Fix dinner, huh? I take it you learned to cook." Robert shot her a teasing grin.

Jessie had frequently offered to fix him dinner when they'd dated, but he'd usually shown up to find dinner burning and Jessie creating a masterpiece. He meant the comment as a joke, but when her eyes clouded, he knew he'd made a mistake.

"It became a necessity early on."

"When did the abuse start?" He asked quietly, unsure whether he really wanted to know.

Jessie stopped walking and turned to look at the lake from the top of the hill they had hiked up. She tucked a lock of hair behind her ear with her casted hand then hugged herself again.

Robert stopped beside her. He was about to apologize and tell her she didn't need to answer when she started talking.

"As soon the honeymoon was over, he started calling a dozen times a day. Wanting to know where I was, who I was with." She shook her head. "If I was with friends, he often asked me to do a favor for him that required me to leave them. If I didn't jump to do what he wanted, he reminded me that if I loved him, I'd want to make him happy."

Jessie raised a fingernail to her lips as if she meant to chew on it, then she dropped it again. "I didn't see what was happening at first, especially since he was so generous, always giving me gifts and showering me with compliments in front of my friends and coworkers. He kept telling me he couldn't live without me."

A tightness filled her voice. "My coworkers and friends thought I was so lucky. But when we were alone, he made his disapproval clear if I did something wrong. He had a way of making me feel guilty for things that weren't really my fault."

She gave a little snort as she started walking again. "Although, looking back, I guess it started while we were dating, I just didn't see it because he was so flattering and charismatic."

Robert shoved his hands into his pockets, where he balled them into fists. "What did he do when you were dating?"

"Little things that were manipulative. Like ordering for me, insisting I would like it, or begging me to try something I didn't like, for him. He showered me with compliments when I dressed up or did my hair a certain way. He was affectionate when I did what he wanted, and I did things just to please him, not realizing I was begging for his attention and approval." She turned troubled eyes on him. "Isn't that what you do for the people you love, though?"

Was she trying to justify falling under his spell and allowing herself to become a victim?

Robert held her gaze. Her amber eyes pulled at his heart. He could so easily get lost in those eyes. He cleared his throat. "It is, if making them happy makes you happy."

He thought of all the things he'd done for Jessie over the years--just to make her happy. Seeing her smile and making her laugh had brought him joy. It was the reason he'd let her leave five years ago, because following her dreams would make Jessie happy.

"Did it make you happy? Pleasing him, I mean."

She turned back to the lake again. "At first, I thought it did, but I often felt so empty afterward. I'm not sure it made him happy, either. It reached a point where, no matter what I did, I couldn't please him." She sniffed. "I remember looking in the mirror on our first anniversary and not recognizing myself. Not just on the outside. I didn't know who I was on the inside anymore." She brushed away a tear that had escaped.

Robert's gut clenched. He wished Pendleton *had* thrown a punch at him today. He would have enjoyed taking the man down.

"I'm sorry," Jessie said with a forced laugh. "Can we talk about something else, please?"

Robert was about to tell her she had nothing to apologize for, but he took in her guarded expression and knew she regretted speaking so frankly. She slipped on a mask he was certain she'd worked hard to perfect over the years.

The rest of the walk passed in relative quiet, with only occasional snippets of conversation. The sun was setting by the time they entered the clearing by the cabin. Clouds on the horizon promised a gorgeous sunset tonight.

In the past, he and Jessie would have snuggled up together and enjoyed it to the very last ray. And still they would have lingered, talking and kissing. He'd always been able to talk to her about anything.

Was that why she'd told him the things she did tonight? Did she feel that old familiar pull toward him, like he did her?

No. I'm only her protector.

"It's getting late. I should probably get going." He stepped toward his Tahoe instead of climbing the steps to the cabin.

Jessie's face fell. "Oh, okay."

"Do you need anything? I can send it with your mom tomorrow."

She stood on the wooden porch with her arms wrapped around herself. "No, I'm fine. Thanks for coming, Robert."

Fighting the urge to suggest they watch a movie together, he climbed into his SUV. He backed up then turned toward the main road before he allowed himself to look at Jessie in his rear-view mirror.

She still stood on the porch, hugging herself. She looked so lonely and vulnerable.

A gnawing feeling spread inside his gut. He shouldn't leave her alone, but he couldn't bear to stay.

CHAPTER 10

Robert climbed into his Tahoe and let out a deep sigh before pulling out of the parking lot of the Benton County District Attorney's office. In a few weeks, Eddie Green, the man who kidnapped his cousin's daughter, would finally be prosecuted for his crimes.

Ben had waited a long time for justice for his first wife.

As Robert braked for a red light, his gaze drifted to a familiar storefront with large, cursive lettering. The sign read, "The Creative Touch."

A familiar tension settled in his chest, as it always did when he thought about Jessie. He'd gone into that store with her more times than he could count. Anytime they came to Pasco together, Jessie turned those gorgeous amber eyes on him.

"Let's stop for just a minute, please."

On the rare occasion Robert could resist her, her pretty, pink lips turned into a pout, and it was his undoing. Because when she pouted like that, all he wanted to do was kiss her. Once he started kissing her, he lost all ability to say no to her.

Honk!

Robert jerked his thoughts back to the green light. He pressed the gas and drove through the intersection, but something tugged at him, and he signaled to pull into the center lane to make a U-turn.

What am I doing? Protector. That's my role. Only a protector.

But he couldn't get the image of Jessie out of his head when he visited her yesterday. She'd looked so lost and alone. So broken and in need of a friend.

She deserved so much more than the cards life had dealt her.

He pulled into the parking lot of "The Creative Touch" and shut off his engine but made no move to get out.

Could be the friend Jessie needed without letting himself fall for her again? If he bought her a few art supplies, would she accept the gift without feeling like there were strings attached?

A chill spread over him as he recalled the images and photographs he'd seen in Jessie's book. He opened his door, letting the hot July afternoon warm him.

Five minutes later, Robert wiped sweat from his brow, feeling glassy eyed. Colorful tubes, brushes of assorted qualities and sizes, sketch pads, and canvases surrounded him.

Did Jessie prefer acrylics over watercolors?

He recalled her touting the merits of this brand versus that brand, but he couldn't for the life of him remember which brand she preferred. All he could remember was how cute she looked when she was passionate about something.

And she'd always been passionate about art.

"Can I help you find something?" A middle-aged woman wearing a long denim skirt and a tie-dye t-shirt smiled at him.

"Uh...yeah. I want to buy some supplies for an artist friend of mine."

"A skilled artist or a beginner?"

"Skilled."

"So, are you thinking of a specialty brush or more paints for your friend's collection? Or perhaps a canvas?"

"She doesn't have a collection anymore."

The woman pressed a hand to her chest and gasped. No doubt an artist herself. "Did she lose it all in a fire or something?"

It probably would have hurt Jessie less to have lost all her art supplies in a fire rather than in the violent, demeaning way he imagined Pendleton had taken them from her.

He rolled his shoulders to clear the tension thoughts of Jessie always caused. "Something like that."

~

JESSIE LOOKED up from sketching in her journal at the sound of tires on the gravel driveway. Her heart skipped a beat. Not because she feared it might be Patrick, but because she knew Robert would visit again today.

She tried to tell herself she was just eager for company, not specifically the company of her former boyfriend. But her heart made up for the skipping a minute later by racing when she opened the door for Robert.

Man, he looked nice in a uniform.

Okay, it wasn't loneliness; she didn't react like this when her mother came to visit. Of course, her mom wasn't tall, broad-shouldered, and didn't have the longest, darkest eyelashes Jessie had ever seen.

"How are you doing?" Robert's deep voice sent a little thrill racing through her. He scratched his jaw, as though needing something to do with his hands.

"Good. Bored, as usual." She remembered how easy it was to talk to Robert two days ago and all the personal things she'd shared with him--things she had told no one else. That piece of her soul that had connected with him when she was seventeen remembered him and wanted to reconnect with him.

Robert scratched his jaw again and looked out the window at his Tahoe, then shifted his weight from one foot to the other.

"Is something wrong? Has Patrick caused trouble for my mom again already?"

"Huh? No, he hasn't returned."

"So why are you acting anxious?"

Robert stopped fidgeting and looked at her. "No reason. I just...would you like to go for a walk again?"

"I'd love to." The offer of a walk was an evasion tactic, but no way would she turn it down. "I have a serious case of cabin fever."

She expected him to laugh at her pun and come up with something equally cheesy, but he barely cracked a smile before stepping toward the door.

He's definitely distracted by something.

Not wanting to push him to talk, since she wasn't keen on sharing her own thoughts, Jessie followed him out the door.

They walked side-by-side in silence for a time, then Robert started talking about his family and what his siblings and mother were doing now. The conversation shifted to reminiscing about Robert teaching her how to drive a stick shift.

"I swear, I had some serious whiplash for that week," Robert said with a chuckle.

Jessi smacked his shoulder. "I wasn't that bad. Besides, it served you right for making me shoot that horrible high-recoil buckshot bullet."

Robert laughed. "I'll never forget the look on your face when it nearly knocked you on your butt."

Jessie joined in the laughter. "I couldn't figure out what happened with that shot. I should have realized something was up when Jake warned me not to trust you as we rode out that day."

Jessie marveled at how easy it was to talk to Robert after all these years. She'd always been comfortable with him and could talk to him about anything.

He'd been her sounding board after her father walked out on their family, and when she'd been trying to decide which college to go to, or when she'd been torn about leaving for a year and a half to study abroad. Robert was patient and supportive; a superb listener, offering helpful advice, never trying to influence her decisions.

"Do you miss it?" Robert asked abruptly, all trace of humor gone.

She shot him a quick glance. Had he read her mind? "Do I miss shooting bullets that leave my shoulder bruised for a week? No way."

"I mean, do you miss the carefree days of our youth? Where all we had to worry about were chores and homework. You know, before we had to start making the hard decisions?"

"Decisions like whether to stay and marry my boyfriend or chase my dreams?" Her voice was so quiet she wasn't sure he heard her.

He stepped in front of her, making her come to a stop. "No, Jessie. That's not what I meant." He raked a hand through his hair. "It's just...we've both been through some rough stuff. Don't you wish we could just go back?"

"Yes," she said without hesitation then silently added, *And I'd choose my boyfriend over my career.*

Her single word answer must have been enough, because he nodded and started walking again. "Me too." After a few strides he added, "Too bad we can't."

"Yeah."

Too bad wishing they could go back didn't change the way things were now. She couldn't help but wonder what difficult stuff Robert had been through, besides her leaving him and losing his dad?

When they returned to the cabin, Jessie put water on to boil for spaghetti, hoping to convince Robert to stay for dinner. She watched him out the window as he split more firewood. Though not bulky, he had a solid, muscular build, with broad shoulders and a trim waist. He loaded his arms full of split wood and warmth raced through her at the memory of being held in his embrace.

Giving herself a mental shake, she turned away from the window. She didn't particularly want to share an intimate meal with him, but she didn't want him to leave yet. The solitude was driving her crazy.

After Robert deposited his armload of wood, he shifted from one foot to the other as though uncertain whether he should stay or go.

"I'm making spaghetti," she blurted when he stepped toward the door. "Would you like to stay for dinner?" She held her breath, waiting for his response. Her stomach tightened in anticipation.

Robert looked out the window at his Tahoe again and rubbed his hands against his thighs. "I'd like that."

Jessie frowned as she turned back to the stove. If he was so eager to leave, why did he agree to stay for dinner?

"Should we watch a movie while we eat?" Robert called from the front room.

Hmm...maybe he's not so eager to leave after all. So why did he keep looking out the window at his SUV?

"Sure. You pick."

By the time dinner was ready, Jessie's stomach had grown so nauseous that she regretted asking him to stay.

Thankfully, Robert chose a comedy instead of a romantic movie. She was also glad he sat in the armchair, leaving her to sit on the sofa alone. Regardless, memories of the many times she'd snuggled into his arms on this very sofa filled her mind. They'd had some amazing intimate moments here.

Pushing aside the memories that made her regret all she'd given up, she focused on keeping her food down. The nervousness over asking him to stay hadn't abated.

When the movie ended, Robert bolted to his feet. "Thanks for dinner. I'd better get going." He stepped to the door, then paused. "I have something for you, Jess."

Her stomach--that had finally settled down--fluttered at the familiar nickname spoken in his low baritone.

Judging by his fidgeting, he either wasn't sure he wanted to give her whatever he had in his truck, or he was afraid of how she might react.

What could cause this kind of anxiety in a law enforcement officer?

"You don't need to give me anything," she said. "You've already done enough for me."

Robert met her gaze, and his words were so quiet she barely heard him. "I want to." Then he turned and exited the cabin.

Jessie waited near the door for him to return. When she saw the familiar logo of her favorite store on the large bag he carried, tears pricked her eyes.

Goosebumps covered her arms. What she wouldn't do for a sketch pad and some decent pencils.

She stepped back as he entered. His cheeks colored as he held out the bag. She hadn't seen him blush since they were teenagers.

She took the bag from him. The brush of his skin against hers sent a warm tingle up her arm, banishing the goosebumps.

The bag was heavy. This was more than a few art supplies. She dropped onto the sofa and set the bag on the coffee table. She couldn't hold back the smile as she pulled out a large sketch pad.

Then she pulled out a large wooden case engraved with a well-known, expensive logo. Her smile faltered, and she gasped. She had always coveted *Ingenuity's* complete artist's collection but could never afford to buy the set outright. Instead, she'd slowly collected the expensive pencils, brushes, and high-quality oil, acrylics, and water-color paints over many years.

She unhooked the metal clasps and opened the case. She ran her fingers over the colorful tubes and pencils before picking up her favorite brush for painting with acrylics; natural hair, size 8, flat brush.

Her hand trembled as she recalled how angry Patrick had been the first time he came home to find her painting and no dinner waiting. He'd snapped her brushes in two like they were toothpicks. Then he'd thrown her easel--canvas and all--across the room. When the wet paint on the canvas smeared against the white bedspread in the spare bedroom, he lost it.

That was the first time he'd beaten her.

He'd often snapped at her and jerked her around to make sure she knew he meant business, but that night was the first time he hit her. And it hadn't been just once.

The paintbrush slipped from her fingers, clattering on the coffee table as a tear fell to her cheek. She swiped at it with the fingers of her casted hand while she picked up the paintbrush with the other.

Aware of Robert's eyes on her, she replaced the brush and closed the case. She looked up at Robert, who watched her warily. "I can't accept this."

A sketch pad and a few pencils were one thing, but Robert must have spent hundreds of dollars on this set.

The muscle in his jaw flexed. "I was afraid you'd say that."

That's why he'd fidgeted all evening.

"Patrick would have a fit if I accepted--"

Robert stepped closer. "You left Patrick. He doesn't control you anymore, Jess." Robert's words were vehement, matching the flash of emotion in his brown eyes.

Oh, how she wished Robert's words were true. She'd left Patrick, but she feared he would always control her. Every thought, every action. She'd never be free of him.

Robert sat beside her. "Consider it a late birthday present."

A lump formed in her throat. "After all these years, you remembered it was my birthday last week?"

Robert's gaze locked with hers as he reached up to tuck a lock of hair behind her ear. "I remember everything about you, Jess."

His words--coupled with the gentle caress--touched something deep inside her. She couldn't fight the emotion anymore. The regret for the poor decisions she'd made, for the things she'd given up, for everything Patrick had taken from her, and the pain he'd inflicted on her all came rushing to the surface.

She turned away from Robert to hide her tears.

His gentle hand on her shoulder pulled her back around, and before Jessie could stop herself, she'd thrown her arms around his neck and buried her face against his shoulder.

His hands rested on her back, light and hesitant at first, but as her tears continued, his arms tightened around her and he pressed his cheek to her hair.

It had been a long time since Jessie had been held with such tenderness, and she reveled in it. Patrick had always apologized for hurting her, but the apology usually came as an explanation of why her behavior had caused him to lash out. It had never been the complete and total acceptance she felt in Robert's arms.

His embrace felt so perfect, so right.

Her tears gradually subsided, and Robert's woodsy, yet tangy, masculine scent along with the warmth of his body permeated her senses. At five foot ten, she was almost as tall as him. He used to joke that they were made for each other because they fit together so perfectly.

If she turned her head the slightest bit, her lips would meet his.

Realizing this was not a direction her thoughts should be going, she pulled away. Robert released her without hesitation, and she looked up to see a flush in his cheeks that matched the warmth in her own.

He bolted to his feet. "I have a couple more things in the truck." He was out the door before Jessie could blink.

More?

Robert soon returned, carrying an easel under one arm and another large bag in the other.

Jessie's breath caught in her throat. In one evening, Robert restored to her everything Patrick had taken away. Though there was a part of her she wasn't sure could ever be repaired. The part that filled her with self-doubt. The part that knew she didn't deserve Robert's kindness and generosity.

He handed her the bag and propped the easel against the wall. "Maybe this will help you fight the boredom."

Her eyes widened when she glanced in the bag. It was full of canvas boards of various sizes and a paint pallet. Tears filled her eyes again when she calculated how much money he must have spent. She blinked them away, confused by why she felt so weepy.

"I know it won't change what that man...did to you, but..." Robert shrugged, letting his words die off.

Jessie dropped the second bag on the coffee table with the first and threw her arms around Robert again. "Thank you."

He had every reason to hate her, but he didn't. And though he no longer loved her as he once had, he cared. Of that, she had no doubt.

Robert returned the embrace, his hands lingering for a moment at her waist before releasing her when she finally pulled back.

Still standing close to him, she searched his warm brown eyes with their long lashes. "Why did you spend so much money on me?"

He leaned toward her. "Because you're worth it, Jess. You probably doubt that right now, but you are worth all of this," he waved his hand at the coffee table, "and so much more." He lifted his hand as though he meant to touch her face. "You--"

Dropping his hand, he clamped his mouth shut and stepped back. "It's late. I'd better go," he mumbled as he turned and walked out the door. "Good night."

His sudden departure left a chill in the cabin and in her heart. What had he been about to say?

You are worth it.

Did Robert understand how little self-worth she had right now?

She gently stroked the art supplies he'd given her. Her fingers tingled as a ripple of excitement once again raced through her. She couldn't wait to start painting. She held up the largest canvas. Her first project would be a gift for Robert.

CHAPTER 11

Robert pulled up to the cabin but made no move to get out of his truck. He looked out at the placid lake, glimmering in the late afternoon sun. If only he could feel so tranquil.

When he was here two days ago, Jessie threw herself in his arms and wept so hard he'd felt his defenses crumbling.

Holding her had felt so right. And she'd smelled so good. Then, when she hugged him again in gratitude, he hadn't wanted to let her go. After telling her she was worth so much more than a few art supplies, he'd nearly kissed her and told her she meant the world to him.

Fortunately, he'd stopped himself, but the realization had rocked him. How, after five years, could she still mean the world to him?

The question had consumed him for the past two days. She'd crushed him when she left for New York, and though he didn't blame her for chasing her dreams, he didn't think he could forgive her. Was it so wrong of him to want her to choose him over her dreams?

So why am I so drawn to her now?

Was it because she'd been so unhappy for the past four years? Because she was so broken? If she'd divorced her husband on amicable terms and returned to Providence, would she still have such a powerful effect on him?

How had deciding he could be a friend to Jessie made everything so cloudy?

Fighting the urge to drive away, he climbed from his truck. *Keep it professional today. You're a protector, that's all.*

He knocked on the door and waited for Jessie. When she opened the door, the air whooshed from his lungs.

She wore his sweatshirt again, with form-fitting yoga pants, her hair mussed, her face void of makeup.

She looked absolutely beautiful.

"Hi. Is it that late already?" Her voice had a breathless quality to it.

His lips turned up at the smudge of green paint on her cheek. He followed her into the house, pleased to see the easel by the large picture window. She'd wasted no time.

He eyed the canvas, but she hurried over and turned it away. She didn't like to let anyone see her work before she finished it. According to Jessie, her reward for finishing a painting was the look on people's faces when they got the full effect of the piece. No matter what she painted, it was always amazing.

He grinned and stepped closer. "Come on, just a peek," he teased.

"No, you know I don't like people to guess what I'm painting." A hint of the old Jessie came through in her tone; passionate and feisty.

He'd seen enough to know she was painting her view of the lake from the cabin. The striking contrast between the vivid-blue sky and the vibrant pine trees surrounding the water took his breath away. And Jessie had only just started. He couldn't wait to see the finished product.

He let it go, but he couldn't stop himself from reaching up to wipe away the smudge of paint from her cheek, like he'd done so many times before.

Fear filled Jessie's eyes before she squeezed them shut. She sucked in a sharp breath and jerked her head away.

The realization that she thought he might strike her hit. He turned away and walked to the other side of the room. "Jessie, I--"

"I'm sorry." She wrapped her arms around herself. "I thought I upset you because I wouldn't show you the painting."

"I'd never be upset about that." He rubbed his neck, trying to ease the tension there.

"I know. I'm sorry. I just...overreacted." She dropped her gaze.

"Don't apologize." He shook his head. "I should have realized how threatening that might look. I only wanted to wipe the paint off your cheek."

Pink colored Jessie's face as she brushed at her cheek.

He stepped toward her. "Look at me, please."

She raised her eyes, and he held her gaze. "I would never hurt you, Jess. You know that, right?"

She nodded, tears filling her eyes. She pressed her good hand to her chest. "In here, I know that. But nowadays I'm afraid...of everyone and everything."

Robert had been here for less than five minutes, and already he ached to pull her into his arms. Instead, he stuffed his hands into his pockets. "Please tell me you don't fear me."

She shook her head. "I don't fear you. You just took me by surprise."

Keep it professional, man.

He cleared his throat. "I'd better go chop some firewood." He needed a physical outlet, or he'd end up doing something they'd both regret.

"Robert." She stopped him at the door.

He looked back at her.

"I trust you more than I've ever trusted another person."

He dipped his head in acknowledgment before closing the door behind himself. Her words both pleased and terrified him. Because he wasn't sure he trusted himself around her.

Forty minutes later, Robert dropped his second armful of split logs in the wood box and looked at Jessie.

She stood behind her easel, so absorbed she hardly noticed he'd come back in. He studied her, refusing to let his eyes linger on the way she chewed her top lip while deep in concentration. Instead, he looked at her eyes, alight with joy. He loved watching her face while she created works of art.

He recalled the way she used to close her eyes while molding clay on the potter's wheel. Watching her hands shape the clay had been one of his favorite pastimes. It calmed and mesmerized him.

He shifted his gaze to her hair. Her brown roots showed through the blond locks that hung straight and slightly tangled.

Jessie could become so absorbed while painting that she often forgot to eat. He wandered to the kitchen and noted a lone cereal bowl in the sink.

"At least she ate breakfast," he murmured to himself. "But it almost seven p.m."

Finding the leftover spaghetti in the fridge, he pulled it out to heat for dinner. Because that's what a friend would do.

He *wasn't* doing it because he didn't want to leave yet.

He hummed absently while he tossed a salad. His hands stilled as he realized what tune he hummed. Tim McGraw's "It's Your Love" had been his and Jessie's song. It was an oldie, but it fit them so well. Heat filled his face, and he stopped humming, only to hear Jessie's softer tones join in.

Did she realize what song she was humming? Or was she too absorbed with her painting?

Fifteen minutes later, he had everything ready on the table. Keeping his distance, so he wouldn't startle her, he called her name. "Jessie, dinner is ready."

She jumped anyway. "Oh, you didn't need to fix dinner."

Robert folded his arms and grinned. "What time is it?"

Jessie turned her gaze to the window. Her eyebrows shot up, and her mouth formed an "O" when she realized it was almost dusk.

"And what did you eat for lunch?"

Fighting a smile, she dropped her gaze to his shoes. Color flooded her cheeks.

Robert chuckled. Hopefully, she'd forgotten for a little while that she was hiding from an abusive husband.

"Come on, let's eat."

Jessie cleaned her brushes, then joined him at the table. "Thanks for this. It's easier to slip back into old habits than I thought it would be."

Was that what he was doing with Jessie? Slipping back into old habits?

As comfortable as Jessie was to be around, he didn't like to think of her as a habit. Because habits--especially bad ones--became addicting. And he couldn't become addicted to Jessie again. He would never recover when she left again.

And she would leave. Because nothing had changed. Jessie was still too talented for this one-horse town.

CHAPTER 12

Patrick watched as Sylvia drove out of the parking lot of Knight's Grocery. He pulled Jessie's Infiniti out and followed Sylvia onto Main Street. Despite his desire to find Jessica, he kept his foot steady on the gas. Drawing the attention of the Sheriff's department that seemed to be everywhere lately was the last thing he needed.

He kept a car between himself and Sylvia so she wouldn't spot him tailing her.

This was the third night in a row he'd tailed her after she left the hospital. Her shift always ended at six, but he'd gotten there an hour early tonight to make sure he didn't miss her. He cursed himself for losing her two nights ago when he got stopped at this hick town's one and only traffic light.

Sylvia hadn't returned home until after dark that night. She'd spend the evening with Jessica, he was sure of it. Wherever that was.

Last night, she went straight home from work and didn't leave her house all evening. Patrick had finally gone to the grocery store and pretended to be a college buddy of Winters, stopping in for a surprise visit. The teenage cashier had been no match for his charm, and she'd not only told him what street the sheriff lived on, she'd described his house.

Patrick had spent hours parked in front of the sheriff's dark house, stewing. He just knew Winters was with Jessie, and the thought infuriated him.

Jessie is mine.

No way would he let some Podunk sheriff have her.

Yesterday had been a complete waste, but Patrick refused to let today be one as well.

Actually, the entire week had been a waste. He had hard time convincing his boss to let him take some personal time off while he tried to figure out where his wife was. In the meantime, projects piled up on his desk.

Tina kept pestering him, too. She was acting possessive, and it grated on his nerves. It was time to cut her loose. But he couldn't think about that right now.

He needed to get Jessica back. The stress he'd been under this past week was intolerable. He needed to find Jessie, get her to drop the charges against him. Then things could go back to normal.

The car between him and Sylvia turned off Main Street, so he dropped back, hoping she wouldn't recognize Jessica's Infiniti in her rear-view mirror. He didn't dare bring his red Lexus back here for fear the expensive car would stand out in this hillbilly town full of rednecks and pickup trucks.

As nice as Jessica's car was, it didn't speak "wealth" like his Lexus did. Presence was everything. That's why he needed his wife back by his side. Tina was pretty and all, but Jessica--despite her simple upbringing--was beauty and grace defined.

Sylvia's aged Camry took a right and Patrick realized why he'd lost her the other night. There was nothing out this way except for a pretentious mansion on the outskirts of town and a vast ranch.

He shook his head. "How can people stand to live so far away from civilization?"

After another fifteen minutes of driving, he feared Sylvia was leading him on a wild goose chase. Then she turned off the road that circled a lake.

He slowed as he passed the driveway Sylvia turned into. There, hidden in the trees, sat a large log cabin.

Bingo.

Now all he had to do was wait for Sylvia to leave. Then he could get his wife back. It had to be tonight. He couldn't risk the chance of running into the sheriff tomorrow.

JESSIE LOCKED and turned the dead bolt on the door behind her mom. She hated to see her go. She'd enjoyed reconnecting with her mother, but more than that, she dreaded being left alone again.

Despite enjoying painting again, she found the solitude and quiet stifling. Anxiety ate at her, tying her stomach into a perpetual knot, often making her nauseous. She pressed a hand to her abdomen, wondering if the fear of Patrick finding her would ever go away.

It surprised her that he didn't cause more waves after Robert ran him out of town. Jessie couldn't hide out here forever and expect Robert to keep taking care of her. Something needed to give.

She walked back to her easel, itching to pick up her paintbrush again. But it was too dark now; she wouldn't get the colors right. Instead, she studied her progress so far. The space and colors were good, but something was off. She focused on the texture she'd given the trees surrounding the lake and realized she'd created too strong of contrast and lost the balance and harmony she'd been aiming for.

At the crunch of gravel outside, Jessie's lungs seized.

Please let it be Mom coming back.

She peered through the glass in the door out into the twilight. The car pulling in, though blue like her mother's, didn't look right. This car was nicer, more silver.

A chill swept over Jessie as she recognized her Infiniti Q50. Her knees buckled. If not for her tight grip on the doorknob, she would have fallen.

Hands trembling, she made sure the door was locked and dead bolted. She spun around, searching for a hiding place. There were two bedrooms upstairs, but she'd be trapped up there with no way to escape. She turned toward the back door. If she got outside...

She couldn't outrun Patrick, but maybe she could hide in the forest? A sharp pain shot through her chest, stealing her breath, and fear clawed at her throat. Resisting the urge to scream and curl up in a ball, she rushed out the back door, pausing long enough to lock it and pull it closed. Locking herself out was stupid, but hopefully Patrick would think she was still inside.

Jessie shivered as she stepped off the back porch. She figured it had less to do with the cool summer night and more to do with the fact that if Patrick got his hands on her, he would kill her. She darted for the cover of the shed where Robert's family stored the canoes. It was probably locked, but she had to try.

The door swung open. She darted inside, banging her shin against a hard metal object. Stifling a yelp, she rubbed her leg while her eyes adjusted to the darkness.

Two hulking shadows claimed the center of the shed. *Four-wheelers?* She hadn't driven one of those in years, but she'd figure it out if she could find a key...

She fumbled around the handlebars but came up empty-handed. Of course, they don't keep the keys on the machines. In fact, they probably kept this shed locked. Robert must have forgotten to lock it yesterday.

Jessie continued to search the small shed for a place to hide. The fishing boat lay on its side against the far wall, and two canoes rested upside down across the rafters overhead. She wrapped her arms around herself as the pressure in her chest increased.

She had nowhere to hide.

She backed out of the shed.

"Jessica!" Patrick's angry bellow came from the front of the cabin, followed by the sharp crack of wood splitting.

Jessie clapped one hand over her mouth and the other over her stomach that had turned rock hard. Blinking back the tears that filled her vision, she turned and bolted to the steep trail behind the shed.

~

ROBERT CLOSED his office door behind Debbie and dropped into his chair. That's what he got for staying late. He scrubbed his hands over his face.

The woman never gives up!

This time she wanted his help to develop a youth outreach program. A great idea, but it was all Robert could do not to bite her head off.

He didn't have the patience for Debbie and her "do-good" programs today. He had more important things to worry about, like helping Jessie. The fear in her eyes as she flinched away from him yesterday had haunted him all night.

Jessie shouldn't be afraid of everyone and everything. She deserved to live a normal life, dressing the way she wanted and doing the things she loved.

An odd sensation--somewhere between a crawl and an itch--swept across his skin.

He loosened his tie and undid the top button of his uniform. The last time he felt like this was years ago, when Jessie was thrown from a horse.

He rolled a pen between his fingers as he thought about Jessie riding out on her own on Honey. He'd wanted to join her, but his father needed his help with a heifer that had fallen into a ravine.

Even before they arrived back at the ranch and realized Honey had returned without Jessie, Robert had been uneasy. Something was wrong. He just knew it. He left his father and pointed his horse in the direction she'd ridden.

His heart had nearly stopped when he found her unconscious on the ground, miles from the house.

She easily aroused when he touched her. But he refused to let her move until he'd checked her over for bleeding and broken bones. Her only injury was a goose egg on the back of her head where she'd struck it on a rock.

"What happened?" he asked, overcome with relief.

"Honey got spooked by a rattlesnake and bucked me off."

Warmth flooded over Robert as he recalled holding her in his arms. She could have suffered serious injuries.

Grabbing his keys and sidearm from his desk drawer, he walked out of the office with barely a wave to Janice. He got in his truck and headed toward the ranch. He needed to talk to Emily.

He didn't know what he'd say, or how Emily could help, but he needed to do something.

Fifteen minutes later, he pulled off the road at the turnoff to the lake. He'd been thinking so intently about Jessie--wishing she'd come back to Providence under different circumstances and hoping she'd stick around--that he'd blown right past the ranch.

He told himself to turn around, go back, but something pulled at him to check on Jessie. Despite remembering how much he'd enjoyed riding double with Jessie after Honey threw her off, the hair on the back of his neck lifted.

Something is wrong with Jessie.

Putting his truck into drive, he made the turn toward the lake, unsure how he'd explain his unexpected visit.

CHAPTER 13

Jessie curled into a ball and hid in the corner of the fort in the oak tree that hung over the shed.

She'd almost raced right past the giant tree in her haste to flee from Patrick. Then she'd remembered Robert taking her there to hide from Riley and Paige, his little sister and cousin, who kept pestering Robert to take them out on the lake.

She prayed Patrick wouldn't spot the old, yet sturdy, structure in the dark.

Trying to stay calm despite the adrenaline coursing through her veins screaming, "*Run!*" she focused on taking steady breaths.

"Jessica!"

She gasped at Patrick's harsh tone.

"I know you're out here. It's time to come home, honey."

Jessie squeezed her eyes closed and held her breath. She clenched her jaw so Patrick wouldn't hear her teeth chattering.

His footsteps crunched on the rocks and twigs in the yard. Then his voice came from directly below her, as though he knew exactly where she'd hidden. "Come on, Jessica. Did you really think you could just come home and pick up where you left off?" The derision in his voice sent an additional chill racing through her. "I saw your painting.

I'm afraid you've lost your touch, honey. Did you honestly think you still have that kind of talent?"

Patrick went quiet and Jessie tried to tell herself not to listen to his mind games, but it hit too close to home. As much as she wanted to, she couldn't pretend the past five years hadn't happened. Why did she think she could still paint when she'd done nothing to foster her talents over the past few years?

A crash came from inside the shed, and Jessie jumped. She clamped her hand over her mouth again, stifling the urge to scream. Her heart pounded so loud she feared it would give her away.

Patrick's cursing grew louder as he exited the shed. "Come on out, Jessica! I just want to talk." A tight edge filled Patrick's voice, and Jessie knew talking was the last thing he intended to do. "We have some things to iron out."

Jessie curled a little tighter, wishing she could make herself invisible.

"The sheriff isn't here to save you." He gave a derisive laugh. "I can't believe you came running back to him. There's a reason he let you leave, Jessica. You weren't worth his time and effort."

Patrick's words tore at her. She wanted to tell him they weren't true, but she couldn't. And not just because she didn't want to give away her hiding spot.

"Did you honestly think he'd want you again? You're a useless, washed up, piece of trash who couldn't even keep her husband satisfied."

Jessie pressed her fingers to her ears. Just because Patrick spoke the truth didn't mean she had to listen to it.

A WEIGHT PRESSED against Robert's chest, and his stomach plummeted as soon as he turned into the driveway of the cabin.

The blue car parked in front of him was not Sylvia's.

He shoved his truck into park and fumbled with his seat belt. He couldn't make his icy fingers work fast enough.

Once free of the blasted harness, he leapt from his truck, not even bothering to turn off the engine. He had to find Jessie and protect her from her lunatic husband.

He sent up a prayer as he ran toward the cabin, unsnapping the holster on his gun as he did so.

Please don't let me be too late.

He skidded to a stop at the sight of the door hanging ajar. A chunk of the door frame fractured on the floor. His senses went on high alert as his heart raced. He'd be lucky if he didn't have a heart attack before he found Jessie.

He stepped through the door to find Jessie's unfinished canvas on the floor beside the easel that lay in a jagged heap. Each leg snapped in two. His adrenalin spiked, and he fought to keep his hands steady as he searched the great room.

The iciness in his veins turned hot as his fear for Jessie shifted to anger at the man who had broken her.

"Jessie!" He spun and looked at the loft.

Nothing.

He swore under his breath. He couldn't afford to waste time searching the cabin if she was already outside. But he didn't want to go racing outside if she and Pendleton were upstairs.

The thought of her running for her life through the dark forest stole his breath. He needed focus so he could find her.

Now.

He paused and sucked in a deep breath, waiting for that feeling that brought him here to guide him.

His gaze shifted to the open back door of the cabin, and his feet pulled him in that direction. He scanned the small yard that lay between the cabin and the shed and on down to the lake.

Fifteen feet beyond the shed, he spotted movement--a dark figure--moving toward the lake.

"Pendleton!"

The shadow froze and vile swear words floated on the breeze.

As the figure moved back in his direction, relief swept over Robert. He didn't know where Jessie was, but Pendleton was alone.

Robert's hand hovered over his holster. "Get on the ground, now! And keep your hands where I can see them."

Patrick stopped walking toward Robert and edged closer to the shed. "I don't want any trouble, sheriff. I just want my wife back. Jessica's mine. She's coming home with me."

Like heck she is. Robert bit back the retort and forced a laugh. "The only place you're going is jail for breaking the restraining order."

Patrick darted to the side of the shed, reappearing seconds later with the ax Robert had forgotten to put away yesterday. "You had your chance with Jessica, and she left you. She's mine now."

Robert's hand hovered over his weapon. It'd be the easiest way to subdue Pendleton, but that seemed excessive when Robert was confident he could disarm him without his gun. It *wasn't* because he wanted to take Jessie's husband down and slam his face into the ground when he cuffed him.

He inched closer to Jessie's husband, reading the other man's body language in the dark. Robert tensed. He needed to get close enough to disarm him but stay out of reach of his weapon.

As soon as the other man shifted to raise the ax, Robert charged. He shoved the hand with the ax upward, then rammed his shoulder into the other man's abdomen. Pendleton fell back on the ground with a grunt, Robert on top of him.

Robert drew back and threw a punch at Pendleton's jaw. He ignored the pain that tore through his knuckles, taking pleasure instead in the satisfying thud his fist made against the other man's face and the groan it evoked. The ax moved in the corner of Robert's vision and he reached out to block it but wasn't quick enough. The back side of the ax clipped him in the temple.

Stars filled his vision, and he felt himself sway. He shook his head, trying to clear it, and made a desperate grab for the arm that held the ax before it swung again. He caught it inches from his face and slammed it into the ground. Pendleton's hand loosened, and the ax fell from his grip.

Robert shoved it out of reach and pulled his hand back to punch Pendleton again. He caught the other man's fist in the abdomen before he could land his own blow. Chiding himself for letting the other man get a shot in, he struck out hard and fast. First to Pendleton's face, then his chest.

As the other man gasped for air, Robert pulled back a third time. Or was it a fourth? He caught himself. He'd love to punish Jessie's husband for all he'd put her through, but he couldn't get carried away. It would only come back to bite him if Pendleton pressed charges of police brutality.

He grabbed Pendleton's shoulder and flipped him onto his stomach, trying not to take too much pleasure in shoving the man's face into the ground.

Reading Pendleton his rights, Robert pulled him to his feet and pushed him toward his Tahoe.

The other man let loose another string of swear words. "Jessie may have come running back to you, but she'll never be yours. She's mine now, and I'll make sure If I can't have her no one will."

Icy fingers snaked around Robert's neck at the deadly tone in Pendleton's voice. The man meant every word of his threat.

As soon as he'd locked his prisoner in the backseat of his Tahoe, Robert radioed Dale, requesting backup.

He turned toward the cabin. He needed to find Jessie, make sure she was okay, and let her know she was safe.

His chest tightened. She had to be okay. He'd never forgive himself if Pendleton had already gotten to Jessie before he arrived.

He stepped into the cabin. "Jessie! It's safe. Come out, sweetheart."

Heat filled his face at the endearment that slipped out. He sucked in a sharp breath. He was traversing a slippery slope here, and he didn't know what to do about it. He wanted to take Jessie far from here and hide away together. Just the two of them. Forever. Where there was no abusive ex-husband, no past hurts or regrets, and no irreconcilable futures.

Even if he could take her far away, would she even want to spend forever with him? There had been a time when he was certain she would have loved exactly that. But he'd let her walk away five years ago. And when she returned, he brought her here and left her alone and defenseless. He'd promised to protect her, but he'd failed.

He wouldn't blame her if she wanted nothing to do with him.

He continued searching the cabin, repeatedly calling her name. Every second that passed with no answer made his muscles bunch and his insides churn.

He pulled his flashlight from his belt as he rushed out to the shed. He searched every corner of the structure before stepping back out into the clearing.

"Jessie!" It was full dark now, with only a sliver of a moon. If Jessie didn't answer his calls, he might not find her tonight. It rarely froze this late in the summer, but temperatures could still drop quite low at night near the lake.

His stomach bottomed out as he looked at the lake. *What if I'm too late?*

No, Pendleton had been walking toward the lake, not away from it, when Robert arrived.

A muffled sniff sounded above him, and Robert raised his eyes and flashlight to the dark sky. The old fort amid the branches of the oak tree created a looming shadow.

He heaved a sigh. *Smart woman.*

Short of running into the forest where she could have easily become lost in the dark, Jessie hid in the one place Pendleton would have been hard-pressed to find her. Even in broad daylight, the tree house was hard to spot in the old oak tree.

"Thank you," he whispered heavenward before he darted to the path that led to the only access to the upper branches.

Robert shivered as he climbed the tree to the clubhouse. The chill of the night air and the adrenaline surging through him made it difficult to grasp the branches.

"Jess." Robert poked his head through the floor of the clubhouse and shone his flashlight around. The beam landed on Jessie huddled in a fetal position, eyes squeezed shut, hands pressed to her ears.

Another shiver surged through him at the sight.

She flinched away from the glare of the flashlight and curled tighter in on herself.

He turned off the light and slipped it into his belt. The night outside was dark, but it was even darker in the tiny structure with only one small window. The tree house that he, Jake, and Ben had labeled a "fort" and their younger sisters had called their "castle" was much smaller than he remembered.

He lifted himself inside and scooted toward Jessie. Reaching out, he felt for her shoulder.

She flinched again and swatted at his hand. "No, don't hurt me again, please."

The plea in her words tore at his heart, and again he silently cursed himself for leaving her here alone, unprotected. "Jess, it's me. I won't hurt you."

He sensed that she lifted her head, though he couldn't see her clearly.

"Robert?" It was little more than a whisper.

Grappling for her in the dark, he gathered her into his arms and pulled her onto his lap.

She trembled as shivers wracked her body. How much of her shaking was caused by the chill of the night air, and how much was caused by fear?

He rubbed his hand up and down the arm that wasn't pressed against his chest. "I'm so sorry, sweetheart. You're safe now."

He didn't chide himself for using the endearment again. In fact, he barely noticed it had slipped from his lips. It felt so right. So natural. Just like it felt so right to hold her in his arms.

Robert hated to think what might have happened if he'd ignored the prompting to come check on Jessie. Or if he'd been even fifteen minutes later. Would Pendleton have discovered Jessie up here?

He tightened his arms around Jessie's trembling body and pressed his lips to her hair.

"I'm s-sorry," she mumbled into his shoulder, shaking her head. "I shouldn't have c-come home. I shouldn't have put you and my m-mom in danger."

"I'm the one who should be apologizing. I promised to keep you safe, and I nearly failed." He swallowed hard to clear the tightness from his throat. "I'm so sorry I wasn't here for you when you needed me."

She shook her head and pushed away from him. She scooted off his lap, leaving his arms with nothing to hold but the chilly night air. "No, it's not your f-fault. It's mine. It's all m-mine. Patrick's right. Why did I think I could c-come back and pretend I still had a p-place here?"

"You do have a place here. This is your home. You still--" He stopped himself before he could say she still had a place in his heart. As badly as his heart hurt for her, and as much as he wanted to take her away from here, he didn't dare let her in again.

"No, I should never have come home."

"Listen to me." Robert scooted closer until his knees bumped hers. He wished he could see her gorgeous amber eyes. "None of this is your fault. I don't know what he said to you but, the man cuffed in the backseat of my SUV is nothing more than the dregs of humanity. You can't believe anything he said."

Jessie shook her head. "He was right. I'm not good enough anymore."

Good enough for what? For whom? Boy, did he regret not punching that jerk a few more times.

He wanted to tell her she was good enough for him. Nothing could ever change that. But he couldn't say the words.

"Yes, you are. You're too good for this small town." He bit his tongue before adding, *too good for me.*

A soft sniffle filled the darkness. "I wish I could believe that."

Robert reached out a hand. As soon as he touched hers, she grasped his. "So do I, sweetheart."

CHAPTER 14

Jessie couldn't believe Robert was here.

The first time he called her name, she thought she'd dreamed it. That she'd blacked out from the terror that overwhelmed her, and her subconscious had brought him to her rescue. But when he touched her, she just knew Patrick had found her, because there was no way Robert had shown up when she needed him most.

When he pulled her onto his lap and wrapped his strong, warm arms around her, she wanted to curl into his embrace, inhale his familiar woodsy scent and let him chase away the fear and darkness. But Patrick's words mocked her. Of course, Robert wouldn't want the woman who had once rejected him. Chosen her dreams over him. A woman who had married a man she didn't love because she couldn't have the man she loved.

But Robert called her "sweetheart," and confusion swamped Jessie. She wanted to believe his words--that she was good enough--but more than that, she wanted to believe she hadn't imagined the affection in his tone.

She wasn't naïve enough to think she could just come back and have all she'd walked away from. She didn't deserve that. In fact, most days she was certain Robert could barely stand to be around her. So why had he let that endearment slip? Twice.

She closed her eyes in the dark tree house and relished the warmth of his hand in hers and the fact she was safe.

Robert squeezed her hand. "Backup is here."

Jessie opened her eyes to see an eerie strobe of muted red and blue lights flash through the small window.

Robert tugged on her hand. "I need you to pack your things while I turn my prisoner over to Dale."

He released her hand and seconds later the bright beam of his flashlight illuminated the hole in the floor of the tree house. Robert shifted, lowering his body down the hole. "Come on. I'll help you down."

Less than a minute later, Jessie reached out a hand to Robert, letting him help her down from the lowest branch of the tree. A loose pebble rolled under her foot as she hit the ground, and she pitched forward against Robert's chest.

Strong arms tightened around her. "Careful, now."

Jessie caught her breath and resisted the urge to wrap her arms around Robert's neck.

His breath tickled her cheek, and his masculine scent surrounded her. She leaned into his embrace, a ripple of warmth sweeping over her. They had always fit so perfectly together.

She didn't deserve Robert, but oh, how she wanted him.

Robert's hands slid up her back, and Jessie's pulsed quickened. His cheek shifted against hers, and her breath hitched. She'd dreamed so many times of being back in Robert's arms with his lips on hers.

His hands shifted to her bare arms. Whether to pull her closer or push her away so he could kiss her, she didn't know, but his warm hands against her cold skin sent a jolt through her.

He sucked in a sharp breath. "You're cold as ice. Let's get you inside and warmed up." He stepped back but kept an arm around her shoulder as he guided her down the short, steep slope behind the shed.

Jessie shuddered. Just when she thought Robert might kiss her, he slipped back into his protector role. Patrick was right: Despite the mixed signals Robert sent her, he didn't want her back. He was only doing his job.

Patrick had often told her she was a horrible wife, and he'd been right. She'd pined for what she'd walked away from, and the fact that she craved Robert's kiss again proved she'd never gotten over him.

Appalled with herself, she let Robert lead her to the cabin. He pulled a throw blanket off the couch and wrapped it around her shoulders before walking out the front door. "I'll be right back."

Jessie followed him, but stopped when she saw the splintered door frame. If Patrick had done that--and she was sure he had--what would he have done to her if he'd gotten his hands on her? A new series of chills racked her body.

She watched as Robert pulled Patrick from the back of his Tahoe and pushed him toward Dale's cruiser.

Before allowing himself to be shoved into the car, Patrick looked straight at her. She couldn't see his face because of the darkness and the still strobing red and blue lights, but she knew he sneered. And she knew the look in his eyes right now--the one she'd seen so many times--said he'd kill her the next time he got his hands on her.

She turned away from the door and dropped onto the couch.

Robert found her there a few minutes later, sitting in a daze. He crouched in front of her, drawing her gaze. "Patrick's gone. You don't need to be afraid of him anymore."

She felt her brow furrow as she fought the urge to give in to hysterical laughter. Because it was laugh or cry, and Jessie couldn't give in to the tears right now. She might never stop crying if she started.

"He'll be back." The voice sounded like it came from somewhere other than her own mouth. She felt as if she were watching herself in a bad dream. Trapped some place she didn't want to be, unable to leave this endless nightmare.

"Dale is going to lock him up."

Jessie pushed to her feet. "But he'll get out on bail again tomorrow. And then what?"

"He's stacked up multiple felony charges against himself. He won't get out so fast this time."

"So, he takes three days to make bail. He'll still get out and he'll come after me again."

Robert stood, too. "When he gets out, I'll make sure he leaves town. I will personally follow him to the county line."

Jessie wished Robert's words comforted her, but they didn't. Patrick would be back.

She pushed past Robert and paced the room, feeling like a caged animal. "You followed him to the county line after he showed up at my mom's. That was less than a week ago. He'll come back, and h-he broke the d-door. I can't e-even lock--"

Jessie sucked in a sharp breath, trying to rein in her emotions.

Robert stepped in front of her and put his hands on her shoulders. "That's why I'm taking you away from here. I should have never left you here alone. I'm so sorry."

She heard the self-recrimination in his voice and wanted to assure him it wasn't his fault, but she couldn't. She was so close to hysterics she didn't dare open her mouth.

"I need you to go pack your things while I make you some tea. Maybe it will help you calm down."

"Calm down? How am I supposed to calm down? My husband wants to kill me, and he doesn't respect the law telling him he can't!"

She obviously hadn't overcome the hysterics yet. She felt bad about taking it out on Robert, though. He'd come to her rescue tonight. If not for him, Patrick might have found her. A sudden wave of exhaustion hit her at the thought, followed by an even stronger wave of nausea.

Jessie dropped the blanket she still held and bolted for the bathroom.

A few minutes later, she washed her face, wishing she didn't still feel like such a wreck. For some reason, vomiting always made her weepy, but after tonight's traumatic events, she couldn't seem to stop the flow of tears. Everything was so out of control.

A knock sounded on the bathroom door. "Jessie? Are you okay?"

"I'm fine. I just need a minute."

She leaned her head back against the door and squeezed her eyes shut, pushing out the remaining tears. Robert had seen her at her worst many times before. She did not want him to see her now, though. She might end up in his arms again, and she could not allow that to happen. It only confused her. Made her want things she couldn't have.

She washed her face and studied her reflection in the mirror. She'd become a master at controlling her emotions in front of Patrick. She could do the same in front of Robert. Never mind that he knew and understood her in ways Patrick had never even attempted to understand.

Jessie opened the bathroom door and nearly collide with Robert, who stood in the narrow hallway. For the second time tonight, she caught her breath at his nearness.

"Are you okay?" he asked.

Drawing in a steadying breath, she stepped sideways. "I'm fine."

"Your tea is almost ready."

"I don't need it." She forced a smile but couldn't make eye contact. "See, I'm calm."

She felt far from calm, but she wouldn't tell Robert that. If she sat down to drink a cup of tea, Robert would sit nearby, watching her. And he would see right through her facade. Besides, the thought of putting something in her stomach right now made it churn.

She stepped toward the bedroom where she'd been sleeping. "I'll pack my bags."

Robert reached out a hand as though he meant to stop her, but then he dropped it. "Okay, I'll pack up your art supplies."

Jessie stopped before closing the door of the bedroom between her and Robert. "Where are you taking me?"

"Home."

A strange sensation rushed through her, stealing her breath, at that single word--a mixture of nostalgia and hope, followed by fear. "Not to my mother's?" She didn't want to put her mom in more danger than she already had.

"No. To the Double Diamond," Robert said as he pulled his phone from his pocket.

A light-heartedness filled her. The Double Diamond had been her second home. There was nowhere else she'd rather go. The thought of being close to Robert every day was both exciting and painful. She couldn't bear to be around him that much, knowing he would never want her again. Not like he once had.

Robert turned away, phone to his ear. "Jake, I need a favor."

THEY MADE the ride to the ranch mostly in silence. The hope Jessie had felt at the mention of the Double Diamond dissipated when she recalled Robert mentioning--during one of their walks--that he'd moved into town and Jake now ran the ranch.

Robert was pawning her off on Jake.

He broke the silence a few miles before they reached the Double Diamond. "I wish I could tell you you're free to come and go whenever you want, but we need to be cautious until we know if Pendleton will make bail or not."

Jessie stared out her window into the darkness. "I understand."

"Your mother is welcome to visit whenever she wants, and I'll come out as often as I can to check on you."

As much as Jessie loved the Double Diamond, she wasn't that eager to return to her home away from home. If she thought the cabin was uncomfortable because it was so full of memories, the ranch would be ten times worse.

"Jake's married now. I think I mentioned that the other day." Robert scratched his jaw, the stubble there creating an abrasive sound that made Jessie want to reach out and stroke his cheek. "His wife, Emily, is really nice. She's uh...a doctor...of psychology."

Robert left the words hanging there like they meant something to her. They didn't. And as Jessie thought about Robert's family, the unsettled feeling in her stomach expanded. She didn't want to face those people who loved Robert the most. The ones who knew how badly she'd hurt him.

When she didn't respond, Robert cleared his throat. "Emily can help you, Jess. If you'll let her."

So that's why he mentioned his sister-in-law was a psychologist. He thought Jessie needed help. Professional help. Mental health. She couldn't help but take offense. She opened her mouth to tell him to mind his own business then closed it, the words still on the tip of her tongue.

She had no desire to talk to anyone, especially not a psychologist. She remembered the counselor her mother had insisted she and her sister see after their father left. She had helped Jessie regain some self-esteem and not feel like a failure as a daughter. But that kind of counseling couldn't restore all that she'd lost to Patrick.

Who am I kidding? I do need help.

Because no matter how hard Jessie tried, she doubted she'd ever be able to overcome the fear that enshrouded her like a heavy cloak. Fear of Patrick. Fear that she'd never be good enough. Fear that she'd never again find the kind of happiness she'd once had with Robert.

"I'll keep that in mind," Jessie murmured. "By the way, thanks for saving me tonight. What made you come to the cabin when it wasn't your night?"

Robert gave her a brief glance before turning off the highway under the iron gate sporting the Double Diamond name and brand. Jessie pressed a hand to her chest as the sprawling ranch house that always took her breath away came into view. Though it didn't look near as impressive in the dark--with only a few windows lit--as it usually did.

Robert didn't speak until he'd brought his truck to a stop in front of the house. "Do you remember that time you rode out on Honey alone and got thrown off when a rattlesnake spooked her?"

Jessie remembered the spiritual lesson eighteen-year-old Robert taught her that night. Although her mom took her and Chelsea to church after their dad left, Jessie had difficulty believing God--a loving heavenly father--could love her when her own earthly father hadn't.

That evening, as she rode back to the ranch house with Robert on his horse Goliath, he'd explained to her how he'd felt prompted to come find her. He'd helped her realize God looked out for her because he loved her. She'd felt the truthfulness of his words that night and had tried hard to maintain that relationship with deity.

But she hadn't felt that love from God for a very long time. She figured it was punishment for the choices she'd made, since she'd distanced herself from Him. Not by choice. It was just one of the many things Patrick had taken from her. But she'd stopped crying unto God, even in her heart.

She whispered a heartfelt, "Thank you," meant for both Robert and the father who felt so far away.

They climbed from the SUV and she followed Robert, dreading facing his family.

Jessie shot a glance toward the front porch swing where she and Robert had spent many an evening talking and planning their lives together. He often played his guitar for her. Did he still play?

The front door opened as soon as they stepped up onto the wooden porch. Jake, a younger, stockier version of Robert and equally as handsome, stood there. He ushered them into the house, his eyes grazing over Jessie before they returned to his brother.

He pointed to the side of Robert's face. "What happened?"

Robert turned his cheek away from Jake, which gave Jessie a better view of his face. A purplish bruise had formed high on his cheek and temple.

"Pendleton clipped me with the backside of an ax."

An ax?

Jessie hated to think how much worse things could have turned out if Patrick had done more than clip Robert. What if the ax had been facing the other way? That queasy feeling took over her stomach again.

"Jessie," Jake's voice pulled her gaze away from Robert's face. "Welcome home."

She shook his outstretched hand. Did he mean welcome back in general? As in welcome back to Providence? Or welcome back to the Double Diamond?

Though brown like Robert's, Jake didn't have his brother's long, thick lashes. But warmth filled his eyes. Jake had always been compassionate and caring, and that hadn't changed.

Jessie didn't see any of the anger or accusation in Jake's eyes that she'd expected. She thought for sure Jake would hate her for the way she'd hurt Robert.

A slender auburn-haired beauty stepped up beside Jake and extended her hand. "Hi, I'm Emily." Twin dimples creased her cheeks.

Right, the psychologist.

Emily seemed nice enough, but that didn't mean Jessie was interested in spilling her guts to the woman. She wondered how Jake met Emily, though. She couldn't see Jake seeking professional help for the mild anxiety he'd always suffered with.

Emily pulled Jessie to the sofa and sat beside her while Robert and Jake carried in Jessie's bags. "Jake tells me you were like one of the family and practically lived here."

Jessie nodded and tried to smile, but she couldn't help feeling a twinge of sadness at Emily's use of the past tense.

CHAPTER 15

Jessie lengthened her stride to keep up with Emily's shorter-legged, but faster pace, wishing her stomach didn't still feel so upset.

"So how did you and Jake meet?" she asked breathlessly.

When Emily told her last night that she always took a quick walk before breakfast and invited her along, Jessie assumed she meant a short walk.

They'd walked at least a mile already, and Emily didn't look like she planned on turning around soon.

Emily flashed Jessie a smile. "Jake was my knight in shining armor last year, after I got abducted and injured in a car accident." Jessie's footsteps faltered at Emily's matter-of-fact admission.

Abducted?

Jessie hurried to catch up to Emily, who'd kept a steady stream of conversation since they began their walk. "Someone kidnapped you?" she asked.

"Yes, after I witnessed a murder."

Jessie stumbled. How could Jake's pretty wife talk about something so traumatic with such ease?

Robert's words filled her head. *Emily's a psychologist. She can help you work through things, if you'll let her.*

Jessie had no desire to talk to anyone about what she'd been through. She didn't want to relive the mental, emotional, and physical abuse she'd suffered.

Would talking to Emily help her put it all behind her?

Emily started talking again. "The psychological trauma I'd suffered caused memory loss, and Jake and Faith took me in while Robert searched for my family."

They continued talking about what Emily went through last year. It stunned Jessie to learn Emily lost both her father and her brother within a short period, yet she was an enthusiastic and optimistic person.

"How did you put it all behind you?" Jessie finally asked.

Emily sighed. "Initially, I didn't handle it well at all. But knowing the men responsible are behind bars helps. I also spent a lot of hours counseling with one of my colleagues, but ultimately, what helped was recognizing that God was in control. It wasn't easy, believe me. But once I realized he had a plan for me, then I found happiness."

Knowing Patrick was behind bars gave Jessie a measure of peace, but she had a long way to go if she was ever going to find true happiness.

Emily started talking again about how much she loved it here on the ranch, and how it became her refuge during the darkest time of her life.

Refuge. It fit the Double Diamond.

Jessie had always felt safe here. Could the Double Diamond become her refuge again?

"So, how did you meet Robert?" Emily asked.

"My family moved to Providence when I was sixteen. My Father up and left us a few months later." Jessie smiled as she told Emily about Robert's perseverance in getting her to go out with him. "He just wouldn't give up. But once I finally caved and went out with him, I couldn't figure out why I'd fought him for so long."

Jessie shrugged as she continued talking. "He just seemed like a player. Every girl in school had a crush on him and I often heard girls brag about making out with him."

"Ah, this must have been after the twin thing?" Emily gave her a knowing smile.

"Yes, that happened before I moved to town, but I heard about him making out first with Trina then Trudy Hansen in the same twenty-four-hour period."

"So you know the girls swapped places on Robert?" Emily asked.

Jessie shook her head. "I didn't know that."

"I guess he'd been dating Trudy for a while," Emily said, "and he'd planned a special date. But Trudy had gotten grounded. She didn't want to mess up her chances with Robert, though, so she made Trina go in her place. Well, Trina and Robert ended up making out that night and Trudy was so jealous that she pulled him into the janitor's closet the next day at school and made out with him." Emily chuckled as she continued to talk.

Jessie hadn't heard about the twins swapping places. Why hadn't he corrected her the one time she'd referred to that incident and called him a player?

Emily continued to ask questions, drawing Jessie out. And Jessie confided how hard the separation from Robert had been when they went to different colleges. "The eighteen months I spent in Europe were the hardest, though. I loved it there, but I missed him so much."

When they arrived back at the ranch, after walking what felt like ten miles, but was only three, Emily sat down on the steps of the back deck and encouraged Jessie to finish telling her how she ended up leaving Providence--and Robert--to chase her dreams.

"Did it hurt that Robert let you go so easily?" Emily's voice was quiet.

Jessie picked at her nails, resisting the urge to bite them. Emily had been doing her psychologist thing for a while now, and Jessie hadn't even realized it.

"Yes. I mean, I know the whole thing was all my fault, but I guess I wanted him to fight for me. Or at the very least, tell me he wanted me to stay."

"Why do you say it was all your fault?"

"Because I'm the one who left. I chose my dreams over Robert."

"Do you think he blames you?"

Jessie was pretty sure five years ago Robert thought it was a bad thing for her to choose her dreams over him. "He hasn't said so, but he has every right to."

"Do *you* feel like it was wrong of you to chase your dreams?"

Jessie had regretted the decision she made that took her away from Robert more times than she could count, but she'd never thought of it like that.

It had proved she really was good enough. Since her father deserted his family, Jessie had felt the need to prove herself. And she'd done that.

Until Patrick took it all away.

"No, it wasn't wrong of me to chase my dreams."

Emily tilted her head. "Then why do you keep blaming yourself for everything?"

Jessie stopped picking at her nails. They needed to be filled. If Patrick were here, he'd insist she make an appointment today to get her nails done.

But Patrick isn't here. And Emily is right. I don't need to keep blaming myself for everything.

After so many years of trying to please Patrick, she had a feeling it would be easier said than done.

"Robert says the same thing. He keeps telling me to stop apologizing for everything."

Emily smiled and stood. "Robert's a pretty smart man. I mean, he didn't get to be sheriff by his good looks alone."

No, but he could have.

"And don't censor yourself. People may not always like what you have to say, but you don't have to apologize for how you feel or what you think."

Emily opened the back door, and Jessie followed her into the house. They stepped into the kitchen, and Lottie, the ranch's housekeeper, who had always been like a second mother to Robert, froze at the sight of Jessie.

Jessie had always liked Lottie, despite the older woman's stern expression and no-nonsense personality. She didn't take crap from anyone, least of all Robert, who liked to tease.

The older woman dropped her spatula and approached Jessie, stopping a few feet away. Lottie reached up and brushed a lock of hair away from Jessie's bruised eye, her touch gentle and confident. She smiled, and a twinkle lit her eyes. "It's about time you came home."

And here came the tears again. Jessie hated roller coasters, especially emotional ones.

Lottie pulled Jessie into her arms and squeezed her tight.

DESPITE ROBERT'S family's unconditional acceptance, Jessie felt like a fraud. She sat on the back patio, staring at her painting propped on a small table.

Patrick's right: It is garbage.

Jessie turned her gaze toward the stables. Why did she think she could still paint?

She recalled hearing the parable of the talents in Sunday School. The man who buried his talents for fear of losing them had them taken away.

God's done the same thing to me.

It didn't take a skilled eye to know that the problem with her painting was more than just a balance issue. The lines were all wrong, and the colors were off.

The tranquility of the ranch couldn't wash away Patrick's voice in her head. Couldn't magically make her something she wasn't. Couldn't take away the unsettle feeling in her stomach.

A niggling voice in the back of her mind told her the frequent nausea and exhaustion were caused by something much more serious than anxiety. But Jessie couldn't even consider that right now; it was too overwhelming.

Instead, she recalled her desire to paint the picture for Robert. But what was the point, now? He'd pawned her off on his brother. Apparently, all those times she'd still felt a connection to him had been one-sided.

Grabbing the painting, she marched around the house and stuffed it in the trash can. It didn't fit, but she didn't care. She was done daydreaming that maybe Robert could forgive her and come to care for her again.

She turned away from the garbage can to find Jake walking out of the stables, leading a horse. His gaze bounced from her to her canvas sticking out of the dumpster and back to her again.

He tipped his hat up as he drew close. "Looks like you could use some horse therapy."

Jake and Emily made the perfect pair. She healed the psyche, and he healed the soul.

Jessie smiled as she walked toward him. "Horse therapy sounds exactly like what I need. But I haven't been on a horse in years."

"It's just like riding a bike. It'll all come back to you once you're in the saddle. Honey will take good care of you."

Honey? Jessie couldn't believe her favorite horse was still here on the ranch. She walked over and ran her hands over the Arabian's shiny, honey-colored coat. The smooth, silky hair calmed Jessie. She closed her eyes and inhaled. The smell of horses, leather, and straw wrapped around her.

Honey gave a soft whinny and pressed her nose into Jessie's neck. A feeling of weightlessness swept over Jessie.

She looked at Jake. "How did you know?" The question sounded cryptic, but Jake would know what she meant.

Jake shrugged. "Never had a problem that didn't seem smaller from the back of a horse."

Ten minutes later, Jake helped Jessie onto Honey's back and adjusted the stirrups.

"Are there rattlesnakes out this time of year?" Though Jessie had ridden Honey dozens of times after getting thrown off, she couldn't help remembering what happened the last time she rode out alone.

Jake patted Honey's neck. "Haven't seen any for a few years. You should be fine."

Jessie turned Honey and led her down the lane, deeper into the heart of the ranch. She relaxed into the saddle, appreciating Honey's smooth gait, and let her gaze roam over the beautiful countryside.

Everywhere she looked, memories assaulted her. The alfalfa fields reminded her of the time she stayed up all night baling hay with Robert and the cattle grazing in the distant pastures, brought to mind the many times she'd helped with calving, branding, and roundup.

A hundred and fifty yards from the main house stood a grove of trees that hid a small meadow. Jessie and Robert had often stolen away to that cozy meadow when they wanted to be alone.

Honey's gait slowed as though she anticipated being led into the grove. But Jessie couldn't go there. Not yet.

Maybe never.

Jessie pulled the reins, turning Honey to the west, and nudged her flanks.

CHAPTER 16

Brady greeted Robert when he walked through the front door of the Adam's County Sheriff's Office the next morning. Cheryl, the weekend dispatcher, must have stepped away from her desk, because Brady lounged in her chair, scrolling on his phone.

"Hey, boss. I wasn't expecting to see you this morning."

Robert glanced at the clock that hung in the foyer. Yep. It was still morning, but just barely. He'd slept late this morning, but he was too keyed up and worried about Jessie to sit around at home, so he'd come in even though he wasn't scheduled.

"I've got a few things to take care of."

"I'll bet. I heard about the excitement last night." Brady eyed Robert's temple. "Looks like Pendleton meant business."

You have no idea. A chill raced down Robert's spine every time he thought about the man's threat concerning Jessie.

He gave a noncommittal response and continued to his office. He still couldn't believe Pendleton clocked him with an ax. Either Robert was slipping, or he'd let his concern for Jessie cloud his judgment.

He settled into his chair, wishing he didn't have a headache settling in already. It didn't help that he hadn't gotten to bed until after midnight. After dropping Jessie off at the ranch, he'd driven out to the county jail to make sure they had properly booked Pendleton on charges of aggravated assault, resisting arrest, trespassing, and violating a restraining order. Then he'd spend over an hour in his office doing paperwork before finally going home to ice his head.

With it being Saturday, the judge wouldn't set Pendleton's bail until Monday. Keeping him behind bars was the only way Jessie would get any peace of mind. He hoped Uncle Dawson, who was the justice of the peace, wouldn't let him down and set a hefty bail, so Robert didn't have to worry about Pendleton going after Jessie again soon.

He picked up his phone and called Knight's Repair Shop. When he got Scott Wheeler on the phone, he couldn't help the smile that stole over his face.

"Scott, this is Sheriff Winters. I need you to do me a favor."

"Sure. What's up?" Scott's voice was considerably deeper than his brother Rudy's, one of Robert's deputies. Of course, Scott was considerably stockier than Rudy, too.

"I made an arrest at my family's cabin up near the lake last night and I need the perpetrator's car towed."

"No problem. Where am I towing it?"

Robert scratched his jaw. Providence didn't have an impound yard, so they had to improvise on the few occasions that impounding a vehicle had been necessary.

"Do you have room in the lot behind the repair shop?" It was one of the few places in town with an eight-foot chain-link fence and a padlock.

"Yep."

"Great, thanks. I doubt anyone will come for it for some time, so if keeping it there becomes a problem, let me know. And if someone does come to claim it, send them my way."

Robert ended the call a short time later, after giving Scott the address of the cabin and the make of Pendleton's car.

He put through another call to Scott's father, William Wheeler, the best handyman in town. After arranging for William to fix the broken door jamb at the cabin, Robert reviewed the report he'd filed last night. His head had been killing him by the time he'd finished, and he wanted to make sure it made sense in the light of day.

A booming voice echoing down the hall broke his concentration ten minutes later.

"Sheriff!" Mayor Conrad stepped through Robert's open office door. "I was planning on visiting with you on Monday, but I saw your Tahoe out front and decided I may as well stop by." Not waiting for an invitation, he settled his robust frame into a chair. "I'm afraid I have some bad news."

"Bad news?" Every muscle in Robert's body tensed, his thoughts immediately jumping to Jessie.

Wait. If something had happened to Jessie, he would have heard about it from Jake. Not the mayor.

"Lewis Jackson filed the paperwork yesterday to run for Sheriff this fall."

Robert's stomach sank. "I thought the paperwork was due in May."

He'd been hoping to run unopposed again. Now he would have to put time and effort into campaigning. It would only distract him from figuring out the best way to keep Jessie safe. Which is what he needed to be focusing on today, not on whether he'd still have a job in a few months.

"It was, if he wanted to be listed on the ballot and featured in the elections' pamphlet that goes out in October. Lewis is running as a write-in, so he won't appear on either. The deadline for write-ins isn't until next week."

Robert leaned back in his chair and rubbed his neck.

"Personally, I don't think you have anything to worry about." Conrad gestured with his hands as he spoke. "You're home grown. Jackson's a nice guy and all, but he's a transplant. He's only been here what, three or four years?"

"Probably closer to six."

The mayor waved a hand in dismissal. "You've done a fantastic job these last four years. Finding Ben's daughter and the man who killed Emily's brother and father will benefit you."

Robert didn't accomplish either of those things without help, but his involvement in both cases shone a favorable light on him.

"You've got plenty of family and friends in Providence, too. You know they won't let you down."

Robert had lived here all his life, as had his father's family. His mom and her sisters were transplants, but they moved here over thirty years ago. Faith, Hope, and Charity were pillars in the community and well respected.

Lewis Jackson and his wife had only lived in Providence for five or six years. He'd worked in law enforcement in the Tri-Cities area the whole time they'd lived here. To Robert's knowledge, he was still a beat cop with no leadership experience.

Mayor Conrad pushed his bulky frame to a standing position. "My wife's expecting me home, so I better go, but I wanted you to know you've got my vote. I wouldn't bother with a lot of new campaign paraphernalia. Just dust off the old posters and signs. They worked for you last time."

"Last time, I ran unopposed."

The mayor waved his hand again. "I see little difference. Jackson didn't file in time to get listed on the ballet. So, I don't think you have anything to worry about."

Robert saw the mayor out, then returned to his office. It wouldn't be wise to assume that just because Jackson was running as a write-in, it was the same as running unopposed. Jackson was a nice man. If he got busy, he could drum up a lot of votes.

Robert needed to do the same. But he needed to figure out how to keep Jessie safe first.

Four hours later, Robert pointed his truck in the ranch's direction. It had been a much longer day than he'd intended, with one thing after another popping up. His body ached, and his head pounded.

He'd been so distracted with everything that had gone on today, he hadn't come up with much of a plan to keep Jessie safe. He felt bad for pushing his responsibilities off on Jake.

Jessie is not a responsibility.

He had to think of her that way though, or the image of her curled in a fetal position, cowering in fear, would cause the walls he'd erected around his heart to crumble.

Jake's determination to keep Emily safe at the ranch last summer made sense to Robert now. He didn't worry about Jake or Zane. They could take care of themselves, but Lottie and pregnant Emily were there, unprotected. And now Jessie.

Moving back to the Double Diamond to provide extra security when he wasn't at work would be the best way to keep them safe. But he wasn't sure he could stand to be around Jessie that much.

As he pulled up beside the ranch house, a large rectangular object sticking out of the trash can caught his eye. It was the picture Jessie had started at the cabin. Unfinished.

His stomach sank. Had the close call with Pendleton yesterday shaken her fragile self-esteem? Or was it something personal against him?

He pulled the canvas from the garbage can and studied it. It had suffered no damage that he could see. The painting was so good it made his chest swell with pride on Jessie's behalf.

She obviously didn't think so if she'd thrown it away.

He tucked it under his arm and walked around to the front door. After a brief knock, he walked in.

Jessie was nowhere in sight. But a sight he'd never expected to see in the late afternoon at the ranch greeted him. Jake sat on one end of the couch with Emily's head in his lap. He pulled a brush through her long auburn hair. The sun hadn't set yet, and his workaholic brother sat brushing his wife's hair.

Robert bit back a comment about Jake's man card. Emily would call him immature, and she'd be right.

Even though he always felt like Emily analyzed everything he said and did, he was happy for Jake. Emily was good for him. And Jake had been just what she needed last year when she suffered such a devastating loss.

"Hey," Robert greeted them.

"Hi," Jake and Emily said in unison.

"Jake, I need to talk with you, but first...is Jessie around?"

Jake motioned over his shoulder with his thumb. "She's out on the back deck."

Robert started toward the back door, but stopped when Emily called his name.

"Be careful. She's incredibly fragile." She shot a pointed look at the canvas in his hand.

Was his disappointment that obvious?

He gave her a quick nod and continued out the door with no clue of what he'd say to Jessie. Jake was good at these kinds of things, Robert, not so much.

He stepped outside and looked around.

Jessie sat on the swing with a closed book in her lap. The book either didn't hold her attention or she had other things on her mind. Heavy things, judging by the furrow between her brows.

"Hey." Robert shot her a smile as he leaned the canvas against the railing and sat on the swing beside her. He probably shouldn't sit so close, but all the other chairs were too far away to promote conversation.

Her feminine scent, a combination of flowers and fruit, hit him harder than he expected. He should have sat on a chair. Way over there.

"Hay is for horses." Jessie said with a small smile.

Robert chuckled as he remembered the familiar exchange from when they were teenagers. Except, Robert was the one who pointed out hay was for horses every time Jessie greeted him with a 'hey'.

"Welcome back to the ranch."

Jessie said nothing. She just sucked in a deep breath and looked out over the pasture where the stock horses grazed.

"You should know, Pendleton's bail won't be set until Monday. It will probably be pretty steep."

"It won't matter. His parents have money." Jessie's face showed no emotion, and that concerned Robert. She was a passionate person and often wore her emotions on her sleeve. "I see you fished that out of the garbage." She nodded toward the canvas.

"I thought you were enjoying painting again."

"I was."

"I take it you had a change of heart."

Jessie shrugged. "Patrick was right."

Robert balled his fists at the mention of her jerk of a husband.

"About what?"

"I can't expect to come home and pick up where I left off."

No. Neither of them could pick up where they had left off. As much as he would like to.

Whoa. Where had that come from?

Jessie was talking about painting. Wasn't she?

Jessie picked at her nails. "I'm not the same person I used to be, and I don't have that kind of talent anymore."

Yes, you do. He wanted to shout the words, but remembering Emily's warning, he bit his tongue. "I think you do. It's just hidden."

"Doesn't the Bible say something about losing the talents we bury?"

"Jessie, you didn't choose to bury them."

"It doesn't matter. The point is: I'm not good enough anymore."

He had a feeling she was talking about a lot more than the decline of her artistic skills. He hated to imagine the things Pendleton had done to crush her so thoroughly.

He shot to his feet, partially out of anger, but mostly to keep from pulling her into his arms and assuring her she'd always been good enough for him. When Jessie shot him a strange look, he relaxed against the railing. Not so far away that she'd think he was avoiding her, but far enough to be out of arm's reach.

"Good enough for whom, Jess? You don't have to measure up to anyone's expectations anymore. Just your own."

Jessie hugged herself as tears gathered in her eyes. "I don't know what I want of myself anymore. I haven't been allowed to think for myself for so long."

She looked at him with those beautiful, pain-filled, amber eyes, and he had to remind himself to keep his distance.

"Somewhere along the line, the pride that kept me from admitting I'd made a mistake and leaving, turned to fear. And not just fear of Patrick. I was afraid to admit I had failed. Failed in my career and failed in my marriage." She sucked in a deep breath as though trying to calm herself. "Patrick always said love is putting the other person first. I thought if I just tried a little harder--"

"Bending over backwards to please that man was not love." His grip on the railing behind him tightened.

She gave him a sad smile. "I know, but he convinced me I needed to prove I was worthy of his love."

More like the other way around.

"If he loved you so much, shouldn't *he* have put *you* first?" He couldn't hide the derision in his voice.

"He did." Her voice dropped. "Or at least that's what he told me. Tracking everywhere I went, monitoring my calls and text messages, that was all for my safety." Jessie's voice carried a note of derision now. "He took away my art so I could devote more time to being a better wife."

Robert gripped the railing so hard he feared he'd get splinters. If he let go, he'd probably end up punching something.

"My nails, my hair, the designer clothing. That was all meant to make me feel better about myself because it made me beautiful."

"You were already beautiful, Jess." He ground out through clenched teeth before he could stop himself. He meant it as a compliment, but he doubted she'd feel flattered since he'd delivered it so poorly.

She gave him a small smile. "You're the one person who always made me feel that way, no matter how horrible I looked."

"Because it's true." He ached to take Jessie in his arms and hold her until she believed him. Realizing he'd released his grip on the railing, he folded his arms across his chest to keep himself from following through on the urge.

Jessie shook her head. "You know what my worst failure was?" She looked out across the pasture. "Me. I failed myself."

Robert couldn't help himself, he sat back down beside her. "What do you mean?"

"I let it happen. I let him take away everything that mattered to me and change me into a different person. I saw it happening, but felt powerless to stop it. Every time I stood up to him, he beat me down. It just became easier not to fight back."

The walls around Robert's heart felt tissue-paper thin.

"He may not have let you use your talents, but he could never take away that integral part of you. And he may have made you change your appearance, but it doesn't make you any less beautiful on the inside." He lifted a hand to tuck a lock of hair behind her ear then thought better of it and dropped his hand again.

"But I don't know who I am anymore. I don't remember why I enjoyed creating things." She looked at the unfinished canvas.

"Because you're still afraid," he said, his voice quiet.

Her gaze locked with his.

Knowing he'd hate himself for touching her, he took her hand in his. "I will do everything I can to keep you safe. But that's all I can do to help you overcome your fear. The rest must come from you. Let the fear go and focus on finding yourself again."

"I don't know how." The words were little more than a whisper, and tears filled her eyes again.

Stifling the urge to kiss her, to remind her--and maybe himself--of how things used to be, he released her hand touched a lock of hair. "Start with the outside, then when you're ready, rediscover yourself on the inside." He dropped his hand, then stood and stepped away to slow his racing heart.

Jessie played with a lock of hair. "You think I should change my hair?"

"I think you should do whatever makes you feel good about yourself. Learn to love yourself again." *Like I still love you.* Glad he hadn't spoken that last part out loud, he cleared his throat and took a deep breath. "Once you learn to love yourself, then you'll find your passion for art again."

"Do you really think changing the outside will help?" She picked at fake fingernails that were long overdue for a manicure.

Was she seeking validation? Did she think she needed his approval?

One thing Robert knew, manicures and haircuts and colors weren't cheap. He'd learned that when he dated a cosmetologist a few years ago. And Jessie had little money. He pulled out his wallet, glad he'd gone to the bank yesterday. Taking out three fifty-dollar bills, he crouched down in front of her and took her hand. He pressed the folded bills into her palm and closed her fingers around it, trying to ignore the tingles racing up his arm.

"What I think doesn't matter, Jess. The only person who matters is you."

Jessie's eyes widened when she looked at the money in her hand. She jerked her hand back. But Robert had expected her reaction and held fast. He closed her fingers around the cash.

"Consider it a loan, if you want."

"You've done so much for me. How can I possibly repay you?" Her gaze softened, and she tilted her head.

Picking up the canvas that looked finished to him--but Jessie would want to add a million finishing touches to--he held it out to her. "When you're ready...finish this."

ROBERT FOLLOWED Jake into his office a few minutes later.

"Listen, Jake, I want to thank you and Emily for being willing to take Jessie in. I know having her here puts everyone in danger. And I'm willing to do whatever is necessary to keep her and everyone else safe, but..." He rubbed his jaw and turned toward the window.

"But you're falling for her again." Jake's tone held no criticism, only compassion.

Robert laced his fingers behind his head and watched the horses grazing in the front pasture. He couldn't look Jake in the eye while he admitted he still cared for Jessie. "I don't want to love her again."

"Did you ever stop?"

He swore under his breath as he spun around. "I swear I tried. Why do you think I dated a different girl every month? It wasn't until Amy came along that I felt any kind of spark." Heat crept up his neck. He hadn't meant to admit that out loud.

Jake laughed. "Does Ben know you had a thing for his wife?"

Robert closed the distance between them and grabbed the front of Jake's shirt. "She wasn't his wife at the time. I don't care if you are stronger than me, I'll pound you if you even hint to Ben that I liked Amy." It had taken no thought at all to step aside when he realized Ben had found love again. Of course, Amy was just as crazy about Ben.

Jake chuckled again, unfazed by Robert's threat. "I knew my big brother was in there somewhere."

Robert released Jake's shirt and plopped down on the sofa. "I haven't really been myself, have I?"

"Which is how I know you're falling for Jessie." Jake smoothed the front of his shirt.

Robert raked his hands through his hair. "I can't do this, again."

Jake leaned against the edge of their father's mahogany desk and crossed his ankles. "I'm not sure you have a choice. With matters of the heart, we're never really in control."

Robert rolled his eyes. "Spoken like a true newlywed, smitten by a woman he barely knew. A woman who didn't even know herself."

Jake didn't bother denying Robert's words. He only grinned that goofy grin he'd been wearing for the past year.

Robert had never wanted to wipe it off his face more than he did right now.

"The question is: what are you going to do about it?" Jake asked.

Robert punched the cushion and swore again, this time aloud.

"Good thing Mom's not around. I'd have to hold you down while she washed your mouth out."

"Sorry." His emotions were getting the better of him. "But you know how I hate to admit when I'm wrong."

"Who said you were wrong?"

Robert glared at Jake. "Are we talking about the same thing, here? How can me falling in love with Jessie again be good?"

"She told Emily she plans on getting a divorce."

"Exactly, so what's stopping her from leaving again once she's free of her husband?"

Jake stared down at his boots. "Jessie's changed. Maybe it'll be different this time around."

"And maybe it won't." The words were little more than a growl. "I'm not sure I can take that chance."

Jake turned sympathetic eyes on Robert. He'd been the one to pick Robert up the last time Jessie left.

No. Robert couldn't take the chance of falling in love with Jessie again. He'd barely survived last time.

He cleared his throat and stood. "I want to do everything possible to keep Jessie safe, but I can't be around her all the time." He turned pleading eyes on Jake.

Jake straightened from his perch on the edge of the desk and opened his laptop. He flipped it around so Robert could see the screen. "It's a good thing I have a plan then."

Ten minutes later, after studying Jake's design for a security gate at the front entrance of the ranch, Robert wasn't sure he felt much better. "The gate sounds like a good idea, but it won't keep Pendleton from climbing through the fence and walking up to the front door."

Jake clicked another tab on his computer. "We'll string two lines--one high, one low--of electric wire along the front fence line. Someone would have to be pretty desperate to get past that."

Robert noted the prices of all the components listed on the computer screen. He let out a low whistle. "That's going to be pricey. You've got...what, eight miles of fence line?"

"Five."

"Felt like fifty every time we had to paint that fence."

They had to paint the metal triple-rail fence every three years. One year, Robert tried cutting corners by painting only the tops. But when rust spots appeared on the bottoms the next spring, he not only had to paint the fence again; he had to sand out the rust spots first.

"That fence has always been sturdy enough to keep horses and cattle in. Adding electricity seems like overkill."

Jake shrugged. "It is."

"Let's hold off on the electric fence and the gate for now. I have a feeling Pendleton's bail is going to be high. If we're lucky, he won't get out of jail for the next five to ten years."

But something deep inside Robert told him they wouldn't be so lucky.

CHAPTER 17

"Did you really have your work displayed at the MET?" Lottie asked as she set two paring knives and a bag of potatoes on the table in front of Jessie.

Jessie had never peeled potatoes with a cast on before, but she wanted to help with Sunday dinner. She'd chickened out on attending church today. The least she could do was help with dinner. She picked up one knife, and Lottie grabbed the other.

"It was a lucky break, really, but yes. It was only for one showing, and it only lasted for a couple weeks, but it was definitely a highlight of my time in New York."

"I'll bet. Your work is amazing, though, so I'm not surprised."

Jessie smiled. Lottie didn't say things she didn't mean, so the compliment meant a lot.

"That's impressive, Jessie," said Emily, who stood at the counter making a salad. "I've always wanted to visit New York City."

They continued chatting about some of New York's sights and tourists' traps, and Jessie shared some of her favorite experiences. Thankfully, no one brought up Patrick.

"Where is she?" A high-pitched, familiar voice floated through the swinging door.

Jessie tensed at the sound of Faith's voice. She'd dreaded facing Robert's family, knowing she had hurt him deeply when she left. Faith had been like a second mother to her. She'd accepted Jessie as part of their family long before Jessie became Robert's girlfriend.

Jessie had never told anyone, but Faith visited her the day before she left for New York.

She hadn't wanted to open the door when she looked out the window and saw Faith's car. She was afraid Robert's mother would chew her out for hurting her son.

Faith blinked red-rimmed eyes when Jessie opened the door. She pulled Jessie into a tight hug. "I'm so happy for you to have this opportunity, Jessie."

Faith released her but kept her hands on Jessie's arms. "I told myself I wouldn't ask you to reconsider because it makes me look so selfish. So, I won't. But I couldn't let you go without reminding you that you're a part of our family. If things don't work out for you in New York, don't let your pride keep you away. You'll always have a seat at our table."

Jessie looked up when the kitchen door swung open.

Faith froze when her eyes landed on Jessie. The woman who had loved Jessie like her own had changed little over the past five years. Her blue eyes still radiated love and acceptance.

Warmth swept over Jessie.

Lottie lifted the pot of potatoes from the center of the table and carried them to the sink.

Faith pulled Lottie's vacant chair around the corner of the table and sat facing Jessie. "Oh, my dear, Robert told me what you've been through." Tears filled the older woman's eyes as she took Jessie's hand.

A band tightened around Jessie's chest. She sucked in a deep breath.

Faith leaned forward. "I'm so sorry your dreams got derailed and life turned out like this for you."

Me too. Jessie swallowed hard to dislodge the lump in her throat. She dipped her head so Faith wouldn't see the tears building in her eyes.

But Faith lifted Jessie's chin. "You don't know how many times I prayed you'd come back to us, but I never meant for it to happen like this."

Jessie lost her fight to hold back the tears. She tightened her grip on Faith's hand. She'd come home, but had she really come back to the Winters family? Did she dare hope there was still a place for her at Faith's table?

And maybe someday, in Robert's heart?

Faith held Jessie's gaze. "I meant what I said five years ago. You'll always have a place here..." She placed her free hand on the table. "Well, this is Jake's table now. But you'll always have a place here." She pressed her hand over her heart.

Faith's love was as unconditional as Jessie's own mother's. Did that mean God could forgive her too, for neglecting her relationship with him?

"Thank you, Faith. You don't know what that means to me."

Robert may never forgive her, but Jessie would not turn down this opportunity to have Faith as a friend.

~

ONCE AGAIN, Jessie struggled to catch her breath, while Emily didn't breathe hard at all. Jessie's legs were longer than Emily's, but the shorter woman took her exercise seriously.

"Robert gave me some money to get my hair and nails done. He told me to find myself." They had been walking for almost ten minutes and had only exchanged menial conversation. Jessie kept expecting Emily to do her psychologist thing and draw her into a conversation about herself and the abuse she'd suffered. But Emily seemed to be waiting for Jessie to take the lead.

"Is it just Robert who thinks you're lost? Or do you feel you need to find yourself?"

Robert had insisted her talents were an essential part of her and weren't gone entirely. Jessie didn't know what to believe.

"Patrick took away parts of me I don't know how to get back. I can't seem to pick up all the pieces. And I'm not sure what to do with the few fragments I have left." Jessie focused on not falling behind while she lifted her hair off her neck and wrapped a hair tie around it. "I'm not the same person who left here five years ago, but I feel like I need to fit back into some mold that's not the right shape anymore or maybe it's just too small."

Emily's voice was quiet when she spoke again. "Do you think you can talk about the things Patrick took from you?"

Jessie didn't want to relive every slap, punch, and kick, but she needed to get it out. The trauma of abuse festered inside her like a deadly disease. She'd never be happy--never find herself--if she didn't purge it.

She took a deep breath. "I lost a piece of myself every time he beat me down." Tears filled Jessie's eyes and thickened her throat, but she continued to talk about the many ways Patrick had abused her. If she didn't get it out now, she never would.

With Emily's questions and gentle encouragement, Jessie talked about how it broke her heart to have her art taken away, and what a nightmare this past year had been with no job, no friends, and barely being allowed to leave the house. Then she talked about how she couldn't seem to get the painting she'd started right and wasn't sure she even wanted to paint anymore.

They were approaching the house when Emily said, "Instead of trying to find the person you once were, decide who you want to be and become that person."

Jessie stopped walking and stared at Emily. "What do you mean? Like filling my wall with positive affirmations to help me reach the goal to become the first female President of the United States?"

Emily turned back and laughed. "You should definitely do that if you have those kind of aspirations. The positive affirmations are a great idea, but what I mean is: don't try to be the same person you used to be." Emily started walking again--a little slower this time--and Jessie fell into step beside her. "Identify the things you like about yourself and the things want to change. Write down your strengths and weaknesses and decide if the weaknesses are worth working or if you're better off letting them go."

Emily stopped walking again and looked Jessie in the eye. "You can choose to let the abuse you've suffered define you, or you can learn from it so you never become the victim again. Focus on becoming the person you want to be now."

Jessie stared at the dusty road in front of her. "I'm not sure I understand how to do that."

"What do you want your future to look like?" Emily started walking again.

An image of Robert walking through the door, greeting her with a kiss, filled Jessie's mind. She shook it away. It was way too early to have those kinds of daydreams.

"Your silence tells me you're overthinking it." Emily said quietly, but Jessie had a feeling Emily knew exactly what she was thinking. "Picture your future one step at a time. Don't be afraid to dream big. Will there be art in your future?"

Yes! She'd been suffocating these past couple of years without her art.

But a career based on her art would likely lead her away from Providence. And Robert.

That thought made it as difficult to breathe as losing her art had.

"Write down all the things you want in your future. Do you want a career? If so: doing what. Will you marry again? Do you want a family?"

Yes. Yes. Yes.

Jessie wanted a career in art again, but not one that took her away from Providence. And yes, she wanted to marry again, eventually. But only if it was to the right man. She wouldn't give that man a name or a face yet, because she didn't have the right to dream of a life with him. But maybe someday she could become the person he deserved, and they could have a family together.

That meant she needed to get divorce proceedings started. The thought of the backlash that would bring from Patrick terrified her.

They'd reached the ranch house, and Emily put her foot on the top step of the back deck and leaned into a hip flexor stretch. "Jessie, you deserve happiness as much as anyone else."

Jessie sucked in a deep breath. How long would it take her to believe in herself the way Robert and Emily did?

Two hours later, after breakfast and a shower, Jessie couldn't find any more excuses to delay doing what Emily asked. But she only had her journal to write in. The journal that chronicled all the abuse she'd suffered at Patrick's hands. The journal that was full of her weaknesses and fears. Just looking at the black faux-leather book made her feel gloomy and heavy. How could she move forward when so much darkness held her back?

She looked at the painting that sat in the corner. All the things she'd seen wrong with it the other day didn't seem so obvious today, but she wasn't sure she wanted to try again. What if she failed?

Instead of picking up the painting, she called her mom to see if they could get their hair done together.

"I'd love to," came her mother's enthusiastic reply over the phone. "I'm definitely due for a trim. I'll see if Naomi has any openings and get back to you. Do you want an appointment for your nails, too? I noticed they need to be filled."

Jessie examined her hands. She hated the acrylic nails. They were too long, and the color Patrick always insisted on--bright red--screamed "Look at me." She felt especially uncomfortable when he insisted she wear the stilettos and form-fitting short dresses he'd bought her.

"Yes, make me an appointment for my nails. But do you think I should get them taken off, instead of getting them filled?"

Her mom remained quiet for a long moment. "It's entirely up to you, honey."

It had been such a long time since Jessie had been allowed to make any major decisions, that she often forgot she could make a choice about anything, even something as inconsequential as what to do with her hair and nails.

A few minutes later, she walked out to the stables, hoping to find Jake or Zane, because she still wasn't ready to face the painting. And sitting around in Robert's room only made her think about him more. She recalled the countless hours sitting on his bed or floor, doing homework, listening to music, or just talking. They weren't allowed to be in there alone with the door closed, but they'd still managed to share a few kisses.

"Time for a little more horse therapy?" Jake asked when he saw her coming.

She smiled. "I think so."

Ten minutes later, Jessie climbed on Honey's back. *After my ride, I'll write what I want my future to look like.*

Or maybe she'd take a nap.

CHAPTER 18

Jessie climbed out of her mom's car and took in the bold purple lettering across the large front window of the salon: "In Style." Some things never changed.

They stepped through the door, and Jessie froze.

Naomi's salon *had* changed. It was larger than Jessie remembered, with two additional stylists' chairs. A colorful, yet classy, sign hung in one corner touting manicures and pedicures while the other corner held signage for facials and waxing.

Naomi had expanded into the neighboring strip mall space. Try as she might, Jessie couldn't remember what had been there. A comic bookstore? A pet store?

"Sylvia, welcome." Naomi, as friendly and buxom as ever, greeted her mom with a quick hug. Then she turned to Jessie. "And here's our talented little artist home from the Big Apple." She gave Jessie a sympathetic look before pulling her into a hug.

Jessie returned Naomi's embrace, but didn't bother correcting her. Not only had Jessie not lived in the Big Apple for the past year, she also wasn't sure she could call herself talented anymore.

Naomi held Jessie at arm's length and locked gazes with her. "Home for good, I hope."

Jessie didn't know what to say. She didn't know what her future held. Maybe if she'd done what Emily asked her to, she'd have a clue.

She smiled and shrugged in what she hoped Naomi would interpret as a *"we'll see"* gesture. Fortunately, Naomi let it go and beckoned Jessie into a salon chair.

"What's it going to be today, sweetie?" Naomi frowned as she ran her fingers through Jessie's bleached blond hair.

Jessie felt flattered to have the owner work on her. With two other stylists to help carry the workload, Naomi was selective about whose hair she did.

"Um... I don't know." Jessie still hadn't decided what to do with her hair. She kept wondering what Robert would find attractive.

Even if she knew, she shouldn't let that guide her choice. This was about her.

At least that's what everyone kept telling her.

"Do you want to keep it long? Or go short, like you used to wear?"

"No, not that short." That much Jessie knew. She wouldn't try to be the same person she was before she left Providence.

Naomi exercised incredible patience as Jessie perused a book of hairstyles. Occasionally, Naomi pointed out one style or another and commented on how they would complement Jessie's high cheekbones, oval face, and long neck.

Finally, Jessie found the style she wanted--an A-line cut that ended midway between her chin and collarbone. Patrick hated her hair the last time she had a similar cut. After that, he'd insisted on a longer style.

"This is going to look great on you. What color are you thinking?" Naomi frowned again at her bleached locks.

"As close to my natural color as possible." No one was forcing her to be someone else anymore, so she needed to be herself.

Whoever that is.

"It's a good thing your roots are showing then, because, sweetie, I don't remember what your natural color was. I only remember how much fun I had dying your hair all those crazy colors."

Jessie laughed, and Naomi joined in. She *had* chosen some crazy colors. Her color choice had stunned Robert a time or two. But no matter how wild her hair had been, he'd always said he loved it and that it fit her larger-than-life personality.

"Okay, dark brown it is. What's your highlight color going to be?"

Jessie stuck a fingernail between her teeth. "I don't think I'm going to do highlights this time."

Patrick had always insisted on more and more highlights, until he'd gotten his way and she'd dyed it completely blond.

Naomi's eyes met hers in the mirror. A deep V formed between her eyebrows for a moment. "Oh, I see, you're going to do lowlights? Maybe a dark red, purple, or blue."

Jessie hadn't planned on doing anything other than dying her hair back to its natural color, but the idea of some dark red lowlights sounded cool. Her hair would look like something a mature, sensible woman would wear, but it would still be fun and flirty. Not that she had anyone to flirt with.

"Sure. Let's go with a dark red." She grinned and wiggled her eyebrows. "Or maybe a deep magenta."

Naomi's face split in a grin. "There's my girl."

Two and a half hours later, Jessie walked out of the salon, looking and feeling like a new woman. The time spent with Naomi and her daughter, Susy, the nail technician, had been a blast and bolstered her self-esteem. Now, if she could only get the sympathetic looks from all the other customers who recognized her out of her mind, then she could enjoy her new look.

"I'm starving." her mother said as soon as they got in the car. "How about you?"

Jessie looked at the clock on the dash. Two o'clock. "I'm sorry I took so long."

Sylvia's trim had taken less than thirty minutes, but she insisted she didn't mind waiting; it gave her a chance to read her book. Although she'd done as much visiting with the other women in the salon as Jessie did.

"You have nothing to apologize for, honey. I'm just glad I could share this experience with you again." Her mom patted her hand.

"Me too." Jessie tucked a lock of hair behind her ear. "Uh...Mom. Did you tell Naomi about me and what...Patrick did?"

Sylvia shifted to face Jessie. "Naomi is a good friend, and yes, I've talked about you to my friends, honey. That's what women do when they get together."

"You *gossip?*"

Small towns were notorious for gossip--since everybody knew everyone else--and Providence was no exception. Jessie didn't realize her mom was such a gossip, though.

"No." Her mother's voice was defensive. "We talk about our families. And when my friends asked about my daughters, I told them what was happening in your lives."

"And they tell their friends, who then tell their friends." Sarcasm filled Jessie's voice.

How many times had Jessie been the subject of discussions here in Providence?

"Listen, honey. When we're concerned about those we love, we talk about it. I've put your name on many prayer lists over the years."

Jessie had no argument for that, except she didn't think God had answered any of their prayers, since Patrick's abuse had never lessened.

"So what if you get a few sympathetic looks? You hold your head high wherever you go because you are a survivor. Do you hear me? You are not a victim. You are a survivor."

The vehemence in her mom's voice brought tears to Jessie's eyes. Her mom was right, and until Jessie started thinking of herself as a survivor, she would always be a victim.

I'm a survivor.

How many times would she have to repeat it before she believed it?

CHAPTER 19

Robert's desk phone rang as he stepped out of his office. He debated ignoring it, since he was ready to call it a day.

He stopped himself. Just because he was eager to go see Jessie didn't mean he could shirk his duties as sheriff.

He grabbed the phone from the far side of the desk, anticipating a brief call. "Sheriff Winters."

"Sheriff Winters, this is FBI Detective Donald Harris with Washington State Internal Affairs."

Internal affairs? Robert's stomach dropped.

The last time he'd worked with the FBI was over two-and-a-half years ago when Ben's daughter Cassey was kidnapped.

"What can I do for you, detective?"

"I'm holding a Federal 1983 complaint..." he rattled off more official numbers and letters Robert didn't recognize, but it didn't matter. He knew what a Federal 1983 complaint was.

The blood drained from his face as he circled his desk and dropped into his chair.

"...Alleging police brutality by Sheriff Robert Winters against Patrick Pendleton." The voice on the other end of the phone droned on, citing date, time, and place, but Robert tuned it out. He knew exactly where and when the incident had taken place, and he knew he hadn't taken things too far, as much as he would have liked to.

Robert's grip on the phone tightened. He couldn't believe Pendleton had stooped to this.

"I'm aware of the details, detective. What are the allegations?"

"Excessive force."

Robert bit back a swear word along with the urge to yell, *'He came at me with an ax! What was I supposed to do? Lie down and let him kill me?'*

He leaned back in his chair, laid his head back, and closed his eyes. He let out a sigh. "What do you need from me?"

Robert listened carefully as the detective requested the full report of Pendleton's arrest, testimony from assisting officers, and any other information Robert felt would be helpful in making the investigation go smoothly and quickly.

By the time the call ended, Robert was ready to punch something. It was a good thing the county jail wasn't attached to the Sheriff's Office or Pendleton would definitely have grounds for a suit.

Robert went in search of Dale. Hopefully, the deputy was still here.

Thankfully, Dale was alone in the office shared by the deputies. He plucked at his keyboard, no doubt filing his daily report before ending his shift for the day.

"Dale, will you come to my office when you get a minute?"

"Sure thing, boss. Be right there."

Dale stepped into Robert's office less than a minute later.

"Close the door, please." Robert didn't mean to sound so gruff, but the implications of the charges he faced and how that might affect his chances for re-election settled on him full force.

Dale closed the door and settled into a chair, a frown on his face. "What's up?"

Robert told Dale about his phone call from IA and the allegations of police brutality.

"That's a bunch of bull." Dale pitched forward in his seat. "You sported more bruises from your skirmish with Pendleton than he did."

Robert rubbed the temple that sported a greenish bruise. He still suffered a headache each day because of it. "I agree, but IA needs to conduct their investigation before any of this can go away."

He explained what Detective Harris had requested and asked Dale to make sure his testimony was detailed and concise. "And thank you, for insisting on taking a picture of my injury that night."

Robert had been so exhausted by the time he'd dropped Jessie off at the ranch, all he wanted to do was go home, take some ibuprofen, and ice his throbbing head. But he had to stop by the office to file his report on the incident, and Dale had been adamant about getting pictures of Robert's head. He'd also insisted Robert go to the ER, but Robert had ignored those orders.

Robert scratched his jaw. "Do you think they'll want to question the other deputies, too? You know, to get a feel for my character?"

Dale shrugged. "Maybe, but you've got nothing to worry about. I doubt anyone here has one negative thing to say about you."

"Thank you for that. I have to admit this has taken me by surprise, and I'm more than a little concerned about what it will do to my reputation with the elections a couple months away."

"Internal Affairs investigations are public records, but no one besides the two of us need to know about it yet." Dale shrugged. "It might become public knowledge as the investigation advances, but don't worry about it; you'll be cleared. And you'll win the election by a landslide."

Robert wished he had Dale's confidence. Full of anxious energy, he picked up a ball-point pen and clicked the end a few times. "Do you think it'll come out that me and Jessie...that we used to be together?"

"So, what if it does? Pendleton may cry foul because he's jealous Jessie came home where her former boyfriend still lives, but facts are facts. She left him because *he* beat her, *he* broke the restraining order, and *he* attacked you with an ax." Dale punctuated his words by ticking them off on his fingers. "*You* were just doing your job."

"Thanks, Dale. Not just for this, but your support over the past four years."

Rumor had it Dale had been preparing to run for Sheriff when Robert's uncle, Dawson Winters, retired from being Sheriff and moved on to Justice of the Peace. But Uncle Dawson had groomed Robert to take his place. That, and the familial support Robert had here in Providence, had ensured he'd win the election. Dale had backed out and Robert ended up running unopposed.

Robert had always shown Dale the utmost respect, and the older man had reciprocated. After the Sheriff's Office received the generous anonymous donation last year, all personnel had received a raise, and Robert had made sure Dale's raise reflected his years of faithful service.

Dale stood. "You deserve it, Robert. Don't let anyone try to tell you different."

Robert hoped he could live up to the older man's praise and that this police brutality suit wouldn't cause everything to come crumbling down around him.

DUSK WAS BEGINNING to fall by the time Robert parked his truck in front of the ranch house. He looked at the bag on the seat beside him. He'd bought another gift for Jessie a couple days ago, but he feared he might offend her if he gave it to her. He didn't want her to feel like he was putting expectations on her.

Leaving the gift there for now, he climbed from the truck. He raked his hands through his still damp hair. He'd taken time to go home and decompress--working out hard for an hour--before showering and heading to the ranch.

He knocked, then walked through the front door without waiting for an invitation. His eyes went straight to Jessie sitting on the sofa, and he forgot to breathe. She looked so different with brown hair, but she looked beautiful. He couldn't remember the last time her hair was all brown.

She usually dyed it or had streaks of hot pink or neon blue. He remembered the time she died it black with purple tips. That one had taken some getting used to, but no matter what she did, it always looked amazing on her. She could pull anything off.

She was the same way with clothing. She looked great no matter what she wore--leggings, ragged jeans, a red satin evening gown. The woman was just plain beautiful.

Jake cleared his throat. "You're drooling, bro."

Heat climbed Robert's neck. He'd frozen at the sight of Jessie sitting there looking like a goddess and hadn't even realized Jake and Emily sat on the other couch.

"Great timing, Robert," Emily said, getting to her feet. "We were just talking about playing a game. It'll be more fun with four instead of three."

Jake grabbed his wife's hand. "Why don't we let Jessie take Robert out and show him the new filly that was born last night?"

Robert shot Jake a grateful look, then turned hopeful eyes on Jessie.

She almost looked shy as she slid to the edge of the couch. "Okay, not that you need me to show you where the stables are, but I'd love to see her again."

He followed Jessie to the back door, and just before he closed the door behind them, Emily whispered, "Good idea, honey."

Robert looked at Jessie to see if she'd heard.

Her cheeks flushed a delightful shade of pink, and he caught a smile before she turned her face away. She acted as shy as she had the first time he'd brought her to the ranch.

He fell into step beside her. "You look nice, Jessie. I like your hair."

"Do you really? I wasn't sure if you'd like it or not."

Robert stopped walking, and she turned back, standing in front of him.

She wrapped her arms around herself. "Did I say something wrong?"

He resisted the urge to take her hand. "No. Jessie, you can say and do anything you want. You have the right to dress however you want and wear your hair any way you want. It doesn't matter what anyone else thinks. You don't need my--or anyone--else's approval."

Jessie lowered her gaze, and he feared he'd hurt her feelings. He lifted her chin. The soft skin against his fingers sent shock waves of electricity through him. "Do *you* like your hair?"

Her lips curved into a slow smile. "I do."

"Good. That's all that matters." And then, in case she still needed some validation, he added, "I do too."

He was a little disappointed, though, that she'd decided to just go plain brown. The color was much darker and richer than he ever remembered her hair being, but he'd kind of hoped she'd find enough courage to put a little streak of color in her hair.

They continued to the stables, and Robert was careful not to touch her again. It didn't stop him, however, from noticing the graceful curve of Jessie's neck as she leaned forward to admire the new filly. He longed to kiss the sensitive area below her ear.

"Isn't she pretty?"

"Beautiful." Robert pulled his eyes away from Jessie before she noticed that he'd hardly looked at the foal. He took in the filly's gangly legs and silky coat as she made her way to the stall door.

He reached over and joined Jessie in stroking the foal's smooth neck, but his gaze drifted to Jessie again. Her silky hair fell forward, blocking her face, and the fluorescent light revealed dark purplish-red streaks in the under layers of her hair.

Robert fought the urge to reach out and run his fingers through Jessie's hair.

They talked for a few minutes about the first time Jessie experienced a colt's birth here at the ranch.

Robert recalled the joy on her face during that moment. "I remember you kept saying, 'It's so magical.'"

"It was." She turned back to the filly. "It still is. It gives you hope, you know?"

Jessie needed hope.

He decided to share the news he'd gotten late yesterday afternoon with her. "Your--Pendleton's bail was set at half a million dollars."

Jessie's knees buckled. Her good hand flew to her mouth while her cast hand reached out for support.

Robert grabbed her around the waist and held her upright.

She leaned into him. "Thank you."

He didn't think she was thanking him as much as she was thanking that heavenly being that he knew looked out for her.

He considered telling her Patrick had pressed charges of police brutality against him, but he didn't want to ruin this moment for her. She didn't need to worry about Robert's problems.

Her subtle perfume drowned out the smell of horses, leather, and straw. He ached to pull her tighter against him until her curves melded with the plains of his body. Did her mouth still taste like perfection--sweet and addicting?

Jessie righted herself and pulled from his arms. "I can't tell you what a relief that is."

Cool evening air rushed between them, and Robert had to shove his hands into his pockets to keep from pulling her back against him.

"I know it doesn't mean he won't still be able to make bail, but I can't see his dad handing over that kind of money," Jessie said.

"I'd like you to stay here at the ranch a little longer until we know if he's going to post bail."

Jessie nodded. "You're right. I don't want to put my mom in danger. At least here, it's not so easy to find me."

Robert wondered if he should stay at the ranch to help keep Jessie and Emily safe. If Pendleton made bail, he'd have to consider it more seriously.

They made their way back to the house, and Robert soon found himself seated at the dining table next to Jessie playing The Farming Game.

He tried to focus on the game. He really did, but Jessie's leg or arm frequently bumped his, sending sparks of electricity skittering across his skin. And every time she leaned in front of him to reach the far side of the game board, he caught a whiff of summer and sunshine.

He kept his hands balled into fists most of the evening. Good thing they weren't playing a card game; he'd have mangled them.

He caught glimpses of the old Jessie as they played. She alternated between bubbly and competitive. It was probably because of the knowledge that her husband's bail was so high, but Robert liked to think his presence had a little to do with it.

Because of her cheerfulness, he decided to give her the gift he'd left in his truck. Once Jake finally won the game and put Robert out of his misery, he asked Jessie if she'd walk him out to his truck.

He led her to the passenger door and opened it before he turned to look at her. The dome light inside the truck cast a pale glare on her face.

Man, she's beautiful.

Robert cleared his throat and shoved his hands into his pockets. "I have a confession to make."

Jessie looked at him, face full of trust, and a lump formed in his throat. His protective instincts kicked in, and he hoped he didn't hurt her with his confession or make her upset her with his gift.

"I uh... I saw your journal at the cabin last week."

Jessie lowered her eyes and wrapped her arms around herself, her posture guarded and tense.

Just thinking about the things he saw in that book made his stomach clench and his blood turn hot. "I didn't mean to be nosy. I just... Man, it kills me, to know that you had to hide your feelings and all the abuse you suffered in those pages."

Jessie lifted her head, but didn't make eye contact. A tear clung to her lower lash. "That was my only escape. I had to keep it hidden with the cleaning products."

"I'm so sorry, Jess, for everything you've been through."

She shook her head. "It's not your fault. It's mine."

"No, it's not. It's that man's. Don't make excuses for him or try to accept the blame for the things he did to you."

"Your right." She brushed away the lone tear that had fallen on her cheek. "Can we please not talk about him, right now?"

Gladly.

Robert reached into the truck and pulled out the bag, but didn't hand it to her. "I don't want you to take this the wrong way. I mean, I don't want you to think I'm trying to influence you or rush you in finding yourself or anything." He held the bag out to her. "I saw this and thought of you. I thought maybe you might like a journal that wasn't so full of...pain and darkness."

Jessie took the bag and pulled out the large journal. This one wasn't black. It was yellow, and the cover was filled with bold pink roses, small purple pansies, and vibrant greenery. She dropped the bag and brought the book to her chest.

Her head lowered, and Robert couldn't see her face.

Uh oh. Should I apologize?

Jessie's shoulders shook and she sniffled.

Without thinking, he pulled her into his arms. "I'm sorry, Jess. I didn't mean to upset you."

She kept her head pressed against his shoulder as she mumbled through her tears. "You didn't. It's just that Emily gave me an assignment. I'm supposed to write down...something." She sniffed. "But I couldn't bring myself to write them in that book."

"So, you're not upset with me for giving you the journal?"

Jessie laughed, but didn't lift her head. "No, in fact, this..." The arm holding the journal shifted against his stomach. "I mean, you just reminded me, again, that God is mindful of me."

He tightened his arms around her. "He is, Jess."

And so am I. Robert couldn't seem to make it through his day without thinking about Jessie a dozen times every hour.

More tears soaked his shirt as Jessie let go of...what? Fear? Feelings of unworthiness? Grief?

He didn't know, but he hoped these tears were healing and would help her move forward.

Gradually, the tears stopped, and her shoulders slumped. Her body relaxed and melted into his. The attraction Robert had fought all evening kicked into overdrive, and he was aware of her perfume weaving an intoxicating web around him. The warmth of her body pressed against his lit a fire inside him, warming him from the inside out.

The desire to press his lips to hers was almost too much to bear. If he did, he'd regret it. One kiss would never be enough, and he couldn't get lost in Jessie's arms or her kisses again.

He brought Jessie here to help her find herself. Of course, he hoped she'd choose to stay in Providence, too. He did not bring her here to get lost in her honey-colored eyes. He couldn't afford to let himself get caught up with her emotionally. If he let himself fall for her again and she left, he'd never recover.

Despite telling himself this, he slowly stroked his hands up her back and back down again.

"You can let me go now." Her breath was warm against his neck, raising his awareness to a dangerous level.

"I don't want to," he confessed in little more than a whisper. He wanted to hold Jessie in his arms forever.

"Good. I don't want you to let go either." She pulled the book from between them.

He felt her fumble to set it on the seat behind him before her arms wrapped around his back.

Good grief. This woman was going to be the death of him.

Robert recalled the time his father caught him and Jessie making out in the loft of the stables. Blake Winters had calmly told Jessie it was time for her to go home and said that Robert would call her later. He'd then set Robert down and gave him the next level of the *"birds and bees"* talk. The one that talked about how powerful hormones were. The one that was full of all the dangers of physical intimacy before a couple was mature enough to make lifelong commitments to one another, because that's what the woman Robert loved deserved. Lifelong commitment.

The love and respect his father showed his mother drove his father's words home and when his dad asked him to make and keep a promise to Jessie that he would never take from her what she should never give him outside the bonds of marriage, he'd made that promise to her.

It hadn't been easy, but he'd kept it. Despite the temptations during the many times they'd made out, Robert had been careful to make sure they never crossed that line. When things ended between them, and Jessie left for New York, he'd been grateful they hadn't.

Now Jessie was back.

Robert bit back a groan. For years, he'd dreamed of holding her like this again. But if he kissed her now, the fragile wall he kept around his heart would crumble, and he'd never be able to erect it again.

He pressed his lips against her hair. "I really want to kiss you right now, but I can't."

Jessie gave what felt like an involuntary shudder. "Why?" Her breath tickled his neck again.

"So many reasons. You're too vulnerable right now. I don't think our relationship--if we even have a relationship--is at that level. And I don't know..."

"Don't know what?"

I don't know if you'll leave me again.

"I just don't know." He couldn't voice his thoughts for fear it might plant the idea in her mind.

"I'm still married to Patrick, so we probably shouldn't kiss."

Her husband's name was like a splash of cold water on his face, but his body still felt the warmth she created in him.

Her arms slackened, but Robert held her tight. He wasn't ready to let go yet.

"Yeah, we definitely shouldn't kiss." He cherished the feel of her in his arms for a long moment before breaking the silence again. "I'm not ready to let you go yet, but you're driving me crazy. You need to turn your face away from my neck."

Jessie laughed against his neck.

This time he didn't even try to hold in the groan that rose in his throat.

She laughed again. "Fine. If I have to turn my head away, then you have to move your lips away from my hair."

It was Robert's turn to laugh. He pressed a brief kiss to her hair before she turned her head. He brought his hand up and gave in to the temptation he'd been fighting all night, and plunged his fingers into her silky hair.

She let out a soft sigh.

"My sentiments exactly."

CHAPTER 20

Jessie stretched and rolled over in bed, still shrouded in feelings of euphoria from last night. She had the most pleasant dreams after being held in Robert's arms.

True to his word, he didn't kiss her, and as much as she wanted him to, she was grateful he hadn't tempted her like that. She had too many things to figure out about her future before she decided if there was a place for Robert in it.

Her smile faded as she recalled his parting words through the window of his truck. "If you need anything, Jess...anything at all, call me. But, despite what we just shared... Actually, because of what we just shared...I probably won't be coming around too often. I think we both need to make sure we're not rushing this."

Robert was right. She couldn't rush into something--even though it felt so right--because she was still married.

She rolled back and reached for the pretty journal he'd given her, but a powerful wave of nausea hit like a Mack truck before she could grab the book. She threw back the blankets and rushed to the bathroom, the room tilting precariously as she did so.

She barely made it to the toilet before her stomach heaved. It didn't take long to empty the contents from her stomach, but her abdomen continued to seize. Jessie dry-heaved again and again.

Weak and exhausted, she sank back onto the floor. Her stomach dropped. She'd tried to chalk the nausea these last two weeks up to stress and anxiety. But she could no longer deny that little voice in the back of her head that said this wasn't anxiety.

It's morning sickness.

She leaned her head back against the wall and let the tears flow. *Why now?*

Why, when she finally found the courage to leave Patrick, was she stuck with this link to him? A baby that would constantly drag him back into her life. She would never escape him now, or the power he had over her.

All the beautiful dreams she'd built last night--where Robert forgave her for leaving and they found a way to move forward together--dissipated faster than her breath on a cold winter day. Robert would want nothing to do with her now. Even if he could someday forgive her for choosing her dreams over him, he wouldn't want to be stuck raising another man's child.

Pulling herself to her feet, she studied her face in the mirror. She still wasn't used to seeing herself with her new haircut. All the thought she'd put into the new hairstyle and worry over whether Robert would like it seemed so trivial now. It didn't matter if he liked it, he'd hightail it the other way as soon as he found out she was pregnant.

The red and splotchy face that stared back at her may as well belong to a stranger, because Jessie didn't know who she was anymore. The confident woman who set off for New York City to chase her dreams was long gone. But she refused to remain the timid punching bag Patrick had made her into.

So who am I supposed to be?

She'd started to develop a plan last night as she lay in bed in a state of euphoria, but those plans had been swept away in a flash flood.

Jessie washed her face and went to dress for her morning walk. She thought about telling Emily she wasn't feeling well and crawling back into bed. Maybe she'd stay there all day, so she wouldn't have to face anyone. But she was too frustrated and upset to lie in bed. Too agitated and resentful. So many emotions roiled around in her, it made her dizzy. No, that was the morning sickness making her lightheaded.

She cast an irritated glance at her bedroom ceiling. God must be laughing at her right now. She'd thought he'd sent Robert in answer to the prayer she'd been too faithless to pray. Not once, but twice--first at the cabin and then with the journal last night. So why had He done this to her?

She lowered her eyes. God didn't do this to her. She did all of this to herself. Robert kept telling her not to blame herself for everything Patrick had done to her, but she *was* to blame. She let him into her life. She'd been so sure she'd never love anyone again, like she'd loved Robert, that she hadn't given a second thought to letting an attractive, wealthy man into her life. It was better than being alone. How wrong she'd been.

She made her way to the kitchen, where she found Emily munching on a piece of buttered toast. A second piece sat on the counter, waiting for Jessie. Over the course of the past week, Jessie had often waited for Emily to finish a slice of toast before they walked, since Emily didn't enjoy exercising on an empty stomach.

By the time they returned, Lottie usually had breakfast ready. But Jessie had gotten into the habit of eating toast with Emily because her stomach was often queasy in the mornings.

Jessie rolled her eyes at herself. How had she missed the signs for so long? It wasn't like this was her first pregnancy. She knew morning sickness for her was often sporadic. She stopped herself before she again experienced the pain and loss associated with the miscarriages that ended those other pregnancies.

Then it hit Jessie. Emily was pregnant, too. She often came home after work and took a nap on the couch. She acted every bit as exhausted as Jessie felt. And Jessie had seen her turn away from certain foods as though the smell made her nauseous.

The knowledge should make Jessie feel better--or less alone, anyway--but it didn't.

"Good morning," Emily said, though it sounded less like a greeting and more like a question.

Could she see that Jessie didn't think it was a good morning? Or was Jessie projecting her own foul mood onto everyone around her?

"Morning," Jessie mumbled as she shoved toast in her mouth.

Emily continued to stare at Jessie as she put on her dusty Nikes between bites of toast. Patrick would have a fit if he could see her expensive running shoes.

Her lips curved in the first smile of the day.

It didn't last long, though, because Jessie knew Emily would expect her to talk about whatever was on her mind while they walked. But Jessie didn't want to talk about it. Any of it. Not the fact that she was pregnant. Nor did she want to talk about how her hopes of building a life with Robert had been dashed faster than they could form.

Within minutes, they headed out the back door, and Jessie vowed to keep up today. They walked nearly half a mile before Emily broke the silence. "So, did you and Robert have a fight last night?"

"Nope. Quite the opposite, in fact." Now why did she have to tell Emily that?

Because, other than my mother, I don't have anyone else to talk to.

But Jessie didn't want to talk to anyone right now. She wanted to sulk and feel sorry for herself. Maybe even throw a tantrum.

"Ooh. I hoped that was the case. You were out there for a long time." Emily's words came out slightly breathless, and Jessie couldn't help the satisfied smile that crossed her face.

"I think we crossed a major bridge, but it doesn't matter."

"What do you mean?"

"Robert might someday forgive me for leaving him, but it changes nothing. He's still not going to want a future with me."

Jessie had taken five strides before she realized Emily had stopped walking. She turned around to face Emily but couldn't make eye contact.

"What's with all the negative talk today?" Emily planted her hands on her hips. "You still haven't written your positive affirmations and what you want your life to look like, have you?"

Jessie couldn't tell if Emily was speaking as a counselor or as a friend. It had been so easy to talk to Emily when they walked, because she treated Jessie like an equal and acted genuinely concerned about Jessie and her problems.

Jessie folded her arms across her chest. "Not yet."

She'd planned on doing that and setting some life goals first thing this morning in her new journal, but those plans had gone south in a hurry. Now she had no desire to do anything. All she wanted to do was curl up in her bed and cry for all the opportunities she'd lost once again.

Emily stepped closer to Jessie. "What's holding you back? Is it fear of failing?"

It had been exactly that, initially. But then she couldn't bring herself to write anything positive in that book that was so full of darkness. Now? Now, she feared failing on a whole new level. The thought of being a single mother who had no way to support herself and her child scared her to death.

"Or are you afraid that no matter what goals you set for yourself, and how positive you may see yourself, that others--namely Robert--won't see you in the same light?"

"Something like that, I guess." Jessie rolled a rock with the toe of her shoe. In a few months, people were going to see her in a whole new light, and the pity glances she'd received the one time she'd bothered going out in public would be even more pitiful. Some might even judge her for leaving her husband when she was pregnant.

"People's opinions only matter if you let them, Jessie." Emily spoke as though she could read Jessie's mind.

"I know, but I have way too much baggage to put it all behind me. And I can't expect Robert, or anyone else, to overlook it."

Emily started walking again at a much slower pace, and Jessie fell into step beside her. "Last summer, I felt much the same way, but Ben reminded me that Jake's shoulders were plenty large and strong enough to help me carry my burdens." She grinned at Jessie. "I think

Robert's shoulders are almost as broad as Jake's." Emily grinned and winked.

"Look, Emily, I don't mean to sound insensitive, because I'm really sorry about your dad and brother and the awful things that happened to you last year. But my baggage is not the kind of burden someone else can carry." *Believe me, I would if I could.* "And it's not a burden that will go away or get smaller with time." She placed a hand on her abdomen.

"How far along are you?" came Emily's quiet voice.

Jessie stopped walking again. She wanted to deny it. Didn't want anyone to know she was pregnant, because she could hardly admit to herself that she was going to be a mother. A single mother.

Emily stopped and turned sympathetic eyes on Jessie.

Jessie wanted to ask her how she knew, but then realized vomiting can be heard through closed doors. And this morning was the second time she'd done it since she'd been here.

"How far along are you?" Jessie countered.

Emily smiled, her cheeks creasing with twin dimples. "Just finished my first trimester."

Jessie wished she were as happy and excited about becoming a mother as Emily. If she was in love with the father of her child, she might feel differently. Instead, she carried the child of a man who'd made her life miserable for four years.

"So, how far along are you?"

Jessie couldn't help the tears that sprung to her eyes. "I don't know. I only just realized this morning that's what's been making me so nauseous the past couple weeks."

Emily put an arm around Jessie. "So, you didn't know you were expecting when you left Patrick?"

Jessie shook her head. "No, and now I'm kind of freaking out. Will it make it harder for me to get a divorce? Will Patrick get visitation rights? What if he tries to take my baby away from me altogether?"

Too keyed up to stand still, Jessie started walking again, and Emily joined her.

"How can I let my child see their father, knowing he might hurt them? And how can I face Patrick every other weekend--whenever it's his turn--without the fear that he'll hurt me or my child?"

The tears streamed down Jessie's face freely now, but she didn't care. She brushed them away and continued talking as she walked. Now that the dam had broken, she felt powerless to stop the water's flow.

"I don't even have a job. If Patrick wants a custody battle, I can't afford to fight him. I don't even know if I want to be a mother right now, and that makes me feel so guilty."

Jessie kicked a golf ball-sized rock. "I'm afraid I'll be a horrible mother. I mean, what if I hurt my baby when I had my wrist x-rayed a couple weeks ago?"

"Didn't they put a lead drape on you?"

"They did, but what if it wasn't enough? And I colored my hair the other day. Isn't that bad for my baby?"

"No, the hair color doesn't get into your bloodstream, so it won't harm the baby."

Jessie continued to express all her concerns--some rational, but most irrational--while they walked.

Emily patiently listened to her vent, offering the occasional comment, but mostly remaining quiet.

By the time they'd returned to the house, Jessie still didn't know what the future held, but ranting seemed to lift some of her burden.

Emily turned to her as she pulled her right heel up to her butt to stretch her quad. "You have plenty of time to figure things out. You don't have to decide right away. But I still think you should make that plan of what you want your life to look like. Only now, you're making it with your baby in mind."

Jessie nodded, but inwardly she shook her head. Despite the pretty journal Robert had given her, she was even less eager, now, to write down what she wanted her future to look like.

Because no matter what she wrote, there was no chance now her life could turn out the way she wanted.

CHAPTER 21

Patrick pulled the ugly, smelly rental car up to the dinky auto repair shop in Providence. His lawyer had requested the car delivered to the county jail for Patrick and instructed him to drive straight back to Seattle.

But Patrick refused to spend four hours in this stinky car, especially when the GPS tracker on Jessica's car said it was here.

He looked around as he climbed from the hideous greenish-brown car. There, behind a padlocked fence, sat Jessica's Infiniti. He tugged the baseball cap he'd bought down low on his head. Knight's Grocery was as much of a general store as it was a grocery store and didn't carry name brand clothing, but he'd bought some clean clothes, at least. It wasn't likely anyone around here would recognize him, but it would be just his luck to cross paths with Winters again. No, he wasn't taking any chances.

Patrick wrinkled his nose at the smell of oil and grease as he walked into the garage. He shoved his hands into his pocket. Heaven forbid he touched something. He had enough of a stench clinging to his skin after a week in that cesspool they called a county jail. Spending the night in the Seattle jail with gang members had been disgraceful enough, but the past week with a psychotic drug addict as a cellmate had been horrendous.

"Can I help you?" A man with broad shoulders and dark red hair straightened up from under the hood of a car.

Patrick smiled and turned on the charm, even though it was the last thing he felt like doing. "I hope so..." He noted the name on the man's shirt. "Scott. I'm here to pick up my car."

The ginger-haired mechanic squared his shoulders and crossed his arms over his chest as he glared at Patrick. Scott stood at least four inches taller than Patrick, and his broad shoulders were pure muscle.

"I'm here for the Infiniti Q50," Patrick said, keeping his distance.

"Figured."

What did that mean? What lies had Winters spread about him in this pit-stop of a town? As if Winters hadn't taken enough from him already.

After everything Patrick had given Jessica, he couldn't believe she'd thrown it all away to come back here.

"Could you please unlock the gate, so I can get my car?" Patrick spat.

"Can't. Not 'til you pay the impound fee at the sheriff's office."

"Impound fee?" It was all Patrick could do to keep from shouting.

He'd already paid the bondsman ten percent of his exorbitant bail as collateral, since his father refused to bail him out a second time.

Since Patrick didn't have enough equity in the million-dollar home he'd purchased last year, he cashed in one of his investments to come up with the fifty grand. *Such a waste.* It had taken all week to free up the funds.

"Yep." Scott made a point of looking at the clock covered in a layer of grime. "I close in thirty minutes."

Patrick resisted the urge to throw a few choice words at the burly mechanic and retreated to his hideous rental car.

He headed in the direction of the sheriff's office he'd seen on Main Street on his previous visits to this backwoods town. Hopefully, he wouldn't run into Winters today. He wouldn't put it past the hillbilly sheriff to arrest him again out of spite.

When his lawyer suggested Patrick sue the sheriff's department for police brutality, he'd been all too eager to sign that.

The blood drained from Patrick's face as a familiar SUV with black and gold lettering on the side pulled out from behind the sheriff's office. His grip on the steering wheel tightened. There was the man who'd destroyed Patrick's life.

Patrick rubbed his jaw that was still a little tender from the beating he'd suffered at the hands of the man. He ached to repay the cowboy Casanova, but another physical altercation with Winters would only land Patrick in more hot water. No, he needed to find a way to take the sheriff down a notch. Strike at him in a way he wouldn't expect.

Making a U-turn, Patrick followed Winters to a diner across the street from the repair shop that had his car. He parked in the corner of the parking lot and watched Casanova go inside. *Great. He'll probably be here for at least an hour.*

A whole hour that he wasn't at home. Patrick sat up a little straighter. If the sheriff was here, that meant he wasn't guarding Jessie.

The man wasn't dumb enough to leave Jessica at the cabin again. Alone and unprotected. So, he probably brought her back to his house. It wouldn't surprise him if Jessie was sleeping with the man again already.

Patrick had always doubted Jessica's innocence. No one that gorgeous was as sweet and innocent as she'd acted when they were dating. Of course, he'd changed that. Jessica wasn't innocent anymore.

He cruised the sheriff's street twice before stopping a couple of houses away from Casanova's home. He sat in his car for a full five minutes, checking out the neighborhood, before getting out. He walked straight to the sheriff's backyard to avoid being seen by nosy neighbors.

It didn't take more than a few minutes of peeking through the windows on the back side of the house to know there was no one in there. Only one room, the master bedroom--judging by its size and furniture in there--had any kind of window coverings, and they were open enough for Patrick to see the room had no occupants.

After checking for gawking neighbors, he quickly peeked in each of the front windows. One room was completely empty, except for a few boxes, and the other had a desk and an office chair. The third window, the front room, revealed no movement inside.

He peeked into a couple of basement windows. Other than more boxes and exercise equipment, the basement was empty and unfinished.

Patrick stepped away from the house and cursed. He was certain the sheriff had brought Jessica back here.

She must be at her mother's.

Like a man on a mission, he returned to his car and drove to Sylvia's house. He did a similar sweep of her neighborhood as he had on Casanova's street, before darting to Sylvia's back yard.

The shrubbery and lengthening evening shadows gave him plenty of opportunity to watch her prepare and eat a solitary dinner before doing some light house cleaning. When she turned off the kitchen light, and he could no longer see her from the backyard, he returned to his car and parked across the street from her house.

He'd just spotted Sylvia reading in a recliner when a police cruiser turned onto the street. Patrick laid his seat back and ducked out of sight. The stench of who knows what kind of bodily fluids in the back seat hit him, and he gagged. He sat his seat upright again as soon as it was safe.

He continued to watch Sylvia for quite some time, but it was obvious she was alone. Not a single other light was on in the house. He considered breaking in and making her tell him where Jessica was, but that was the last thing he needed to add to the list of charges against him.

Patrick pounded the steering wheel with the side of his fist. He'd been sure Jessica was here or at the sheriff's house. He wanted her out of this hillbilly town and back where she belonged. She owed him. She had disobeyed him one too many times and for that, she would pay.

But it would have to wait. If he wasn't at work on Monday morning, he would lose his job. One more thing he would exact payment from Jessica for.

Another Sheriff's cruiser turned down the street, deciding for him. He tugged his baseball cap lower and turned his head when the car passed, then he started the disgusting rental car.

Patrick didn't think the sheriff was dumb enough to leave Jessica at that cabin by herself again, but he'd drive by just to make sure before heading home. He yawned, not looking forward to the drive to Seattle before he could shower off the filth that clung to him like a second skin. One shower wouldn't be enough.

Tomorrow, he would rest up, determine exactly what he needed to do to keep his job, and figure out how to get Jessica back.

CHAPTER 22

Robert pulled his cell phone from his pocket as he stepped through his front door. "What's up, Brady?"

It wasn't terribly late, but he was exhausted. It had been a long week, and the last thing he needed was an emergency.

"I just spotted a driver of a brown Honda who looked an awful lot like that Pendleton fellow. He wore a baseball cap, so I can't be sure."

Every muscle in Robert's body tensed. It had only been a week since they'd booked Patrick into the county jail. *With a bail of half a million dollars, he can't be out already, can he?*

Was he back to do what he'd failed to accomplish last time? Did he know where Jessie was?

"He drove by while I was gassing up my cruiser," Brady said. "I've been driving around looking for him for the last ten minutes, but I haven't found him yet. Thought you ought to know."

"Thanks, Brady. Keep your eyes open tonight. Cruise by Sylvia Sorenson's house frequently. Let's make sure he doesn't give her any trouble. And keep an eye on his Infiniti parked in the lot behind Knight's Repair Shop. I'll check on Jessie."

Robert ended the call and punched in the number for the county jail. "Please tell me Patrick Pendleton is not out on bail," he said into the phone as soon as his call was answered.

"Please hold," came the gruff voice at the other end of the line. After an interminably long twenty seconds, the voice returned, and Robert's blood turned cold. "He made bail and walked out of here around four o'clock."

Robert swore.

"Look, when we get orders that someone's made bail, we gotta let 'em go."

The man was right, but that didn't help the frustration coursing through Robert. He ended the call with a sharp jab.

When Robert pulled up to the ranch twenty minutes later--after hurriedly packing a bag and giving Sylvia a heads up--the dark house surprised him. Jake rarely went to bed this early.

Robert let himself into the house.

He couldn't sleep in his old room, since that's where Jessie slept. He pushed the image of her in his old bed out of his mind. Sleeping in Riley or Jake's old room, wouldn't make him an effective as a guard.

He found a pillow and blanket in the hall closet and tossed them on the couch. Figuring he should let Jake know he was here, he stepped to the door of the master bedroom and raised his hand to knock.

Emily giggled on the other side of the door, and Robert's hand froze. At Jake's growl, Robert smiled. No wonder he went to bed so early nowadays. Jake probably wouldn't welcome the intrusion. A squeal from Emily followed by Jake's deep laugh told him Emily wouldn't either.

Backing away, Robert returned to the couch, pulled his boots off, and attempted to get comfortable. An odd sensation burned through his abdomen, and his chest grew tight. He contemplated for a moment if he was having a heart attack, but he knew it was worse than that.

He envied his younger brother. He wanted a relationship like Jake's and Emily's. Again, his thoughts turned to Jessie. If things had turned out differently years ago, Jessie would be his wife and they would have a couple of kids by now. He would be the one making his wife giggle and squeal.

Knowing nothing good would come from this train of thought, he forced his thoughts to Pendleton. Was he really in town? Did he intend on doing Jessie harm? Judging by her fear and the murderous look on Patrick's face the last time Robert saw him, he didn't doubt the man could kill Jessie with his bare hands. Could Robert really protect her from him?

Yes. I'll do whatever it takes.

He'd promised Jessie he would protect her, and he meant it. He'd never broken a promise to her, and he didn't intend to start now. He remembered the promise he made to Jessie many years ago after her father left. "I promise I'll always be here for you, no matter what." He meant those words twelve years ago, and he meant them now.

No matter what.

But how could he keep her safe and guard his heart?

ROBERT STEPPED out of the bathroom the next morning only to run into Jake coming from the master bedroom carrying his boots.

"What are you doing here so early?" Jake asked, surprised.

Robert shot a pointed look toward the sofa where the blanket and pillow lay in a heap. "Brady called last night." Robert kept his voice low so Jessie wouldn't hear if she was awake. "He thought he spotted Pendleton in town. Apparently, Jessie's husband made bail yesterday. I figured I'd sleep here to provide protection."

"You should have let me know. I would have taken a gun to bed," Jake said as he sat on the couch to put his boots on.

"Funny thing... I was going to let you know I was here, but it sounded like you were..." Robert coughed dramatically into his hand, "busy."

Jake grinned. "Oh, you came that early, huh?"

"I figured you'd rather be surprised this morning to find me on the couch than to have been surprised last night," Robert said with a laugh.

"You figured right."

"I can't believe the sun has been up for over an hour already and my little brother is finally waking up."

"I've been awake for a while," Jake said with a sly grin. "I've discovered there are more enjoyable things to do in the morning than feed animals." Jake leaned back, clasping his hands behind his head, and gave Robert a smug smile.

"Seriously? Last night...and this morning?" And there was that jealousy again.

I really need to get a life.

"What can I say? We're still newlyweds, and Emily is pregnant. You know what they say about pregnancy hormones."

The last thing Robert needed to think about was pregnant women and hormones. The only woman he ever thought about was Jessie. And the thought of her carrying his child was a dream that could never come true.

"Are you bragging or complaining there, bro?"

Jake responded with a laugh and a smug smile.

Robert picked up his pillow and threw it at Jake. It hit Jake square in the face. "Looks like your extracurricular activities have slowed your reflexes."

A bedroom door opened down the hall, followed by the slamming of the bathroom door, drawing the men's attention. Robert heard the toilet seat that he'd been certain to put down hit the back of the toilet, followed by the unmistakable sound of someone vomiting. He turned to look at Jake, only to find him gone.

Jake was halfway out the back door. So much for slow reflexes.

"Was that Jessie? What's wrong with her?" Robert's words stopped Jake in his tracks, but Jake didn't turn to meet his eyes. He crossed to where Jake stood. "What's the matter with her?"

Jake pulled at his collar and cleared his throat. "She's uh...she's been...a little under the weather lately."

"Did she pick up a flu bug? Is anyone else sick?"

"No...um, I'm sure she'll be fine. She just needs...a little time." Jake pushed past Robert. "I've got work to do."

Robert stared at Jake's back. Something was up. He'd never known Jake to be evasive. And Jake never went out to work without his hat, but he did today.

Robert closed the back door and turned to see Jessie coming out of the bathroom, her face pale. He stepped toward her, and their eyes met.

Jessie's eyes widened. She pressed a hand to her stomach and hurried to her room, closing the door behind her.

She didn't look good at all, but why did she feel the need to avoid him?

"I thought I heard your voice," Lottie said from behind him, startling him.

"Hi, Lottie." Robert gave his second mother a quick hug.

She took in the blanket and pillow on the couch. "Was there trouble last night?"

"No, but my deputy thought he spotted Jessie's...ex, or soon to be ex, in town last night, so I stayed here as a precaution."

"Well, make sure you stick around for breakfast. I need someone to eat my food. Besides my Zane, Jake is the only one with much of an appetite lately."

I'll bet Jake has an appetite, Robert thought as he went to take a shower.

Twenty minutes later, he sat at the table with a steaming plate of food sitting in front of him. If he ate like this every morning, he would gain weight for sure. He worked out regularly, but his job wasn't active enough to burn this many calories.

Jessie came in and walked straight to the toaster. After dropping in two slices of bread, she turned around. Their eyes met again, as they had in the hallway. Her face still looked pale, but she looked better than she had earlier.

Jessie looked away.

Robert fought the urge to go to her and ask her if she was okay. He felt like a jerk for telling her he needed to stay away because he wanted to make sure they weren't making a mistake. But he didn't know how else to protect his heart.

"Jessie, can I get you some pancakes, eggs, and bacon?" Lottie asked.

She gave Lottie a weak smile and mumbled, "Thanks, but I think I'll just start with toast."

Jessie looked relieved when the toast finally popped, giving her something to do. She finished buttering the second slice as Emily walked into the kitchen. His sister-in-law walked straight past Robert to the toaster as well. Jessie held a slice of toast out to Emily, who took it with a smile.

Emily turned around and spotted him at the table. "Robert," she said around a bite of toast. "I'm surprised to see you here so early."

"He spent the night," Lottie said.

"Is everything okay?" Emily's brow furrowed as she sat down at the table. "I remember the last time you felt the need to spend the night at the ranch."

Robert knew Emily thought about the night the dogs had alerted Jake to a late-night prowler at the ranch after Emily remembered witnessing her brother's murder last year.

"Not so serious as that, but..." He directed his gaze toward Jessie, who still stood across the room. "Patrick made bail, and one of my deputies thought he saw him in town last night."

Jessie's eyes widened. She dropped her partially eaten toast on the counter, walked to the table, and sank into the chair across from him.

"Everything is going to be okay, Jess," Robert assured. "No one has spotted Pendleton since last night. It's possible it wasn't actually him that Brady saw."

Jessie nodded and met his gaze. "Thank you. I appreciate the precautions you're taking." Then she looked away again.

Jake came in through the mudroom door. After washing up, he sat at the table with them. A palpable tension filled the air as Jake avoided eye contact with Robert. Jessie wouldn't look at him. Even Emily fidgeted.

What's going on?

Lottie placed a heaping plate of food in front of Jake.

Jessie's eyes widened. "Excuse me." She clapped a hand over her mouth and shoved her way through the swinging door, setting it swaying wildly.

She looked like she was going to be sick again. Robert looked back at Jake and Emily, who shared a sympathetic look but didn't look at him. There was something going on here that no one wanted to talk about. He didn't press because he wasn't sure he wanted to know what was happening.

He focused on his food.

After a few minutes, he asked Jake if he could keep a ranch hand posted as guard for a few days. "We're not a hundred percent certain Pendleton is even in town. And if he is, I doubt he knows where Jessie is. But I'd like to know someone is keeping an eye out, just to be on the safe side."

"I think we've got enough men we can keep someone posted." Jake took Emily's hand in his. "Kind of like old times, huh?"

Robert finished his breakfast and left without seeing Jessie again. She probably went back to bed. Hopefully, whatever she had would pass quickly, and she'd feel better soon.

CHAPTER 23

Robert drove back to the ranch after an early dinner at the diner. Like most days, he hadn't been able to get Jessie off his mind. He tried to keep his distance because the more time he spent with her, the deeper he fell. But after seeing how sick she looked this morning, he'd worried about her all day.

How long had she had this bug?

When he arrived at the ranch, he grabbed the bag sitting on the seat beside him and went in search of Jessie.

He found Emily resting on the couch in the otherwise empty great room.

"Hi," Robert said when she opened her eyes and smiled at him. "Is Jessie around?"

"I think she's out on the back patio."

"Thanks. Sorry to disturb your nap." Robert walked out before Emily could say anything else. He was always afraid she would psychoanalyze him.

He spotted Jessie laying on a lounge chair as soon as he stepped out onto the back patio. He froze for a moment, waiting for his treacherous heart--that took off at a gallop--to settle.

Why did it always act like this every time he saw her? She was still married to another man. Even if she wasn't, he could never really let himself care for her again. Not like he used to. She wasn't content to stick around this small town five years ago. Why should he think she'd be willing to stick around once the threat of her abusive husband was no longer an issue?

As he stepped closer, he realized her eyes were closed. She was napping, too.

She opened her eyes and gave him a faint smile. "Hi."

A flutter worked its way from his stomach up through his chest. She was so beautiful, especially when she smiled. He sat on a nearby chair, facing her. "Are you feeling any better?"

"A little." She shrugged and looked away.

He set the bag from the diner on the small nearby table, next to a water bottle and an open package of saltine crackers. He perched on the edge of the other lounge chair, resisting the urge to scoot it closer to hers.

"I know you have Lottie here to cook for you, but I thought you might like some of Aunt Charity's chicken noodle soup."

"That sounds good. Thank you. I've had a hard time keeping some foods down lately." The words were meant for him, but she aimed them at her clasped hands.

Robert lifted the Styrofoam container from the bag and handed it to her, along with a spoon.

Jessie lifted the lid and raised it to her nose. "It smells delicious."

Then suddenly, she lowered the lid, closed her eyes, and clamped her mouth shut, taking deep breaths through her nose.

She gave Robert an apologetic smile. "I think I'll save it for later." Placing the container on the table, she picked up a cracker and took a bite.

She placed her casted hand on her lower abdomen as she fought the nausea, and a sense of déjà vu hit him. In recent months, he'd seen both Amy and Emily frequently place their hand protectively on their stomachs, like Jessie did now.

The air whooshed from Robert's lungs as though someone had

punched him. No wonder Jake and Emily wouldn't look him in the eye this morning and tell him what was wrong with Jessie.

She's pregnant.

Shock reverberated through his body, and all of Robert's nerves reacted. He hadn't felt this all-consuming confusion since he had to endure the mandatory tazing at the police academy. He bolted to his feet. He needed to move. Needed to leave.

Jessie's head jerked up at his sudden movement, and their eyes met.

Her brow furrowed.

Robert took a step back. "Um...I've gotta go. I hope you feel better soon." He turned on his heel and hurried down the back steps.

Walking away like that was rude, but he needed time to process this revelation.

Jessie was...is married. So why did the knowledge that she carried another man's child rip his heart in two?

Without thinking, he walked straight to the stables, hooked a lead rope on the first horse he came to--a black Friesian stallion--and led him to the hitching post. He ducked inside the tack room and grabbed his gear that still hung where it always had.

The stallion pranced sideways as Robert saddled him. The horse was as eager to run as Robert was.

Jake rounded the corner of the building as he mounted the stallion a few minutes later. "Robert, what are you doing?"

"What does it look like I'm doing?" The horse again pranced sideways, ready to run Jake over.

"That's Zeus you're riding."

"So?"

"He's strong, fast, and stubborn."

"Good." Robert eased Zeus around Jake, pointed him east, and shook the reins.

The stallion took off.

Robert rode Zeus hard for nearly an hour in a wide-sweeping arc--around the alfalfa fields, up the ridge, then across the summer grazing pastures. He eventually reined the stallion in and circled back toward the northwest and the ranch house. The muscles in his thighs burned from the exertion of keeping himself in the saddle. Without realizing where he'd ridden, he guided Zeus into a grove of trees not far from the house.

This was his favorite place on the whole earth. His and Jessie's grove. It wasn't the prettiest spot on the ranch, but he and Jessie had often walked here when they couldn't take off for a long ride. They'd spent hours here, talking, doing homework, kissing. Sometimes, Robert brought his guitar and sang country music songs while Jessie sketched in her notepad.

He dismounted and looped the reins around a low branch, giving Zeus enough slack to graze near the tree. As if of their own accord, Robert's feet carried him to his and Jessie's tree, the one where he'd carved their initials.

Memories came unbidden, tightening his chest as Jessie's voice from so many years ago played in his head.

"Why did you ask me out, Robert?"

"Which time?" Robert joked. "The second through eighth times were because you kept saying 'no.'"

Jessie laughed, a light, cheerful sound that made him smile.

"I mean, what did you hope to gain by asking me out?" When Robert didn't answer right away, she went on. "Do you plan on making me another one of your conquests?"

"Conquests?" Robert couldn't help but take offense.

Sure, he dated a lot of girls and had made out with a few of them, but that had been mostly their idea and he'd made no promises to any of them. He wasn't ready to get serious about a girl yet.

But there had been something about Jessie the first time he saw her after her family moved to town that wouldn't let him forget about her.

"I want to be your friend. I promise I'll always be here for you, Jessie. No matter what."

Jessie was always so somber. She looked like she desperately needed a friend. Then her father left his family, and Robert felt bad for her. He'd invited her to come to the ranch to ride horses. He hadn't considered it a date, but Jessie was reserved, and Robert was persistent.

She'd finally agreed to go out with him, so he'd leave her alone.

A smile pulled at Robert's lips. Jessie was cute when she got angry.

She'd enjoyed riding horses with him that day, so much so, she agreed to ride with him again the next week. And the next. Sometimes they rode four-wheelers instead of horses, but Robert loved watching her come alive on the ranch.

They could talk about anything; nothing had been off limits. She'd complained about menstrual cramps every time her cycle started, and he'd lamented that Jake might someday be stronger than him. He'd confided in her that as much as he loved the ranch, he didn't want to be tied to it his whole life. He couldn't tell his father because he couldn't bear to disappoint him. And she'd told him of her dreams that she didn't think would ever come true. Dreams of working at the MET.

They'd come here often. They felt like the only two people on earth when they were in this secluded grove. It had been here that she'd confided in him about how abusive her father had been. And she'd sketched Robert for the first time in this clearing. That was the day he'd realized how talented she was and that she was destined for big things.

He'd fallen for Jessie the first time he took her riding, but she'd friend-zoned him hard. He'd let her because he recognized how badly she needed a friend. It terrified her to care about someone for fear of being hurt, like her father had hurt her when he left his family.

Robert rested his forehead against the smooth bark of the quaking aspen and closed his eyes. He remembered the taste of her lips when they shared their first kiss here. It had taken him months to find the courage to push past the friend barrier.

Jessie didn't slap him or push him away like he feared she would. She simply asked why he'd kissed her.

"Because I want to be more than your friend, Jess. I'll do whatever it takes to earn the right to always be by your side. I promise I will always protect you."

Jessie had simply smiled and said, “Good.” Then she’d kissed him back.

He told her he loved her for the first time in this grove, and six months later, he carved their initials into this aspen tree before they left to go to different colleges. They had promised to call and write to each other, but they’d also agreed they should date other people while they were apart. Robert had taken a few girls out--mostly because his roommates talked him into it. But he couldn’t wait to see Jessie. He lived for the long weekends and summer breaks when they could be together again.

He traced their initials encircled by a heart in the soft bark. The tree had grown. The carving sat higher than he remembered. Bark and sap had peeled outward, making the letters thick--like a painful scar. They looked like Robert’s heart felt.

When Jessie left for New York, he told himself she deserved the opportunity to chase her dreams. He didn’t blame her for leaving. He’d been happy for the possibilities that awaited her. But it still crushed him.

Less than a year later, he heard she was engaged. He’d raced to the ranch that day and ridden for hours. At that point, he knew she’d never come back to him. He’d tried to get over her and move on, but it hadn’t been easy. He’d loved her for eight years. He’d never truly convinced himself there was no use pining for someone who was never coming back.

“But she has come back,” he whispered to the tree.

Not back to him, but back to Providence. Was he an idiot for thinking that maybe things could work out for them this time?

All his buried feelings for Jessie hadn’t wasted time in taking up residence in his heart again. But now she was pregnant with her husband’s child. Would she decide to go back to that monster for the sake of the baby?

Deep down, despite telling himself she was never coming back and would never be his, he couldn’t picture any other woman as his wife or the mother of his children. He’d considered taking a chance with Amy almost two years ago, but Ben fell in love with her, and Amy felt the same way about Ben. It had taken no thought from Robert to step aside and let them find happiness.

He wanted that happiness, too. He wanted what Ben and Amy and Jake and Emily shared, but despite the many women he'd dated over the years, he'd never imagined finding that happiness with anyone but Jessie.

When Robert finally returned to the stables with Zeus, exhaustion consumed him, both emotional and physical. Zeus was a powerful horse, and so were the memories and feelings that pulled at him all evening. He unsaddled and brushed down the stallion before putting him back in his stall and feeding him.

He'd planned to talk to Jake before leaving to discuss security measures, but no matter how hard he tried, he couldn't make his feet carry him to the house.

Jessie might be in there, and he wasn't ready to face her yet.

When he got back to town, he sent Jake a text, letting him know he could lift the guard since no one had spotted Pendleton again. Then he told him he wouldn't be around for a few days.

Jake's simple reply of *no problem* told Robert his brother understood what he was going through, and he'd keep Jessie safe.

So why did Robert feel like he was letting her down in so many ways?

CHAPTER 24

Robert walked out of the city office building after a lengthy meeting with the mayor and slipped on his sunglasses. He sucked in a deep breath of fresh air. Mayor Conrad liked the sound of his own voice and always droned on too long.

It didn't help that Lewis Jackson running for Sheriff came up again. Apparently, the man had been busy trying to solicit donations and votes. At some point, Robert needed to get serious about his campaign.

He pulled out his phone and sent Ben a text: *You free for lunch? I can pick up something at the diner and bring it to your office.*

He leaned against his Tahoe, waiting for Ben's reply. He couldn't shake the unease that had plagued him ever since he fought Pendleton at the cabin. Sitting around, waiting for Jessie's ex to make a move, left him restless and irritated. He'd like to think they had seen the last of the jerk, but Pendleton was out of jail, and Robert knew the man would be back.

Would Jessie's pregnancy force her back into Pendleton's grasp?

The thought stole his breath. *She can't go back to that monster. I won't let her.*

Not that he could stop her if she wanted to leave. And therein lay his problem. He didn't have a claim on Jessie's heart.

Robert's phone pinged.

Ben: *Sure. I can meet you at Charity's if you'd rather.*

Robert: *No. I'll come to your office.*

Robert enjoyed eating at his aunt's diner, but not today. He needed to vent to Ben, and he didn't want an audience. Besides, Amy worked at the diner and if things were slow, she'd join them. Robert liked Amy--she made Ben happy--but he wasn't in the mood for her cheerfulness today.

His phone pinged with another text.

Ben: *Sounds good. Everything okay?*

Robert didn't bother to respond because he didn't know how. He couldn't tell his best friend through a text his life was unraveling. And it had all started three weeks ago when Sylvia walked into his office.

Twenty minutes later, Robert walked into Ben's office laden with to-go bags.

Ben stood. "Should we eat in the conference room?"

The conference room wasn't much larger than Ben's office, but it had an open doorway on either end and it sat right across from Sheila's desk.

"This is fine." He set one bag on the corner of Ben's desk.

His cousin gave him a long, piercing look before he shifted some files, making room for the other bag.

Ben left his office and returned a few seconds later with two water bottles, leaving the door open behind him.

Robert closed the door before sitting in the chair opposite Ben.

"Okay, what's wrong?"

"Nothing, I just thought it would be nice to have a quiet lunch." Not that there had been any noise coming from outside Ben's office.

"That's a bunch of bull." Ben's eyes pinned him again.

Robert lifted the Styrofoam container from the bag closest to him. But his stomach had twisted in so many knots he no longer had an appetite. He set it on the desk without opening it and dropped back into his chair with a heavy sigh.

"I guess you've heard Jessie Soren--" Robert stopped himself from calling Jessie by her maiden name. But he couldn't bring himself to call her by her married name either. "Jessie's back."

"I heard." Ben pulled his lunch from the bag and opened it. "I ran into Sylvia in the grocery store a while back and she told me you took Jessie to the cabin. She also said Jessie wanted to file for a divorce and would contact me."

"But she hasn't yet?" Robert shifted in his seat.

"If she had, I wouldn't be discussing her with you."

Right. Ben might be Robert's cousin and best friend, but he took his clients' privacy seriously. He never told Robert who the anonymous donor was last year that gave over four million dollars to the city of Providence. Not that he and the rest of town hadn't figured it out.

"She's at the ranch now," Robert said, pulling his thoughts back to Jessie.

Ben finished chewing the bite he'd taken from his club sandwich before speaking. "I've heard that too. From Jake. What I want to know is why I had to hear any of this from someone other than you?"

"I've been busy, man." *And I didn't know what to say. My old girlfriend's back, and I think I'm still in love with her.*

"Yeah, fighting her husband and getting hit in the head with an ax, from what I hear."

Robert recalled how close he'd come to blacking out. He hated to think about what might have happened to Jessie if Pendleton had gotten the upper hand on him. He touched his temple that was still tender, even though the bruise had faded. "It wasn't as bad as it sounds."

Ben raised a skeptical eyebrow. He pinned Robert with another one of his piercing gazes. Ben had the uncanny ability to see right through a person, and Robert hated when he looked at him like that.

Ignoring his food, Robert picked up a letter opener off Ben's desk. He rotated it in his hands, alternately pressing his middle finger and thumb against either end.

"Pendleton pressed charges of police brutality against me."

"What?" Ben pitched forward in his seat. "What do you need me to do?"

"Nothing yet. I'll let you know if it looks like I'm going to need representation."

Ben leaned back in his chair, still scrutinizing Robert. "If you don't need a lawyer, why are you here? You're obviously not hungry." Ben motioned to Robert's unopened food.

"Jessie's pregnant," Robert blurted.

Ben's eyebrows shot up.

"I'm surprised Jake didn't tell you. He's practically ghosted me."

"Why?" Ben asked.

"Probably because he didn't want to have to be the one to break the news to me."

"Can't say I blame him. Who told you?"

"No one told me. I figured it out the same way I figured out Emily was pregnant."

Ben pitched forward again, eyes wide. "Emily's pregnant?"

Heat rushed up Robert's neck. "Oops, forget I said that. I think Jake said they were going to wait awhile to announce it." He gave Ben his sternest look. "My mother doesn't even know."

"Obviously. If Aunt Faith knew she was going to be a grandma, the entire town would know about it." Ben bit back a smile. "My lips are sealed."

"Yeah, until the next time you kiss Amy. Then I bet you blabber to her. And we all know she can't keep a secret for nothing."

Ben laughed. "True, but you've put me in a precarious situation. When Amy finds out Emily is pregnant, I'll be in the doghouse, if she figures out I already know."

"Then you'd better hope she doesn't find out." *And hopefully, Jake will forgive me.*

"So, how do you know Jessie is pregnant, if no one told you?"

Robert balled his fist around the letter opener and squeezed as he told Ben about hearing Jessie's morning sickness firsthand, twice.

First, at the cabin and at the ranch a few days ago. Then he told him about Jessie's reaction to the soup. "She put her hand on her lower abdomen just like both Amy and Emily do when they are trying not to lose their lunch."

"Thankfully, Amy's better now that she's into her second trimester. But I agree, it sounds like Jessie's pregnant, but you should wait for her to confirm it before you get all bent out of shape."

"I'm not bent out of shape," growled Robert.

Ben quirked an eyebrow again. "Right." He took another bite of his sandwich and took his time chewing. "So, let's say Jessie *is* pregnant. How does that make you feel?"

Robert snorted. "You've been hanging out with Emily too much."

Ben's gaze didn't waver from Robert's face. He expected an answer. A truthful one.

Robert pressed the point of the letter opener into the tip of his index finger. The uncomfortable sensation distracted him from the ache in his chest. "I don't know, man. How am I supposed to feel? It's not like I have any claim on her."

"Then why does her being pregnant bother you so much?"

Robert gave a barely audible grunt. "I'm worried about her, I guess. I'm afraid she's going to decide to go back to that...jerk, just because she's carrying his child."

"I'm worried about *you*." Ben's words were quiet.

Just like Jake had recognized, Robert wasn't acting like himself; Ben saw, too, how erratic his behavior was. But everyone's concern for him couldn't change things. It couldn't make Jessie stay in Providence. Couldn't make Pendleton disappear. Couldn't restore the five years Robert and Jessie had lost.

After a lengthy silence, Ben spoke again. "I know I'm not alone when I say I'd hoped things might work out for you and Jessie this time."

Robert lifted his head and looked at his cousin. "Some days, I hope that might be the case, then other days..."

"Other days, what?"

"Other days, I tell myself to stay as far away from her as I can. I can't go through that heartbreak all over."

"You don't think after everything she's been through, she'll be willing to stick around Providence?"

"Why should she? Providence wasn't good enough for her back then. I wasn't good enough." Robert's throat constricted at the admission, because nothing had changed. He still couldn't bear to leave this small town he loved. He cleared his throat before speaking again. "Why should this time around be any different? Once she's free of Pendleton and feels safe, she'll pick up and leave again."

"You don't think she regretted leaving Providence?"

"Not until her husband started abusing her." Robert ran the letter opener along the crease of his uniform pants. He couldn't hide the sarcasm in his voice when he added, "She finally finds the courage to leave him only after she's carrying his child."

Abandoning his food, Ben propped his elbows on the armrests of his chair and steepled his fingers in front of him. "What bothers you more, the fact she might leave again, or that she's carrying another man's child?"

Robert scowled.

"Or is it the fact that you have no control over any of this, *Sheriff*?"

"All the above." Robert's voice fell flat.

"Want to know what I think?" Ben's gaze bore into Robert's.

"No, but I have the feeling I'm about to find out." Needing a distraction, Robert pressed the tip of the letter opener against the flesh of his middle finger.

"You came to me, remember? I think knowing Jessie is pregnant--and fearing she will leave again--is eating at you, because you still care about her. More than you want to admit even to yourself."

A flash of anger filled Robert. Ben was right. As much as he didn't want to care about Jessie, Robert had never stopped loving her.

"Easy, man." Ben said, eying the letter opener Robert pressed against his finger. "I don't have a Band-Aid."

Robert looked at his finger, mesmerized by the paleness of the flesh surrounding the tip of the letter opener. How much more pressure would it take to break the skin? How much more pain could his heart take before it shattered?

Tossing the opener onto Ben's desk, he scoffed. "I'm sure plenty of paper cuts happen around here. Surely there's a Band-Aid somewhere."

Ben put the letter opener into his desk drawer. He gave Robert a sympathetic look. "You're probably right, but I don't think we have one big enough for you."

He held Ben's gaze. There was no trace of humor in the blue eyes.

Robert shifted his gaze to look out the window. *There isn't a band-aid big enough to fix me.*

He let out a heavy sigh. "I just wish I knew if she's considering going back to that...to her husband, because she's pregnant."

"Put yourself in her shoes for a minute." Ben paused, waiting for Robert to look at him. Ben was a brilliant lawyer because he always considered both sides of an argument. "I expect she feels like she's all alone in this, and I imagine she's scared, if the things Sylvia told me are true."

"They are. Pendleton will kill her if he gets his hands on her again."

"So, imagine how difficult this is for her. If she feels safe, then she won't feel pressured to make a decision that will harm her or her baby. Give her the time she needs to figure things out. And you do the same."

"What's that supposed to mean?"

"It means she's facing a life-changing event, and she probably feels all alone."

"She's got her mother. It's not like she's totally alone."

Ben nodded. "Yes, and I know Sylvia would do anything for her, but she doesn't have the baby's father by her side to help her through this."

Robert snorted and tipped his head back to study the ceiling. "And I'm supposed to step in and fill that role?"

"I didn't say that. But you should consider whether you *could* be that man. For Jessie's sake and the baby's."

Robert looked out the window again. He didn't respond. He couldn't. Could he be there for Jessie? He didn't know if his heart could handle that. Besides, he wasn't sure she wanted him to be there for her.

"Let me ask you something," Ben said after a lengthy silence. "A couple of years ago, when you took Amy to lunch every Friday, did you ever think the two of you might have a future together?"

"Okay, this just got awkward."

"Did it bother you that Amy had a child from a previous relationship? Did you ever think things might develop to where you had to decide if you could be a dad to Kallie?"

Robert shrugged. "I don't know. Maybe. I mean, I liked Amy, and Kallie was a cutie. I was... I am ready to be a father," he admitted, his voice dropping to a whisper.

"It didn't bother you that Kallie wasn't your biological daughter?" When Robert's only response was another shrug and the shake of his head, Ben continued. "Why is this any different?"

"I don't know. It just is." Robert dropped his head to his hands, barely controlling the anger that boiled inside him. "Pendleton doesn't deserve to have a woman like Jessie carry his child."

"I agree. And we both know what kind of man Amy's ex was. He wasn't even there for Kallie's birth. Lance wasn't fit to be a father, but Kallie deserved a father who would love her and care for her." Ben's voice grew husky. "I love that little angel like she was my own and I want to be the father she deserves." Ben paused a moment before continuing. "I think this is different because you care more for Jessie than you ever did Amy. The question is, can you be the father Jessie's baby deserves?"

"I don't know." Robert let out a deep sigh.

Ben slapped his desk. "What's wrong with you, man?"

Robert's head jerked up, heat filling his veins. Ben had no idea how torn Robert felt at the magnitude of making such a decision. Especially if Jessie didn't want his help.

"You lost her once because you weren't willing to fight for her. Do you want to lose her again?"

Robert bolted from his chair, his heart screaming an emphatic "*No!*" He walked to the window and took a deep breath. "I let it her go... because it's what she wanted. I was afraid if I fought to win her over, she would always resent me."

But what kind of message had that sent to Jessie? Had she thought he didn't love her enough to fight for her?

CHAPTER 25

Jessie stepped out onto the back deck and pulled the door closed. When Jake made himself comfortable on the sofa after dinner, pulling Emily's feet onto his lap, Jessie decided to get some fresh air. It was only a matter of time before the foot rub or hair brushing turned into snuggling and kissing.

She dropped onto the porch swing and set it in motion. Jessie had no problem with public displays of affection, but seeing the newlyweds get cozy made her uncomfortable. Mostly because Patrick had never looked at her in the adoring way that Jake did Emily. He'd frequently complimented her in public, but when they were alone, he became a different person.

Years ago, Robert had looked at her like that, but now his eyes were broody and distant. She didn't look forward to telling him she was pregnant. It's not like he cared, but he needed to know he wasn't protecting just her anymore.

Her morning sickness hadn't subsided much, but she'd learned to take preventative measures to combat the nausea. And her emotions were leveling out. She'd finally written in the journal Robert gave her almost two weeks ago.

I'm pregnant. Those had been the first words she'd written. Followed by *I'm scared. For myself and for my child.*

Once she'd started, she couldn't stop. She'd written for hours. First, trying to purge her fears for herself and her baby, worrying about what her obligation would be in telling Patrick. Then she'd listed the hopes and dreams that had barely sprouted before reality dashed them to pieces. She'd filled up page after page, finally finding the courage to make a list of things she wanted to be a part of her future.

Robert's name appeared at the top of the list, followed by art, and staying in Providence. Each of those things felt like a pipe dream, but it didn't keep her from wanting them.

Concern for how she would support her child had finally prompted her to pick up the painting Robert wanted her to finish. She'd stared at it a long time before deciding she could fix it. She'd finished it a few days ago, but she wasn't sure she was ready to give it to him yet. Despite their lengthy hug, she'd hardly seen him since, and everything felt so up in the air between them.

He hadn't been back to the ranch since he brought her the soup a week ago. It had been such a sweet gesture, and she'd looked forward to visiting with him, but then he'd taken off and gone for a ride and she never saw him return.

Jake often mentioned that Robert checked in with him, but Jessie couldn't help feeling like he was avoiding her. She couldn't blame him.

She'd finally scheduled an appointment with Ben for next Tuesday. Hopefully, her pregnancy wouldn't hinder her ability to file for a divorce. Of course, it might not be an issue if she ended up miscarrying this baby, like she did the others. A twinge of heartache stole her breath at the thought of the other two babies she'd lost.

She'd also scheduled a doctor's appointment to find out how far along she was. She guessed about six to eight weeks.

The familiar drone of Robert's truck brought Jessie to her feet while butterflies swarmed her stomach. *I'm only anxious because I need to tell him I'm pregnant. My reaction has nothing to do with the fact I haven't seen him for an entire week.*

Jessie followed the wrap-around porch to the front of the house. She should save him the embarrassment of walking in on Jake and Emily.

Her breath hitched when Robert climbed from his truck wearing faded jeans and a red t-shirt that emphasized his dark lashes. The boy she'd fallen in love with had filled out and developed into a very attractive man. He looked handsome in his uniform, but there was something about the way he wore his jeans--snug and low on his hips--that made women look twice.

Robert came to a stop at the bottom of the porch steps when he saw her. He smiled, and Jessie's heart raced.

"Hey..." Robert drew out the word as though he changed his mind about what he wanted to say.

"I'm pregnant," Jessie blurted, then cringed. Afraid she would lose the courage to tell him she was expecting, she broke the news in the worst way possible.

His eyebrows shot up, and his lips quirked. "Hmm...seems to be a lot of that going around." A light twinkled in his eyes as one corner of his mouth turned up.

Jessie sighed in relief. This was the Robert she fell in love with so many years ago. The one who lightened the atmosphere during tense times.

"You knew?"

"I've been around enough women with morning sickness lately, it wasn't hard to figure out." Robert's brow furrowed as he looked beyond her shoulder. "Jess, I need to know-- Does this change anything?"

It changes everything, she silently screamed. It was one thing to fail at her career and marriage, but to have another human depending on her when she had no means to support a child overwhelmed Jessie.

At the thought, a sudden surge of love filled her chest, stealing her breath. And just like that, Jessie knew she'd do whatever it took to care for her child. She placed a hand on her abdomen. She'd do everything in her power to protect this child from his or her father.

"If you mean, does this change my decision to divorce Patrick? The answer is no. It only strengthens my determination to stay as far away from him as possible."

Robert's shoulders relaxed as he let out an audible sigh. "Good. Then I want you to know I'm here for you. No matter what."

Gratitude swept over her at his selflessness, filling her chest and weakening her knees. She grabbed the handrail and dropped onto the top step. This man had every reason to hate her, but he didn't. For him to offer any help she needed considering this crazy recent development spoke volumes about the kind of man he was.

He placed a foot on the second step and leaned forward. His face, mere inches from hers, filled with concern. "Are you okay?"

She nodded. "I'm fine. I just..." The lump in her throat blocked her words. "Thank you. That means a lot to me."

He braced an elbow on his thigh and continued to study her.

Jessie held his gaze, spotting the golden flecks in his brown irises. He had the most gorgeous eyes. His familiar scent--woodsy, masculine and oh, so heavenly--swept over her. It would be so easy to lean forward and close the distance between them.

It had been years since she'd kissed Robert, yet she still remembered the feel of his lips on hers. Warm and tender, asking permission, while gently probing. Kisses that filled her with passion and longing.

"I mean it, Jess. This is a...complicated situation, but I want what's best for you and your baby."

Was it her imagination, or did Robert's voice drop, taking on a husky tone? His gaze dropped to her lips, and her mouth watered. She sucked in a sharp breath and looked away before she did something crazy.

Like kiss him.

What's wrong with me?

She'd heard pregnancy hormones often made women more passionate, and wondered if Emily experienced this...influx of desire. She'd chalked the affection between Emily and Jake up to them being newlyweds, but now she wondered if hormones drove a lot of it.

Jessie had never felt the desire to kiss and be kissed with her previous pregnancies like she did now. Of course, any affection she'd felt for Patrick had vanished after the abuse started.

Robert cleared his throat and straightened. "So, have you been on a horse yet? Would you like to go for a ride?"

The thought of riding with Robert like she had in simpler times appealed to her, but a sudden concern for the child she carried gripped her. She didn't want to do anything to harm her baby. "I rode twice last week, before I realized..." She still had a hard time admitting she was pregnant. "I'm not sure I should ride in my condition."

His brow furrowed. "Are women not supposed to ride horses when they're pregnant? I'm pretty sure I remember my mom riding when she was pregnant with Riley." He grinned and slapped his forehead. "Of course. That's what's wrong with Riley."

Jessie laughed because there wasn't a single thing wrong with Riley, except that the poor girl had to put up with two older brothers who teased her relentlessly because they adored their younger sister.

Remembering Emily's counsel to not censure herself, she rose to her feet. "Honestly, I don't know if women can ride when they are pregnant. I just know I don't want to lose another baby."

Robert's brow furrowed, and his face paled. "Another baby?"

Maybe I should have said that with a little more delicacy.

Robert deserved to hear the truth. "I've miscarried twice before. During the first trimester each time."

The remaining color in Robert's face vanished, and he pivoted and dropped onto the second step.

"Are you alright?" Jessie sat beside him.

He gave her a tight smile and held up a hand. "Yes, I...just need a minute to...process this."

Is that why it had been so long since she'd seen him last? Because he'd figured out she was pregnant and needed time to come to terms with it. Did he ever think about the plans they had made to raise a family together? Jessie always hoped their daughters would get his long, thick eyelashes. They'd even discussed names for their future children. He'd wanted to name their first son after his dad. Jessie had always liked Blake Winters. Like Faith, he'd made her feel welcome and part of the family.

She shook her head. She'd never have that with Robert.

Being around him again had awakened a lot of old feelings in her, but it didn't mean he felt the same. She didn't deserve a second chance with him.

For the hundredth time since realizing she was pregnant, sorrow washed over her. She was alone in this.

Robert bolted to his feet. "Would you like to go for a walk?"

Sensing his pent-up energy, she rose, too. "Sure."

Robert led the way toward the northern grazing pastures, keeping a break-neck pace. After a few minutes, she stopped trying to keep up with him and let herself fall behind. He didn't seem to want to talk, anyway.

How long would it take him to realize she no longer walked beside him?

Judging by the direction he walked, she thought he might be headed to their grove. A place so full of memories, Jessie hadn't had the courage to visit it yet.

As if suddenly realizing where he was going, Robert's footsteps faltered. He abruptly changed direction, then walked on, leading them toward the ridge that rose about a mile north of the ranch house. After another thirty yards, he stopped and looked back at her. Pink tinged his cheeks, and he lowered his gaze as he shoved his hands into his pockets.

Jessie bit back a laugh. Robert didn't embarrass easily.

"Sorry," he said when she drew near.

She waved away his apology. "I've done plenty of stomping around this ranch myself since I realized I was pregnant."

"So, you didn't know you were pregnant when you left him?" Robert started walking again at a much slower pace.

She fell into step beside him. "No. We had only just started trying again a couple months ago. I didn't expect it to happen so fast."

Especially considering he probably slept with Tina as frequently as he did with me over the last few months. She certainly hadn't minded the decrease in intimacy with Patrick. That had become as unpleasant as every other interaction with him.

"Do you mind telling me what happened with the other pregnancies?" Robert's gentle voice pulled her from her musings.

"Nine months after we were married, Patrick's dad insisted he wanted grandkids. So, Patrick made me go off the pill, even though I thought having a baby just because his dad wanted us to was a bad idea. I prayed I wouldn't get pregnant, but a part of me hoped maybe a baby would mellow out Patrick."

Robert snorted beside her, understanding that her hopes had been a foolish dream.

"It took us about five months to get pregnant. I had horrible morning sickness and could barely make it through work, let alone keep up with the cleaning, laundry...and the cooking." A shudder rippled through her as she remembered Patrick's anger the night she miscarried. She hugged herself.

Robert stopped walking and let out a low growl. "Let me guess, he beat you when you didn't have dinner on the table by five."

Jessie stopped, too. "It took little to set him off," she whispered. Sucking in a deep breath, she steeled her emotions. "I was only eight weeks along when I miscarried after...one of Patrick's rages. When I lost the baby, he said I wasn't ready to be a mother yet if I couldn't take care of myself and the house while I was pregnant."

Robert sucked in a sharp breath.

She didn't want to upset Robert, but she needed to get this out, so she pressed on. "I felt so guilty after I lost the baby."

"Jess, you shouldn't--"

She held up a hand. "I didn't feel guilty because I didn't think I'd be a good mother. I felt guilty because I didn't want to be a mother."

Robert's brow furrowed as he frowned at her. She and Robert had made enough plans together before she left for New York that he knew she didn't mean it.

Jessie lowered her eyes. "I loved that child in the few short weeks I carried it, but I didn't want to bring it into an abusive environment."

Letting out another growl, Robert shook his head. He bent and picked up a baseball-sized rock. He tossed it in the air a few times, catching it each time it fell, then he swung his arm back and let the rock fly. It soared through the air in a high arc before hitting a boulder thirty yards ahead of them with a sharp crack.

"Nice throw. Coach Wilson would be proud," she said, thinking of Robert's high school baseball coach.

"Yeah, except I was aiming for the boulder to the right of that one." His face reddened as he mumbled the admission.

Jessie bit back a laugh as she judged the distance between the two boulders to be about ten feet. It looked like Providence's all-star pitcher had lost his edge.

Had his skills deteriorated because of lack of practice, like hers? Or did he miss because his emotions clouded his judgment? She hated to see him upset because of the things she shared with him.

He started walking again, and she joined him, wondering if she should have kept this to herself. They walked in silence for several minutes before Robert spoke.

"What happened with the second pregnancy?"

"I lost that baby at twelve weeks." The hitch in her voice betrayed the pain she felt at the loss of that child.

"Was it *his* fault, again?" Robert's voice was low, bordering on dangerous sounding.

"No, it was a genetic abnormality in the embryo's formation. It simply didn't develop properly. When the doctor couldn't detect a heartbeat at eight weeks, he said not to worry because it was still early. But at twelve weeks, there was still no heartbeat. He told me my body was getting ready to abort the pregnancy, and he sent me home to wait until it happened. If it didn't happen within the week, I was supposed to go to the hospital so they could induce labor. Two days later, I started cramping. I don't know if losing the baby upset Patrick as much as it did me, or if he just felt sorry for me, but he didn't lay a hand on me for almost a month."

Jessie sucked in a deep breath to fight the emotion that clawed at her throat. In the twelve weeks that she carried that baby, she loved it with her whole heart. Losing it had nearly killed her.

"I'm so sorry you went through that." The sincerity in Robert's voice brought tears to her eyes.

Did it cross his mind that if Jessie had never left, he would have been the father of her child, or rather children, and they would have shared that loss? Or maybe she wouldn't have lost either baby, and she and Robert would be well on their way to having the family they'd always wanted.

Stop it. Stop pining over something you can never have. You walked away, remember?

She'd pined plenty over Robert, already. She'd never tell him, but she'd taken more than one beating because of him; every time Patrick caught her looking at Robert's pictures, wishing things had turned out differently. Even after he'd burned the pictures of Robert, he still accused her of thinking about her former boyfriend. Truth was, she did often long to return to a happier time where she hadn't lost Robert's love.

They continued to walk in silence for the next ten minutes, each lost in their own thoughts. When they reached the top of the ridge, they sat on a large boulder and faced the setting sun.

Jessie let out a sigh as golden rays arced upward, piercing the clouds. "I had forgotten how beautiful the sunsets were out here."

"Hmm?" Robert's voice sounded like his mind was far away. "Oh yeah, we definitely get our share of amazing sunsets."

They lapsed into silence again. Jessie resisted the urge to chew on her nails as she watched Robert roll a small rock around with the heel of his boot.

If he wanted to talk about what was on his mind, he would. And if he didn't, no amount of inane conversation would get him to share his thoughts.

She didn't have to wait long for him to speak, but the words that came out were the last thing she expected to hear.

"I came to New York, you know."

Jessie's heart stalled.

"What did you say?" Jessie asked, certain she hadn't heard him correctly.

"I came to New York."

"When?" An odd sensation rippled through her--a combination of loss and regret, coupled with hope.

"About six months after you left." When she gave him a confused look, he continued. "I promised myself I'd ask you one time to come home with me... If you refused, I had decided I would move to New York, so we could be together."

Tears again filled her eyes. Robert had been willing to leave his family and the small town he loved to be with her in New York?

"But I never--"

"I chickened out. The night I showed up at the MET there was a big fundraiser gala thing going on. Obviously, I didn't have an invitation, but I bribed a guard to let me in." He scratched his jaw. "And I may have promised to make a large donation."

Jessie's mind raced back to the night of the benefit gala for the children's hospital six months after she'd arrived in New York. Not only had she been the principal organizer, the chief curator of the museum had also insisted on showcasing some of Jessie's work. It was the happiest night of her life since arriving in New York. Had she known Robert was there, it would have been the best night ever.

"Why didn't you tell me you were there?"

"I saw your work that night and recognized your style even before I saw your name posted nearby. Those pieces were truly magnificent, Jess, and you were so beautiful in your red evening gown. You had finally realized your dream, and I knew I couldn't ask you to walk away from that. And with each minute I spent in that city, I realized I didn't belong there. My wranglers and blazer could never compete with all those tuxedos and evening gowns. And everywhere I looked there were so many people."

Jessie remembered feeling claustrophobic when she first arrived in New York. She missed the wide-open spaces of home, and even though she'd been surrounded by millions of people, she'd never felt so alone.

She couldn't get over the fact that Robert had stood in the MET close enough to see her and she'd never known he was there.

“I wish you had come and talked to me.”

“It would have made things harder. I could see you weren’t ready to leave New York, and, despite my promise to myself, I didn’t think I could stand to stay.”

It must have killed Robert to break a promise--to himself, of all people. “You’re right, I wasn’t ready to leave, but I would have loved knowing you cared enough to come after me.”

“Of course, I cared. I loved you, Jess, like I’ve never loved another woman.”

His words should have filled her with hope, but instead heat filled Jessie’s chest. “You were sure quick to send me on my way when I told you about the internship.”

Robert sprang to his feet. “What was I supposed to do? You chose New York over me. Besides, you sure didn’t take long to get over me. I mean, you’d barely been there a year before you got engaged.”

Jessie nodded her head, her eyes burning with unshed tears. “You’re right. I did.” She’d taken a broken heart to New York. Torn completely in two--her love for Robert warring with her dreams. She knew she’d never love like that again, so she didn’t even try. She figured affection for an attractive man was the best she could hope for. Her voice dropped to a whisper. “And I’ve regretted it ever since. The night of the gala... That was the night I met Patrick.”

Robert turned and looked at her, his gaze pinning her. As his brown eyes held hers, she could practically see the wheels turning in his mind. Was he coming to the same conclusions as she had? If he’d only talked to her that night... It might not have changed things between them, but she was certain she wouldn’t have welcomed the attention of a stranger if the love of her life stood beside her.

Robert dropped back down onto the boulder beside her. He braced his elbows on his knees and laced his fingers together, keeping his eyes glued to the ground between his boots. “I’m sorry. I didn’t know.”

She watched the fading rays of the sun shrink toward the horizon, wishing she could bring back its warmth and light. “It’s not your fault.

We can't change the past, so we need to let it go." She wanted to add *and learn from our mistakes,* but didn't.

That's what she intended to do, but she wasn't sure how, or even if, that applied to Robert. He might feel bad for the way things turned out for her, but it didn't mean he could get over the hurt she'd caused him and ever consider moving forward with her. If Robert learned from his mistakes, it meant he'd never trust her with his heart again.

"We'd better head back or it'll be pitch black before we get home." He stood and reached out a hand to pull her up.

Without thinking, Jessie placed her hand in his. Electricity raced up her arm at his touch, as strong as ever. As soon as she was on her feet, she pulled her hand away, and he released it without hesitation.

The walk back to the ranch house passed quickly and quietly. They kept a fast pace, the darkness closing in with each step. As soon as they reached the yard, Robert bee-lined for his truck.

Jessie followed, planning on saying good night and going into the house.

Robert turned to her before opening his truck door. "I don't know when or if Patrick will make another move. Even though it has been quiet, I doubt he's backed off for good."

"He hasn't." Of that, Jessie was certain.

"I'd like you to stay at the ranch for a while longer. Overall, I think it's safer here." He opened the driver's door, leaned in, and pulled out a small bag. He held it out to her. "I thought this might give you a little freedom to come and go on your own, though."

She pulled a cell phone from the bag.

"I've pre-programmed it with your mom's number and mine as well as most of my family."

"I can't take this, Robert." She pushed the phone and bag in his direction. "You've done too much for me."

He stepped back. "No, I didn't do enough." He rubbed the back of his neck with one hand. "I should have talked to you that night in New York. I was a coward. As soon as I saw you, I knew you belonged there, and I'd never measure up to your glamorous lifestyle. I couldn't bear your rejection again." He shook his head as if ridding it of an unpleasant thought, then gave a rueful laugh. "You're right. We need to let go of the past. We could *'what if'* and *'should have'* ourselves to death, but it won't change anything." He leaned back against his truck and folded his arms over his chest.

He looked out toward the distant hills, hidden in the darkness. Tension filled his voice when he spoke again. "I want to keep you safe, Jess, but I can't be here all the time."

The words she heard didn't match his tone. His posture, the lack of eye contact, and the tension in his voice told her what he really meant was, *I can't stand to be here all the time.*

Robert continued talking, explaining the features of the phone. Much of what he said didn't register, but she didn't care. She just wanted him to leave already.

"Keep location sharing turned on, so if something happens to you, I'll know where to find you."

Jessie's body tensed as heat flared in her.

Robert was as bad as Patrick--wanting to control her actions when he wasn't around. He'd pulled her painting out of the trash, telling her she should finish it. Then he gave her money and insisted she get her hair done. He didn't dictate how she should have it done, but he'd been the driving force behind that change. And now he wanted to track her location with a cell phone he provided?

He must have sensed her tension, because he held up both hands, palms outward in a pacifying motion. "Jessie, I know how controlling Patrick was. Please believe me when I say that's not what I'm trying to do. I just worry something will happen to you when I'm not around and I won't know where to find you."

She hung her head at the sincerity in his voice. She'd overreacted. Robert was nothing like Patrick. Jessie knew that, but she obviously still had trust issues. She'd have to talk to Emily about that.

Swallowing her pride, she nodded. "I accept the phone and I won't turn off location sharing. Thank you."

She let herself into the house a few minutes later, after Robert drove away, to find the great room empty. Jessie locked the front door and went through her bedtime routine. She climbed into bed, trying to still her mind from the evening's turmoil.

I came to New York, you know. Robert's words filled her head as pain filled her heart. He was right. She could *"what if"* and *"should have"* herself to death, and it wouldn't change anything. But oh, how she wished things were different.

I loved you, Jess, like I've never loved another woman. Did that mean he still loved her, like she did him?

Maybe, but Robert had pride, and he'd never open himself up to heartache again. Just like Jessie didn't know if she'd ever fully trust a man again.

She rolled onto her side and hugged the extra pillow close, powerless to stop the tears she'd been fighting all night.

Stupid hormones.

CHAPTER 26

Jessie looked up from her sketch pad when unfamiliar footfalls sounded on the back deck.

Jake and Zane were the only ones who used the back door during the afternoon, but their boots made a much heavier sound than the quiet tapping of the high heels the woman who now approached wore.

The slender, yet busty, woman with red hair bore a familial resemblance to one of Jessie's high school classmates, whose name Jessie couldn't recall at the moment.

The woman with fiery red hair and striking blue eyes crossed the deck like she owned the place and gave Jessie an appraising look. "So, you're Robert's ex-girlfriend." There was an edge of contempt in the woman's voice.

Ex-girlfriend sounded so much worse--more final--than former girlfriend, especially when Jessie hoped to be his girlfriend again, someday.

"I am." Jessie sat up a little straighter in her chair. "I'm Jessie Pen--uh, you can just call me Jessie."

The other woman's eyes studied Jessie as though trying to figure out what Robert had ever seen in her. "Sylvia Sorenson's daughter, right?"

"Yes. And you are?"

"Debbie Wheeler. I believe you went to school with my younger sister Joy."

"Right, yes, I remember Joy." Surprised Debbie made no move to shake hands, Jessie wondered why the woman had come.

Debbie wandered around the spacious deck with cat-like grace. "I've heard you and Rob--the sheriff used to be an item. Before you up and left him, for a career in New York."

Jessie struggled not to cringe. Debbie made it sound like Jessie's decision to leave Robert and go to New York was something she'd done lightly. But it couldn't be further from the truth. Walking away from him was the hardest thing she'd ever done. Even harder than enduring years of abuse.

Jessie bit her lip to hold back a rude retort.

"So, how do you know Robert?" Jessie got the impression--even though her mother said he dated a lot--Robert wasn't currently dating anyone.

Debbie gave a light laugh. "We've worked closely together on several of my philanthropic projects."

How closely? Philanthropic projects must be Debbie's way of telling Jessie she was wealthy.

Debbie stopped walking and studied her fingernails. "He could really use my support, what with him being up for re-election this fall."

Unsure of what Debbie was getting at, Jessie kept her mouth shut.

"I worry about what people will think of him getting involved with a married woman."

"I'm getting a divorce." The words squeaked out of Jessie's tight throat. She had an appointment with Ben this afternoon and she hoped he'd guarantee her she could get a quick and easy divorce even though she was pregnant, and her husband would most likely refuse to sign divorce papers.

Her and Robert's relationship wasn't anybody's business, but their own. Jessie's trip to the hairdresser a couple of weeks ago had reminded her how people in small towns liked to gossip. With Robert being a public official, people were sure to talk about him and Jessie, especially since they had a history.

"I'm not sure it's in his best interest to get involved so quickly with a woman who just left her husband. You know how critical people can be in small towns." Debbie's last statement sounded like it held a warning.

Surely, she wouldn't hurt Robert's chances of getting re-elected. Would she?

Debbie planted herself right in front of Jessie and leaned against the railing. "From what I hear, he was pretty broken up when you left years ago. He's a good man. I'd hate to see him get hurt again."

Jessie lowered her eyes. No one had ever pointed out how torn up Robert was when she left, but she knew she'd broken his heart. It had broken *her* heart to walk away.

Jessie never wanted to hurt Robert again. That was part of the reason she struggled with finding herself. She shouldn't encourage a relationship between them if she couldn't be content here in Providence.

"I have no intention of hurting him again." Jessie wanted to stay here in Providence, where she could have a second chance with him, but she needed to find a way to support herself and her baby.

Debbie's gaze narrowed on Jessie as though she didn't believe her. "He deserves a woman who will put him first and support him no matter what. Not someone who sees him as a back-up plan."

Jessie reeled, as though Debbie had slapped her.

The woman was right, though. Robert deserved a woman who loved him with her whole heart and didn't put him second to her career.

I couldn't commit to him five years ago, because I was selfish and wanted to chase my dreams. And now, I don't feel like I can commit to him, assuming he even wants me, until I have a place and a purpose here in Providence.

Why couldn't loving Robert be her purpose?

No, it would give him too much power over her. She'd never let a man have that kind of ultimate control over her again.

If there was one thing she'd learned from the past four years, it was that she was responsible for her own happiness. She couldn't put her happiness in someone else's hands. And she couldn't love Robert with all her heart if she didn't love herself first.

Could she love herself enough to be the woman he deserved?

Jessie considered the sermon at church last Sunday about grace. Grace made up for her weaknesses. Instinctively, she knew that if she and Robert could take a chance on one another again, his love would be enough to fill all the empty places inside her. And she would love him with her whole heart again.

"You're right." Jessie held Debbie's gaze. "And if I'm lucky enough to get a second chance with Robert, I promise he will be my priority for the rest of my life."

Jessie stood and gathered up her sketch pad and pencils. "If you'll excuse me, I have an appointment I need to get ready for."

CHAPTER 27

Robert's truck finally came to a stop. "Any idea where we are?"

Jessie reached up to lift the blindfold he'd put on her at the ranch. Although she trusted him, it had been difficult to let him blindfold her. His eagerness over the surprise he had for her was the only reason she'd given in.

She'd struggled to breathe the entire time he stood close, tying on the bandanna. It had been all she could do to not reach up and touch the spot on her neck where his fingers had momentarily lingered after he'd finished tying the bandanna.

"No, don't take it off yet. Guess first." Robert pulled her hand away from her face and continued to hold it, sending warmth radiating up her arm.

"I have no idea. I thought I knew until a couple turns ago. I have a feeling that wherever we are, you didn't take the direct route to get here."

"Nope." He laughed. "I couldn't make it too easy." He reached over and took the blindfold off, his fingers once again brushing her neck.

Jessie's brow furrowed when she spotted the brick wall with a door in front of them. "Where are we?" She pivoted in her seat and looked out the back window. Her eyebrows lifted when she spotted the football field. "Your big surprise is the high school?"

Robert got out and hurried around to open her door. "My surprise is a certain room in the high school."

"Okay..." Jessie let the word draw out as she slid down from the truck, letting Robert know she thought he was crazy.

He waved a hand at the door in front of them. "Don't tell me you don't know what's on the other side of that door."

Jessie looked around again. Her stomach dipped, then leapt to her throat when she realized what door that was. "The ceramics lab?"

"Bingo," he said, but he shook his head. "I'm disappointed it took you so long to figure out, though. You threw pots almost every day during our senior year while you waited for me to finish football or baseball practice."

Jessie leaned toward him and shook a finger in his face. "See, that's where you're wrong. You practiced every day while you waited for me to finish throwing my pots."

Robert laughed, but didn't contradict her. "I suppose you're right, since I usually had to wait for you to clean up before we could leave."

He grabbed her hand and tugged her closer, wrapping his other arm around her.

Jessie sucked in a sharp breath. His presence took her breath away every time he got close. The way his tangy, yet woodsy scent enveloped her made her feel like she'd come home. And when he touched her... She felt powerless to break the spell he had over her.

His eyes clouded with worry and he watched her face, as though he feared she might feel threatened by his actions. His gorgeous brown eyes held her mesmerized, and she felt herself relax into him.

He tightened his hold the slightest bit, and his eyes dipped to her mouth.

Was he thinking about all the kisses they'd shared outside this door? Or was he thinking about creating new memories?

She couldn't go there with Robert. With the hormones raging through her lately, one kiss wouldn't be enough. And she shouldn't be kissing other men while she was still married to Patrick. Besides, until she knew exactly what his relationship with Debbie Wheeler was, she didn't dare take a chance.

"Don't, please." Her plea came out breathy and not very convincing, but it was all she could muster when she wanted so badly for him to kiss her.

Robert released her and shook his head. "Sorry."

He probably thought she didn't want him to kiss her, but that couldn't be further from the truth. He pulled a key from his pocket and turned toward the door.

"What are you doing? Please, don't tell me the sheriff is breaking into the high school."

"It's not breaking in if you have the key," he said with a grin.

"Do you have a key to all the buildings in town?"

"No, I got the key and permission from Aunt Hope."

Jessie had forgotten Robert's aunt was the high school principal. Even if the principal wasn't his aunt, Jessie had the feeling he could sweet talk anyone into letting him do just about anything he wanted.

Robert opened the door and turned on the lights, making a sweeping gesture with his arm. "After you."

Jessie had learned well over the course of the last four weeks that she couldn't simply expect everything to be like it used to be just because she'd come back. The high school ceramics lab would never be the haven it once was to her.

But what if it could be?

Determined to keep an open mind, she stepped into the room and took a deep breath.

She didn't expect to feel the peacefulness she'd always felt here as a teenager. But the earthy scent of fresh clay surrounded her, and a lightness filled her. The tension she'd carried for the last month melted away, and she once again felt like she'd come home.

But she didn't dare get her hopes up that she still had the talent she used to have. Robert meant well, but this felt like a cruel joke.

"What are we doing here?"

Robert tilted his head, eyebrows raised. "Throwing pots, of course."

Jessie teetered between excitement and anxiety. She stepped toward the door. "No, I can't. I don't do that anymore."

Robert grabbed her hands, preventing her from retreating further. The arc of warm electricity she experienced every time he touched her shot up her arms.

"Come on, you need a break from the ranch. This used to be one of your favorite past times. Your cast is finally off, so why not let yourself have a little fun?"

She gave him a skeptical look. He didn't expect her to produce a magnificent work of art. He simply wanted her to have fun.

A warm tingling sensation pricked her fingertips. It was the same sensation she used to get every time she got an idea for a new vase design.

She tugged her hands from Robert's. She hadn't thrown a pot for over three years. Since before they'd left New York, where she'd paid a monthly fee to show up and throw as many pots as she wanted. The warehouse where the pottery studio was located also housed a small gift shop where, if an artist chose, they could sell their work. Jessie had sold several pieces there.

"Mr. White insisted you help yourself to any supplies you need. School started this week, so if you throw something you want fired, just leave it on the drying shelf with his students' work and he'll throw it in the next time he fires up the kiln."

"Mr. White still teaches here?"

Jessie thought of the tall, slender, gray-haired man who'd taught her to mold her talents in all mediums of art. Mr. White was exceptionally talented, and Jessie had always felt he'd wasted his talents as a high school teacher. She'd even told him so one time, and he'd responded with, "Fostering a love of the arts in youth and helping shape their talents is more rewarding than having hundreds of pretty paintings throughout the world."

Jessie understood what he meant, but she still thought maybe the man was too afraid of failing to try to succeed as a world-renowned artist.

"Yep. He considered retiring a couple years ago, but his wife still had two years before she could retire from the post office. So, he kept working. Besides, they couldn't find anyone to replace him. It's not that easy to find an art teacher who wants to tie themselves to a one-horse town." His voice held a tinge of sadness, and Jessie wondered if his words held a double meaning for her.

Was he hinting that Jessie didn't want to stay in this little one-horse town?

As much as she loved it here, she couldn't help wondering if there was something more for her out there. She wasn't sure she ever wanted to return to the New York; she'd felt so alone there. That's why she'd welcomed Patrick's attention so easily.

Nothing had changed about this small town, though. Could Jessie find a way to do what she loved *and* be happy here?

Was Robert hinting she take Mr. White's place?

He examined a small vase he'd picked up off a shelf, his body language relaxed.

It might be dreaming on her part that Robert hoped she'd stay in Providence, so that maybe they could have a second chance at working things out, but she knew he'd never try to change her into something she wasn't. And she definitely wasn't a teacher.

She stepped away from Robert and dragged her fingertips across the cool surface of the nearest Formica-topped table. She wandered the art room, noting all the things that hadn't changed.

On the back wall hung the same painting that had been there for years, of two hands holding a globe. A sketch of Mr. White's, where he'd sketched an image of himself sketching another image of yet another image of himself, occupied the wall at the front of the room. One of the watercolor landscapes Jessie did of the Double Diamond still hung on the wall to the left.

When Mr. White asked if he could display it her senior year, she'd gifted it to him as a thank you for all he'd taught her. Out of everything she'd painted, it was still one of her favorite pieces.

Jessie crossed the room to study a new painting on the opposite wall: a beautiful seascape with clean lines, vibrant colors, and excellent use of space. She appreciated the artist's attention to detail and talent.

She wandered to the adjoining room--the ceramics lab--looking at the pieces of pottery that lined the shelves. She recognized a few pieces she created thirteen years ago. Mr. White hadn't replaced them.

Jessie itched to get her hands on some fresh clay. Within minutes, she found a sizable hunk of clay in the same cabinet where Mr. White had always stored it. She looked over the pottery wheels; they all looked brand new. They must have cost the school a fortune.

Sitting at the closest wheel, she pulled the clay from the plastic bag and broke it into three chunks. Her breathing quickened as she rolled them into balls. She didn't realize how much she'd missed this. She plopped the first ball on the center of the wheel.

Robert set a small bucket of water and a sponge beside her.

She smiled up at him.

His smile was almost as big as hers. Was he as excited to see her give this a shot as she was to try again? Once again, she had the urge to kiss him. He was honestly the most thoughtful man she'd ever known.

Grasping the clay in both hands, she bent over the lathe and tucked her elbows close to her sides for stability. The scent of the minerals in the clay filled her nose as the cool malleable mound bobbed and ebbed with the pressure of her fingers.

After several long moments, the mound centered, and she smiled. Dipping her hands into the water, she shaped the clay, slowly raising it into a perfect cylinder. She dripped water from the sponge over the clay.

The mesmerizing spinning of the wheel and the clay's conformity to the pressure of her fingers eased a knot deep inside her. A knot that had been there long before she left Patrick. This was exactly the therapy she needed, especially since she couldn't ride horses anymore.

Although Dr. Young hadn't forbidden her to ride, he'd cautioned against it, considering her previous miscarriages.

Finding out she was already ten weeks along in her pregnancy had shocked Jessie. She must have gotten pregnant almost immediately after going off the pill this last time. A part of her still wished things had turned out differently, but hearing the baby's heartbeat at her doctor's appointment earlier this week had only strengthened her resolve to be a good mom to this baby that had been entrusted to her.

She only hoped Patrick signed the divorce papers Ben was filing for her without contesting so they could have a quiet divorce. Jessie hadn't asked for anything, hoping it would hurry the process along. But deep down, she knew he wouldn't sign them. Patrick would not let her go easily.

Unfortunately, she had to declare in the paperwork that she was pregnant. It also meant she would have to go to court to have the divorce finalized. But Ben had assured her a judge could not deny the divorce just because she was pregnant.

She'd taken her black journal with her to her appointment with Ben, and her throat tightened--nearly blocking her airway--when she handed it to him.

His jaw repeatedly clenched as he flipped through its pages. He didn't even make it halfway through the book before closing it. "I'm sorry. I can't read anymore. And I'm so sorry you had to endure all of that."

He looked at her for a long moment as he gripped the book. "I know this won't be easy to share with the judge, but this will help ensure you not only get your divorce, but that Patrick spends time in jail. As far as sole custody goes... We can't file for that until after the baby is born." He held up the book. "But I don't think you'll have much trouble, especially since he will do jail time for the charges currently pending against him. I'll file the divorce paperwork and we'll see how things play out with his other legal issues."

Jessie only hoped the judicial system did its job before Patrick found her again.

She pressed on her clay, making the cylinder wider and shorter. Pushing her index and middle fingers down into the center, she watched the clay spread outward, creating a dip that widened to a bowl. With the gentle pressure of her fingers on the inside and outside of the bowl, she raised the sides. Her wrist dropped a little, and instantly, the bowl sagged on one side, then the whole thing toppled.

Robert laughed, and she scowled at him. "I'm sorry. That just makes my heart feel good since, you know, I threw that rock and missed by a mile."

"Maybe you should go practice." She tilted her head toward the door.

Robert's voice lowered. "No way. Watching your face while you create is a lot more fun than throwing a ball."

She tried to ignore the seductive tone of his voice. "What do you mean?"

He bent down, putting both hands on either side of the bowl that surrounded the pottery wheel. The motion brought his face so close to hers, she felt the warmth of his breath on her cheek. She bit her lip and dug her fingers into the clay to keep herself from reaching out and pulling him closer.

Robert smiled. "You pucker up your lips when you're focusing on centering the clay. Then, when you finally have it centered, you get a triumphant smile. Did you know when you raise it up you raise your eyebrows too?"

"Stop it. I do not."

"Yes, you do. And your eyes close when you're really getting in the zone."

Jessie let out a small gasp. She didn't realize anyone had ever noticed the way she liked to close her eyes and let herself become one with the clay. She rarely did it with a piece she intended to fire, but she loved shutting out the world and focusing on the feel of the cool clay between her fingertips.

"Go away." She rolled her eyes as she flung her hand out, flipping water across the floor. "You know I don't like having an audience when I create." That wasn't entirely true. She'd always loved the quiet support Robert gave her. But his nearness distracted her.

Robert winked before straightening. It was so quick, Jessie thought maybe she'd imagined it. "Fine. I know when I'm not wanted. I'll just go sit over here in the corner. All alone."

She laughed at him because it was better than telling him how much she wanted him. But he'd been involved with Debbie until recently. She should come right out and ask him about the pretty redhead, but she wasn't sure she wanted to hear the answer.

Pushing away thoughts of Debbie, Jessie smiled as she scraped her lathe clean and grabbed another ball of clay. She may not produce something worthwhile tonight, but she was having a blast.

A few minutes later, soft rock music filled the room, and her lips turned up again. Robert had connected his phone up to the speaker Mr. White kept at the back of the room, and he'd remembered her favorite choice of music.

She let the music and clay carry her away to a time she didn't have to worry about an abusive husband or a child who would depend on her for everything. The cool clay obeyed her fingers, and her eyes drifted closed as she relished the feelings of freedom, acceptance, and the power it gave her.

Robert's voice came from the back of the room, barely louder than the music. "And now her eyes are closed."

Jessie smiled, marveling that he could still read her so well. She opened her eyes again and study the delicate vase taking shape in her hands. Only a few moments ago it had been a shapeless lump. But it had the potential to be so much more.

Affirmations from her mom rang in her head: *You're a survivor. You're stronger than you think.*

And from Emily: Y*ou deserve happiness as much as anyone else.*

Jessie had potential to be more than a battered wife. It would take work, but she could become something beautiful and precious.

CHAPTER 28

Robert slowed his stride as he and Jessie approached the back door of the ranch house. He didn't want this time with her to end. He could probably find an excuse to stick around a little longer, but it wouldn't be wise. The more time he spent with Jessie, the more he wanted to pull her into his arms and kiss her like there was no tomorrow.

He'd already pushed the boundaries tonight by holding her hand. After the third time of her hand brushing his as they walked side by side, he'd given in to temptation and clasped her hand, threading his finger through hers. He'd half expected her to pull away, but she didn't. She'd simply given him a quick smile, then looked away again.

He and Jessie had settled into a comfortable friendship. They didn't talk about the future, or whether she planned to stick around. She still needed time to find herself, and he didn't want her to feel pressured. He tortured himself by pretending Jessie wouldn't leave again, but he couldn't seem to stay away.

Robert released her hand before opening the back door. No sense advertising what a lovesick pup he was. They were three steps into the great room before he realized something was wrong.

Lottie, with tears in her eyes, stood beside Zane, who wore a heavy expression that looked somewhere between angry and worried. Jake and Emily, both wearing concerned expressions, stood a few feet away. Their conversation died when Robert and Jessie entered the room.

A feeling of dread settled over him. "What's wrong? Who died?"

"No one died, but..." The words died on Jake's lips as he looked at Jessie. "Robert, maybe you better come with us into my office."

The group headed toward Jake's office, and the knot that had taken over Robert's stomach tightened. He felt bad walking away from Jessie, but he needed to know what was going on.

She must have felt the same dread, because her face paled. "Is it Patrick? Is he back?"

"No, this has nothing to do with Patrick," Jake said. "I'm sorry, Jessie. I didn't mean to alarm you. This is just a family matter that we need to discuss with Robert."

Family matter? Jake's words may have eased Jessie's mind, but they didn't ease Robert's. He gave Jessie's hand a quick squeeze before following the others into Jake's office. He appreciated the words of assurance Emily whispered to Jessie before joining them in the office.

As soon as the door closed behind Emily, Robert whirled on Jake. "What's going on?"

Jake looked at Zane and Lottie.

Lottie gave Zane a tearful nod and sat on the small sofa in Jake's office. She buried her face in her hands.

Zane cleared his throat. "We just got a call from Daniel. He's been arrested. Charged with being drunk and disorderly. Got in a bar fight."

Robert stifled the swear word that came to mind and sat down beside Lottie. He put his arm around the woman who had been like a second mother to him.

She leaned into him.

A jumble of emotions tumbled around inside him. Zane and Lottie's son Daniel was like a little brother to him. He'd gotten especially close to Daniel last year when the kid had to do community service and serve time in jail because he'd caused an accident while intoxicated. Robert had been right there with him every weekend as he served his time.

He wanted to pummel Daniel for turning to alcohol again and putting his parents through this pain, but Daniel struggled with demons Robert would never understand. Because both of Daniel's grandfathers were alcoholics, he faced a daily struggle to stay sober since he made the mistake of taking that first drink.

Last year, during one of Daniel's Saturday nights in jail, he'd confided in Robert what had driven him to drink. Robert's heart hurt for the kid he thought of as a brother when he heard about the accident Daniel had been involved in that resulted in the death of a five-year-old boy. Guilt consumed Daniel, even though the accident wasn't technically his fault.

Jake looked at Robert. "We'd just gotten off the phone with Ben when you walked in the back door. He should be here in a few minutes. Then we can discuss the best way to help Daniel."

"It won't be easy," said Emily. "Especially if he's been drinking for some time. His dependence on alcohol will be much more difficult to overcome this time."

Robert stepped to the door of Jake's office. "I'll be back in a few minutes. Don't start without me when Ben gets here, and whatever we do for Daniel, count me in."

He went in search of Jessie. He found her sitting on his old bed with the door open. She had the journal he'd given her on her lap.

She looked up as he leaned against the door frame. "Is everything okay?"

He walked in and sat on the edge of the bed. He scratched his jaw. "I hope so. It sounds like Zane and Lottie's son Daniel has gotten into some trouble."

"I'm sorry to hear that."

"Me too," Robert sighed. "I just wanted to let you know this has nothing to do with Patrick. And I might be away for a few days, but don't worry, I'll make sure Jake or one of my deputies are here at all times."

He hated leaving Jessie, but he wanted to be there for Daniel at his hearing.

~

ROBERT DROVE his truck down the lane, past the ranch house. As much as he'd love to see Jessie, tonight he was here to visit Daniel.

Zane had gotten a call early yesterday morning before he, Robert, and Ben had started the long drive to Portland, saying that the charges against Daniel had been dropped and he was being released.

Robert and Ben decided to stay home at that point, and Zane and Lottie made an overnight trip to Portland. Robert had gotten word from Ben yesterday afternoon that Daniel's involvement in the bar fight had been because he was defending a waitress from an aggressive drunk biker. The bar owner had dropped the charges against Daniel once he got the full story from the waitress.

It pleased Robert to know Daniel hadn't gone so far off the deep end that he'd completely forgotten the morals he'd been raised with, but he still wanted to throttle the kid for turning back to alcohol.

Robert parked his truck in front of Zane and Lottie's cottage-style home. He climbed from his truck and reached into the back seat for his guitar case. He hadn't touched the thing for five years--except to move it to his new house--but he'd do it for Daniel.

To distract himself from the withdrawals while he was drying out last year, Daniel had learned to play the guitar with the help of You tube tutorials. Robert had visited with Daniel on multiple occasions and played his guitar a few times, but he hadn't touched his own until today.

He'd lost all desire to play after Jessie left.

Emily walked out the front door of the cottage. "Leave it in your truck."

Robert released the guitar case and turned to Emily. "That bad, huh?"

She shrugged. "Bad enough he won't be playing for a few days. I could hardly get him to talk to me."

"Should I even bother talking to him?"

Emily played with a lock of hair. "I don't know. It might help him to know people care about him, but..." she shook her head.

"He feels guilty for going back to the bottle?" Robert guessed.

She nodded. "He feels like he's disappointed everyone."

Robert leaned against his truck. "He has, but I we understand he's been through some rough stuff."

Emily frowned. "Unfortunately, he experienced something equally difficult several months ago that triggered the drinking again."

Robert hated to think that things had been so bad for Daniel that he felt the need to turn back to alcohol, but it relieved him to hear the kid hadn't started drinking again just for the heck of it.

Robert decided to give Daniel a day or two, but then he'd be there for the kid. No matter what. Even if it meant facing his own demons and picking up the guitar, he hadn't played for five years.

CHAPTER 29

Patrick ducked into his office and slid into his desk chair. He was almost an hour late, but he doubted anyone had noticed, except Tina. She'd scowled at him, then flipped him off before walking the other way.

She'd been angry when he dumped her a couple weeks ago and had badmouthed him to their coworkers ever since, calling him unfaithful and an adulterer. Normally, that would tick him off and he'd even the score, but he had bigger things to worry about. Like keeping his job.

He turned on his computer. Between the week he spent in the Adam's County jail and the few days he'd take off over the course of the last two weeks to go to Providence, he'd almost exhausted his personal time off. He had to figure out where Jessica was. After frequently tailing Sylvia and the sheriff--in different rental cars each time--he figured out Jessica was staying at a ranch called the Double Diamond.

What a pretentious name.

That's why he was late getting to work today. He hadn't gotten home until almost two in the morning and had overslept. Once he'd figured out where Jessica was, he'd lingered as long as possible to try to figure out the best way to get to her.

He'd watched the place from a distance long enough to know that two couples lived on the ranch--one older, one younger--and a half dozen ranch hands. Not to mention Sylvia and Winters, who came and went frequently.

Patrick's phone rang before he could check his email.

He picked it up. "Pendleton."

"Mr. Pendleton," Eleanor Turnbaum's nasally voice came through the phone. "Mr. Matthews wants to see you in his office right away."

Patrick bit back a curse. Eleanor was the big boss's executive assistant. "Thank you. I'll be right there."

Patrick pounded a fist on his desk before walking out of his office and down the hall. He buttoned his suit coat as he neared Mr. Matthews's office. Eleanor ushered him into the corner office so fast Patrick didn't have time to prepare himself mentally to face the shrewd executive. A week wouldn't have been enough time.

"You wanted to see me, sir?" Patrick stood erect, hoping the older man didn't detect the tremor in his voice or the stubble on his jaw. He should have taken the time to shave this morning despite oversleeping.

"Sit." Mr. Matthews didn't smile, didn't shake Patrick's hand, and didn't offer him a cup of coffee. He simply stared at Patrick from underneath bushy eyebrows.

Patrick dropped into a chair and stared right back, resisting the urge to fidget.

Matthews rose and stood behind his chair, towering over him. Patrick recognized the intimidation tactic; he'd seen his father do it enough.

Patrick clenched his jaw when his pulse kicked up a notch.

"When I hired you, I thought I was hiring an aspiring, goal-oriented broker who would give one hundred percent to this firm and our clients." Mr. Matthews leaned forward.

Patrick squared his shoulders. "You did, sir."

"But I got a call four weeks ago telling me you'd been arrested for assault and battery."

Patrick leaned forward too, his defenses rising. "I told you it was all a misunderstanding."

"You did, but you've yet to inform me that you and your wife have worked things out." The older man's eyes narrowed. "Instead, I get another call from your lawyer telling me you're in jail again. This time for aggravated assault."

"Those charges are bogus." It was all Patrick could do to stay in his seat.

"Right." Mr. Matthews gave a clipped nod. "That's why I approved you taking some time off to get things sorted out." He pointed a finger at Patrick. "As long as you kept up with your accounts."

"I have been, sir."

"Then why did I get a call from Henry Rosenberg this morning telling me he lost two million dollars yesterday because you didn't sell the stocks he'd requested?"

Patrick swore under his breath. He swallowed hard before speaking. "I'm sorry, sir. I was out of town, and the motel I stayed at had unreliable Wi-Fi. I couldn't complete the transaction."

He hadn't even tried, hadn't even bothered to check his email, but Matthews didn't need to know that.

"That's unacceptable, and you know it!" The veins in Matthews' forehead stood out much like Patrick's father's did when he got angry.

Patrick slumped back in his seat, resisting the urge to cower.

"How much PTO have you taken in the past two weeks, Pendleton?"

"Four days."

"And are you any closer to getting things straightened out?" The older man's voice softened a bit.

"I'm trying." If he could only get Jessica back home, then he could work on convincing her to drop the charges against him. That would help with the other charges he faced. Patrick's lawyer was trying to build a case of self-defense in his altercation with Winters, but he'd warned Patrick to expect to do some jail time.

Patrick couldn't do that. He wouldn't go back.

He sat up straighter and looked Matthews in the eye. "The hearings won't be for several weeks."

"Then I suggest you use the next few weeks to pass off your clients to Hendricks." Mr. Matthews sank into his chair, an air of defeat surrounding him.

"But sir--"

Matthews held up a hand, cutting Patrick off. "I don't employ criminals, Pendleton. If you're cleared of all the charges, then you still have a job here. But until then..." He pointed a finger at Patrick again. "One more mistake and you're gone."

Patrick gripped the wooden arms of his chair so tightly his hands ached.

"You have less than ten hours of PTO left; use them wisely. And if I get even a single inkling that you've let one client down, you're gone. Do you understand?" Matthew's face turned beet red.

"Yes, sir."

"Now get out of here and figure how to recover some of Rosenberg's money."

Patrick stood and exited the corner office before Matthews decided to terminate him.

Instead of going straight back to his office, he entered the nearest bathroom. After making sure he was alone, he kicked a stall door, making it bang and swing wildly. He stopped himself inches from kicking the stainless-steel trash can, too.

He propped his hands on the granite countertop and swore. This was all Jessie's fault. If she hadn't left him, he wouldn't be in this mess right now. Winters played a big part, too. Why couldn't the cocky sheriff have stuck to the schedule and stayed away from the cabin that night?

NINE HOURS LATER, Patrick let himself into his house while juggling his Chinese takeout and the mail he'd neglected to collect all week. He couldn't wait to take a hot bath after dinner. Working all day with Hendricks, who gloated about becoming the company's youngest broker, had given him a headache.

He was halfway through sorting out the junk mail when the doorbell rang. Recalling who was on the other side of the door the last time it rang late in the evening, Patrick braced himself as he opened the door.

Relieved it wasn't a police officer who stood on his porch, Patrick smiled at the young man who wore a too-big navy-blue blazer with an insignia on the left breast.

"Patrick Pendleton?" The kid had a deeper voice than Patrick expected.

The hair on the back of Patrick's neck raised. "Yes."

The young man held out a tablet. "Sign here, please."

"What am I signing for?" Patrick asked warily.

The kid shrugged. "Official documents from an attorney's office."

Had Patrick's lawyer sent him more papers to sign? Did they have something to do with the charges of police brutality he'd filed against the sheriff?

Patrick signed the tablet and took the large envelope the kid pulled from under his arm.

"You've been served." The young man smiled and walked away.

"Served?"

What the...?

Patrick waited until he'd closed the door to inspect the envelope. Attorney Benjamin Young appeared on the return address label. Confused, he read the rest of the address.

Providence?

His blood grew warm. He ripped open the envelope, nearly dumping the papers on the floor.

He straightened the pages and looked at them. His gaze was halfway through reading Superior Court of Washington... when the words **Petition for Divorce** jumped out at him from lower down on the page.

He let loose a string of curses as heat shot through him. *How dare Jessica file for divorce?*

No way would he let her go. He'd meant it when he told that hot-shot sheriff if he couldn't have Jessie, no one would.

Red shadows blurred the edges of his vision and he staggered into the table in the wide entryway, knocking over the vase on top of it. It was one of Jessie's.

The last one.

Her best work.

He picked it up and flung it at the framed piece of modern art that had cost him almost a thousand dollars. Shards of glass and chunks of pottery scattered across the floor. He'd bought the hideous picture to spite Jessica, because she didn't like that abstract style.

Here's something else she won't like.

He ripped the papers he held in two, then fourths before storming into his home office. He turned on the paper shredder and fed the divorce papers in.

"Jessica is mine!" His shout echoed through the sparsely furnished room.

Jessie was coming home, whether she liked it or not.

And he'd make Winters pay too.

CHAPTER 30

Jessie sucked in a slow, deep breath as her hands caressed the moist clay. This was only her second time here, and already she was becoming addicted.

She'd made Robert promise to bring her back again this week before they left last Wednesday.

He'd easily agreed. He seemed to enjoy watching her as much as she enjoyed getting her hands dirty and being creative.

He didn't watch her tonight, though. He'd brought a laptop and said something about needing to get some work done.

Jessie had left two small vases on the drying rack last week. They weren't as delicate as she would have liked, but they'd turned out smooth with graceful curves. If nothing else, they'd make a nice gift for her mother or sister for Christmas.

She set aside the first of tonight's vases and took a seat at the wheel again. The soft rock music, the scent of the rich minerals, and the feel of the cool clay taking shape under her hands carried her away.

I could get used to this.

A familiar voice from the past greeted Robert over the music, and she caught her breath as feelings of tenderness filled her chest. She wiped her hands on a nearby towel and turned to look at the man who had influenced her more than any other person.

Mr. White had recognized her talents as she struggled through a troublesome time in her life. He'd become a surrogate father figure to her and taught her to believe in herself and nurture her talents in a way that made Jessie fall deeply and irrevocably in love with art.

Her favorite teacher had aged over the past five years, and although he had a slight stoop to his frame, he was still large in stature. His full head of hair was fully gray now. A smile split his face, and his blue eyes twinkled as he opened his arms wide.

"Jessie Sorenson."

She didn't hesitate to walk into his outstretched arms and return the embrace. She didn't bother correcting him with her name. In fact, she'd written the initials *J.S.* on the bottom of the vases she'd left to dry last week. It felt more natural than putting *J.P.* on the bottom when she was trying to leave that part of her life behind.

Mr. White hugged her tight, then released her and stepped back. "You're still as beautiful and as talented as ever."

"I don't know about that." Jessie laughed.

"Believe it, dear. As soon as I saw the two pieces you left on the rack last week, I knew they were yours. You have a style all your own."

Warmth filled her cheeks. A compliment was nice, but a compliment from her hero meant the world to her. "Thank you. And thank you for letting me exercise my creative juices in your classroom."

Mr. White waved away her thanks. "Talent like yours needs to be nurtured." He walked over to the shelf of drying pottery and pointed at the pieces she'd thrown last week. "I was hoping you'd consider selling me these two. It's mine and Elizabeth's forty-second anniversary next month and I think she'd love them." He held up hands that trembled, and Jessie's heart broke for her idol. "I haven't thrown a decent pot in years."

"I'm sorry, they aren't for sale. But you're welcome to have them."

Mr. White followed her to the opposite corner of the room, where they discussed what color of glaze his wife might like on the vases after they were fired. Together, they decided the rose granite glaze would make the vases look regal yet delicate.

"It does my heart good to see you, Jessie. You were always one of my best students. I have a young lady in one of my classes now who reminds me a lot of you. I'd love for you to stop by seventh period sometime and look at her work. I think you could help her elevate her talent in ways I no longer can."

With the tremors Mr. White now suffered in his hands, holding a paintbrush and demonstrating specific techniques would be nearly impossible. "I'd like that. I'll stop in one day next week."

They continued discussing art and life, while Robert returned to his computer. Thirty minutes later, the older man hugged her before making his way to the door. "I have to admit, I'm surprised to see you've returned home from New York City. I thought once we lost you to the glitz and glamour of the Big Apple, we'd never see you again. But I hope you're back to stay."

He obviously hadn't heard the entire story behind her abusive marriage and her return to Providence. And Jessie had no interest in enlightening him.

"I guess I just couldn't stay away." She smiled and waved as he left. She turned to find Robert grinning at her. "What?"

He followed her back over to the pots she'd been working on earlier. "Nothing. I just think it's funny that someone beat me to the punch. I was going to call first dibs on last week's vases and offer to buy them for my mom. It's her birthday next month. I guess I'm going to have to buy tonight's vases instead."

"Whatever."

Jessie wasn't contradicting Robert concerning his mother's birthday. She knew Faith's birthday was exactly one month after her mom's. But she felt like he only offered to buy her vases out of pity. She'd seen enough pity in everyone's eyes since she'd returned to last her a lifetime. She didn't need his.

"If you want the new vases, you can have them. I mean, what else am I going to do with them?"

"You could sell them, Jessie. For a lot of money. They are that pretty."

She shook her head. "There's not a market for my creative puttering here in Providence."

"How do you know? You've never tried to sell your work around here? People who have been lucky enough to be gifted one of your pieces--whether it's a painting or one of your pottery pieces--love them. I know there are plenty of people around here who would spend money to have a Jessie Sorenson original in their home."

Jessie didn't bother to correct him on her name, because her chest tightened as a glimmer of hope warred with confusion. Did Robert suggest that because he truly believed she could make a living with her art in Providence, or was he just desperate for her to stay in this small town?

"And then what?" Her words came out sharper than she intended.

He frowned. "What do you mean?"

"Let's say I want to support myself and my baby with my art and I crank out paintings and pots galore and rent a corner in Miss Hattie's craft store to sell them." The words rolled easily off her tongue because it was something she'd already considered, along with the end result. "Let's pretend they sell well and all of Providence's thirty-five hundred citizens buy a piece. Actually, it would be less than that since a least a third of Providence's population doesn't even drive yet. But what then? Where does that leave me in a year or two?"

"I'm sure you could expand and sell in neighboring counties or even online. My mom sells her baby blankets and afghans on Esty."

"I don't want to have to rely on Etsy to support my child." The hurt Jessie felt manifest itself in her tone. It felt like such a put-down. Like saying her work wasn't good enough anymore to be on display at the MET.

Who am I kidding? My work isn't good enough. Maybe someday, but not yet.

Robert let out a deep sigh. "I'm sorry if I offended you, Jessie. I just wish you could see how talented you really are and believe in yourself the way I do."

He was right. Despite all the progress she'd made, Jessie still had a tough time believing she could be a successful artist if she stayed in this small town. Was she trying too hard to fit into the mold everyone expected her to slide back into? She didn't know if she even wanted to be in that mold anymore. Art or not, Jessie didn't have a purpose in life.

Robert walked back to his computer, frustration and disappointment apparent in his posture.

Jessie returned to the pottery wheel, her enthusiasm for the project waning. Throwing another pot now seemed more of a chore than a pleasant distraction. She just wanted to go home.

The ride back to the ranch was long and full of tension.

She broke the silence as Robert drove down the lane to the house. "You can have tonight's vases. I'll glaze them in a few weeks. What color do you want?"

He put his truck into park and looked at her. By the light of the front porch, she saw him smile. He reached over and slid his hand into hers, lacing their fingers together.

"Whatever color you think will look best."

Jessie couldn't think about colors or anything else right now because of the zings of electricity shooting up her arm. She curled her fingers around his and tightened her grip on his hand.

"Jessie, I hope you will let me pay you for the vases."

"You don't need to do that. You have given me so much already. I'm the one who needs to repay you."

"No, you don't." He stroked the back of her hand with his thumb, sending a warm tingling sensation across her hand. "I'd like to think of the things I've done for you as an investment."

"An investment in what?" Was he expecting her to become some world-renowned artist?

Robert's hand loosened and slipped from hers. "If you don't understand what I mean, then there's no point in me explaining." He faced forward, jaw set, and put both hands on the steering wheel.

Jessie didn't understand what he expected from her, because she didn't even know what she expected of herself. The sting of tears pricked her eyes, so she kept her mouth shut and opened the truck door.

She slid out with a mumbled, “Good night,” and hurried into the house.

She probably should have apologized, but she wasn’t sure what for.

~

JESSIE SETTLED into a table across from her mom at their favorite Italian restaurant in the Tri-Cities area. They’d spent the morning shopping and were now getting lunch. Well, her mother had shopped, and Jessie had spent the morning telling her mom she didn’t need maternity clothes or all the baby paraphernalia yet.

It had been three weeks since she realized she was pregnant, and she’d finally told her mom last week. Her mother had shared Jessie’s concern about how this would affect her ability to distance herself from Patrick, but she’d been so excited for Jessie.

Sylvia stared at Jessie after they placed their orders. Her brow furrowed.

“What?” Jessie asked.

“You tell me?”

“What do you mean?”

“You’ve been quiet and sullen all day. What’s going on?”

Jessie wanted to say “nothing,” but she couldn’t. Despite walking and talking with Emily every morning and working through much of the trauma she’d suffered, she still felt like there was more wrong in her life than there was right. She’d started painting again, but she didn’t know where it would lead her. She had no direction in her life. But she had a baby on the way, so she needed to find her purpose soon.

Jessie chewed on her fingernail for a moment before speaking. “Do you think me getting my hair done with money Robert gave me is giving him control over me?”

She’d thought a lot about what Robert said the other night, about everything he’d done for her being an investment. And she wasn’t sure if she should feel offended or flattered. Offended because it made it sound like he viewed her as someone he could own. She'd been there, done that, and refuse to travel that road again.

Or flattered, because maybe he felt like making her happy was something that might ensure a happy future for the two of them. If that was the case, then she needed to understand exactly what Debbie meant to him. She still hadn't asked him about her. She wasn't sure she wanted to hear the answer.

"Is that how you feel?" Her mother's brows furrowed. "Do think Robert is trying to control you. Like Patrick did?"

"Not necessarily. I mean, I think he's just trying to help me find myself but..." She shrugged, then rambled on, hoping that verbalizing all the thoughts tumbling around in her head would help her make sense of them. "He gave me money and told me to get my hair done, and I did. He gave me an amazing, expensive art kit and suggested I paint, and I did. He gave me a phone and asked me to keep location sharing on, and I am. And he's taken me to the ceramics lab at the school twice now to throw pots, and I have."

Despite the tense discussion with Robert concerning the vases she made this week, Jessie smiled as she recalled how pretty they had turned out.

"I know he's just trying to help me find myself. But I don't know if I want to find the old me."

"Was there something wrong with the old you?" Her mom frowned.

"No, but what if I'm not content to stay here in Providence? The old me felt so trapped in this small town."

"Is this a question of finding yourself, or feeling like you have to find the person you think *someone else* expects you to be?" The emphasis her mom placed on someone else clearly meant Robert.

Was that Jessie's problem? She struggled to find herself because she was trying to become the person Robert wanted her to be. Did she not want to be that person again? Or was it because she feared never measuring up to the woman he deserved?

Jessie wasn't sure how to answer, so she didn't. The server brought their salads, giving her an excuse to remain quiet.

"Let me just say this..." Her mom picked up her fork and pointed it at Jessie. "You've known Robert for what...thirteen, fourteen years? In all that time, did you ever feel like he wanted you to be someone other than who you are?"

"No." Any time Jessie got down on herself, Robert had always been quick to say he loved her just the way she was.

"And during the past thirteen years, did you ever feel like he had ulterior motives in giving you the gifts he did?"

Jessie thought about the many gifts Robert had given her over the years for birthdays, Christmas, Valentines, anniversaries, and just because he was thinking about her. He'd never made her feel like he expected favors or wanted something in return. He only wanted to make her happy.

Just like he's been doing the past two months.

Jessie propped an elbow on the table and pressed her forehead to her palm. *Did Patrick mess me up so badly that I can't trust my oldest and dearest friend?*

That's all she could consider Robert to be right now. A friend. Maybe someday they could be more, but there was still too much unsettled between them.

Things had been interesting between them for the past few weeks. She no longer felt like he avoided her, but she still only saw him twice a week. They texted frequently though, and Jessie saw frequent glimpses of the boy she fell in love with so many years ago in those texts.

He'd held her hand once--Wednesday night didn't count because it didn't last near long enough--and put his arm around her twice. But that was it. More than once, they had exchanged a heated glance where Jessie was certain he wanted to kiss her as badly as she wanted him to.

But they hadn't kissed. They hadn't even talked about kissing again, and they hadn't talked about a future together.

Jessie considered his investment comment again and wondered if she hadn't been so clueless, would that have led to a discussion about their futures?

She lifted her head. "No, Robert would never do that. He'd never try to control me. I guess I'm looking for signs that aren't there."

Her mother frowned as she patted Jessie's hand. "It's good to be wary, honey. But don't let what you've been through make you afraid to love again."

"How come you never remarried, Mom?"

Sylvia shrugged. "I just haven't found the right man, I guess. Now, back to you... Do you *want* to stay in Providence? Or do you want to go somewhere else? Back to New York, maybe?"

"No, I don't want to go back to New York."

That much she knew. There were too many terrible memories there. But she craved the fulfillment she'd experienced there. She'd been so close to becoming a successful artist. Until Patrick took it all away.

"I'd like to stay in Providence. I love it here." Yes, people were nosy, but they cared about one another.

It was where Robert was, after all. She'd never ask him to leave--especially since he was up for re-election as sheriff--assuming there was a future for them. But that was something she couldn't depend on. What if she stayed here and things didn't work out between them?

"So, you want to stay in Providence, but you're afraid you won't be content here? And you're enjoying painting and making pottery again, but you're not sure you want those things to be a part of the new you?"

"I want those things to be a part of my future, but how will I make a living doing them here in Providence?" Despite Robert's insistence that she should try selling her art here in town, Jessie wasn't convinced it would be enough.

Her mom was quiet for a minute while she took a long drink of water. As she set her glass back down, her eyes sparkled as though someone had turned on a light bulb. "I've got an idea. Didn't you tell me that your boss at the MET... What was her name? Vivian?"

"Violet."

"Right. Didn't Violet hook you up with a smaller gallery where you sold several of your pieces? Maybe you could reach out to that gallery owner and see if he'd be willing to sell some of your work again."

Jessie pictured Mr. Ramo. He was such a kind man, even if he was a little funny looking with a bulbous nose and big ears. She hadn't made a ton of money on the pieces she'd sold there, but it had helped supplement her income.

It wouldn't be enough to support a child, but it might be a start. She also pictured Mr. and Mrs. Becker--the sweet little husband and wife owners of The Pottery Cottage, where she'd thrown pots every Wednesday evening. Until Patrick forced her to quit. She'd sold several of her pieces in their gift shop.

A light, fluttery feeling skittered through Jessie's abdomen and she wondered if the baby was moving or if hope was trying to push its way up? If she reached out to Mr. Ramo and the Beckers and they agreed to sell her work, would she be able to make enough money to support her child? Maybe she could find galleries in other big cities too that would feature her work.

She looked at her mom. "Do you really think I could make enough money to support myself and my baby?"

"I say it's worth a try. You're certainly talented enough. I took the painting you gave me last week for my birthday to work to show my coworkers and everyone loved it. It may not provide a large, steady income, but I think you could open up a studio right here in Providence and sell your work." Her mom leaned forward to make sure she had Jessie's attention. "You will never know until you try, honey."

She sounded like Robert.

The thought of trying and failing scared Jessie to death. But her mom was right. She would never know until she tried.

CHAPTER 31

Robert cranked up the air conditioner as soon as he started his Tahoe. The temperature already this morning promised a warm day. They'd probably hit mid-nineties by this afternoon. Not unexpected for late August but also not typical for south eastern Washington.

A flashy red and blue sign caught Robert's eye as he stopped at the entrance to his subdivision.

Jackson for Sheriff.

That was not the same sign Jackson put up last week. This one was larger, more colorful, and eye-catching. The sign was much higher quality than the dozen signs Jackson had originally put up.

How had Jackson come up with the funds for additional signs?

Similar signs mocked Robert from almost every corner on his drive to work. He let out a low whistle. Jackson was getting serious about this election.

Robert needed to, as well. He'd finally dusted off his old signs last weekend, but he'd decided he couldn't reuse them because they said "Elect" not "Re-elect." It looked like he'd better get on the ball and drum up some campaign funds. Judging by the quality and number of Jackson's signs, Robert needed some substantial funds.

He knew a certain wealthy young widow, who would love to contribute to his campaign, but Robert would not go there. He didn't want to be obligated to Debbie in any way.

As soon as Robert arrived at work, he turned on his computer. He wanted to figure out how Jackson could afford so many new signs. He'd just accessed Jackson's campaign finance report, which was a public record, when Dale knocked on his open office door.

"You should be home in bed," Robert said by way of a greeting.

"I'm headed there, believe me, but there's something I need to discuss with you."

Every muscle in Robert's body tensed at the serious tone in Dale's voice. His mind raced, concerning all the things that might have gone wrong last night, and every one of them landed on Jessie. Surely if something had happened to her, someone would have notified Robert.

Dale dropped into the chair opposite Robert. "I'm afraid I have some bad news."

Robert's stomach churned, sending burning acid shooting up into his chest. "Spit it out, man," Robert said when Dale pulled out his knife and started cleaning his fingernails.

Dale's hands stilled, and he lifted his gaze to meet Robert's. "Saw Pendleton last night."

A sudden spike in temperature in the small office sucked the air from Robert's lungs. "Where?" the single word came out low and gruff.

He knew it was only a matter of time until Pendleton showed up again.

"Spotted him putting up one of Jackson's new campaign signs. Almost didn't recognize him. His hair's longer and he has a beard now." Dale went back to digging at his nails. "I followed him out to the Sleepy Inn Motel. He stared right at me and grinned as he got out of the car and walked into his motel room."

Pendleton was here in town, staying at a motel out by the county line? Robert sprang from his chair and pulled his firearm from his desk drawer.

Dale pocketed his knife and got to his feet, too. He blocked the doorway. "You know you have no grounds to arrest him, right?"

"But Jessie's in danger."

"Relax. I made Kyle park his car at the gate of the Double Diamond and keep watch all night while I did the patrols, including frequent passes by the motel. To my knowledge, Pendleton was there all night. Vickie spelled Kyle off about an hour ago."

"Why didn't you call me last night?"

"So you could do what?" Dale pinned Robert with a glare. "Go after the man half-cocked while you've got Internal Affairs breathing down your neck?"

Robert rolled his shoulders and popped his neck. "You're sure it was really Pendleton that you saw?"

"Yep. Ran the plates on the car he was driving. It's a rental leased to Patrick Pendleton. I called the rental company this morning--that's why I'm still here--and they said Pendleton rented this one two days ago."

"This one?"

"Apparently, he rents a different car every few days."

"Why?"

"My guess? To stay off our radar. After I got a good look at him last night, I realized I might have seen him a couple days ago on Main Street, driving a different car, of course."

Robert swore under his breath as he dropped back into his chair. "How long has he been in town?"

"Manager at the Sleepy Inn said this is the third time he's rented a room in the last four weeks."

Pendleton had been here in town almost every week since being released from the county jail and Robert hadn't a clue? His shoulders bunched as the urge to punch something filled him.

How could I have been so stupid? Robert propped his elbows on the desk and plunged his hands into his hair.

He'd been watching his tail for the red Lexus since Pendleton got out of the county jail, because they still had the Infiniti Q50 impounded behind Knight's repair shop. Robert had never considered

Pendleton would drive a rental car. How many times had Pendleton following him and Sylvia to the Double Diamond?

Did Pendleton know where Jessie was? Robert's stomach bottomed out at the thought.

Dale yawned. "What I can't figure out is why he was putting up one of Jackson's campaign signs? I planned to ask Jackson before I got off shift, but I was on the phone with the rental car company and the motel longer than I expected." He stifled another yawn. "Maybe I'll have Brady do it."

"No, I'll do it," Robert said.

At the mention of Jackson's name, Robert turned back to his computer. Jackson had only half a dozen contributions listed on his finance reporting form, but the last one may as well have been in bold with flashing arrows pointing at it.

Ten thousand dollars donated by Patrick Pendleton.

Robert turned his laptop so Dale could see the screen. "Apparently Pendleton is a major contributor to Jackson's campaign."

Dale let out a long, low whistle. "Why would Pendleton donate that kind of money to a campaign where he has nothing to gain?"

"He's making it personal. I think he views me as having taken Jessie away from him. He's going to great lengths to taunt me, which concerns me. What other plans does he have?"

"Whatever they are, we can't engage until he does something illegal."

"I know," Robert growled. But what happened when they learned Pendleton's intentions too late?

An hour later, after informing his deputies to keep an eye on Pendleton, Robert pulled to a stop in front of Lewis Jackson's house. Relieved to see his Pasco City police cruiser still parked in front, Robert slid from his SUV and approached the front door.

He didn't know Jackson well--they'd never had much occasion to socialize--and he'd only seen him in passing since Jackson announced his intentions to run for sheriff. He didn't want this to be an awkward situation, but Robert needed to know Pendleton's end game.

He knocked long and hard to be heard over the baby crying on the other side of the door.

The door opened and Robert smiled at Carrie Jackson, who bounced a red-faced baby on her hip. "Is Lewis at home?"

The petite woman's eyes widened. "Is something wrong, sheriff?"

"No, not at all. I just have some questions about his campaign."

Carrie gave him a wary look before asking, "Would you like to come in?"

A toddler started crying behind Carrie as another child darted out of the family room, yelling, "It's mine. You can't play with it."

Robert smiled at Carrie again. "Thank you, but I'll just wait for him out here." No need to add to the woman's stress.

Less than a minute later, Lewis stepped out onto the porch wearing sweatpants and a rumpled t-shirt. "Sheriff?" He wore the same wary expression as his wife.

"Looks like I drug you out of bed."

Lewis ran a hand through his messy hair. "Yeah, I'm working nights this month."

"Sorry, man. I'll keep this quick so you can get back to sleep." Robert scratched his jaw and squared his shoulders. "How do you know Patrick Pendleton?"

Lewis's brow furrowed. "I don't, not really."

"The man contributed ten thousand dollars to your campaign!" Robert sucked in a sharp breath and reminded himself to stay calm.

"Yeah, but I didn't solicit his donation. He just showed up on my doorstep a couple weeks ago and handed me a check along with a pamphlet from a print graphics company who'd already agreed to do a rush job on my campaign stuff."

"Did he tell you why he wanted to make such a large contribution?" What did Pendleton hope to gain?

A red flush filled Jackson's cheeks. "When I asked him the same question, he said, 'the sheriff needs to be taken down a notch'."

So it is personal. Pendleton is playing mind games.

Robert hated to admit it was working. Not because he feared he might lose the election to Jackson, but rather because Pendleton was way to close to Jessie, and Robert couldn't do a single thing to stop the man.

Pendleton was an idiot if he thought keeping Robert from getting re-elected would somehow help him get Jessie back?

"I swear I never saw the man before he showed up on my doorstep a couple of weeks ago. Then he showed up last night insisting on helping me distribute my signs. I don't know how he knew I picked them up yesterday."

"Apparently he has a lot of free time on his hands, and he's been watching more than just you."

"What do you mean? Is there something I should know about him?"

Robert debated over how much to tell Lewis about the kind of man Pendleton was. He certainly didn't want to advertise that there was a police brutality suit against himself. Jackson could leverage that in his campaign if he wanted to.

"He's a dangerous man whose wife has sought refuge here in Providence." Robert took a step back, preparing to leave. "Do me a favor?" when Jackson nodded, Robert continued. "If you talk to him again and you get a glimpse of what he might be planning, let me know, please?"

"Sure." Lewis nodded. "I uh... hope there are no hard feelings about me running for sheriff."

Robert waved a hand in dismissal. "Of course not. I am curious why you decided to run, though. I half expected you to apply to join the sheriff's department when we hired new deputies last fall."

Lewis shifted from one foot to the other. "I considered it, but at the time my wife and I were planning on moving back to the Tri-Cities area. But then the house we were looking at buying fell through. We took that as a sign that we were supposed to stay here."

"Well, if you decide you're ready to give up the commute, let me know. We can afford to bring on another deputy." Robert stepped off the porch before turning back and smiling. "And depending on the outcome of November's election, I hope you'll consider keeping me on as a deputy if you get elected."

"I think we both know my chances of getting elected are slim."

Lewis scratched his jaw. "I just wanted my wife to know I was serious about truly sinking down roots here now that we've decided to stay."

"You never know, Lewis. I mean, you didn't expect to receive such a generous donation to your campaign either."

They said their goodbyes, and Robert pointed his truck toward the ranch.

~

JESSICA KNEADED the dough she'd made under Lottie's tutelage for dinner rolls and cinnamon rolls. Baking wasn't one of her favorite past times, but there was a certain sense of satisfaction that came with kneading dough.

Instead of using the Bosch mixer, Lottie insisted Jessie needed to feel the dough in her hands so she would know when to stop kneading.

The swinging door opened, and Jessie sucked in a sharp breath at the sight of the handsome man standing there dressed in a sheriff's uniform. No matter how he dressed, Robert took her breath away. But something about his grim expression and the fact that he never came to the ranch at ten thirty in the morning made it difficult to breathe.

"What's wrong?" Her voice came out a croak.

"Can I talk to you for a minute?" If his serious expression hadn't put her on high alert, his lack of greeting and the gruffness of his tone did.

Jessie's gaze darted to Lottie, as if the other woman could somehow make everything better.

The older woman's face looked equally grim. She patted the dough and gave a curt nod. "It's ready. I'll put it in a bowl and cover it. It'll need to be punched down in about thirty minutes." She jerked her head toward Robert. "Go on."

Jessie washed her hands and followed Robert out of the kitchen and onto the back deck.

Robert spun to face her as soon as the door closed behind her. "I owe you an apology, Jess."

"For what?"

"For everything. For not believing you. For letting my guard down and not doing my job properly."

Jessie wrapped her arms around herself. "It's Patrick, isn't it?"

Robert propped one hand on his gun holster and rubbed his neck with the other. "Apparently, he's rented a motel room out by the county line a few times and he's been driving around town in rental cars."

Jessie gasped. "He's here in Providence?"

She knew they hadn't seen the last of Patrick, but she'd gotten lulled into a false sense of security. Carried away in thinking she could build a new life here.

"Yes, and I can't touch him," Robert said in a voice akin to a growl. "Not until he breaks the law or the restraining order."

"So I just wait for him to come after me?" Her voice broke on the last word.

"No, Jess. You live your life." He grabbed her shoulders and looked into her eyes. "Don't let fear hold you back from doing the things you want to do. Trust me with your safety. I know I haven't exactly warranted your trust thus far, but I'm going to make sure we have a guard here around the clock. We'll continue to make sure you never leave the ranch alone and whatever you do, please keep your phone's location sharing turned on."

Jessie nodded, despite the fear clawing at her throat. She trusted Robert, but he didn't know Patrick like she did. He didn't know how conniving and self-serving Patrick could be. Didn't know how irrational Patrick became when he lost his temper.

Robert must have sensed her fear, because he pulled her into his arms. "I'm going to take care of you, Jessie."

She wrapped her arms around his waist and let his embrace comfort her. *He's right. I can't live my life in fear, but how do I let it go while Patrick is still out there?*

The thump of cowboy boots sounded on the back deck, and Robert pulled away. They turned to see Jake approaching.

His gaze pinned Robert. "I didn't expect to see you here this time of day. Is everything okay?"

Before Robert could answer, the back door to the house opened, and Emily stepped out. "What's going on? Why is Robert here?"

Emily worked mornings at the hospital as a counselor, but now that school had started again, she spent the afternoons at the high school working with troubled students. She often came home for lunch, especially if her last appointment before lunch canceled. Which must be the case today.

Lately, after school, Emily spent hours at Zane and Lottie's house talking with Daniel. Jessie didn't fully understand what was going on with him, but from the snippets she'd overheard, he was going through a rough patch.

Robert cleared his throat. "I found out this morning that Pendleton's in town."

Jake's jaw clenched, and he squared his shoulders as if prepping for a fight.

Emily put an arm around Jessie. "So, what's the plan?"

"I want a guard here around the clock. I'm going to ask Daniel to stand guard during the night." Robert shifted his gaze to Emily. "Do you think he can handle it?"

She nodded. "It'll be good for him."

"As far as the daytime goes, I'll work out a schedule for me and my deputies to make sure someone's here at all times."

"You don't have that kind of manpower, do you?" Emily asked.

"Not really." Robert looked at Jessie again. "But I'm not taking any chances."

A tingle of warmth--that had nothing to do with today's rising temperatures--shot through Jessie.

"We can play this like we did last year when Emily was in danger," Jake said. "I've got a ranch hand who dislocated his shoulder yesterday. He's out of commission for the rest of the season. I was considering letting him go, but it sounds like I should keep him on and shift his responsibilities."

Emily smiled. "That sounds like a great idea. Let Jake worry about who stands guard. You've got other things to worry about, Robert."

Three sets of eyes turned to Emily, including Jessie's.

"What?" Robert asked, confusion filling his face.

"I saw Lewis Jackson's signs all over town."

Robert smirked and rubbed his neck again, a sure sign of his tension. "Hard to miss, huh?"

Jake asked the question Jessie wanted answered. "What signs? What's Jackson got to do with anything?"

Emily turned to Jake. "I couldn't drive a single block without seeing," Emily made finger quotes, "Elect Lewis Jackson for Sheriff." Emily shook her head. "I have no idea how he came up with the funds for that kind of signage."

Robert tensed beside Jessie and shot her a quick glance before shifting his gaze to the stables.

Jessie stepped in front of him, drawing his gaze. "What?"

"Pendleton gave Jackson ten thousand dollars for his campaign and even put the signs up for him."

Jake whistled.

Jessie's mouth dropped open. Patrick never spent money on anything unless he felt like it was a sound investment. How could contributing to Robert's opponent in the upcoming election benefit Patrick? It was obvious he was mocking Robert, but did he really think he could get Jessie back if Robert didn't get re-elected?

Had she inadvertently cost Robert the election?

"You haven't put up a single sign yet, have you?" Emily asked Robert.

"I haven't had time. I dug my old signs out last week but they should say 'Re-elect' not 'Elect'. Besides, I've got bigger things to worry about."

"What things?" Jake's eyes narrowed on Robert. "I told you we'll keep a guard posted."

Robert darted another glance at Jessie then dropped his gaze. "Nothing. Don't worry about it."

There was something that had to do with her or Patrick that

Robert didn't want her knowing about. It should probably infuriate her that he was hiding something from her, but knowing Robert, he was doing it to protect her.

Jake and Emily shared a long look before Jake shook his head and shrugged. Emily spoke first. "Jessie, I think we have need of your artistic skills. If you design new posters for Robert, Jake and I will pay for them." She grabbed Jessie's arm and pulled her inside the house, leaving the men alone.

Within minutes, Jessie found herself at the dining table surrounded by papers and markers. It wasn't long before the men came through the back door talking about installing a security system.

Whatever Robert was dealing with, he didn't plan on telling her.

She didn't know whether to be pleased or upset, but she owed him for keeping her safe. She'd design him the best campaign signs Providence had ever seen. But first she needed to punch down some bread dough.

CHAPTER 32

Jessie stepped back and looked at her canvas. The portrait of Jake and Emily was turning out nicely.

The painting was a gift for Jake and Emily; Jessie's attempt to repay Emily--in a small way--for all the counseling she'd done with Jessie. She'd offered to find a way to pay her, but Emily refused, saying she enjoyed walking and talking with her. But Jessie benefited much more than Emily did.

She wouldn't finish the today, because Emily would be home soon, so Jessie needed to get the wedding picture she'd borrowed off the wall in the great room put back.

Jake knew what Jessie was doing, so it wouldn't be a surprise for him, but he seemed content to let her do her own thing. He and Emily had both been so gracious in letting Jessie know she was welcome to stay at the ranch as long as she'd like.

Jessie was content to stay here because she wasn't ready to give up her early morning walks and talks with Emily. She'd shed a lot of tears during those walks, but she'd made excellent progress and was slowly finding herself. And with Patrick roaming around town, the ranch felt like the safest place.

Jake and Robert had installed a security system on all the doors and windows. One of the ranch hands stood guard on the front porch during the day, and Daniel stood guard at night. Add in the dogs, who were quick to bark when a stranger came near the place, and the Double Diamond felt like Fort Knox.

She cleaned her brushes a few minutes later and was almost done clearing up her mess on the deck when the back door opened. She rotated her new easel--the one her mother insisted on buying to replace the one Patrick broke--before looking up.

Jessie expected to see Emily coming out of the house, but it was Faith... No, wait. She looked closer. It was Hope who walked toward her. This petite woman, who looked so much like Faith, was the high school principal, and she took her job seriously. Though she smiled plenty, she'd mastered the stern expression. Her features today were somewhere in the middle.

"Hi, Jessie. I'm sorry for stopping by without calling first." Hope extended her hand.

Confused about why Hope was here, Jessie shook her hand.

"How are you doing?" Hope sat on the suspended swing, her short legs dangling.

"I'm doing good." Still wondering why Hope was here, Jessie leaned back against the railing. She visited with Robert's aunt last weekend at the Labor Day barbecue, so Jessie couldn't fathom why Hope felt the need to come visit her today.

"I'm going to cut to the chase because I can see you're confused why I'm here. Mr. White had a heart attack yesterday afternoon."

Jessie pressed a hand to her chest. "Oh, no. Is he going to be okay?"

He'd looked a little stooped when she saw him in the ceramics' lab last week, but he'd still been larger than life.

"He's having double bypass surgery tomorrow. The doctors seem confident he'll be back on his feet in no time, but he's decided to retire, effective immediately."

"I'm so sorry to hear that. He was such an amazing teacher." The knife in Jessie's chest twisted. Mr. White had always been her favorite teacher, probably because she'd always sensed that he loved teaching and he made the students feel like they really mattered.

"His wife retired last year from the post office, so they're determined to do some traveling once he's back on his feet."

"I'm glad to hear that."

"So, I suppose you can guess why I'm here."

Jessie shook her head.

"We need an art teacher." Hope tipped her head toward Jessie and gave her a pointed look.

"What?" Jessie dropped onto the swing. *Hope couldn't be serious.* "You want me to teach art at the high school?"

"I can't think of anyone more qualified."

"But I'm not a teacher. I'm only an artist."

"Only an artist," Hope scoffed. "You studied art all over Europe, and you worked at the Metropolitan Museum of Art. Talent like yours needs to be shared."

Jessie agreed, but she wanted to do that through her art, not by teaching.

Hope continued, "Besides, you have something most teachers who've gone to school to get a teaching degree don't have."

"What's that?"

"Passion." Hope smiled. "You know art, you love it, you've lived it and breathed it."

Jessie's chest swelled a little more with each of Hope's statements. She loved art, and there had been a time in her life when she'd lived for her art. She'd breathed art in the oldest cathedrals and coliseums in the world. Images of all the amazing things she'd experienced filled her mind, and she itched to share them with others.

"But I know nothing about teaching." Jessie stood up and paced.

"You can learn. I wouldn't be here if I didn't think you'd make a fantastic teacher. But I guess you'll never know what an amazing teacher you'll be unless you try."

Jessie really hated that phrase: "You'll never know until you try."

It means leaving my comfort zone. But she wasn't exactly comfortable with her current situation. She needed a job.

"You already have a bachelor's degree," Hope said. "It wouldn't take much for you to get certified as a teacher. I think you can even take most of the classes online. Initially, we'd hire you as a long-term substitute, then once you're certified, you'll have a permanent position at Providence High School."

Jessie liked the sound of a permanent position, but it didn't still convince her she'd make a good teacher. "Can't you just get a long-term substitute until you hire an actual teacher?"

"These students deserve more than a substitute who knows nothing about art. Besides, we tried to hire an art teacher two years ago, but we weren't successful. We could try again, but it could take months."

Jessie watched the horses graze in the nearby pasture as she remembered what Robert said about no one being willing to tie themselves down in a one-horse town. *Didn't I complain to my mom about the opposite problem just last week?*

Teaching--she still found the thought ridiculous and horribly overwhelming--would be the anchor she needed to support herself and her baby in Providence, and she could do it while teaching a topic she loved.

She turned to Hope and pasted a smile on her face. "When would I start?"

"Tomorrow."

Jessie dropped back onto the swing. How would she teach without making herself more of a target to Patrick?

JESSIE CHEWED on her fingernails as Robert brought his Tahoe to a stop in front of the high school.

He shut off the engine and turned to look at her.

"I don't think I can do this." She pressed a hand to her stomach, unsure if morning sickness caused her nausea or the fact that she had to walk into a classroom of students and pretend she was a teacher.

Or maybe she felt like she might lose what little breakfast she'd been able to choke down because her designer jeans had grown too tight over the past few weeks. She needed to buy maternity clothes soon. She was almost halfway through her pregnancy.

Emily and Jake had announced their pregnancy a few weeks ago, and Emily was now wearing maternity clothes. Although Jessie wasn't keeping her pregnancy a secret, she wasn't ready for maternity clothes yet. Even though Dr. Young assured her everything looked great, she still feared she might lose this baby.

Robert took her hand, distracting her from her nausea. He laced his fingers with hers and squeezed. "Yes, you can. You're going to be an amazing teacher, Jess."

Warmth crept up her arm, and she squeezed back. "What if the kids don't like me? Or won't listen to me?"

"I can pretty much guarantee all the boys are going to have a major crush on you by the end of the week. And the girls will definitely admire your talent."

Warmth filled her cheeks. She wasn't sure if Robert was teasing or flirting. Or just being Robert. He'd always made her feel talented and beautiful.

He had sounded so pleased last night when she called and told him she had a job. There had been something in his voice that sounded a lot like relief. Was he thinking the same thing Jessie had? That this might make a second chance between them more plausible?

Despite the spark of hope the thought ignited in Jessie, it hadn't brought relief. In fact, her anxiety had flared, and she'd spent the evening fighting waves of nausea. What if this made it easier for Patrick to get to her? She'd never left the ranch by herself yet; Robert, her mother, or Emily always accompanied her.

Robert had sensed her hesitation and promised to drive her to and from school each day. When she protested, he held firm. "Just until we're certain Pendleton is nowhere around."

It had been over a week since Robert told her Patrick was in town. Since that day, he'd not been spotted again. That he'd been here at all made Jessie ill. She didn't know what kind of mind games he was playing, but he was planning something. She was sure of it.

He pressed his lips to the back of her hand and the sensations that rippled through her effectively distracted her mind from teaching. "You've got this, sweetheart."

Jessie's breath caught at the endearment. The last time he called her sweetheart, she was certain he hadn't meant to let the endearment slip out. But today, he smiled and winked at her after saying it.

She sucked in a slow, steady breath, gave him a smile, and tugged her hand from his before reaching for the door handle. Facing a bunch of teenagers seemed a lot safer right now than staying in this truck with Robert. She couldn't afford to let herself get too carried away.

Yet.

Providence High School was relatively quiet when Jessie stepped through the front doors on shaky legs. She had forty minutes to get started on some of the paperwork Hope said needed to be filled out before the bell rang. The rest would have to be done during third period--her prep time.

Jessie's hand shook as she filled out the papers Hope and the secretary put in front of her. She kept repeating Robert's words, *'You're going to be an amazing teacher,'* as she focused on taking slow, steady breaths.

By the time Jessie walked to her classroom--ten minutes before the bell rang--the halls were filled with loud, active teenagers. Her chest tightened as she read over Mr. White's lesson plan for today's classes. There wasn't near enough information there to fill a full class period. Nor was there any clear assignment for the students to work on.

I guess that's what happens when you've taught for thirty years. You become so comfortable teaching you hardly need any notes.

Jessie fought the urge to give in to the panic rising in her and concentrated on remembering the details of the get-to-know-you art activity her favorite professor had done on the first day of one of her advanced art class.

Before she knew it, the room was full of curious students whose faces looked skeptical, as though questioning whether their new teacher knew anything about art.

"Good morning, everyone. My name is..." Even though she'd filled out all the paperwork with her married name, having the kids call her Mrs. Pendleton didn't seem right, since she planned on changing her name after the divorce. But Ms. Sorenson didn't feel right either. "My name is Ms. Jessie."

She turned to the whiteboard. When had they gotten rid of the chalk boards? She picked up a dry erase marker and prayed this activity didn't fall flat.

"We're going to do a get-to-know-you activity today. Everyone needs to think of one thing that represents them to add to our class mosaic. There are only two rules: Each addition to the mosaic needs to attach to a previous piece of the picture, and you only get one minute to draw your part." She pulled the cap off the marker. "I'll go first. I need someone to time me."

She watched over her shoulder until someone said 'go', then she quickly sketched a horse as best as she could with the dry erase marker. *This is a first.* She'd have to get used to this.

When the student called time, she hesitated before signing her horse. She wanted each student to sign their picture so she could learn their names, but she wasn't sure how to sign hers. Finally she did her swooping *J.S.* on the horse's flank, like a brand.

She turned around. "My favorite thing to do, besides painting and creating art, is riding horses." She held the marker out. "Okay, who's next?" When no one volunteered, she added, "It doesn't matter your artistic ability. There's no judgment here. And keep in mind, the longer you wait to take your turn, the more challenging it will be to figure out how to attach your drawing to the mosaic."

Four hands popped up, and Jessie smiled.

CHAPTER 33

Jessie heaved a sigh when the bell rang. She'd done it. She'd make it through her first week of teaching.

Jessie sank down in the chair behind her desk and took a long drink from her water bottle. She'd survived. Barely. She'd basically been treading water all week, but she'd made it. She'd even enjoyed it. But she wouldn't admit that to anyone yet.

She grabbed a granola bar from her bag. The best way to fight her intermittent morning sickness was to eat small, frequent meals. She washed down the granola bar with more water as she contemplated the week. Overall, she supposed it had been a success.

Mr. White's simple outline hadn't been easy to follow, so she'd improvised a lot, but the students seemed to enjoy the activities she'd thrown at them. Next week, she'd start with the basics by teaching the elements of art and assign projects that illustrated each principle.

"You did it," Emily said as she walked into Jessie's classroom. "You made it through an entire week of teaching."

Jessie grinned. "Technically, it wasn't a full week, since I didn't start until Tuesday, but I made it."

Emily perched on the corner of a table. "Don't hate me for

pointing out that you're smiling right now. I know the thought of teaching terrified you, but you're practically glowing." Dimples creased Emily's cheeks as she smiled.

"I'm pretty sure I can chalk the glow up to pregnancy." Jessie laughed, and Emily joined in. "Teaching still terrifies me." She gave a sheepish grin. "But maybe it's not as bad as I thought it would be. I mean, I get to talk about art all day, what can be more fun than that?"

Emily rolled her eyes. "I enjoy talking about feelings. So tell me, how are you feeling right now?"

Jessie chuckled again as she grabbed a piece of scratch paper off her cluttered desk, balled it up, and threw it at Emily's face.

Emily caught the makeshift ball and laughed again. "Seriously, Jessie, you look really happy. Teaching suits you."

Jessie sobered as she thought about Savannah Reed, the talented junior in her seventh period class. It had only taken Jessie fifteen minutes to identify her as the student Mr. White had talked about.

Jessie had a lot of talented students, but Savannah was truly gifted, and she needed someone to help guide her to fully develop her talents.

Jessie smiled at Emily. "Thanks. I never--*ever*--dreamed of being a teacher, but I think I want to really give this a shot."

"I'm glad to hear it." Emily stood. "I've got a little paperwork to do, then I'll be ready to leave in about thirty minutes. Does that work for you?"

Instead of making Robert interrupt his workday to drive her home, Jessie rode home with Emily.

"Sure."

Thirty minutes wasn't near enough time for Jessie to prepare for next week, but neither would all weekend be. Ideas had flooded her mind throughout the week as she recalled lessons Mr. White and many of her college professors had taught her, and she was eager to develop them and make her own lesson plans.

Her thoughts turned to Robert. Would they do something together Saturday night?

Over the past several weeks, they'd fallen into a routine. They spent Wednesday evenings at the ceramics lab and hung out at the ranch on Saturdays. They'd taken walks, ridden four-wheelers, and done some target practice. Robert had even hinted once about taking her for a carriage ride.

She recalled how he watched her face after making the comment. They'd gone on many romantic carriage rides over the years, and the idea of taking another romantic ride in the Winters antique carriage with Robert appealed to her. But it would feel too much like a date.

Jessie wouldn't feel right about dating Robert while she was still married to another man. Without Patrick's cooperation, the process of getting a divorce was slow.

Robert's smile had turned stiff before she'd answered him. "I'd love to go for a ride in the carriage with you." She smiled to soften the rest of her response. "But I don't think this is the right time."

His face fell. "You're right. I guess I keep forgetting that you're still married."

Jessie wished she could forget.

Patrick was always in the back of her mind. And until she was truly free of him, she couldn't pursue a relationship with Robert.

ROBERT SLUMPED into his office chair and let out a lengthy sigh. He'd just spent the last hour in the small conference room talking to Detective Harris, where he'd recounted the entire incident with Pendleton. He'd left nothing out--from the other man's vile language to every punch, including nearly blacking out after being struck by the ax, to Pendleton's threat that if he couldn't have Jessie, no one would.

"He sounds like a real piece of work," Harrison said.

"He is." Robert was glad the detective seemed like an honest man who simply wanted to sort out this complaint.

"Do you think he'd actually kill her, given the chance?"

"Yes," Robert said without hesitation. "The look I saw in his eyes that night...I've only ever seen that on one other man. A professional hit man." Robert hadn't planned on sharing this next part, but if it helped the detective understand the seriousness of the situation, he shouldn't keep it to himself. "When I found Jess--uh Mrs. Pendleton, she was curled in a fetal position, crying, 'Please, don't hurt me anymore'."

The detective's jaw clenched. "It's a good thing Pendleton is behind bars, then."

"He was."

"You're kidding me. He made bail after being charged with aggravated assault?" Harris shook his head in disbelief.

"Half-a-million-dollar bail. He was out within a week." It still chafed Robert that Pendleton had made bail at all. "And we've spotted him around town a few times since."

Robert hadn't told Jessie that Brady had seen Pendleton walking out of Knight's Grocery store last week. He didn't want to worry her, but it irritated Robert that they couldn't touch Pendleton. That hadn't stopped Brady from following Pendleton for the rest of the evening, though.

"He sounds determined," Harrison said. "I don't envy you, sheriff. I hope Mrs. Pendleton is somewhere safe."

"As safe as can be."

I hope. They'd done everything they could to keep Jessie safe, but it still didn't feel like enough. He'd never forgive himself if something happened to Jessie, Emily, or Lottie.

Needing a distraction, he opened his laptop. He couldn't think of a single thing he needed to do right now, but he needed to find something to occupy his mind.

As he'd feared, Harris had requested to speak individually with each of the deputies. He wasn't afraid the deputies would slander him, but he worried Harris might find out he and Jessie used to be a couple. Because that might make it look like Robert had a motive to use excessive force on Pendleton.

Brady filled his doorway.

"You finished already?" Robert asked. "That didn't take long."

Brady sat in the chair opposite of Robert and shrugged. "He just wanted to know what kind of man you are in your personal and professional life. He asked if I had any idea why Pendleton would feel the need to file a federal suit against you for police brutality."

Robert's heart stalled. "What did you tell him?"

"Said I'd never met the man, but he seems to be a classic textbook narcissist displaying characteristics of entitlement, authoritarianism, and aggressive behaviors."

Robert laughed. Brady always liked to use big words to confuse people, despite being one of the biggest rednecks Robert knew.

"So, you didn't tell him Jessie and I...used to be a couple?"

"Should I have? You told me yourself that was a long time ago. You said you'd do your job, just like anybody else. And you are." Brady looked Robert in the eye. "I don't care if you're sleeping with her..." He raised his hand to cut off Robert's protest. "Of course I know you're not sleeping with her. You're not that kind of man. But my point is, no matter what happened between you and Jessie in the past, or may happen in the future, it doesn't excuse Pendleton's behavior. You're an excellent sheriff who does things by the book, and Pendleton is just trying to avoid taking responsibility for his actions. That's what I told the detective." He waved his hand in the air. "Just the last part about doing things by the book, not the sleeping with Jessie part."

"Thanks, man." Robert picked up the weighted stress ball from his desk and threw it at Brady's face.

Brady caught it, like Robert knew he would. "My pleasure. Seriously, dude, don't sweat it. All of us deputies have decided we're going to keep this to ourselves. So you don't have to worry about this messing up your election or anything."

Robert nodded and ducked his head. It wouldn't do for one of his deputies to see him get emotional. He couldn't have asked for a better group of people.

An hour later, Harris walked into Robert's office and shut the door before sitting down.

Robert's stomach dropped. If the detective felt the need to close the door, he probably wasn't delivering good news.

"I'm going to be straight with you, sheriff. I came here expecting to encounter a cocky law enforcement officer with a bone to pick. Bone or not, I've learned you're an honest, highly respected man. I'm aware you have a history with Mrs. Pendleton, but as far as I can see, you haven't let that cloud your judgment. If it'd been me making the arrest, Pendleton wouldn't have fared so well."

"Thank you, detective."

"As far as I'm concerned, you're cleared of all charges. Pendleton strikes me as the type who, if he's got to be miserable, is going to make everybody else miserable with him."

Relief filled Robert, making his limbs feel like jelly.

They talked for a few more minutes about Pendleton before the conversation shifted to politics and sports. By the time Robert walked Harris out to his car, he was ready to celebrate. A craving for Amy's chocolate cake or Aunt Charity's peach pie hit him. He just might have to have both.

A few minutes later, Robert swung the door to Charity's diner open and froze. There, in front of him, on her way out of the diner, was Debbie Wheeler.

He stepped back and held the door open for her to exit, hoping she'd do just that and be on her way.

Debbie stepped out of the diner, but she didn't step away. "Robert, I wish I'd known you were coming here for lunch today. I would have waited for you, and we could have eaten together."

"Debbie, I've made it clear I'm not interested in joining you for lunch, or dinner, or anything else that might suggest a relationship between us."

Debbie tapped him playfully on the arm. "I don't know why you play so hard to get. You and I both know there are not a lot of single men and women in this town. Do you really want to grow old all alone?"

Was that a hint of desperation in Debbie's voice? A sudden image of Debbie as an old woman sitting all alone in her enormous mansion filled his mind, and Robert felt sorry for the wealthy young widow.

Robert had no intention of growing old all alone, though.

He took Debbie's arm and stepped aside with her as another

couple approached the door. He let go as soon as they were out of the way. "Listen, Debbie, you are an attractive, generous woman, but I'm just not interested in you romantically, which is not fair to you. I'm sure someday you will find someone to grow old with. And they will appreciate you for your many talents." He should probably name some of her talents, but for the life of him he couldn't think of one at the moment.

Debbie's gaze dropped, and she examined her nails. "Are you turned off by the fact that I've been married twice before?"

Robert shook his head. That was just one of many reasons he didn't care for Debbie, but he wouldn't say it to her face. Honestly, who wanted to be some woman's third husband?

Yet he couldn't deny wanting to be Jessie's second husband.

It was different with Jessie, though. He couldn't explain what made it different. It just was.

"Is it my money?" Debbie propped a hand on her hip.

"No, Debbie. You're very generous with your money and I admire you for that, but admiration isn't the same as attraction or affection."

Debbie's lips turned down in what looked like a genuine pout. "Is it because I'm three years older than you?"

"No, it has nothing to do with your age." Robert pinched the bridge of his nose. He didn't know how to get through to Debbie without outright offending her.

"It's that artist, isn't it?" Debbie folded her arms across her ample chest. "I've heard how close you two were. I guess you'll be getting back together, huh?"

I sure hope so. But there were still so many obstacles to overcome.

"Yes," he said, finally seeing an out. "I fell in love with her when I was seventeen and I've never stopped loving her." The words came out more forcefully than he'd intended.

It was the first time Robert had admitted his feelings out loud to someone else. Just hearing the words out of his own mouth drove them home. He was completely and irrevocably in love with Jessie.

Debbie's finely arched eyebrows rose. She tilted her head, watching him intently. "I heard she was married."

And pregnant.

"Our relationship is...complicated, but it doesn't change the way I feel about her."

Debbie's expression softened. "You really care about her, don't you?"

"I do."

"Then I hope you're happy." She turned away, then turned back. "I hope she deserves you, Robert."

"Thank you, Debbie, but it's the other way around. I hope I can be worthy of her."

And Robert meant it. He needed to reclaim Jessie's heart and convince her to take a chance on him again.

JESSIE DROPPED into the chair behind her desk in her classroom.

Her classroom.

I'm a teacher.

It still felt surreal to Jessie. But she'd survived her second week, and it had gone even smoother than the first. She'd only gotten a month's worth of lesson plans organized last weekend, but the more she taught, the more ideas came to her and the more she enjoyed it.

"Hey, Ms. Jessie." Tall, slender, ginger-haired Savannah Reed stepped into the classroom. "I forgot my cell phone."

Jessie's head jerked up. She still hadn't gotten used to being called Ms. Jessie. Even though that's what she'd asked the kids to call her.

She smiled at Savanna as she got to her feet. Jessie had enjoyed teaching this gifted girl some simple techniques that took her artwork to the next level.

"Yeah, you don't want to forget that. It would make for a very boring weekend if your friends couldn't get a hold of you."

"Oh, I don't really have that many friends." Savannah shrugged. "I need a phone so I can check in with my dad after I get my brothers from the elementary school."

Not that many friends. Savannah reminded Jessie of herself when she first moved to Providence.

"Oh, does your dad work late often?" To get to know her students, Jessie struck up conversations with them as often as possible.

"Most days." Savannah shrugged. "He likes to be there to get us off to school, but that means he doesn't get home until seven or sometimes later."

No wonder she didn't have many friends if she had to tend her brothers every day.

"Does your mom work, too?"

Savannah looked down at her feet. "She's not around, anymore."

"I'm sorry to hear that, Savannah." Jessie stepped a little closer to the girl. "My Dad walked out on us when I was sixteen. It's tough."

Savannah looked at Jessie as though trying to decide whether to believe her before nodding.

People always said, "I know how you feel," but very few had ever experienced the crushing belief that if they had just been a better child, dad--or mom--wouldn't have left.

Savannah stepped toward the door. "I better go or I'm going to be late."

"Savannah, I want you to know my door is always open...if you ever need anything."

"Thanks, Ms. Jessie." She stepped out the door, then hurried back into the room. "By the way, I'm glad you're our teacher. I mean, I feel bad about Mr. White, but I think you're doing a fantastic job."

"Thank you, Savannah. I feel bad about Mr. White too. And I'm glad I get to be your teacher as well." Warmth filled Jessie's chest as she said the words. She meant them. Every word. More than she ever thought she would after only two weeks of teaching.

If she could make a difference in even one student's life, especially a student as gifted as Savannah, then all the hard work she would need to put in to learning how to teach would be worth it.

Now she understood why Mr. White never felt like being a teacher prevented him from doing something worthwhile with his life. *Teaching children is worthwhile.*

A feeling of lightness spread through Jessie's chest. She was exactly where she was supposed to be.

Jessie wouldn't let this sense of fulfillment keep her from sending her paintings and pottery to New York City to be sold, though. Especially since Mr. Ramo and the Beckers had both responded to her email, saying they'd love to sell her work.

She could be a teacher and an artist from right here in Providence.

CHAPTER 34

Robert pulled his truck into his driveway and killed the engine. He dropped his hands to his thighs and wiped his damp palms against his jeans.

Jessie sat beside him, looking more beautiful than ever.

His heart rate accelerated. Just being near Jessie did that to him. Add in bringing her to his house for the first time, and he feared he might have a heart attack.

When he signed papers to start construction on this house just over five years ago, he'd done it with Jessie in mind. He'd chosen this house design because he thought it fit Jessie's tastes, and he'd selected this lot so the bedrooms on the front side of the house would face south. He'd always intended one of the bedrooms to be Jessie's art studio.

"What do you think?"

"It's a beautiful house. Who lives here?"

"I do."

"This is your house?" Jessie's eyes widened. "When you told me you lived in town, I assumed you were just renting a small house. But this is a gorgeous home. Did you buy this or are you just renting?"

"I built it about five years ago." Robert watched her to see if she would make the connection.

He'd planned to surprise Jessie with the announcement that the builders had already broken ground on their home after he proposed to her on that carefully planned night at the cabin.

But he never ended up proposing and never told her he was building a home for her.

Jessie's brow creased. "Did you start this before I..."

"Yes. I was going to surprise you."

"I don't know what to say..." Jessie let out a short, but heavy, sigh. "I wish saying I'm sorry would make it so I could take it all back. Hit rewind somehow. You don't know how many times I've wished I could go back five years and do it all again."

He shifted to face her and took her hand. "You don't mean that, Jess. You know you never would have been happy settling here, always wondering what opportunities you missed out on."

Tears filled her eyes. "You're right, but I think I regret the opportunities I missed out on here even more."

Robert's heart pounded so hard in his chest he suspected Jessie could hear it. He'd hoped the night would eventually head in this direction. He just didn't think they'd have this discussion before they even got out of the truck.

"Those opportunities were only delayed. They're still here." The words were little more than a whisper.

Robert feared saying them too loud might make them more fragile. Like a giant bubble that hung in the air suspended, waiting for the slightest touch to burst it.

Jessie's hand tightened around his, but she shook her head. "I don't deserve a second chance."

He reached up and wiped away the tear that fell on her cheek. "You deserve it more than anyone, Jess. You've had your fill of pain and suffering. Now it's your turn to enjoy some happiness."

"And you're telling me that happiness can include you?" She pressed her cheek against his palm, her eyes full of questions, as though she didn't dare hope that things could really work out between them this time.

She looked exactly like Robert felt.

"I'm telling you I want to discuss it with you and make a plan together." He cleared his throat and chuckled. "But I hadn't planned to do it until much later in the evening. I'm dying to kiss you already and we haven't even had dinner yet."

Jessie's laughter joined his, but her eyes held that heated look that mirrored the desire simmering in him.

He released her hand and opened his door. He needed to put a little distance between them, or he'd end up doing something he'd regret.

No. He wouldn't regret it, but it wouldn't be right to kiss Jessie while she was still legally tied to another man.

Robert led her into the house. "I'll let you wander through the house and show yourself around." He scratched his jaw before pointing over his shoulder toward the kitchen. "I need to get the grill fired up."

He wanted more than anything to show Jessie around the house he'd built with her in mind, to see her reaction. Wanted to know which room she'd pick for her studio and which room she'd want for a nursery. He wanted to see the look on her face as she walked through the spacious master bedroom and saw the jetted tub in the master bath.

He didn't dare accompany her on the tour, though. Walking beside her through the home he'd built for her would feel too much like cementing his dreams.

If he and Jessie didn't have the same dreams at this point, he wouldn't be able to stay in this house. He'd have to sell it and move to the other side of town. Maybe he'd even move to the next county and let Lewis Jackson have the sheriff's badge.

Robert lit the barbecue grill and pulled t marinated chicken--recipe courtesy of Amy--from the fridge. Amy had also coached him on how to make a savory rice dish and a fancy salad with spinach and strawberries. She'd even given him a couple of generous slices of her famous chocolate cake for dessert.

After putting the chicken on the grill, he set a timer as per Amy's instructions. *"Don't overcook the chicken. No longer than seven minutes per side, or you'll dry it out."*

He stepped back into the house to find Jessie staring at the portrait she'd painted of him and Goliath. Even though the picture had hung in his home for five years, Robert still marveled at Jessie's talent every time he looked at it.

He stood behind Jessie. "Can you see what an amazing artist you are?"

"I can't believe you still have it after all these years."

"Of course I still have it. It's my most prized possession. If this house burned down, that is the one thing I would miss." He put his hands on her shoulders and she leaned back into him, like he'd hoped she would. "It's irreplaceable, and so is the artist who painted it."

Jessie rested her head against his jaw, and he fought the urge to turn her a little further and press his lips to hers.

"No one has ever believed in me like you do, or made me feel the way you make me feel."

"How do I make you feel?" the words came out a hoarse whisper. He'd never intended for things to become so intimate this evening, but he needed to hear her answer. He slipped his arms around her waist, feeling the firmness of her rounded abdomen. A burning desire to protect her and her child filled his chest.

"You make me feel like I could conquer the world. Like I'm invincible."

That wasn't the response he was hoping for, but he'd take it.

"You make me want to be a better person." Jessie turned in his embrace and slid her arms around his neck.

Robert pulled her closer. The subtle, firm mound of her stomach pressing against his reminded him she carried another man's child. A man she was still married to. He remembered the promise he'd made to himself and her after struggling for an entire week with the revelation that she was pregnant.

I'll always be there for you, no matter what. He'd let her down once, but he'd never do it again. He tightened his arms around her.

"You make me feel irresistible and beautiful."

"You are," he groaned against her hair.

Darn it. He didn't care if she was married to another man. He wanted to kiss her. He wanted to reclaim her heart and make her his.

He pulled back a little, intending to press his lips to hers.

Beep. Beep. Beep.

Robert froze at the annoying sound of the timer on his phone. He silently cursed Amy. He'd rather kiss Jessie and eat burnt chicken than to lose this moment with her. Jessie pulled away, and Robert let her, even though it was the last thing he wanted to do. He pulled his phone from his pocket and silenced the dang thing.

"Saved by the bell." Jessie's eyes reflected the regret that was surely mirrored in his.

"Perhaps you're right." If he'd allowed himself to kiss Jessie, the chicken would undoubtedly burn to a crisp. As much as he would like to ignore dinner altogether and pull Jessie back into his arms, his goal tonight was to impress her and show her how perfect they still were for each other. Although kissing her might prove the passion was still there, he wanted to show Jessie he was capable, ready, and willing to take care of her and her child.

He backed toward the patio door. "Make yourself at home. I just need to flip the chicken."

When he returned to the kitchen, they worked together to set the table and get the food on. Robert lit the candles he now regretted placing on the table before going to pick up Jessie. He'd been going for a romantic dinner, because he'd wanted his intentions toward Jessie to be clear.

But romantic meant intimate, and he'd forgotten how powerful that intimacy could be. He felt like a teenager all over again. There had been plenty of times in the past when he and Jessie had made out, that he'd been hard pressed to keep the promise he'd made to her and not cross the line they'd agreed upon, but now that she was back, he never wanted to let her go.

Jessie's eyes closed in appreciation when she took her first bite of chicken. "Mmm...this is delicious. I can't believe you made this all by yourself."

"Hey, I can cook...a little. Actually, Amy coached me with all of this." He made a circle above his plate with his fork.

"It's amazing."

Robert couldn't appreciate the food's taste because of the knot in his stomach. He had a lot he wanted to say to Jessie, but he wanted to make sure she wouldn't reject him first. They ate in silence for a while before he found the courage to broach the subject.

"So, how is school?" He forced himself to take a bite of the seasoned rice, so she couldn't tell he was holding his breath.

"Crazy and very stressful. But I loved it. I can't wait to finish developing my lesson plans for the rest of the year."

Yes! Robert sucked in a sharp breath, inhaling into his airway the last few grains of rice in his mouth. He coughed again and again until tears blurred his vision.

"Are you okay?"

He took a drink of water, trying to calm his irritated esophagus. "I'm fine. In fact, I've never been better." He cleared his throat. "I'm glad you're enjoying teaching."

He lifted his glass for a second drink because his throat still felt like it was trying to kill him.

"There's something I've been meaning to talk to you about for a while now." Jessie took a quick breath, then continued. "Who is Debbie Wheeler?"

Robert spit water across his plate. *Jessie had met Debbie?*

"Um...when did you meet Debbie? What did she say to you?"

Jessie's eyebrow raised, and her lips turned up in a slow smile. "Why don't you tell me about Debbie? Who is she to you?"

Robert stifled the urge to groan. "She's a nuisance."

He noticed Jessie didn't answer either of his questions, but he was determined to be completely honest with her. He told her how Debbie returned to Providence a few years ago as a widow. She'd married a wealthy, older man, who left his fortune to her when he died.

"She has chased Ben, Jake, and me relentlessly over the past couple of years. She's generous with her money, so I'm sure she's a pleasant person, but she gives off this vibe of desperation. It's very off-putting."

"It must have been difficult to see both Ben and Jake get married."

"You have no idea." And not just because Debbie doubled her efforts to get his attention. He'd envied his brother and cousin, desperately wanting a wife to come home to every evening. What was the point of having this big house when he had no one to share it with?

"Debbie is very attractive," Jessie said, watching him.

Robert shrugged. "I suppose, if you like that type."

"But you don't like her type?"

"Nope," Robert said without hesitation. "She's not my type."

"What is your type?" Jessie leaned forward, a twinkle in her eyes.

You. You're my type. It's only ever been you, Jess.

Robert bit his tongue to keep from blurting the thoughts racing through his head. He smiled. "Hmm... I need to think about that."

He took a bite of his chicken, pretending to think while he chewed. Jessie was right; it was delicious.

"I like tall women with two-toned hair and amber eyes that sparkle when she's angry or excited."

Jessie smiled, and her eyes sparked into little twin flames.

"I like strong, independent women who aren't afraid to chase their dreams. Talented women who enjoy sharing their gifts with others."

Jessie's smile faded, and her eyes dimmed.

Shoot. What did I say?

He'd planned this whole evening hoping to convince Jessie to take a second chance on him. And now he was ruining it.

"Don't you want a woman who puts you first?"

Where is this coming from? Did Jessie honestly think he was that selfish? That he was like Patrick?

"Sure, I want a woman who loves me so much, she thinks about me all the time. But I don't want a woman who feels she needs to base every decision and action on what I want. What good is her devotion to me if she's not there for her family and friends when they need her?"

He reached for her hand across the table. It felt so delicate in his. "I want a woman who loves herself first."

Tears filled Jessie's eyes, and Robert prayed they resulted from something he'd said right, not something he'd said wrong.

He cleared his throat. "I have some things I need to say to you, Jess, but I need you to listen to everything before you comment. And if you don't want to comment, that's okay too, I guess. But I really hope you have something to say when I'm done."

He sucked in a deep breath, and Jessie laughed. "Quiet. I'm trying to be serious here." He tightened his hold on her hand. "Okay, here it goes. I love you." Jessie's lips turned up, and Robert's pulse raced. "I fell in love with you when I was seventeen and I've never stopped loving you. I tried to get over you the past five years. A time or two I thought I'd succeeded, but the minute you waltzed back into my life, I was sunk."

He leaned forward in his seat, needing to get it all out before he lost his courage. "If you feel you need to leave Providence to follow your dreams or build your career, I will follow you. To the ends of the earth. Even to New York City. I could give up law enforcement and become a stable master or groom, or whatever they're called, for some rich senator or actor who has some land. That way, I wouldn't feel too claustrophobic, hopefully. And if you're going to be some famous artist, then you could basically support us."

Jessie burst out laughing. "I am not going back to New York City. Ever." She clapped her hand over her mouth. "I'm sorry. Were you done? Is it my turn yet?"

"I have more to say, but first, I want to hear more about you never going back to New York."

She squeezed his hand. "I'd never ask you to leave Providence. Especially when you're up for re-election."

"Getting re-elected as sheriff isn't near as important to me as never losing you again. And if that means leaving Providence so you can have the career you want, then I'll do it in a heartbeat."

It wouldn't be easy, but Jessie was worth the sacrifice.

CHAPTER 35

Jessie leaned forward and squeezed Robert's hand. "I love you too, Robert."

The smile that took over Robert's face took her breath away. She ignored her racing pulse and focused on what she wanted to say. "I'm so sorry I left five years ago. Except for the glimpse of success I had with my art, I was never happy in New York." Her voice dropped as she continued. "That's why I went out with Patrick, because I was so lonely. The affection I felt for him was nothing compared to the love I have for you. I wonder if that was the problem between us. I couldn't love him enough."

Robert shook his head. "Don't start blaming yourself again and please don't excuse that man's behavior."

Jessie held up her other hand. "You're right. It's not my fault. I understand that now. The affection I felt for him could have grown, if he hadn't crushed it along with the rest of me." She was making progress. It was slow, but her psyche was improving.

"Jess--"

She waved away his protest. "Okay, I'm done with my pity party. Now, where was I?"

"I believe you just said you loved me," Robert said, with a gleam in his eyes.

"I did?" Her eyes widened in mock surprise.

"Don't play games with me, sweetheart." Robert's Adam's apple bobbed.

Jessie gave him a contrite smile. "I do love you. I always have and I always will. You were my first love, and you'll be my last."

Robert let out a tortured groan.

"Did you just growl at me?" Jessie's surprise was genuine this time.

"Yes, because a couple usually kisses after declaring their love for each other. But--"

"But I'm still married. And I wouldn't feel right about kissing you while I'm still married to Patrick."

"Just like I don't feel right about kissing a married woman." He rubbed his jaw, and Jessie wanted to reach out and stroke the smooth skin. "That's where I was going with all of this, by the way." He waved his free hand toward the candles and their dessert plates. "I want to marry you and give your child the father he or she deserves. I'll try not to rush you, but as soon as your divorce is final, I want to put my ring on your finger and make you my wife."

Jessie's heart swelled, and tears filled her eyes. She didn't deserve a man as amazing as Robert.

"I want that too. With all my heart." She took a quick breath. "Oh, with all the craziness of teaching, I forgot to tell you, I have an appointment in two weeks to get my divorce finalized."

Robert's grip on her hand tightened. "Say the word, Jess, and I'll put a ring on you so fast and take you to the courthouse, or the church, or wherever you want. I'll even spring for plane tickets to Vegas if that's what you want."

They both laughed, because years ago they had joked about eloping to Vegas before Robert went to the police academy.

Then Jessie sobered. "Please don't joke about stuff like that. Let's agree not to discuss this again until my divorce is final, and you have a ring."

"I've got a ring." Robert held her gaze.

He's not joking.

Her brow furrowed, and she tilted her head, trying to make sense of his words. "When did you buy a ring? I only decided yesterday that I absolutely wanted to stay in Providence."

"I'm not sure it would do any good to tell you." Robert scratched his jaw and dropped his gaze.

Jessie's chest grew tight, and a sense of foreboding swept over her. She had a feeling she was about to be served another giant helping of regret.

"How long have you had the ring, Robert?"

He released her hand and stood. "Let's discuss this later, after your divorce is final."

Jessie stood, too. "No, we need to discuss this now. I need to know."

"I bought it...five years ago. I was going to propose to you...that night."

She dropped back into her chair. "And I dropped a bomb on you, by telling you I was leaving before you could. No wonder you were so upset. I ruined all of your plans for us." She looked up at him, her eyes full of tears again. "I'm so sorry. I was such an idiot. I was so focused on chasing my dreams that I didn't see how hard you were working to make *our* dreams come true."

He knelt in front of her and took her hands in his. "Jessie, don't. It won't change anything."

"You're right. Regret changes nothing." She blinked the tears away. "I won't dwell on it. And my admitting to being an idiot doesn't change the fact that you were an idiot too."

"Me?" He released her hands and stood again.

"Yes, you were an idiot." She stood too and smacked his arm. "You had a ring in your pocket, yet you let me walk out of your life. Only an idiot lets the woman he loves walk away. Besides, what man builds a house without consulting the woman he plans to share it with?"

"You're right, I was an idiot." Robert grinned.

"I love the house, by the way. It's beautiful."

Robert puffed his chest out in a show of pride. He cupped her face in his hands. "I intend to learn from my mistakes, sweetheart. I promise to never let you go again."

His gazed dipped to her lips and his hands tensed. He wanted to seal his promise with a kiss--she could see it on his face.

She wanted that kiss.

He let out a deep groan-like sigh and lowered his hands, his fingertips leaving a trail of fire down the length of her neck. He tugged her into the family room. "Come swing dance with me. I need upbeat music and lots of movement or I'm going to break down and kiss you."

Jessie had a feeling swing dancing would do nothing to dampen the attraction and desire building between them.

ROBERT SENT Daniel a quick text to let him know he was bringing Jessie in before he slid from his truck and walked around to Jessie's door.

He'd kept Jessie out much later than he'd planned, but having her in his home after all these years...

He never wanted her to leave.

Jessie turned to him as they reached the front porch, and once again he fought the urge to pull her into his arms and kiss her. His restraint tonight had been tested to the limits. He should qualify for sainthood.

"Wait here. I have something for you." Jessie disappeared inside the house.

Despite the chilly late-September night, Robert opted to wait outside on the porch, rather than face Daniel's knowing grin. The kid was doing much better, and his joking personality had returned. He frequently teased Robert about marrying Jessie already.

If only it were that easy.

Jessie came back out the door carrying a large, flat package wrapped in brown paper. She gave him a shy smile as she handed it to him.

Warmth settled over Robert, and he sucked in a sharp breath. "You finished it?"

"A while ago." Jessie stuck a fingernail between her teeth.

Why hadn't she given it to him sooner?

Had she been waiting for the time to feel right, just like he'd been waiting to make sure she wouldn't leave again?

He lifted the picture and grabbed the edge of the paper.

"Don't open it yet." She grabbed his hand.

He shot her a questioning glance. She usually liked to see the recipient's reaction to her gifts.

She smiled, and he looked deeper into her amber eyes. He saw a light there that radiated inner peace. Jessie didn't need validation from him that her work was amazing. She knew she'd painted her best work.

He held the picture up in front of his chest to keep himself from pulling her into his arms again. "Thank you, Jess. I can't wait to open it." His next words came out through a clenched jaw. "Now go inside before I kiss you."

She giggled and backed toward the door. "Goodnight, Robert."

"Goodnight." He stepped down a step, then hurried to his truck, knowing Daniel would make sure the door got locked behind Jessie.

In fact, it was a good thing Daniel was in the house, or Robert might have followed Jessie inside.

Anticipation of opening Jessie's painting helped Robert get home much faster than usual. It's a good thing he didn't cross paths with Brady working the night shift; the deputy would have pulled him over just to give him a hard time.

After parking in his garage, he pulled Jessie's painting from the back seat. His hand stilled as he looked at the guitar that had ridden there for the past few weeks. He'd played it several times with Daniel just for fun, and he'd been toying with the idea of learning a new song for Jessie. But he hadn't quite found the courage.

Yet.

He picked up the guitar case with his free hand.

He let himself into the house and set the case on the couch beside him. Laying the painting across the coffee table, he gently pulled back the paper.

His lungs stalled. The painting had looked amazing when he pulled it from the trash, but the finishing touches Jessie had put on it made the image look so real. He could practically smell the fresh air--scented by pines trees and the fresh-water lake--and hear the birds singing in the trees. The gentle waves lapping at the shore appeared to be in motion.

The painting blurred.

Robert blinked away tears and sucked in a sharp breath. *Jessie is so incredibly talented.* He'd meant it when he said he'd support her in her art and follow her to the ends of the earth.

She wanted to stay in here, though.

His chest swelled with gratitude. He'd make sure she never regretted her decision to stay in Providence.

He pulled down the painting of him and Goliath and took it to his bedroom. Tomorrow, he'd hang it--where it would be the last thing he saw at night and the first thing he saw in the morning--but this new painting would sit at the heart of his home. The home he hoped to share with Jessie soon.

He hung the new painting, then stepped back and stared at it. Looking at the beautiful scene would never get old.

Finally, he sat on the couch and pulled his guitar from its case. It was late, but it was time to work on a new song for Jessie.

And he knew just the song.

CHAPTER 36

Patrick lugged the five-gallon jug of gas from the trunk of this week's rental car into the old barn north of Providence. He'd driven past here enough times on his way to the Double Diamond to know the old farmer who owned this remote barn didn't farm anymore. The overgrown weeds and grass in the surrounding fields attested to that.

The barn stood empty except for a few bales of straw, a couple of old wooden buckets, and some rusted farm equipment. Patrick kicked up dust as he crossed to the straw bales. He uncapped the gas can and started pouring.

This was an asinine move but his life was falling apart. Unraveling faster than his Aunt Hattie's crocheting always did. Patrick had to take drastic measures.

Matthews had put him on an unpaid leave of absence weeks ago after a client complained about losing out on millions because Patrick didn't buy the stocks he wanted fast enough. And of course, Patrick was racking up the debt with motel bills and rental cars.

He'd drained his savings several weeks ago to support that Jackson fellow in his campaign for sheriff. A horrible investment, but if it kept Winters from getting re-elected, it was worth it.

Yes, this was a rash, but he needed Jessica to come home, so she could help him pick up the pieces of the life she'd destroyed. He hadn't been able to get close to her yet.

Jessica never left the ranch alone; her mom, the sheriff, or the rancher's pretty wife always accompanied her. And any time he got close to the ranch, the dogs started barking. Patrick was pretty sure he saw a man with a gun on the front porch.

The timing of this distraction was crucial. He needed to get to Jessie before she left school with the rancher's wife.

He grinned as the sweet, yet pungent, aroma of gas filled the musty barn. The last ten weeks, since he'd gotten out of the county jail, had been an exercise in patience. But the countless hours he'd spent watching Sylvia, Winters, and Jessica were all about to pay off.

Patrick would get back what belonged to him.

Winters couldn't focus on his election and keeping Jessica safe if he was trying to find an arsonist. And when Patrick was long gone with Jessica before the flames were even out...

Well, then he will have won.

He dribbled a trail of gasoline to the door, then tossed the jug on the ground. Casting a last look around to make sure he was still alone, he pulled a lighter from his pocket. Flicking it, he watched the flame dance for several long seconds before dropping it on the ground and walking away.

He climbed into his rental car and drove down the dusty lane. This car was barely a step up from the raunchy, puke-colored one his lawyer rented for him months ago, but at least this one didn't reek.

His breathing sped up as he approached the outskirts of town without passing a single other car. It wouldn't have mattered if he had, because he drove a plain white sedan that looked like dozens of other cars here in this backwoods town.

He pulled into the high school parking lot and drove around the back of the building. He still couldn't believe Jessica fancied herself a teacher.

The school bell split the air, and within seconds, the parking lot was chaos. No one paid attention to him as he parked outside the ceramics room. He checked his watch, waiting for his signal.

His heart raced, hammering against his ribcage at the thought of getting Jessica back. They'd leave this Podunk town for good and never look back. Once he had her away from here, he'd convince her to drop the assault charges, and from there, they'd work on getting him cleared of the other charges against him.

The trial for the bogus charges that hot-shot sheriff pressed against him was in three days. His lawyer planned to make it look like the sheriff attacked Patrick, and he'd only defended himself. Apparently, Internal Affairs had already cleared the sheriff of any charges, but Patrick's lawyer still planned to maintain his innocence.

Regardless of the outcome of that trial, Patrick was facing some jail time. But after a full week in that cesspool of a county jail, he refused to go back, even for a few months.

His lawyer would have a heart attack if he knew Patrick was here. But he was determined to get Jessica to drop the assault charges against him before the aggravated assault trial. He needed Jessica by his side.

Not only was the trial for assault and battery against Jessica next week, her lawyer had informed him of a hearing to complete the divorce scheduled for next week as well. But Patrick wouldn't let Jessica go. His entire world was crumbling around him, and he couldn't fight the desperation that kept him imprisoned.

A siren split the air, and Patrick grinned. *Perfect timing.*

The crowd of students leaving the school had thinned, and Patrick climbed from the rental car, confident the few remaining students in the back parking lot weren't paying him any attention. When a second siren joined the first, he tucked the gun he'd brought along--in case Jessica wasn't cooperative--into the back of his waistband.

The last thing he wanted to do was hurt her, but if she didn't do what he said, he'd make her. He had too much at stake right now.

He stepped to the back door of the ceramics lab as a second and third siren joined the first and tried the knob. It was unlocked.

Just like it had been two afternoons ago. He'd almost gotten Jessica then, but she'd left the art room--presumably for a faculty meeting, judging by the announcement he'd heard--as he entered through this door. Forty minutes later, when the janitor came to clean, she still hadn't returned. So Patrick had sneaked out the back door.

Yesterday, Sylvia had appeared out of nowhere right after school, and she and Jessica had driven away. He'd tried to follow them, but he'd gotten stuck in the crush of crazy teenage drivers in the back parking lot and lost her.

Today, he had a plan. While all the emergency personnel and concerned citizens headed north of town to fight the barn fire, he'd be heading south with Jessica.

He stepped into the pottery room and closed the door behind him. It stunk as bad as it had the other day. He'd hated it when Jessica came home smelling like dirt from that pottery studio she used to go to all the time in New York.

That had been one of the first changes he'd made to her routine. Getting her away from her job had taken a little longer because they had needed her income until he'd gotten the raise with his move to Seattle.

At the sound of voices in the adjoining art room, he froze and made sure he was out of sight. He recognized Jessica's warm, alto tones. "This looks amazing, Savannah. You've got great spatial awareness and depth going on here."

The other voice was softer and younger. "Do you really think so, Ms. Jessie?"

Ms. Jessie?

It irked him that she'd gone back to her art after all, but it didn't surprise him. What did surprise him was that she wasn't making the kids call her Mrs. Pendleton. Or maybe she'd gone back to her maiden name.

The blood pulsing through his body heated a few degrees.

"I don't have to tend my brothers tomorrow. Is it okay if I stay after to paint?"

"You're always welcome, Savannah. I'm sorry I had to leave early yesterday for my doctor appointment."

Doctor appointment? So that's where she disappeared to. But what was wrong with her? She wasn't still having problems with her wrist, was she?

It took several seconds for Patrick to realize the student had left and the other room was quiet except for the rustle of papers.

Pasting on his most charming smile, he leaned against the door frame adjoining the two rooms. "Hello, Jessica. Did you miss me?"

CHAPTER 37

No. It can't be.

Jessie dropped the water bottle she'd been drinking from and grabbed her desk. Her hands turned ice cold while her legs melted like hot rubber. How was that possible?

She stared at the man in the doorway.

The voice was Patrick's but the man before her looked nothing like the suave, debonair charmer she'd married. The man she'd married wore nothing less than business casual, unless he was headed to the gym. Yet this man wore faded jeans and a rumpled hooded sweatshirt. Patrick hated hoodies. He thought they looked sloppy, and that only gang members dressed like that.

He also hated facial hair because it looked unprofessional. But the man slowly approaching Jessie had shaggy, unruly hair and a beard. A full beard and cold, hard eyes.

Jessie had seen many unpleasant emotions displayed in Patrick's eyes before, but never any as deadly looking as what she saw there now.

Her racing heart caused her body to tremble, or maybe the trembling was from the sudden chill surrounding her. She stepped sideways, keeping the desk between her and Patrick.

"W-what are you doing here?" She grimaced inwardly at her stutter. "You're not supposed to come within five hundred feet of me."

Patrick held up his hands, palms forward in a pacifying motion. "Come on, honey. I just want to talk to you. Can't we have a nice, civilized conversation?"

Right. It only stays civilized when it goes the way you want it to go.

Jessie didn't for a second believe he'd come just to talk. Patrick always had an ulterior motive. Besides, the cold, menacing look in his eyes didn't match the placating tone of his words.

Jessie's gaze darted to the door, willing Emily to open it and say she needed to leave early today. Every nerve in her body screamed, *Run!*

She'd never be able to outrun Patrick. She glanced at the phone on her desk, wishing she could dial 9-1-1 before he could get to her. But since he was less than eight feet away from her now, there was no way.

She folded her arms across her chest. "Fine. Talk."

He took a step closer. "You're cute when you're being obstinate. Still so beautiful even though you've let yourself go. I'm not a fan of the hair. Brown is so boring. And the baggy shirt? Really, it just makes you look like you've put on weight."

Jessie resisted the urge to press her hand to her stomach. She expected him to say something about her being pregnant, but he didn't. In fact, he didn't seem to have noticed her rounded belly at all. The last thing she wanted was to draw attention to it.

She'd declared her pregnancy in the divorce paperwork, but knowing Patrick, he was probably so furious when he received the paperwork, he'd destroyed it without even reading it.

Compared to how much Emily showed with her shorter, more petite frame, Jessie was barely showing. But she felt the difference in her own body. A difference that necessitated wearing leggings instead of jeans and loose t-shirts.

Jessie still hadn't gotten around to buying maternity clothes yet, because she still feared she might lose this baby. After seeing her perfectly formed baby in the ultrasound yesterday, though, and finding out she was having a boy, she'd felt so closely connected to her child. She'd be devastated if she lost him.

She recalled something Emily said weeks ago when Jessie admitted she was having a hard time getting Patrick out of her head. "If you understand his motivations for treating you like he did, then you'll stop falling for his mind games. He'll no longer have any power over you."

Jessie had thought long and hard about that. She remembered the cutting, spiteful way Patrick's father spoke to him every time they were around the domineering man. She'd quickly learned to keep her mouth shut around him. Just like Patrick's mother did. No matter how hard Patrick tried to please his father, he never seemed to measure up to the bar Parker Pendleton set for his only child.

And no matter how hard Jessie tried, she couldn't measure up to the bar Patrick set for her. It didn't help that every time he raised the bar; he cut her down first. Jessie refused to play his mind games. She wouldn't allow him to hurt her with his words.

"You drove four hours to stand here cutting me down with your passive-aggressive compliments?"

He folded his arms too, mimicking her posture. Except his stance was wider, his shoulders broader, his demeanor hard and unrelenting. "Why don't we take a drive, so we can find a quiet place to talk?"

No way! If she left with him, she'd never see her mother or Robert again. Her stomach revolted. Of all the times for her sporadic morning sickness to surface, now was the worst. She sucked in a slow, deep breath through her nose.

"It's quiet here." Jessie congratulated herself on how calm her voice sounded when she felt anything but.

"Until the janitor comes." Patrick looked at the clock above the classroom door. "In about twenty minutes, right? Or the rancher's pretty wife tells you she's ready to leave."

How did he know that she usually left with Emily? Or when the janitor came to clean her room?

Unless he's been here before.

Another icy chill swept over Jessie, and she felt the blood drain from her face.

"You're mine, Jessica." The coldness in Patrick's voice matched the chilling temperature of his gaze. "I told you I'd never let you go, and I meant it." He unfolded his arms and stepped closer to the desk.

Jessie stepped back.

"I know everything about you, honey. I know you're still staying at the Double Diamond. I'm know you think you're protecting your mother by staying away, but between you and me, she looks kind of lonely in the evenings. I also know you go out with that hot-shot sheriff on Wednesdays and Saturday nights." Patrick's lips curled in an evil grin. "The two of you looked pretty cozy last Saturday."

How long had Patrick been following her? Though his words sounded like casual observations, his tone was anything but. They may as well have been outright threats.

Another chill swept over Jessie, and she struggled to take in a deep breath. The warmth that filled her every time she thought about how swing dancing with Robert had led to them slowly swaying to the music, their bodies pressed close together, vanished.

If I don't go with him, he'll hurt my mom and Robert, maybe even Emily. But if I go with him, he'll kill me.

"It's time for us to go, honey. While Winters and his deputies are busy with the fire."

"Fire?" Is that where all the sirens she heard a few minutes ago were headed? "What have you done, Patrick?"

"Only what needed to be done. I couldn't have witnesses... I mean, an audience while I took my wife away from this backwoods town."

"I'm not going anywhere with you." Jessie stood her ground, even though she trembled inside and feared she might vomit any second.

"Oh, but you are." He pulled a gun from the back of his waistband. "I'm sure you understand it's the only way to keep your mom and your beloved sheriff safe."

Jessie feared her heart might explode as her inner trembling took over her entire body. "Please don't do this Patrick. This is not who you are."

"You have no idea who I am anymore!" Patrick snarled. His eyes filled with wild desperation, like a trapped animal ready to lash out at the first sign of a threat. "You ruined me! And your boyfriend..." the word was full of contempt, "attacked me and put me in jail. I was incarcerated for an entire week. Trapped like a common criminal with a filthy psychotic drug addict."

Patrick still hadn't learned to take responsibility for his actions. Everything that had gone wrong in his life was always someone else's fault.

"You hurt me, Patrick. Again and again, you beat me." Jessie fought to keep the emotion out of her voice. If Patrick knew how terrified she was, he'd used it to beat her down.

Patrick sneered. "Only because you couldn't learn your place. You brought your punishment upon yourself. Just like a dog who disobeys his master."

Jessie couldn't believe the words she was hearing. There had been many times when Patrick had been irrational, but he'd never sounded this deranged.

She squared her shoulders. "I am not a dog, and you are not my master."

With lightning speed, Patrick darted around the desk.

Jessie bolted for the door, but he grabbed her arm and jerked her back, nearly pulling her off her feet.

"You're coming with me." He shoved the barrel of the gun into her ribs. "Or else."

Jessie gasped. "Okay. Calm down, please. I'll go with you." She didn't have a choice. Did she?

No. Not if I want to protect my mother and Robert. Her heart broke at the thought of never seeing Robert again. Her disappearance would crush him.

"This is calm, honey. If you don't believe me, I dare you to try me." Patrick shoved her toward the back door.

Jessie fought the tears that sprang to her eyes. She'd finally found where she belonged, found fulfillment in her life. And now it was all being taken away.

Why would God do this to her? Was she still being punished for walking away from everything He'd given her five years ago?

When Patrick pushed open the door to the back parking lot, her gaze darted around, searching for help. But the lot was nearly empty, with only a smattering of cars. Two lone boys stood in the far corner watching the secondary fire engine with the volunteer firefighters drive past, sirens wailing.

If she screamed, no one would hear her.

Patrick opened the back door of a white Nissan. "Get in!" When Jessie resisted, he grabbed a handful of hair and jerked her head back. "You get in the back seat and lay down, or I'll shove you into the trunk."

Not daring to fight him, but knowing going with him meant she'd never see Robert or Providence again, she climbed in the car and lay on the back seat. She squeezed her eyes closed to keep the tears at bay and pressed her hands to her chest.

Her fists met the hard plastic of her cell phone between her breasts. When she'd dressed in her leggings this morning and found herself without pockets, she'd slipped her cell phone down her bra. She normally left it on her desk during school, but she'd forgotten to take it out after lunch.

"Keep location sharing on." Robert's words filled her head.

Hope shot through her like an electric shock.

She kept a close eye on Patrick as he pulled onto Main Street and turned south. As soon as she was sure he was focused on his driving, she pulled the cell phone from under her shirt. Keeping her right hand pressed to her chest, she moved her left hand with the cell phone down by her hip, out of Patrick's line of sight, should he look back.

Robert was the last person she'd texted, so it didn't take long to find his name. Her thumb swiped across the keyboard in a frantic motion: *He found me*

She hit send with an urgency that mounted with every passing second.

If Robert was dealing with a fire, would he even get her text?

Desperate, she sent a second text: *He has a gun*

CHAPTER 38

Robert's phone vibrated in his pocket as he directed the fire truck driven by the volunteer firefighters closer to the burning barn while he kept the onlookers at bay. He didn't have time to answer any calls or texts right now.

It vibrated again, and the persistent feeling that drove him to the cabin the night Pendleton came after Jessie hit him like an ice-cold wave that warred with the heat coming off the barn behind him.

Check your phone.

Unable to argue with the voice in his head, he pulled the phone from his pocket. His blood turned cold as he read the texts from Jessie on its screen.

He found me

He has a gun

Robert's heart stalled. He looked at the old structure being consumed by the flames. The barn was far enough gone that the firefighters were focusing the spray from their hoses onto the surrounding grass to prevent this from turning into a wildfire. There was nothing he could do to make a difference here. But if he hurried, maybe he could save Jessie.

He turned toward the closest deputy--Brady.

"I need to go. Pendleton's got Jessie, and he's armed."

"Go. We've got this." Brady said without hesitation. "Call if you need back-up. I'll call Rudy and Vickie, see if they can come on duty early."

Robert shouted instructions at him about keeping everyone away from the fire as he headed to his Tahoe. He climbed into his SUV and opened the app that tracked Jessie's phone. He wanted to call her to see if she was okay, but he knew that would only endanger her more.

If she'd been able to send him a text, Pendleton obviously didn't know she had a phone. He checked Jessie's location as he started the engine. Her blue dot moved south on U.S. 395.

His heart sank. *He's taking her away.* If Pendleton made it to the Tri-Cities area with Jessie, or heaven forbid, back to Seattle, it could make it more difficult to find Jessie.

He started his truck and cranked the wheel, spraying gravel as he floored it. His lights were already flashing, and as soon as he pulled away from the fire, he turned on his siren.

What if I don't get to her in time?

He checked his phone. The blue dot still moved. That was the only thing giving him hope right now.

She's going to be okay. She has to be. I can't lose her again.

He glanced at the blue dot a few minutes later as he entered the interstate. His heart stuttered. The dot had stopped moving.

Keeping an eye on the road, he repeatedly checked Jessie's location. The dot stayed frozen on the outskirts of Pasco. Robert tried to recall what was in that area. The gravel pit? A trailer park? A seedy motel?

He radioed the office. "Janice, I need you to ping this number and give me an exact location." He rattled off Jessie's number and waited several long, tense seconds--his foot heavy on the gas--until Janice got back to him.

He was more grateful than ever that he'd used some of the donation money last fall to invest in the high-tech location services program.

Thank you, Emily.

"It looks like it's at the Lazy Daze Motel just north of Pasco." Janice's voice filled his vehicle.

Motel. Was that a good thing or a bad thing? Pendleton wouldn't take Jessie to a motel if he intended to kill her outright. Would he?

Imagining Jessie suffering more violence--any kind of violence--at the hands of that man enraged Robert.

"Find out if anyone by the name of Patrick Pendleton or someone fitting his description has a room. And remember he's got facial hair now."

"Sure thing. What's going on?"

"I'll fill you in after you get me a room number." Robert ended the call.

He checked again to make sure the dot hadn't moved, then stuffed the phone into its holder so he could focus on the road. Fortunately, traffic was light, and he quickly closed the distance between him and Jessie.

Please don't let me be too late.

He jumped when his radio crackled. He snatched it up. "Go, Janice."

"There's no one by the name of Pendleton registered there, but when I described him, the motel clerk and he said that sounded like the guy in room twenty-three."

"Twenty-three. Got it, thanks."

"Robert, what's going on?"

"Pendleton's got Jessie, and he's armed."

"Please tell me you're not going after him alone. Have you got back up?"

"Contact the Pasco police and have them send some. I have to go."

He should have brought some of his own deputies, but they were needed at the fire, and he couldn't wait for the Pasco police to arrive.

He needed to get to Jessie now.

JESSIE'S STOMACH lurched when the car came to a stop much sooner than she expected, although it felt like they'd been driving forever. She was both relieved Patrick wasn't taking her any farther away from Robert and scared to death about what he intended to do to her.

She checked the floor behind the front passenger seat, where she'd hidden her cell phone to make sure it wasn't visible. If Patrick killed her and left her here--wherever here was--he'd take evidence with him.

He opened the back door. "Get out!"

Jessie scooted from the car. Her stomach took a nosedive at the sight of the dilapidated motel surrounded by barren fields. Only two other cars sat in the long, narrow parking lot.

Nowhere to run and no one to hear her scream.

The fear that filled her, combined with the morning sickness and car sickness, was all it took to bring her lunch up. She tried to turn away from Patrick, but he had her pinned against the car.

She tried to shove him back, but he didn't budge. "I'm going to be sick!"

Patrick jumped back, but not fast enough. Vomit splattered his jeans and shoes. He let loose a string of swear words.

He grabbed Jessie's arm in a bruising grip and dragged her toward the motel. Fishing a key from his pocket, he unlocked the door, cursing the entire time.

She grabbed the door frame as he tried to push her into the room. If he got her behind closed doors, she was in trouble. The chance of someone seeing them out here was slim, but at least there was a chance. He'd be less likely to hurt her if they had an audience.

Patrick leaned against her back with the gun pressed to her ribs. His breath, hot against her ear, sent a shudder of revulsion through her. "If you don't move, Jessica, I will move you."

Before she could even shift her body, he wrapped a hand around her waist. His palm pressed against her slightly rounded abdomen. He gasped and shifted his hand across her stomach, feeling the swell of the child that grew inside her.

Without warning, he shoved her through the door. "You filthy little--" Not even the slamming of the door could mute the string of vile labels he hurled at her.

Jessie stumbled into the dim hotel room, catching herself against the bed. She stood and backed away from him, placing a protective hand on her stomach.

He pointed the gun at her, a sneer on his face. "You must have jumped into bed with him the day you left me."

It was clear he thought she carried was Robert's child, and Jessie didn't bother to correct him. Patrick was so far gone right now she doubted knowing the baby was his would change anything.

"No, the day I left you, I spent the night in the hospital with a concussion and a broken wrist."

Patrick whirled on her, leveling the gun at her abdomen. He pulled a dingy padded chair away from a small desk. "Sit!" He motioned to the chair with the gun. "And don't even think about moving."

Jessie thought about moving alright. She thought about bolting out the door and screaming for help. But Patrick stood between her and the door, and there was no one outside to help her.

She sank into the chair but stayed wary, her eyes never leaving him. When he unzipped his pants, Jessie realized he intended to change out of the vomit covered jeans. She let her eyes roam the room, searching for something--anything--she could use as a weapon.

She grimaced at the dingy olive-green bedspread as the stench in the room hit her--a musty combination of dust, stale body odor, and bodily fluids.

She shuddered. *What a dive!*

Why had Patrick rented a room in such a seedy motel?

Her stomach bottomed out. If he intended to leave her for dead, what better place to do it than in some hovel.

The only thing movable, besides the chair she sat in, was a tall lamp with a thick ceramic base. Her gaze followed the cord to the cracked outlet cover on the wall beside the desk. It wouldn't be difficult to yank the cord from the wall, but the lamp shade would make swinging the lamp difficult.

"Here's the deal." Gun in hand, Patrick--now clad in clean jeans--

stood stocking-footed on carpet that made the bedspread look clean enough to snuggle in.

She marveled at the depths Patrick had sunk to. He was right: She didn't know him at all. Which made him even more terrifying.

"You're going to call the Seattle Police Department and tell them you want to drop the charges against me."

"It doesn't work like that, Patrick. If I make the call under duress, it won't be legally binding."

He grabbed a pen and a 5 X 7 pad of paper from the desk drawer and slapped them down in front of her. "Then start writing! As soon as you're done, we'll head back to Seattle and you can deliver your statement first thing in the morning."

No way would she go back to Seattle with him. It terrified Jessie to defy Patrick, but if she didn't stand up to him, his power over her would forever haunt her.

She pushed the pad and pen away. "I won't write it. You need to pay for what you did to me."

Patrick was on her in a flash. He grabbed hair and yanked her out of the grimy chair. "You'll do what I tell you, do you hear me?"

Pain seared Jessie's scalp as tears stung her eyes. She bit her tongue to keep herself from screaming out. It would only anger him more.

The words Jessie had written on the last pages of the black journal--before putting it away and vowing to never get it out again except to take to court next week--filled her mind.

The letter Emily had counseled her to write to her abuser had filled several pages. The exercise helped her siphon off the negative emotions that kept her from moving forward in her life. She'd unloaded her heavy emotional baggage on those pages and in the process gained a measure of freedom.

But now, writing the words in a letter she never intended to send didn't feel like enough. Patrick should hear them from her. They probably wouldn't help her situation, but she needed to say them.

"I'm sorry," she said, barely above a whisper.

His hold on her hair loosened. "You'd better be."

"No, I'm sorry I couldn't love you the way you wanted me to. I kept thinking if I just tried a little harder to be a better wife, I could make you happy."

Patrick released her hair and stepped back, eyes wide.

Jessie took an additional step back. "But I've realized something since I left. You can't love someone else if you don't love yourself first. And despite your confidence and charm, I don't think you ever loved yourself."

Patrick's face turned crimson, and he lashed out so fast Jessie didn't have time to flinch.

The handle of the gun struck her cheek below the right eye with a force that knocked her off her feet. She fell against the small desk, hitting her stomach against the corner.

Half bent over, supporting herself with one hand against the desk, she wrapped her other arm around her stomach to protect her baby. Pain ricocheted through her side and face, blurring her vision. A sensation of warmth crept down her cheek. *Blood.*

"How dare you mock me?"

She sucked in a deep breath, trying to block out the pain. "I'm not mocking you. Over the past few months, I realized why you're this way. Nothing you did was ever good enough for your father. You never learned to love yourself because he didn't love you. And your mother never stood up for you for fear of retaliation from him."

The strike this time came from the left, and with nothing for Jessie to catch herself on, she went down, cradling her stomach. Her head slammed into the leg of the chair, and darkness crowded in.

Patrick loomed over her with the gun as she fought to stay conscious.

Knowing it wouldn't help, Jessie did the only thing she could. She screamed.

CHAPTER 39

Robert turned off his siren as he approached the Lazy Daze Motel. No need to alert Pendleton of his presence. He stopped his Tahoe a few doors away from room twenty-three and jumped out.

He skidded to a halt.

Get your vest! The voice inside his head that had guided him so many times in his life screamed at him now.

He hated wasting precious time to put his bulletproof vest on because Jessie could be bleeding to death.

Robert took a deep breath. He needed to be smart about this and do this by the book, not with his heart. As badly as he wanted to race in and save Jessie, he wouldn't be any good to her if he got shot.

He watched the window of unit twenty-three as he darted to the back of his vehicle. He pulled his vest from the SUV and strapped it on. He checked his firearm to ensure it was loaded with the safety off.

He sent a prayer heavenward as he approached the door of room twenty-three. *Please don't let me be too late.*

Robert attempted to get a look inside through the window, but the curtains were closed too tightly. He deliberated whether to knock and announce himself or to kick the door in. Would announcing himself give Pendleton the opportunity to hurt or kill Jessie? Provided he wasn't already too late.

A vice tightened around his heart. *I can't lose her again.*

A woman screamed on the other side of the door, and Robert's heart thundered in his chest.

He braced himself, back to the door, and kicked with the force of a wild stallion. Spinning, he pulled his gun from its holster and stepped into the room, willing his eyes to adjust to the dim light inside.

A dark figure in the middle of the room swung toward him.

Jessie screamed just as Robert saw a bright flash and heard the deafening report of a gun. A sharp, searing pain tore into his left shoulder. Instinctively, he fired at the still shadowy figure, aiming at where the flash had been.

His own gun flashed, followed by a second flash from the shooter. The bullet hit Robert's chest, knocking the breath from him and propelling him back.

He went down hard. His head struck the concrete, and dark, heavy shadows filled the edges of his vision.

"No!" Jessie screamed when Robert went down. Pain ripped through her chest at the horror of seeing him take a bullet.

I need to get to him. She put her hands on the filthy carpet to push herself upright.

Her fingers met the barrel of Patrick's gun.

Patrick moaned and shifted.

Jessie's fingers wrapped around the butt of the handgun, and she pushed herself upright until her back rested against the bed.

I won't let him hurt me again.

Groaning, Patrick staggered to his feet. A dark red stain discolored his hoodie high on his left shoulder. His eyes frantically searched for the gun. He froze when he spotted it in Jessie's hand, his eyes widening. Then, as though he'd flipped a switch, he smiled and turned pleading, puppy-dog eyes on her.

She used to think he was cute when he did that while they were dating. Now, it only sickened her. Because she recognized it for the manipulative ploy that it was.

"Give me the gun, Jessica." His voice held only the slightest hesitation.

She swallowed hard. "No."

The pleading expression turned to one of contrition. "Honey. I'm so sorry for hitting you. I promise I'll never do it again." He stepped closer.

"You're right, you won't. Because I won't let you." Jessie had heard his lies too many times before. She refused to be his punching bag any longer. She raised the gun a little, and he stopped advancing.

Disbelief flashed across his face before turning to rage. His cheeks turned red, and the veins on his forehead bulged. "The little mouse finds herself a new man and starts painting again, and now suddenly she's full of confidence? Too bad the sheriff only wants you for your body."

He pulled the lamp off the desk and yanked the cord from the wall in one fluid motion. It took him only a second to dispose of the bulky shade. "If he really cared about you, he wouldn't have abandoned you at that ranch. I guess it doesn't matter now though, does it? Since I killed him."

Jessie's eyes burned with unshed tears as a piercing ache consumed her chest. She wouldn't fall for Patrick's mind games again. Everything Robert had done, he'd done because he loved her. He knew what Jessie needed better than she did, and he'd given it to her. The Double Diamond was exactly where she'd needed to be these last few months.

Patrick loomed over her, sneering and threatening. "You're too gutless. You'd never dare pull the trigger." He raised the lamp above his head. "You're just a worthless piece of--"

Jessie blocked out Patrick's degrading words and gripped the gun with both hands. She aimed it at his chest.

No. I don't want to kill him.

She lowered the gun a few inches, closed her eyes, and squeezed the trigger.

~

JESSIE'S SCREAM pushed its way through the dark fog filling Robert's head.

I've got to get to her.

Sitting up, he gasped for air. He shook off the dizzying effects of hitting his head and winced at the pain shooting through his skull.

Jessie's soft voice reached him again, followed by Patrick's deeper one. Robert couldn't make sense of the words, but Pendleton's angry tones drove him to his feet. He retrieved his gun that lay a few feet away and grabbed a hold of the door frame, waiting for the world to stop spinning and wishing the burning in his shoulder would go away already.

Pendleton blocked Robert's view of Jessie, but he could tell she cowered on the floor near the bed. Pendleton raised a thick lamp above his head, and Robert's blood turned cold as he read the man's intentions.

Patrick could kill Jessie if he struck her hard enough.

He tensed, preparing to shoot the man in the back.

A gunshot exploded through the air, and Robert jerked. It took him a full three seconds to realize he hadn't taken another bullet.

Jessie.

Robert's mind reeled. Had Pendleton somehow exchanged the lamp for a gun and shot Jessie? His stomach dropped at the thought.

Robert surveyed the room. The smell of gunpowder hung in the air.

Pendleton lay on the floor, groaning, and Jessie sat--back to the bed, eyes closed--gripping a handgun.

"Jess!" Relief flooded over Robert, weakening his knees. He holstered his weapon and stepped into the room.

Jessie's eyes popped open. "Robert? You're alive?" She tossed the gun on the floor as though it had burned her. "Did I kill him?"

Pendleton groaned again as Robert dropped to one knee beside him. He checked the bullet wound he'd given him--in the shoulder--and the one Jessie had given--him in the thigh. Both had ripped clean through the muscle and didn't bleed profusely. They would hurt like crazy, but Pendleton wouldn't bleed to death.

"Nope." Robert said. It was a good thing Jessie was the one who shot the man, because if Robert had shot him, Pendleton *would* be dead.

Robert flipped Pendleton over amid a howl of pain and cuffed him. He left him lying face down on the disgusting carpet that now sported smears of Pendleton's blood. With two bullet wounds, he wasn't going anywhere.

He turned to Jessie. His gaze roamed over her body, searching for signs of injury. Relief washed over him when he didn't see any immediate signs of injury. His blood turned hot, however, at the sight of blood on her cheek and the bruises forming there. He dropped to his knees in front of her and carefully placed a hand on her cheek and searched her face for signs of pain.

"Are you hurt anywhere besides your face? Is the baby okay?" If something happened to her baby, he'd never forgive himself for not being there for her when she needed him. He didn't want Jessie to lose another baby. And he didn't want to lose Jessie.

"I'm fine, I think." Putting her hand to her side, she winced as she sat up straighter. "I hit my side on the corner of the desk, but I think it's just bruised."

Robert saw the concern in her eyes, though. He couldn't stand it any longer. He pulled her into his arms. "Oh Jess, I was so afraid I wouldn't make it to you in time. I can't bear to lose you again."

Jessie clung to him. "I knew you would come. You've always been there for me. But I saw him shoot you--" She choked back a sob and pulled back enough to study his bullet-proof vest. She poked at the bullet embedded in the chest of his vest, and her eyes filled with tears.

"I'm fine," he said. "I promised I would always be here for you. I meant it then, and I mean it now."

Giving in to the emotionally charged atmosphere between them, he pressed his lips to hers in a heated kiss, releasing all the fear of the past thirty minutes and the frustration of the past three months. Jessie was still married, but Robert didn't care. The man lying in handcuffs didn't deserve her, and Robert needed to let her know how much she meant to him.

Jessie's lips parted, and she returned the kiss, matching the passion that ignited inside him.

Kissing Jessie had always given Robert a glimpse of heaven, and today was no different, despite this filthy motel room and the fact that her sorry excuse of a husband lay behind him. Robert took his time exploring her mouth. Her kiss tasted the same as it always had, but the flavor was richer and deeper than he remembered.

Jessie's lips moved with his and he realized it was a good thing they hadn't allowed themselves to share this intimacy before now, because Robert didn't want to stop. He never wanted to let her go.

Jessie gasped and pulled back. She put both hands on her stomach. "The baby's moving. What a relief."

"Are you sure?" He put his large hand near her belly and paused. She took it and pressed it to the right side of her abdomen. After a moment, a soft bump tapped his palm, and something expanded in his chest.

A smile took over his face. "I felt him. That's so cool." His smile faded. "I'm glad he's okay, but you're still going to the hospital." Squeezing the button on the radio clipped to his collar, he radioed Janice giving her a report of the situation and requested two ambulances.

"What about you?" She asked. When he frowned at her, she pointed to his arm. "You need to go to the hospital too."

Robert raised his sleeve and winced. He was so relieved Jessie was okay that he'd blocked out the burning in his shoulder. But now, it felt like someone pushed a hot branding iron into his skin.

"It's just a flesh wound." His voice came out tighter than he intended.

"Yeah, that's what they always say...in the movies." Then her voice grew serious. "But this isn't a movie."

"No, this isn't a movie, and it hurts like crazy, but tell me..." He gently stroked her bruised cheek. "Do I at least get the girl?"

Jessie wrapped her arms around his neck and pulled him in for another kiss.

Robert needed no more invitation than that. He gathered her in his arms and got lost in her kiss.

CHAPTER 40

Robert's Uncle James, also known as Dr. Young, tied off the last stitch and clipped the thread. "I kept the stitches small, but with ten of them, you're going to end up with a nice scar."

Just what Robert needed, a reminder of how close he'd come to losing Jessie today. He shifted to slide off the table, but Uncle James stopped him with a hand on his shoulder.

"Thank you." When Robert frowned in confusion, Uncle James continued. "I'm sure you're smart enough to realize, if you hadn't put your vest on..." He looked at the ugly bruise on Robert's left pectoral, right below where his badge usually rests. "I'd be doing your autopsy tonight instead of stitching up your shoulder."

Robert acknowledged his uncle's words with a nod. And sent another silent *"thank you"* heavenward. It wasn't the first he'd sent today, and it wouldn't be the last. He had so many things to be grateful for tonight.

He thanked his uncle, then slipped out of the ER. He needed to find Jessie.

"Robert!" Uncle James called him back. "Wait a second." He ducked into a nearby room and came out a few seconds later with a blue scrub top. He tossed it at Robert. "You better cover up or you'll have all the nurses swooning and wanting to tend to your wounds."

Robert laughed as he caught the shirt. For all his uncle's seriousness, he had a cool sense of humor.

Less than a minute later, Robert knocked on the door of Jessie's hospital room before slowly opening it. His heart raced at the sight of her sitting on the bed.

"How are you?" he asked.

"I'm fine." She smiled, and his heart skipped a beat. She was so incredibly beautiful.

He sat on the edge of her bed. She scooted over, making more room for him, and he claimed it.

"If that were the case, the paramedics wouldn't have insisted on bringing you to the hospital."

She looked fine other than the bruises on both cheeks, including a small butterfly bandage over her right cheekbone. But her blood pressure had been high, so the paramedics had insisted she go to the hospital.

Watching her leave in the ambulance had been hard, but he was glad someone was looking after her. Especially since he had to stay behind and give a statement to the Pasco police and fill out the mountain of paperwork every cop faced after firing their side arm.

He'd been sure in his written testimony to specify that Pendleton had been about to strike Jessie over the head with the heavy ceramic lamp. A blow that could have killed her. Jessie shooting her husband was clearly self-defense.

"Yeah, well after a good night's rest, I'm sure my blood pressure will be fine." She picked up a paper from the bedside table and handed it to him. "And I have ultrasound proof that the baby is fine, too."

Robert took the picture and stared at the grainy black-and-white image. He'd never seen an ultrasound picture--except the one Jake had so proudly shown him last month. When his brother had pointed out the head and balled up fists, Robert had to hold back a laugh. Because he couldn't make sense of what Jake was so proud of. But in this picture, he recognized what must surely be the baby's head and the bones in his legs bent up close to his chest. He also had one tiny hand by his face, waving.

Robert counted five tiny, perfect fingers. The feeling of expansion he'd experienced at the motel pressed against his chest again, stealing his breath. He locked gazes with Jessie, letting his hand hover over her abdomen, seeking permission to touch her.

"He's not moving right now, but you're welcome to feel." She pressed his hand to her stomach, keeping it pinned there with hers.

Robert had never been so in awe. The child she carried wasn't his, but he was ready to stake his claim as the baby's father. He cleared his throat to rid it of the lump that formed there.

"I thought your mom would be here."

"She was, but I told her to go get some dinner. Knowing her, she'll be back in about thirty minutes and will probably end up spending the night here."

Good. That gave Robert a little time alone with Jessie. He wanted to insist he be the one to spend the night with her, but he was so exhausted he could barely stand up straight.

After nearly losing Jessie and the baby today, he didn't want to leave her side, but if he didn't, he feared she'd see him break down. He needed a little time alone to process and compartmentalize what had happened today before he could let it go and move on. Not only had he almost lost Jessie today, he'd nearly shot a man.

He didn't want Jessie to witness his weakness. He needed to be strong for her.

Her brow creased. "Please tell me he won't get out of jail again."

"With two counts of attempted murder on top of his aggravated assault, and the arson charges, he'll be behind bars for a good twenty years or more."

Relief filled her face.

He cupped her cheek with his hand. "I'm so glad you're okay."

"I'm glad you're okay, too." Jessie leaned into his hand. "When I saw you go down after that second shot..." Her voice wavered.

"Sh... I'm fine and you're fine. That's all that matters."

"No, it's not. What matters is that I love you, Robert. And I'm so sorry for everything I put us both through--recently and five years ago."

Robert pressed a finger to her lips. "I'm sorry, too. I never should have let you leave. I should have worked harder to give you a reason to stay. Because I've loved you since our first date." He leaned in and pressed a kiss to the hollow below her ear, smiling when she shivered. "I promise I'll never let you go again. No matter what." He gently kissed her temple. "And if you want to leave Providence someday, I'll go with you. I don't care where you go, I will follow you."

He pressed his lips to her forehead, then replaced his lips with his forehead. "I want to kiss you again like I did at the motel, but I don't dare."

"Why?" The single word came out breathy.

"Because it's not appropriate for me to kiss you the way I want when you're technically still married." He played with a lock of her hair, trying to distract himself from the desire coursing through him.

"Patrick broke our wedding vows a long time ago. And as far as I'm concerned, he ceased being my husband the minute he tried to kill me."

She slipped a hand behind his head and pulled him in until his lips touched hers. The kiss was hesitant. He stopped resisting and pressed his lips more firmly against hers. The kiss was suddenly no longer gentle. It held all the pain and sorrow of years filled with regret and disappointment mixed with the passion of their youth.

Robert reveled in the feel of her mouth on his. So familiar, yet new and different. Jessie was the one he was meant to be with forever. He'd never tire of kissing her.

"I'm not going anywhere," she whispered when the kiss finally broke. "I should have realized a long time ago Providence has everything I want and the only thing I really need. You."

He resisted the urge to pull her back into his arms and kiss her again.

"I love you, Robert, but I don't want to jump into a relationship too quickly." She chewed on a fingernail, and Robert's heart sank at her words. "Please don't be mad. I just need a little time to make sure I know who I am without Patrick's threats hanging over me. You deserve a whole woman when we get married."

Robert couldn't help the grin that took over his face.

"Why are you smiling? I thought you'd be mad."

"I'm smiling because I don't recall asking you to marry me, yet," he teased.

"I'm pretty sure I remember you saying something about putting a ring on my finger and springing for tickets to Vegas last weekend?" She laughed and smacked his bad shoulder.

He winced and flinched away.

"I'm so sorry. I didn't mean to hit you there." She put her hand on his chest and though she didn't press hard, the flesh below the scrub shirt was tender enough that he captured her hand and held it in his.

"I'm also smiling because you *are* going to marry me, eventually. I'm a very patient man, in case you haven't noticed." He kissed her knuckles. "Take all the time you need, but just know that I plan to make myself a nuisance, because I'm not letting you out of my sight again."

CHAPTER 41

Robert relaxed and put his arm across the back of the sofa in his family room. Jessie snuggled into him like he'd hoped she would.

"Phew, finally, a weekend that we don't need to go to Seattle," said Jessie as she laid her head against his shoulder.

Robert had made three different trips to Seattle with Jessie over the past three weeks. The first, for her divorce hearing, where the judge, after learning of the abuse Jessie had suffered along with all the charges against Patrick, not only granted the divorce, but awarded Jessie half of all Patrick's assets.

The second trip had been for Jessie to get anything she wanted from the house in Seattle, which had been very little, and to sell Patrick's Lexus along with her Infiniti. And last week's trip had been to Patrick's lawyer's office to sign paperwork for her share of Patrick's investments, and paperwork for the estate sale.

"Is Patrick's lawyer going to take care of the sale of the house and everything else from here on out?"

"Yes, he'll split the proceeds from the estate sale and the equity of the house after it sells, and send me a check. There's not much equity in the house, since we'd only been in it a year, but the real estate agent said the market is good right now."

"That's good." Jessie would have a sizable nest egg when everything wrapped up.

Not that she needed it, because Robert had every intention of marrying her as soon as possible. Then he'd take care of her and their child. He hoped she'd be willing to have few more children in the coming years.

As if on cue, Jessie put her hand on the side of her belly. "He's moving."

Robert placed his hand beside hers and gently pressed. He'd been able to feel the baby moving often lately. It was always only just a slight bump against his palm, despite Jessie's growing belly, but it made Robert's chest swell.

The child she carried wasn't biologically his, but he'd vowed to love him and raise him as his own. He couldn't wait until he could see the baby's movement, like Ben now could on Amy's belly.

Jessie turned and looked up at him. The joy on her face filled him with happiness. Oh, how he loved this woman.

Baby forgotten, he lowered his lips to hers, and she shifted her body toward him. He moved his hand from her stomach to her hair, pressing his mouth more firmly against hers.

They had shared many passionate kisses over the past few weeks, each one becoming a little more reckless. The passion between them grew deeper each time they touched, and Robert feared he would burst into flames one of these days. He ached to be one with Jessie.

Having to take her home each night was torture. He wanted to bring her into the home he'd built for her, carry her to the master bedroom, and shut the world out for a long, long time.

The desire that had been burning in him for the past four weeks intensified, and Robert knew he'd be in trouble if he didn't put some distance between him and Jessie. He tore his lips away from hers with a groan.

He'd promised her he would be patient, but with Pendleton

permanently behind bars, and Jessie's divorce final, his patience had worn thin.

He pushed himself off the couch and stood in front of the window, looking into the darkness of his backyard. He still couldn't believe Pendleton had been here and watched him and Jessie, and Robert had no clue. The thought sickened him and made him feel like a failure as a law enforcement officer.

"Is something wrong?" Jessie's hand landed on his shoulder.

"Nothing I can't handle." The words came out a growl. *Maybe.*

She slid her arms around him and rested her cheek against his back. "Talk to me, please."

"I can't right now, sweetheart."

"Why?" That one word held so much tension.

"Because I promised I wouldn't rush you."

"Does this have to do with that thing we agreed not to discuss until my divorce was final?"

Robert gave a grunt of agreement.

Jessie walked around in front of him and slipped her arms around him again. "My divorce was final two weeks ago."

"Yep."

Her rounded stomach pressed against his. And Robert hoped they'd get to have a honeymoon before the baby came.

"But I told you at the hospital I didn't want to rush this."

"Yep."

Jessie looked at him through half-closed lashes. "What word am I supposed to say?"

"What do you mean?" Robert's heart leapt in his throat.

"A few weeks ago, you said all I had to do is say the word, and you'd put your ring on my finger and book the church. Or was it Vegas?" She gave him a smile so big his heart stumbled. "But I don't know what word I'm supposed to say."

"Please don't toy with me, Jess. I've waited way longer than any man should have to wait to marry the love of his life."

"I'm not toying with you. I'm confident with who I am now, and I know what I want." She smiled again, and his heart raced again.

"Are you sure? It might kill me, but I can wait until you're ready." He puffed out his chest in a show of bravado.

Jessie rolled her eyes. "Tell me the word I need to say."

Robert couldn't hold back a grin. "Tell me you love me and promise to never leave me again."

"That's..." She thought for a minute. "Like ten words." But before Robert could comment, she cupped his face and gazed into his eyes. "Robert Blake Winters, I love you with all of my heart. And I promise I will never leave you again. Ever."

She leaned in to kiss him, but Robert leaned back. He was so thrilled he couldn't resist teasing her. "That was a lot more than ten words."

"Well, now you know I do a good job of making a promise. And I intend to kee--."

Robert couldn't wait any longer. He crushed his mouth to hers. He kissed her long and hard, letting his lips communicate his desire for her.

They were both breathless by the time he pulled away.

"Don't move. I'll be right back." Robert rushed to his bedroom and pulled out the drawer where he'd kept the ring he bought for Jessie over five years ago. In his excitement, he pulled too hard and the whole drawer fell out. He caught the sidearm he stored there before it hit the floor. But everything else scattered at his feet.

"Shoot!" He set his gun on the dresser and dropped the drawer.

"Is everything okay?" Jessie called from the other room.

No, everything was not okay. Robert didn't see the ring box anywhere. "Yes, I'll be right there."

He dropped to his knees and looked under the dresser. Too dark. Heart in his throat, he pulled the cell phone from his pocket and turned on the flashlight.

No ring box, but he definitely needed to move the dresser and vacuum under it. Robert's heart sank. *Where did it go?* It was there just this morning.

The bed was far enough away, he didn't think the box could have rolled that far, but he crawled over anyway. He shined his flashlight. It illuminated a black velvet ring box.

"Yes!"

"Robert, are you okay?"

He grabbed the box, sprang to his feet, and darted back to the family room. "I'm great!" He took Jessie's hand and led her to the sofa. "Have a seat." Dropping to one knee in front of her, he opened his mouth, but his mind went blank. He couldn't remember a single word of the proposal he'd rehearsed so carefully five years ago. He couldn't even remember other variations he'd been considering for the past few weeks.

Robert took a second to catch his breath, then he cleared his throat. "You'd think with thirteen years to prepare for this moment, I'd have something eloquent and profound to say, but all I can think of is: It's always been you. Only you." He squeezed her hand. "I love you, Jess. Way more than I did five years ago, and I want to reclaim your heart. Will you be my wife, my friend, and my partner forever?"

Robert opened the ring box to reveal the solitaire surrounded by smaller diamonds.

Jessie gasped, and tears filled her eyes. "You've had this beautiful ring for five years?" He nodded, and she smacked his shoulder.

He fought the urge to wince. His shoulder was still tender from the bullet wound.

"You really were the biggest idiot," she said. "If I'd know how much you'd invested into our future, I wouldn't have gone to New York." Her expression turned sad, regretful.

"But we both know you would have felt like you were settling without ever finding out what might have been."

She let out a heavy sigh. "You're right, but I'm not settling now. Now, I'm chasing my dreams and I promise to never put my art or my career before you again. Now put that ring on my finger and kiss me."

Robert complied, slipping the ring onto her finger, then slid onto the couch beside her before pulling her into his arms.

Several long minutes later, they came up for air.

Robert pushed away from her. "I want to play you a song." He retrieved his guitar from the case he'd left sitting in the corner.

Jessie grinned. She faced sideways on the couch with legs tucked under her. "I've missed listening to you play and sing."

"Don't get too excited. I'm kind of rusty, because I haven't played for a long time until recently." He strummed the guitar before she could question why he'd stopped playing.

Jessie clasped her hands, her smile broadening, as he played the first notes of Ed Sheeran's "Perfect." Tears filled her eyes when he sang about just being kids when they fell in love.

His voice grew huskier as he sang about seeing her in that dress and wishing he'd talked to her that night in New York.

She stared at him for a long moment, hands pressed to her chest, after the final notes of the song faded away. "That was incredible. So beautiful." She wiped the tears from her cheeks.

Robert set his guitar aside and pulled her into his arms again. They sat in silence for several long moments, enjoying the perfectness of the moment.

Jessie asked as she admired the ring on her hand. "So, when do you want to get married?"

"Tomorrow."

She laughed and looked at him, but Robert wasn't laughing. He wasn't even smiling. He was dead serious. He couldn't wait to make Jessie his wife.

"We can't get married tomorrow."

"Why not? I know you probably want a big, fancy wedding and if that's the case that's what we'll do, but as far as I'm concerned it can't happen fast enough."

"No, I don't want a big wedding. But I think you need to wait a couple days after you get the marriage license before you can get married. Besides, elections are next week, I don't want to do anything that might mess that up for you."

Robert pulled back and looked at her. "What do you mean?" Had someone said something to her to make her think getting married would hurt his chances of winning the election?

There had been rumors flying around that the child Jessie carried was his. Never mind that she was already two months pregnant when she returned to providence. If Jessie hadn't heard those rumors yet, he wasn't about to tell her. Robert didn't care what people thought. As far as he was concerned, the child she carried was his.

When she didn't respond, he continued. "Everyone in town knows we're together. Getting married before elections won't hurt my chances of winning. If anything, it will help. Four years ago, there were several old biddies--I mean, older ladies--who thought it was inappropriate for the sheriff to be single." He waved his hand in the air. "I stopped worrying about the election a long time ago. It's not near as important to me as you are."

"That's just about the most romantic thing anyone has ever said to me," Jessie teased.

But Robert was in no mood to laugh. "Jess, I have waited thirteen years to make you my wife. I don't want to wait a minute longer."

"How about we get married next Saturday?" She placed a hand on his chest.

"Are you serious?" Robert's heart raced.

"I think with my mom's and your mom's help we could pull together a simple little wedding."

Robert pumped his arms in the air. "Yes!" He looked up at the ceiling and whispered, "Thank you." Then he pulled Jessie into his arms again. "Oh, don't forget Lottie. And Amy and Emily. I'm sure they'd all love to help. My aunts too."

Seven more days, and Jessie will be mine. Finally.

CHAPTER 42

Robert looked up from the year's budget report on his desk at a knock on his office door. He smiled as Sylvia Sorenson stepped into his office. The woman was finally his mother-in-law.

The last three months with Jessie as his wife had been absolutely amazing, and Robert couldn't be happier. He'd been re-elected Sheriff on November second and married the love of his life four days later. They'd waited until Jessie was out of school for Christmas break to go on a honeymoon, but the two weeks they'd spent together in the Bahamas were the best of his life.

"Come on in, Sylv--Mom. How are you?"

"I'm doing good but..." Sylvia bit her lip. But it didn't look like she was concerned. It looked more like she was trying not to smile.

"Is something wrong?" Robert's stomach sank as his mind raced through all kinds of possibilities of bad things that could happen to those he loved. It landed on Jessie and the fear that somehow Pendleton had gotten out of jail.

"Nothing is wrong, but I need you to do me a favor."

"Anything."

"I need you to get in your SUV and calmly drive to the hospital."

Robert's heart plummeted, joining his stomach low in his gut. "What's going on? Who's injured? Please tell me it's not Jess--" Emotion choked Robert's throat.

Sylvia held up both hands. "No one's hurt. Although Jessie is in a fair amount of pain."

"What?" Robert stood so fast his chair rolled back and slammed into the wall. His heart and stomach both leapt to his throat, blocking his windpipe. "What happened to her?"

"I was calmly trying to tell you to go to the hospital because Jessie is in labor."

"What? She can't be." He quickly covered the few steps it took to get to his office door before turning back for his keys. "It's too early. She still has three more weeks."

Jake and Emily just had their baby last week. His little brother Jake, one of the strongest men Robert knew, was so cute with his precious little son, Adam. It made Robert eager to hold his own son.

"It is a bit early, but Dr. Young says the baby is measuring big enough that he's confident he'll be healthy."

He opened his desk drawer, then slammed it again when he didn't spot his keys. *Where did I put them?*

The next drawer he checked held his firearm. Out of habit, he pulled it out and slipped it into his holster. He was checking the third drawer when Sylvia laughed.

"Jessie warned me you were going to freak out, and she was right."

"I'm not freaking out. Where are my da--darn keys?"

Sylvia stood and picked up the key ring off Robert's desk. Instead of handing them to him, she dropped them into her purse. "Rudy is standing by to drive you to the hospital."

"I can drive myself to the hospital, Sylv--Mom."

"Right. And do you plan on standing by your wife as she gives birth while wearing your gun?"

Okay, Sylvia was right. He was freaking out. But it was because he was so excited and worried about Jessie and the baby. What if something went wrong?

Sylvia put both hands on his shoulders. "It's going to be okay. Take a deep breath. Put your gun back in the drawer. I'll make sure it's locked up. Then Rudy is going to take you to your wife so you can see for yourself that she's fine. In the meantime, I'm going to your house to pack a bag for Jessie and the baby, and I'll pack a bag for you, too."

"For me?"

"Do you want to be wearing your uniform when you hold your son for the first time?"

"Good point." Robert nodded as he slipped his gun back into his desk. "Thanks." He gave Sylvia a quick hug and walked out of his office. "Rudy! Get out here and drive me to the hospital! I'm about to become a father!"

JESSIE LOOKED up when the door to her hospital room opened, surprised the doctor had returned already.

But it wasn't Dr. Young who walked through the door. Her heart leapt, then raced when she saw her handsome husband.

Robert froze for a moment and stared at her. His gaze raked over her as though assuring himself she was okay.

"Hi, Honey." The words came out breathier than she expected. If her heart didn't stop racing before her blood pressure monitor cycled again, it would set off all kinds of alarms.

Robert stepped next to her bed. "Don't you 'Hi, Honey' me. How long have you been in labor? And why did I have to find out from your mother? She scared me to death. I imagined all kinds of terrible things happening to you."

"I'm sorry." She grabbed his tie and pulled him in for a kiss.

"Mmm..." Robert sat on the edge of the bed and gathered her into his arms.

The passion that flared between them raised Jessie's heart rate another notch.

"Stop distracting me, and answer my questions," Robert said when the kiss ended.

"I've been having contractions all day, but they didn't get bad until halfway through sixth period. I came straight here after school to see if it was real labor or just Braxton Hicks." Just then a contraction hit, and Jessie felt like her abdomen might rip in half. She sucked in a sharp breath and pressed a hand to her stomach.

Robert grabbed her other hand. "That definitely doesn't look like false labor. That looks like it hurts."

Jessie didn't respond for several long seconds as she focused on taking slow, deep breaths. "It does, and the breathing exercises we learned in last week's Lamaze class aren't cutting it anymore." They were supposed to have two more classes over the course of the next two weeks, but it looked like Jessie was graduating early.

"You don't have to suffer, sweetheart. You can get pain medicine any time you want. No one is going to think less of you if you have an epidural."

Emily gave birth last week without the help of any drugs and she swore it was the best way to go, but Ben's wife, Amy, whom Jessie had a lot in common with and had become good friends with, swore an epidural was the only way to go.

Jessie had suffered enough pain in her life, physically, mentally, and emotionally. She didn't see the need to suffer unnecessary pain on what should be one of the happiest days of her life, when she had a choice.

Besides, labor really hurt.

"I know. I've already requested an epidural. The anesthesiologist will come soon."

"Good." Robert smoothed the hair back from her temple and tucked it behind her ear. "So, why didn't you call me?"

"I was going to, but I was afraid you'd freak out, since the baby is coming a little early and we're not really prepared. My mom was working when I came in, and when Dr. Young said I was in labor and needed to be admitted right away, Mom said she'd go home and pack me a bag and make sure you got here safely. Admit it, you freaked out, didn't you?"

Robert's ears turned pink. "Maybe a little. But only because we weren't expecting the baby to come early."

"Well, the doctor said everything looks good, and we should have ourselves a healthy baby in a few hours."

"A few hours?" Robert's voice was tight, and his face looked strained, like Jessie felt.

She was more than ready to have this baby out of her tummy and in her arms. She couldn't wait to be a mother, but she knew the honeymoon bliss she and Robert had been living in for the past three months was about to end.

Another contraction hit, and by the time Jessie had breathed through it, the anesthesiologist had arrived.

Robert held her while the epidural was administered. For a second there, Jessie thought he might faint, but he pulled himself together and became the support she needed.

Over the next five hours, he never left her side except to change out of his uniform when her mother returned. They talked about what life would be like with a baby and how anxious they were to meet their son.

And they kissed.

A lot.

Robert fed her ice chips, smoothed her hair back, and held her hand as her labor progressed. And when the doctor said it was finally time to push, he encouraged her and told her she was doing great.

When their baby's first cry sounded, Jessie cried, too. She was so exhausted, yet full of joy.

Doctor Young placed the tiny, slimy bundle of squirming flesh on her abdomen, and Jessie thought her heart might burst.

"Okay, Daddy. Are you ready to cut the cord?"

Robert's face filled with the same amazement Jessie felt. He took the scissors Dr. Young offered.

A few seconds later, the doctor placed a tightly wrapped bundle in Robert's arms. "I'll let you present your son to his mother."

"He's so perfect, Jess." Robert's eyes filled with tears as he gently took the tiny bundle. After a long moment of rapidly blinking while he stared at their baby, he lowered the infant into her waiting arms.

"He is, isn't he?" Jessie's heart swelled with pride as she held her son against her chest. She could see definite signs that the baby would take after his biological father, but she refused to let that dampen her joy.

Robert stroked the baby's cheek, then caressed his little fist. The baby splayed his tiny, perfect fingers, then wrapped them around Robert's big, strong one.

Robert pressed his lips to Jessie's forehead. "You were amazing." His tears dampened her temple. "Thank you for letting me be his father."

Jessie pressed her free hand against Robert's cheek. They stayed like that for a long while, both to overcome with emotion to speak.

Finally, Robert pulled away. "Now you need to decide on a name. Does he look like a Gavin or a Cole?"

Those were the two names she'd narrowed it down to, but the baby didn't look like a Gavin or a Cole. She'd suggested naming him after Robert once, but he'd said, though he wasn't opposed to using his name as the baby's middle name, it would be too confusing having two Roberts in the house.

Jessie thought that--although Robert seemed devoted to her and the baby--maybe he didn't want to give his name to a baby he didn't father biologically. But he was going to be an amazing father, and she wanted their son to carry his namesake to help him always remember what an exceptional man he had for a father.

"Well, I thought since Ben and Amy named their son James after Ben's dad..." She smiled at Dr. Young, who beamed as he cleaned Jessie up. "And Jake and Emily named their son Adam after Emily's dad. I thought we could name our son after your dad. How does Blake Robert Winters sound?"

Fresh tears filled Robert's eyes. "I think he looks exactly like a Blake." Robert pressed his lips to her temple again. "Thank you for coming back into my life and making me the happiest man on earth."

"*Thank you* for reclaiming my heart and trusting me with yours again."

The End

If you enjoyed Reclaim, please consider leaving a review on Amazon.

Not ready to leave Providence yet?

Check out Debbie's story.
Leveling Up - Choosing Providence Book 1
Free on Kindle Unlimited, or from Amazon.

He's not comfortable in her world, but she dreams of being a part of his.

Debbie "Widow" Wheeler has everything money can buy--except the one thing she wants most: a family of her own. Tired of waiting for the right man to come along, and dealing with the disappointment of infertility, she decides to become a foster mother. Her plans are right on track--until she runs into single dad Austin Reed.

Too bad he wants nothing to do with her.
Or does he?

You can also check out Daniel and Riley's story.
Love Rebranded - Seeking Providence Book 1
Free on Kindle Unlimited, or from Amazon.

They grew up together, then they grew apart. Now they're both back at the ranch trying to pick up the pieces of their broken lives.

Daniel Hamilton needs to get on with his life, but he doesn't dare leave the ranch. Every time he does, he sinks deeper into his alcohol addiction. After enduring a traumatic assault, Riley seeks the security of the Double Diamond. Can Daniel and Riley find their happily ever after, or have they changed too much from the best friends they once were?

And when Riley's attacker catches up to her… Will their demons tear them apart once and for all?

Be sure you join my newsletter, so you don't miss a new release. www.jillburrell.com/newsletter

ACKNOWLEDGMENTS

SPECIAL THANKS to my friends Shelley and Lynda. Thank you for sharing with me the difficult things you've been through and reading this story even though it must have been hard for you. Thank you to my beta readers Marie, Jenessa, and Tia.

Thank you to my critique group for helping me figure out how to write a narcissistic antagonist. And thank you to my nephew, Cliff, for sharing his legal knowledge with me and patiently answering all my questions.

A huge thank you to my editor, Daniel Rodrigues-Martin, for once again challenging me and helping me become a better writer. Thanks for making this book better. Thank you to Kelli Ann Morgan at Inspire Creative Service for designing this amazing cover. Thank you Tia for the chapter heading art.

As always, thank you to my biggest supporter and the love of my life. It's always only ever been you.

ABOUT THE AUTHOR

JILL HAS always been an avid reader, and romance has always been her favorite genre. If she's not writing or folding laundry her head is usually in a book.

When her father told her, "I've got a story I want you to write," she didn't think she'd ever actually do it.

But after twenty years of being a stay-at-home mom with seven children, the idea of writing and publishing a book sounded less terrifying than entering the workforce again. Boy, was she wrong!

Keep in touch with Jill Burrell
www.jillburrell.com

amazon.com/author/jillburrell
facebook.com/authorjillburrell
goodreads.com/authorjillburrell
bookbub.com/authors/jill-burrell
instagram.com/authorjillburrell

www.ingramcontent.com/pod-product-compliance
Lightning Source LLC
LaVergne TN
LVHW020659110826
845149LV00012B/2054

* 9 7 8 1 9 5 5 5 0 7 0 7 3 *